Critical acclaim for Sarah Diamond

Remember Me

'*Remember Me* is a masterly performance, deeply atmospheric and supremely confident ... a chilling account of compulsion and repressed emotion ... quality writing which shines like – well, like a diamond' Mike Ripley, *Birmingham Evening Post*

'Rachel lives with her soulmate and has a rocking career, but the arrival of her estranged best friend threatens to destroy everything by revealing haunting secrets from the past. Chilling stuff in this disturbing psychological thriller' *Heat*

'Brilliantly composed ... a compelling psychological thriller from an author sure to become one of our leading crime queens' www.thebookplace.com

Cold Town

'Sarah Diamond's *Cold Town* ... goes for the psychological jugular in a traditional tale of compulsion, secrets and lies, confirming her unsettling talent for small epiphanies and the horrors of so-called normal life'

Maxim Jakubowski, *Guardian*

'A psychological thriller that is cold, scary and as compelling as staring at a maggoty corpse ... *Cold Town* isn't easily forgotten'
Mark Timlin, *Independent on Sunday*

Sarah Diamond was born in 1976 and grew up in Weymouth before studying English Literature at Reading University. She now works as an advertising copywriter and lives in London. Her three previous novels, *The Beach Road*, *Cold Town* and *Remember Me*, were published to wide critical acclaim.

By Sarah Diamond

The Spider's House
Remember Me
Cold Town
The Beach Road

The Spider's House

Sarah Diamond

ORION

An Orion paperback

First published in Great Britain in 2004
by Orion
This paperback edition published in 2005
by Orion Books Ltd,
Orion House, 5 Upper St Martin's Lane,
London WC2H 9EA

1 3 5 7 9 10 8 6 4 2

A CIP catalogue record for this book is available
from the British Library.

ISBN 0 75286 486 6

Typeset by Deltatype Ltd, Birkenhead, Merseyside

Printed and bound in Great Britain by
Clays Ltd, St Ives plc

www.orionbooks.co.uk

*To Catherine Diamond and Anna Bowles,
who helped me babysit Kevin*

Prologue

I find it very hard to look back to the time before it all started. When the name Rebecca Fisher meant no more to me than it did to anyone else. A blurred black-and-white photograph in the public domain, a name from yellowed newspaper cuttings and out-of-print true crime novels, from people's darker recollections of the late 1960s. The name Rebecca Fisher had a faded notoriety; a name you never heard spoken but somehow recognised.

Imagining it scrubbed clean of resonance is virtually impossible, these days – in the light of what came later, it verges on the surreal. But at a cerebral level I'm well aware that, once upon a time, I'd never given a conscious thought to the Teasford murder. While I was vaguely aware of its place in a long list of anonymous horrors – the nurse who'd killed more than eighty patients, the man who'd left work smiling one evening, gone home and bludgeoned his family to death – it held no special significance to me.

So much for an author's intuition. For better or worse, however, my memory's a lot more impressive than my sixth sense. Even now, when I look back to the evening it began, I can remember every detail: the blustery, dispiriting March of 2002, Carl's preoccupied mood when he got home from work. It's a scene that comes back to haunt me rather too often. A memory that feels like being trapped in someone else's body, seeing through someone else's eyes.

Anna, he says during dinner, laying his cutlery down. *I've got something to ask you.*

Remembering the way I'd felt then is worse than anything – like looking at a photograph of myself laughing at a party, knowing I'd been paralysed for life on the drive home. *At last*, I say cheerfully. *What is it?*

He looks awkward. *Look, I don't know how you're going to take this, but anyway* . . .

He keeps talking. In my memory the scene goes to slow motion, and takes on a nightmare quality. I'd give anything to reach back and tell myself what's going to happen – scream at myself that, if I say what I did before, it's all going to start unfolding again. It'll put me on a direct collision course with Rebecca Fisher, and the murder of Eleanor Corbett, and the truth.

And the words I'm dreading at last, in my own offhand, unsuspecting voice. *Well, I wouldn't mind moving. Not if it means that much to you* . . .

1

Friday afternoon, and the end of an era. Four years and five months that seemed like half a lifetime: melting summer afternoons eating lunch on a bench outside this building, windy autumn mornings travelling in here by bus, winters when I'd have given a week's wages for another hour's warmth in bed. An infinity of trips to Boots in the lunch-hour, of phone calls to and from Carl during the day. Ringing telephones and familiar faces and a reception area I knew as well as the flat I lived in. When today was over, I'd almost certainly never be here again.

Everything was done. The next few hours were as pointless as the front row of seats in a cinema, as necessarily unoccupied – I couldn't take any more work on, and I'd finished tying off the loose ends so the new PR officer wouldn't be stuck picking up after me on Monday morning. But I couldn't leave before six, when they'd be giving me my card and leaving present and expecting me to make a little speech. All I could do was enjoy the sunshine through the window, and say a last private goodbye to this broom cupboard of an office.

I looked around as if making a final inventory – the personal leaving cards I'd arranged round the monitor in a riot of colour, the desk that was usually buried under sheaves of paperwork. Time passed too slowly and far too fast, as the minutes ticked out on the wall clock. When the knock at the door yanked me abruptly from reverie, I had to make a conscious effort to get my feelings under control. It had been a good job, but it had *only* been a good job; it was ridiculous that the prospect of leaving it should stir such a complexity of emotion.

'Come in,' I called.

My immediate boss entered, present and card under his arm. A dozen or so of my colleagues followed him, crowding into the confined space and plugging the doorway. My little exclamation of gratitude and joy was unfeigned, but still seemed to tell only half the story; behind it was something diffuse and tender and nameless, the feeling of something long-term and well-liked, coming to a formal, inevitable end.

'You sure you don't want to stop off at the pub for a quick one?' asked Kim. 'I know we went out for a drink this lunchtime, but still . . .'

We were walking out of the building together, Naomi and Kim and myself; the kind of amiably casual workplace alliance that didn't quite extend into personal lives, that limited itself to lunchtime gossip and the occasional drink after hours. Deep down, I knew it wouldn't survive my leaving, and felt the bittersweet pang return – this was probably the last I'd see of either of them, and they'd soon be filed under Memories.

'I'd love to, but I can't.' It was the truth – sharp regret pricked me as I spoke. 'I'm meeting someone in fifteen minutes: you know Petra, I must have mentioned her hundreds of times. It'll be the last we see of each other before the big move.'

'That's a shame,' said Naomi. 'Still, we'll have to stay in touch. You've got our email addresses, we've got your home one. It's going to feel weird without you, to be honest . . . the place just won't be the same.'

'It'll probably be better organised.' But, while I spoke

flippantly, I couldn't quite disguise my feelings. 'I'm going to miss you too, as it happens. Both of you.'

'What did you think of your leaving card?' asked Kim unexpectedly. 'It was our idea to do it like that, you know, looking like the front of your novel and all. I thought the IT bods did a pretty good job on it.'

'They did a great job,' I said, 'I loved it.' The first part was true, but the second wasn't, not entirely. 'Thanks a lot.'

'No worries,' said Naomi comfortably. 'Just think, now you're becoming a lady of leisure, you'll be free to start another novel. You're going to, aren't you?'

'Well, who knows?' My voice sounded natural enough – still, I couldn't help being a little evasive. 'I'll just have to wait and see if another idea turns up, I suppose.'

We said our last goodbyes outside the big shopping mall that provided my short-cut into the town centre, all awkward hugs and *take cares* and vaguely anticlimactic finality. At last, I turned and walked into the near-empty mall. Its dead quiet implied a lot of people in pubs and heading home – empty escalators trundled up to an equally deserted cafe area, a desolate plastic forest of bolted-down seats and tables. The piped music was reedy, echoing.

I stopped by the escalator, where a fountain ran on and on in a place of lush fake greenery, in front of a closed chocolate shop. The music seemed louder here, a tinny instrumental version of 'Your Song'. I caught a glimpse of myself in one of the square-edged, mirrored pillars nearby – too tall, too skinny, too much curly dark hair. *Plus ça change.*

Taking my leaving card from under my arm, I extracted it from its envelope and looked at it again. The cover of my first and only published novel, a moody black-and-white shot of a streetlight next to a house. Where the original said A DEEPER DARKNESS, a near-identical font spelt out GOOD LUCK. And, in place of ANNA JEF-FREYS, the card spelt out ANNA HOWELL – my married name, the one I worked under. It touched and flattered me that they'd gone to so much trouble to make it look authentic. However, it wasn't quite what I wanted to be reminded of. Replacing the card carefully in its envelope, I tried to ignore a subtle sense of regret. I'd get another idea sooner or later, I told myself. I was bound to.

Then I was walking on, tucking the envelope under my arm, hurrying on to meet Petra in the Fez and Firkin.

'So I'm meeting up with him tomorrow, in Murphy's,' Petra was saying. 'Jim and that lot from work are going to be there too, so it should be a good night.'

We were sitting by the window, over our first drink. As always, Petra's voice was slightly too loud, but not in a jarring, strident way that would make occupants of nearby tables smirk and raise dubious eyebrows at each other. Even in a pub crowded with strangers, she had the air of a well-liked insider – the kind of size fourteen that looked curvy rather than fat, with dark-blonde shoulder-length hair and a sweet, round, snub-nosed face. Petra Mason was the only person I'd ever met who lent immediate physical reality to that tired old cliché, *twinkly-eyed*. 'He seems really nice, anyway,' she continued. 'Fun. Sexy.'

'You said that about the last one,' I reminded her dryly. 'Right up to the point where you dumped him.'

'Oh, *Rob* – he wasn't right for me. And it was getting too serious. I still feel way too young to settle down.' Her expression was suddenly and comically horrified. 'I can't believe we're both twenty-seven. And you're *married*; you're going to be a full-time *housewife*.'

'Full-time writer.' My affronted dignity gave way to something else almost instantly, something frank, humble, rueful. 'Well, sort of. It's like Rebel Without a Cause – Writer Without a Story.'

'Sort of? Come on, Anna. You're published, for God's sake – got good reviews as well, didn't you?'

'For all the good it did. I've lost count of the number of people from work who told me they couldn't find my book anywhere, as if they thought I'd really want to know.' I waged a brief but desperate battle against the black gloom such acknowledgements always dragged along with them – this was a time for laughter and togetherness with my closest friend. 'Anyway, I won't be hearing bad news from them any more. Won't be hearing anything from them. I can't quite believe I've seen the last of Reading Borough Council.'

'Wish I could say the same for the *Evening Post*. So much for my dreams of Fleet Street.' We laughed, but it tailed off uneasily. I saw Petra looking at me closely. 'You *are* looking forward to moving, aren't you?'

'I don't know. I know I should, but . . . I really haven't got a clue *how* I feel.' It was maddening, as ever, a kaleidoscope of feelings and impulses and instincts: I'd love the country, I'd loathe every minute there, it would be a whole new life, it would be the end of everything I'd known. 'Still, you never know,' I said, with determined cheerfulness. 'Dorset might just inspire me.'

'Worked for Thomas Hardy.' Petra smiled, rose from the table. 'Anyway, my round, isn't it?'

She went off to the bar while I sat and gazed out of the window. Beautiful early evening quietness looked back at me: closed shops, rosy shadows, occasional people passing – too convivial to be suburban, too reassuring to be at the sharp edge of big-city life. Martha and the Muffins were playing on the jukebox. There was something nostalgic about the old song this evening – as if, already, I could feel the world around me turning into a haunting memory. This time tomorrow, I'd be somewhere else completely . . .

Then Petra was returning to the table with two bottles of Becks, and I dragged my eyes and mind determinedly back to the here and now.

'So what's the new house like?' she asked curiously, as she sat down. 'You haven't said a word about it.'

'It's— well, sort of a cottage, I suppose. Two bedrooms. Big garden.' I was amazed by how little I could really remember of it, the all-important details that made a place three-dimensional in the mind. I had no real sense of it at all, and no idea what it might be like to live in. 'It was a real bargain,' I said quickly. 'It's a lovely house.'

'You'll have to invite me down one weekend, when you've settled in. Could do with a trip to the country.' Her voice was amiable and throwaway until, noticing my expression, she spoke more seriously. 'Don't worry about it, Anna. You'll have a great time there. Be right at home in no time.'

We talked about this and that for a little longer, topics that had no real resonance in either of our minds, that had the advantage of distracting my thoughts from tomorrow. Setting her drink down, Petra suddenly glanced at her watch. 'God, look at the time. I'm really sorry, but I've got to run – I'm supposed to be having dinner with the family.'

'Don't worry about it. I told Carl I'd be home by eight.'

We finished the last of our drinks, and walked out into cooling sunlight. Words kept assembling themselves in my mind, and I kept forcing them back awkwardly before realising they'd have to be spoken. 'Listen, I'll give you a ring when we've moved in, okay? I can give you our new number then.'

'Of course.' Petra laughed. 'You don't have to sound so apologetic about it, Anna. I'd be really pissed off if you didn't.'

'Well, great.' We were approaching my stop now. As we reached it, I turned to her. 'Anyway,' I said, 'have a great weekend.'

'You too, and best of luck with the move. I'm going to miss you – we really have *got* to stay in touch.'

It was Petra who initiated the hug, and I returned it awkwardly – her side of it was fluid and impulsive, my own as stilted as bad stop-motion photography. Over her shoulder, I couldn't help but be relieved at the sight of the bus drawing in. 'That's mine,' I said, pulling away. 'Well. Better go.'

By the time the bus set off, she'd vanished from sight. It was perfectly natural that she should have done, but still, her absence intensified an unease that had haunted me for hours. As if my last permanent link with this place had stopped existing. Looking out of the window, I watched the town centre fading around me for the last time, and waited for home and Carl to arrive.

2

My husband was the only man I'd ever wanted that I'd actually got. Partly, that was to do with him – he was a great guy, and I adored him – but maybe, just maybe, it had more to do with me.

I knew a lot of people, perfectly normal people with no apparent forcefield of wealth or glamour or brilliance to protect them, who could extend an invitation to lunch or bed or the beginning of a friendship or relationship as casually as offering a packet of crisps. The idea of doing that terrified me. I found it too easy to imagine the face falling behind the bright social smile; at best the quick scramble for a convenient excuse, at worst the cruel and stinging rejection that would haunt me for weeks. It wasn't natural to me as dark eyes and long fingers were; I knew enough about psychology to understand that, to realise my shyness had been etched into me like a scar. Still, understanding why and how it had been created didn't stop it existing – from early childhood, I'd only ever been confident from a distance.

I suppose it was no real surprise that, throughout my life, every single one of my close friends had been built along the Petra lines, the sort of people who meet someone new and quite like them, and – sensing a potential friend or boyfriend – have absolutely no trouble asking them if they'd like to come and see that new film some time, if they'd like to meet up for a drink over the weekend, whatever. If I met someone like me, we'd both be too scared of rejection to do any such thing, and would inevitably drift straight back out of each other's lives. And, now I come to think of it, that had probably happened quite a few times.

With friends, that wasn't necessarily a bad thing. Sometimes, it was like getting something for Christmas you hadn't asked for, and realising it was exactly what you'd wanted. But when it came to boyfriends, different story. I'd been told I could seem difficult to approach, and it meant I got the kind of men who approached the kind of girls who seemed difficult to approach. This type of man came in all shapes and sizes – intelligent, dull, handsome, ugly – but they invariably had two things in common: the Teflon hide of the truly inspired double-glazing salesman, and an honest belief that they were God's gift to womankind.

The first time I met Carl with Petra's brother, I knew straight away he wasn't going to ask me out. It had happened to me too often before – a lively conversation with an attractive male friend-of-a-friend, a smiling good-bye, a backward glance. A lingering sense of regret. He was tall, blond and blue-eyed, with a nice smile and straight-forward good looks that seemed to imply other qualities: intelligence without pomposity, confidence without ego-mania, sense of humour, but serious about important things. I'd never understood women who complained such-and-such was *too nice* or *too conventional*. It was all I'd ever wanted in my perfect man – from an early age, my subconscious probably figured I had enough hang-ups for both of us.

It wasn't going to happen, he wasn't going to ask me – but he did. As the evening progressed, we got chatting in earnest. Eventually, he asked me if I'd like to meet up for lunch some time. That was how it started.

Maybe I loved him slightly too much. I could get a bit

obsessive about the things that really mattered to me, sometimes.

But that didn't matter now. Sitting at the back of the bus, things flashed hard and fast behind my eyes – a house I couldn't really remember, a village I didn't know at all – the entire course of my life so far trembling on the brink of the unknown.

We had a takeaway that night. The stripped, impersonal look of the kitchen seemed to demand it. We ate pizza out of grease-speckled cardboard boxes and drank beer straight from the can, in a living room that seemed bigger and chillier than usual; all its personal touches had been carefully packed away, leaving nothing but the sofa we sat on and the widescreen TV that flickered unwatched in the corner.

'This is so weird,' I said. 'I feel like a bloody squatter.'

Carl laughed. 'Is that good or bad?'

'I don't know. It just seems . . .' But I couldn't quite define the taste of incipient upheaval, even to myself, and I laughed as he did, cuddling up to him. 'Want some garlic bread?'

We ate for a while in companionable near-silence. Beside me, he looked carefree and five years younger, a clean-cut student relaxing after a hard day's lectures – his responsible, slightly earnest work-face was nowhere in evidence. It was the way he looked on holiday sometimes, in a hotel room, on a beach; as if day-to-day concerns had been packed away like the furniture, temporarily but completely out of sight.

'You're really looking forward to moving, aren't you?' I asked quietly.

'Of course.' Looking at me, he frowned slightly. 'Aren't you?'

'I think so.' But, while it was true, it still seemed to require further clarification. 'I'm going to miss things here, though. Work. Friends. The town centre. This flat, even . . .'

'Don't forget the traffic. And the crime.' His broad face creased into a grin. 'And that wonderful kebab shop over the road. You're going to lie awake at night *dreaming* we could have that place back.'

I couldn't help smiling myself – the kebab shop was the kind of domestic annoyance that could quickly develop into a mordant private joke, and it had done. 'It's not going to be the same without the three a.m. drunks every weekend,' I agreed. 'There's nothing like waking up to the sound of top-volume swearing.'

'The Saturday night fights.'

'Pavement sick on a Sunday morning.'

'The joys of city life.' Finishing his last slice of pizza, he put his arm round me, reassuring, expansive. 'It's going to be great in the country, Annie. Peace and quiet. A gorgeous house. More money.'

'I'll be a kept woman.' I was only half-joking. 'It's great you've been offered this promotion, but – I don't know – it's going to feel funny, not working. I don't think I was cut out to be a housewife.'

'Who says you have to be? You can get a job in the area if you start feeling too bored. Or you can start writing again. Get going on that second novel.'

'I'll have to be inspired first.' My thoughts turned back to that well-designed, well-meant leaving card, on the kitchen counter where I'd left it. 'I hope I get another idea soon,' I said. 'I really miss writing, you know.'

'I do know. But I'm sure you will.' I saw him do a small double-take and check his watch, becoming momentarily serious again, the Regional Sales Manager that he'd be in our new life. 'Oh, yeah, I'd better call Mum and Dad. Remind them we're off first thing tomorrow.'

'Give them my love.'

'Will do. Won't be long.'

He got up, went out towards the hallway phone. I found myself listening carefully. Perhaps unsurprisingly, I'd always been interested in other people's families and how they differed from each other. Carl's couldn't have been further removed from Petra's, who seemed to see each other as everything from loan companies to lodgers to confidantes as the situation arose. Carl, his younger brother and his parents never seemed to call each other just to chat, but would never have dreamed of ignoring a formal milestone – in this case, our last evening in Reading. Hearing Carl talk to them, I was always obscurely reminded of a Japanese tea ceremony; created and driven by protocol, charming, amiable, but essentially formal.

'All right, Dad,' he said at last, 'we'll look forward to it. Thanks a lot, I'm sure we will. Give our love to Nick when you see him. Bye.'

I heard him hanging up, his footsteps in the hallway. He came back into the living room and sat down, looking cheerful. 'Well, that's that done,' he said. 'Dad says they're going to send us a little moving-in present – probably a set of saucepans, knowing Mum. I spoke to her as well. She sends her love.'

I couldn't help asking, even though I wasn't sure I wanted to know the answer. 'What did she say?'

'Oh, just the usual. She hopes you don't get lonely there, you can always give her a ring if you do.' Seeing my expression, he came up behind me and closed his arms round my shoulders. 'Come on, Annie, it's nothing to get upset about. You know she means well.'

'I know, I know. I'm just being silly.' I hurried to

change the subject. 'What time did you say the removal van was turning up tomorrow?'

'Half seven – I rang to double-check with them this afternoon. Better get an early night.' The comforting pressure of his hands on my forearms became something else, moving downwards, inwards, gradually melting from practical into sensual. 'It's our last night here, after all. It would be a shame not to celebrate.'

'Sounds good to me.' I turned slightly, he bent down, we kissed. A giddy, weightless holiday feeling came out of nowhere to become an intense aphrodisiac, as if our drive tomorrow would end in some airport concourse; sitting in a cafe that faced out onto walkways and perfume shops, drinking coffee, waiting for our flight, and preparing ourselves for a whole new world.

3

'I spy, with my little eye . . .'

We'd been driving for quite a while, in the separate-isolation-booths silence that tended to fall unexpectedly during long journeys and set amazingly fast. Carl's ironic voice took me by surprise.

'Let me guess,' I said. 'It's something beginning with M.'

He grinned. 'How did you guess?'

'There's nothing to see *but* motorway. Doesn't seem as if there has been for hours.' Beyond the car windows, it extended stark and two-dimensional as an old computer game – black tarmac, blue sky, featureless green stretching out on both sides as far as the eye could see. 'How much longer?'

'Next to no time, now. The removal guys are probably there already.'

Silence fell again, the beginnings of a bad headache buzzing in my mind – another key symptom I associated with too-long, too-featureless drives. But yesterday's uncertainty had vanished without a trace. Now it was blown effortlessly away by spring breezes and sunlight – so clear, so pale, so fresh – like a nightmare that had faded beyond recognition three seconds after you opened your eyes.

We turned off the motorway onto a medium-sized road, then almost instantly onto a narrower one.

'Well,' said Carl, 'here we go.'

It was extraordinary, how quickly our scenery had changed. Through the windows, the relentless brutal ugliness of our surroundings was gone without a trace. I saw fields like brown corduroy, hay stacked in neat bales; the May afternoon suddenly becoming beautiful as it touched on old honey-coloured farmhouses, a grey-dappled pony grazing idly in a field.

'You know,' I said quietly, 'I'd forgotten how lovely it was.'

'Like something from a postcard, isn't it?' He laughed – unexpected elation affected us in different ways, making me dreamy and thoughtful, filling him with a vast, undiscriminating good humour. 'Almost makes me want to pack in Taylor's Furniture and start my own farm. Can just see myself milking the cows every morning.'

Down another narrow side road, trees closed in around and above us. Entering the shadowy canopy of dark-green leaves was like diving into an outdoor pool in summer; the chill through the open windows was immediate and welcome. A sign came into view to the left. ABBOTS NEWTON.

'I'll get a state-of-the-art company tractor,' Carl was saying. 'You'll just *love* feeding the chickens and making the jam.'

'It might just grow on me.' He was joking, but everything around us sold the picture-postcard idyll in earnest; pretty little cottages, lush greenery, an infinitely seductive advert for placid, constructive, semi-rural pursuits.

'I might take up gardening here, you know. No, really. I think I might like it.' Carl turned right, and we entered the village equivalent of a town centre. I saw only three cars, and they were all parked outside a Tudor-looking building I'd have bet on being the real thing. The sign swinging over the door in the breeze read THE BULL INN, three stars. Across the road from it, the smallest shop I'd ever seen announced its identity as ABBOTS NEWTON STORES.

'For your sake,' Carl said, 'I really hope that place sells fags.'

'If not, I'll just have to stock up in bulk. Come to think of it, I'm dying for one now ... where the hell did I put them?'

But we were almost there, no point in lighting up now. I vaguely recalled our surroundings from our brief house-inspecting trip in March, and recognised the handful of other houses we passed before turning into a driveway.

Our driveway, I had to remind myself, *it's ours, now.* I found it impossible to fully take in. What had probably been built as a single house in the late nineteenth century was now knocked into two, and a waist-high privet hedge bisected the front garden. The facade of the house was blinding white, the tiled roof the colour of bitter choc-olate, and surrounding trees and bushes were dark or light green depending on where shadow fell. I had an impres-sion of colours squeezed fresh out of the tube, laid thick and unblended on canvas, the world coloured in with the unrealistic precision of a diligent ten-year-old.

'I can't believe I never noticed how gorgeous it was,' I murmured.

'I know what you mean.' For a second or two, I saw him drinking in the scene as I did before becoming practical – his gaze moved to the removal van already there, the two men carrying our Reading coffee table through the open front door. Everything in his demean-our changed from reflective to businesslike. 'Suppose I'd better go and give them a hand,' he said, then, with a quick backward smile, 'welcome home, Annie.'

I couldn't share his no-rest-for-the-wicked urgency, not today. A dreamlike feeling had settled over me, and I moved as if in slow motion. He'd entered the house before I unbuckled my seatbelt, got out, leant against the passenger door. I inhaled the scent of this place as if I could somehow make it part of me, discovering something I'd never expected to find here: a bone-deep hunger to belong.

'Hello, you must be one of the new neighbours!'

The voice across the hedge startled me, and I glanced round sharply. A woman had come out of the adjacent house, and its front door stood wide open behind her. She could have been anything between forty-five and sixty, plump, pleasant-faced, barely-lined; she wore a short-sleeved shirt, and her forearms were white to the elbows. 'I'd shake hands,' she said apologetically as she approached the hedge, 'but I'd get flour all over you – I'm afraid I've been baking. I just saw your car pull up, and thought I'd pop out to say hello.'

'It's nice to meet you.' We smiled at each other, and I noticed more details – the slightly anxious blue eyes, the wisps of mid-brown, probably-dyed hair, escaping from a makeshift bun. 'I'm Anna Howell. My husband Carl's off helping the removal men.'

'I'm Liz. Liz Grey.' She turned and called towards her open front door, her voice startlingly loud in the near-silence. 'Helen! Come on out and meet the new people!'

The woman who emerged was easier to put an age to than Liz, around forty-five. She looked even taller than me, about five foot ten. Her colouring struck me as vaguely Nordic, or perhaps just more Anglo-Saxon than most people's.

'Helen lives just off the village square,' Liz explained as the woman came over. 'She's helping me get some things ready for a bring-and-buy sale in Wareham tomorrow. Helen, this is Anna.'

'Hi,' I said, extending a hand.

'Hello.' My hand was shaken rather perfunctorily – Helen's smile didn't quite reach her eyes, and something about them said she always took everything absolutely seriously. 'Welcome to Abbots Newton.'

'Thanks. It does seem lovely.'

'It's a very nice place, dear,' said Liz. 'You'll have to pop round for a proper chat, when you're all settled in. Come whenever it suits you; if my car's here, so am I.' She gestured towards the little powder-blue Fiat in her driveway.

I smiled again, nodded. 'Thanks very much,' I said. 'I'd love to. Look, I'm sorry to run off, but I'd really better go and give my husband a hand.'

Goodbyes all round, and we headed towards our separate front doors. The shadows through my own were unfamiliar and intriguing, and I could hear Carl and the removal men upstairs. First things first, I thought – I was dying for a cigarette now. Standing just inside the door, I lit up, and felt the reality of this place slotting into place around me.

Our first week in Abbots Newton felt so much like a holiday that – no matter how often I reminded myself that we lived here now – a deep-rooted part of me remained stubbornly convinced that we didn't. Underlying my thoughts and feelings, there remained an inexplicable conviction that this was a temporary escape from Reading's events and stresses and concerns; that I'd be walking back to work next Monday morning refreshed and pleasantly regretful, thinking back fondly to the white-painted, oak-beamed house we'd rented for a single idyllic week.

It wasn't simply the change of scene that made me feel

like that – it was everything in the atmosphere, the situation. That week, we seemed to exist in isolation, a couple with no wider network extending around us, romantically and lazily adrift as if the world had become a gondola and we were the only two people in it. There was nothing and nobody else to affect anything we said, thought or did – no managers or colleagues intruding on our private selves with praise or criticism or indifference, no brusque outside world making its own demands in the form of traffic jams and gas bills and late-night drunken fights outside the kebab shop.

I knew that some people would have been bored and enervated by this, people like Petra, people who could easily grow restless with a one-to-one conversation in a deserted pub, who seemed to have a raging desire for strangers' voices in the background, and nights out in big groups, and casual acquaintances everywhere they looked. I also knew that Carl was happy to live like this for a single week, comfortably aware that normal service would resume next Monday. Personally, however, I'd have been only too delighted to spend the rest of my life in this way – just the two of us together, with nothing to care about but each other, and the straightforward beauty of our surroundings.

Of course, there was inevitably some activity: the man from the phone company arriving to reconnect us, the carpet fitters, the postman lugging the carefully-packaged set of saucepans that had been Carl's parents' inevitable moving-in present. But that didn't seem to count. They were strangers who drifted in and out like ghosts and left no trace of themselves, disappearing to leave us absolutely free to turn any impulse into reality.

The house itself enraptured us, that first week – it was so different from anything we'd known before. Its low ceilings, its narrow curving staircase, its arched doorways Carl would have had to bend to get through if he'd been much taller than his five foot eleven. And its walls, bare and white as fresh sheets of paper, waiting for whatever marks of our personalities we cared to inscribe.

Long, aimless, laughing walks around the quiet village, car journeys that had no specific destination and no purpose other than the joy of discovery, three-hour lunches in country pubs we'd just happened to pass, endless lovemaking in the bedroom's afternoon sunlight – the petty, querulous, demanding clock I'd taken for granted in Reading had suddenly fallen silent. We smiled at strangers, saw them smile back at us, and knew nobody.

At any given moment, it seemed that we saw something new – the middle-aged couple walking four Labradors in the village square, the sprawlingly functional farm on the outskirts of neighbouring Wareham, the field in which white ponies grazed like a beautiful hallucination. And constantly, constantly, the sunlight, cool breezes, drifting smells of earth and wildflowers – a sense of the world standing poised and alert, preparing to dive smoothly into summer.

On Thursday Carl went to pick up his new company car. I drove him to Wareham Station in the sporty little white Mazda we'd arrived here in, which would be mine from today.

'Honestly,' I said, as we approached the station, 'I don't mind driving you all the way into Bournemouth. Really.'

'Don't worry about it, Annie. There's no point us both having to come back from there – I might as well get the train. Anyway, I won't be long.' I pulled up outside the little station. 'Be back about two thirty,' he said, opening the passenger door. 'See you then.'

Driving back on my own felt strange. I told myself I just wasn't used to being behind the wheel – in Reading I'd generally relied on public transport. Still, I was aware that there was far more to it than that. Approaching Abbots Newton, my surroundings looked different and their inviolate peace took on an alien edge: trees rustling, a flock of birds taking off unexpectedly, not a single sound that could have been made by people.

You're being ridiculous, I told myself, *it's just the way things are in the country; it's nothing to be afraid of.* But most of my not-quite-subconscious mind was entirely preoccupied with keeping that worry at bay all the way home. As the front door closed behind me, my mind dropped its guard for just a second, and I had a momentary glimpse of something appalling beyond words, a vast and unknown world extending like an ocean around me, a memory of another time and place when I'd felt exactly the same way.

Almost immediately it was gone, as my subconscious redoubled its efforts to hold it back. Even so, knowing that it *could* come back disturbed me. As if in self-preservation, my thoughts twisted away from the idea, focused hard on the powder-blue Fiat I'd seen a few minutes ago in next door's driveway. *You'll have to pop round for a proper chat*, Liz had said. *If my car's here, so am I.*

I'd normally have felt very awkward about just dropping in, even though she had extended a sort of invitation – for all I knew, this could be a bad time for her, she might not even have meant it, might have spoken out of politeness alone. But I was driven out by something even deeper-rooted than my fear of intruding. I couldn't stand being on my own with my fears till Carl came back, feeling them inch in further and further, inexorable, preparing to engulf everything.

I wasn't sure if you had to lock up here, or if you could just leave the door on the latch, but, deciding it was best to err on the side of safety, I took the key with me, locking the front door on my way out. I went round to Liz's front door and rang the bell. Distant chimes, a wait of maybe thirty seconds before the door opened, and she was there.

'Anna!' She spoke amiably and brightly, as if she'd been expecting me for several minutes. In my mind, she'd faded into near-facelessness – I saw the plump, smiling woman with the grey-blue eyes as if for the first time. 'What can I do for you, dear?'

Her apparent welcome gave me something close to Petra's confidence. 'Oh, nothing. I just thought I'd come round and say hi properly. You're not busy, are you?'

'Not at all. Come on through – I'll put the kettle on.'

I followed her through a hallway crowded with ornaments and framed photographs. As she walked, she turned her head slightly, addressed me briskly over one shoulder. 'Really, dear, come round whenever you feel like it. It's the best thing about a little place like this, no need to worry about being neighbourly – everyone's very nice round here, so there's no danger of falling in with the wrong people.'

'Oh, really,' I said quickly, 'I wasn't worried about *that*.'

'I wouldn't blame you if you were, dear. As my late husband always used to say, you can't be too careful.'

We entered a kitchen as crowded, domestic and welcoming as the hallway: intricately carved pinewood, a library of well-used cookery books, a vague unplaceable smell like flour and nutmeg.

'Take a seat,' she said. 'Would you like ginger biscuits with your tea?'

'That would be lovely. Thanks a lot.'

I sat down at the table in the middle of the big, sunny

room, and a silver-framed photograph on a nearby shelf caught my attention. Two little brown-haired girls smiled out at me side by side, exuding dimpled, prepubescent confidence; I realised Liz was looking at me, and knew I'd have to mention them. 'Aren't they pretty! Your grand-daughters?'

'Daughters. Taken a long time ago, mind, but they've only got prettier over the years, bless them.' She bustled across the kitchen with a proprietorial air, and her small, plump hand indicated first one, then the other. 'That's Katie, and that's Alice.'

'How old are they now?'

'Katie's thirty-seven, Alice is thirty-five. I married young; it was the done thing in those days. Neither of them stayed in Britain, more's the pity.'

Everything about her manner actively invited further questions as she returned to the kettle. Looking at the photograph again, I felt an odd kind of jealousy. 'Where do they live these days?'

'Katie's working as an English teacher in Germany – she's very bright, always has been. Alice married an American man and went to start a family over there; they've got three children now. Come to think of it, she sent me a photo only the week before last – that's it there, by the fruit bowl.'

It had been framed as carefullly as the first, and I picked it up afraid I'd damage it. A tanned long-legged woman in pristine khaki shorts posed in some well-manicured outdoors setting. Three small, wholesome-looking kids surrounded her. 'I've been over to visit, of course,' Liz went on, making the tea. 'They're just lovely. A very happy family, and doing very well for themselves.'

'That's great.' But the jealousy came back again, insidi-ous, wistful. 'You must be very proud.'

'Oh, I am, dear. If only they could have stayed in the country. They take after their father, I suppose, he was the travelling type, too – he was a pilot before we got married, although he gave it up to go into business soon after that.' She brought the tea and plate of ginger biscuits over on a tray. Carl and I always made do with mugs, and the delicate cups and saucers with the little silver teaspoons on the side struck me as intimidatingly formal. 'Next time you come round I'll have to show you our wedding pictures, but I'm afraid I haven't got them to hand.'

On our initial meeting, she'd struck me as a woman who'd grow on me very quickly, but I was startled to realise that, if anything, my feelings were going in the opposite direction. While she still seemed essentially kind and well-meaning, her manner was slightly overbearing, as if she'd always existed on the side of the judges rather than the judged. Whether she realised it or not, that drove an immediate wedge between us; I sensed she'd led a sheltered life in every possible sense, and knew that she'd never understand my own past.

'That's a shame,' I said, only half-meaning it. 'I'd love to see them.'

A moment's pause before she spoke again, unexpectedly. 'Do you work at all, dear?'

'Well, I did in Reading – that's where we lived before. I was a PR officer for the council.' Suddenly, I wished she'd carried on talking about her family. I'd come here precisely so I wouldn't have to think about these things. 'But here, well, I suppose I'm going to be a housewife from now on.'

'You're awfully young for that, I'd have thought. You should get a little job in the area, just to pass the time. I work for a few days each week in Wareham Library, and I keep myself quite busy with the local WI. It's a very good

26

way to meet people. I've made some wonderful friends there.'

If I was young to be a housewife, I was *embarrassingly* young to belong to the WI – but there seemed no polite way of saying that, and I had to smile back as if grateful for the advice. The slightly ajar back door creaked open and a large ginger cat padded in, plump and plushly-furred as an expensive stuffed toy. 'This is Socks,' Liz announced. 'He's a funny little thing. Do you have pets yourself?'

'No, I'd like to, but Carl's allergic to cats *and* dogs.' Socks glanced at me with polite indifference and I reached out a hand to stroke him. He acquiesced with a kind of feline shrug. 'He's lovely, isn't he?'

'He certainly is.' Socks wandered out into the hallway with a last incurious glance back at me. 'Would you like another cup of tea?'

'Thanks very much, but I'd better be off. Carl should be back soon.' We both stood. 'Well, it's been great to meet you properly. You'll have to pop round yourself, soon.'

'That would be nice, dear. I do hope you like it here.'

As I let myself into our empty house, I realised that I hadn't told her anything about my writing. It wasn't as if I'd deliberately hidden it – the conversation just hadn't turned in that direction – but I couldn't help but feel relieved. Ridiculous as it seemed, it wasn't something I was altogether comfortable discussing with strangers, or even casual acquaintances; as a topic it was too personal, carried too much baggage I couldn't easily unload.

Still, I was glad I'd conquered my fears and popped over. Suddenly, the nonspecific anxieties of earlier that day had vanished completely. Part of me was aware that they might only be hiding, but, for as long as I didn't have to face up to them, I could easily convince myself that they weren't really there. It was, after all, only Thursday, and

Monday morning still seemed a comfortable distance away.

Through the living room window, I saw the gleaming black Audi pull up outside about half an hour later. Carl's expression as he got out told me exactly how he felt about it; I opened the front door and stepped out, smiling. 'I take it you're satisfied?'

'That's an understatement. Isn't it *terrific*? I was like a little kid with a new toy, driving back. Makes the one they gave me in Reading look like a three-wheeled van.' He leant across to the passenger seat, lifted out a bulky, paper-wrapped parcel. 'Come on, I know you're not that wild about cars, but even you've got to admit it's pretty stunning.'

'I'm getting quite jealous – it's a *car*, for God's sake.' I found his passion for hi-tech status-symbols of all kinds both incomprehensible and oddly endearing. As he stepped towards me with the parcel, curiosity overcame half-humorous exasperation. 'What have you got there, anyway?'

'Well, I was just walking out of Bournemouth Station when I passed this little antiques shop, and something in the window just caught my eye.' He walked past me into the house and through to the kitchen, and I hurried after him. 'You know we were talking about buying a new lamp for the living room?' he said, starting to unwrap the package at the table. 'I thought you'd like this one. I must admit, I quite liked the look of it myself.'

He peeled away the last layer of bubble-wrap and I stared, delighted. 'My God, Carl, that's just beautiful. Never mind the car, that's something I can get excited about.'

'Hey, it's not that thrilling.' Pushing the discarded

wrapping to one side, he set the lamp upright. 'It's pretty nice, though, isn't it?'

It was a Tiffany-style lamp: an intricate steel framework held glass shards of varying shapes and colours, deep, vivid primary shades of blood-red and jade-green and midnight-blue. The wrought-iron base was curved, fluted, delicate. 'Well chosen,' I said, kissing him impulsively, 'I *love* it. I have to see what it looks like switched on. Where did we put those spare bulbs the other day . . .'

I bent down and opened a cupboard at random. It was entirely empty apart from a dark shape at the back. 'Looks like the old owners left something behind for us,' I said, peering in. 'Now, what have we here . . . ?'

I pulled it out, and frowned at the studded leather dog-collar in my hand. 'Well, *that's* not much use to us. I didn't know they had pets here, did you?'

'Maybe they didn't. Maybe they were just into hardcore S and M, you never know.' I laughed, and Carl went over to the cupboard beneath the sink. 'I was sure I put the bulbs in this one . . . Yeah, here we go.'

He took one out as I looked at the collar again dubiously. 'Do you think we should throw it out?'

'We *could* give it pride of place on the mantelpiece, I suppose . . . Come on, just bin it, Annie. I don't think they're likely to turn up demanding it back.'

'Consider it officially binned.' I went over to the swing-bin and dropped it inside. As I turned back, I saw he'd put the bulb in and plugged the lamp in temporarily next to the kettle. Even in the bright sunshine, the quality of its light was atmospheric – luminous carnival colours both vivid and muted, seeming to set a final seal on our residence here.

4

On Monday, there had been a reassuring infinity of days ahead of us – even by Thursday, we'd seemed to have more than enough. But the days ran out like cigarettes, from five in the packet to one in the blink of an eye. By Saturday night, I'd begun to understand that this was home now, and that most of the time, I'd be here alone; Carl would soon be spending his days far away from me, in a distant office.

I woke early on Sunday morning; the bedside clock said it was seven a.m., and Carl was fast asleep. I lay awake beside him for some time, flat on my back with eyes wide open, breathing slowly and deeply. Feeling the future suspended above me like a dead weight. The uncertainty that had whispered to me on Thursday afternoon now spoke again, horrifyingly louder and closer as if it had first filtered through from a distant room, and now came from directly behind my shoulder.

Inactivity seemed only to make that feeling worse, and I got out of bed quietly, hoping Carl wouldn't wake up until I had it under some kind of control, not wanting to ruin his last day of leisure with a worry that didn't even have a name. Heading into the bathroom, I opened the window to let in the crisp greenery-smelling morning air. While the fittings around me were new-looking – mixer taps and power-shower pristine and shiny as if fresh out of the showroom – they seemed incongruous with the room itself. Its sense of age lingered like a smell. I couldn't rationalise that feeling beyond its low ceilings and doorway, the odour of decades piled on decades, of a house that had already been standing perhaps fifty years when my mother was born. Colder than it had any apparent right to be, and the merest hint of damp on the air that evoked claw-footed tubs streaked with rust, carbolic soap, one bath a week whether you needed it or not.

The view from the window only reinforced it. Looking out, an involuntary shudder ran through me. Beyond our large but undistinguished back garden, a dense dark-green cluster of trees swept over the horizon, beneath an empty sky that was the white-blue colour of sun-faded ink. Nothing moved. My thoughts turned back to the Reading flat with unexpected longing; if you'd opened the tiny frosted-glass bathroom window there, you'd see reassuring hints of strangers' lives from two storeys up: the bus shelter and the phone box and the kebab shop that attracted such an infuriating stream of drunken, noisy, late-night custom. Even if there was nobody walking past, you knew that someone would be, soon . . .

For the first time, I allowed myself to open my ears and mind to the silence. With Carl drowsing peacefully in the next room, it was deafening. I couldn't help but wonder how loud it would become when he wasn't around.

Suddenly, urgently, I needed the reassurance of his company, and hurried back into the bedroom and under the duvet, movements now the exact opposite of stealthy, trying to wake him up without speaking a word. The sharp creak of the mattress made him turn, shift sleepily, reach out for me.

'Morning, Annie. Well . . . looks like it's our last day of doing nothing . . .'

I held him a little tighter, and we kissed – drowsy companionship blurred into the kind of lovemaking that felt more than anything like the natural progression of a morning cuddle. I tried to lose myself in it, at least partly succeeded; only when it was over and we were lying side by side did my worries come creeping back, shadowy in the half-light that filtered through the curtains. At first, his caressing hands were idle and reflective, then his touch changed, and I felt it focus on specific muscles with a physiotherapist's concern.

'What's the matter? You feel so tense! You're all knotted up.'

'Oh, it's nothing.' But I'd always been as honest with him as I was with myself. 'I just went into the bathroom earlier, when I couldn't sleep, and ... I don't know. It feels so *quiet* here. So *old*.'

'It's a quiet area. It's an old house.'

'I know,' I said reluctantly, 'but it's all so different. I never really thought about that before, not till now. Everything's going to be different, here.'

'Not *us*.' His voice was reassuring as he held me a little closer. '*We're* still the same, aren't we?'

There was no arguing with that, and I knew it. He was unquestionably right; I was being silly. Still, as the minutes passed, I found it impossible to relax or fade back into sleep. Restlessness gripped me, a longing to explore, to come to terms with the simple fact of living here, to reassure myself that our surroundings held nothing essentially alien.

. 'Listen,' I said, sitting up abruptly. 'I'm wide awake now. Think I'll get washed and dressed and pop down to the local shop. Don't know if it'll be open, but it's worth a try. I'm almost out of cigarettes, and it's about time I saw what it was like.'

'Jesus. It's early, isn't it?'

'For a Sunday. It's past half-nine.' His vaguely apprehensive look made me laugh, and I spoke again quickly.

'Don't worry, I'm not hassling *you* to come. I wouldn't dream of ruining your lie-in.'

Cautious, slightly guilty hope in his eyes. 'You sure? I don't mind—'

'Of course I'm sure. Just call me an intrepid explorer.'

'You may be gone for some time,' he said, lying back down. 'Well, if you're not home by noon, I'll send out a search party.'

I showered and dressed quickly, left the house and started walking along the grassy roadside verge that was the nearest thing to a pavement. While our address was Four Ploughman's Lane, the impression it gave of a wider community was entirely misleading, and it was a good five minutes before I passed another house. I tried to enjoy the peace and the beauty around me, but, despite myself, irrational panic was taking the place of delight; it was far lovelier than Reading had ever been, but there was too much space to be alone, and think, and worry.

I approached the village square, which had a kind of wooden bandstand in the dead centre, brightly coloured notices posted on one side behind clear glass. Pretty terraced cottages faced onto it from two sides. My watch said it was approaching ten o'clock, and the sky had darkened to a vivid blue. As Abbots Newton Stores came into sight, I saw a car pull up outside the Bull Inn and quickened my step, somehow reassured by the evidence of other life here.

A bell jangled sharply as I came in the shop, but there was nobody behind the counter where the cigarettes were kept. Inside, everything was musty-smelling, twilit with shadows, crowded as I'd never known a shop could be. I saw baskets of shrunken, elderly-looking vegetables piled on top of each other on a waist-high glass-fronted fridge that served as the off-licence. Beside it, cardboard boxes of crisps had been stacked into a precarious Tower of Pisa. The shop didn't seem to sell papers or magazines, but other, stranger things exploded from random corners – balls of wool and knitting needles, boxes of candied fruits, assorted arcana that seemed to have no place here.

I felt somehow embarrassed to call out, and was standing there wondering what to do when I heard voices coming from the open doorway behind the till. At first they were distant, then closer – then they stayed where they were, muted but still clearly audible.

'Oh, come on, Julie.' A slightly aggressive young male voice, bullying rather than entreating – I had a clear mental image of its owner's hand clasped round a female forearm in the narrow hallway. 'Stay outside with me a bit longer. Won't do no harm.'

'I *can't*. Nan'll kill me if she finds out.' The girl's voice expressed the full helplessness of wanting to please everyone at once, having to make a choice. 'She'll be back this afternoon. What if someone says they been in and there wasn't no one serving?'

'Some chance. Don't look like your nan has any customers from one month to the next.' Clear contempt in the male voice, now. 'Don't know what you wanted to come and stay the weekend here for. It's a right boring dump.'

'Didn't have no choice, did I? Mum made me.' Irritable, now, increasingly resentful. 'You didn't have to come down today, you know.'

'Maybe I wanted to, innit? See if I could spot the famous Rebecca Fisher.'

'I told you. She's gone.' A new hushed note, shades of a car-crash rubber-necker. 'They said they'd kill her if she stayed.'

The voices started coming closer again, getting louder. 'For real?'

'For real. My nan heard about it off Uncle Harold. It was dead creepy.'

On the last word, they appeared in the doorway behind the till – a large, spotty redhead who looked about fifteen and a lanky young man with greasy black hair in a ponytail. He barely reacted to the sight of me, but she did. 'Oh, I'm ever so sorry,' she said. 'You been waiting long?'

'No time at all,' I said, 'don't worry about it. Twenty Benson and Hedges, please.'

Afterwards, passing the village square again, I thought about what they'd said, and wondered what they'd meant by it. I found myself hurrying to a trot, longing to share this new turn of events with Carl.

When I let myself in, the house was in silence. I went upstairs to find him sitting up sheepishly in bed as I entered our room. 'I know, I'm a lazy sod – just want to make the most of my last good lie-in for a week,' he said. 'Looks like you survived the local shop, then?'

'It seems mostly harmless. A bit spooky, but harmless.' Sitting down on the bed, I went on quickly. 'You know, I heard the weirdest thing when I was in there. Some teenage girl and her boyfriend talking – they seemed to think Rebecca Fisher used to live in the village.'

'What, *the* Rebecca Fisher?' He looked every bit as startled as I'd felt hearing it from them. 'That's *insane.*'

'Well, it's what they said, all right. They said someone threatened to kill her if she didn't leave.'

He frowned. 'How did they know who she was?'

'God, I don't know – I just overheard them talking. I couldn't exactly ask them for a recap. I felt like a bit of an eavesdropper as it was.' I could read his carefully neutral,

35

noncommittal look too clearly after almost two years of marriage. 'You don't believe a word of it, do you?'

'Sounds like some sort of sick joke to me, Annie. Things like that don't really happen. Not in a sleepy little place like this, anyway. My guess is, one of them was winding the other up. You know what teenagers are like.'

In the shadows of Abbots Newton Stores, the revelation had had the power of oracle. Suddenly, however, it seemed ridiculous, transparently false. I felt as if I'd been breathlessly telling him about some spectacular news story – an ice-skating cat, a plant that could cure all known diseases – only to have him amiably point out that it was April the first.

'Anyway, suppose I'd better get up at last,' he said, swinging his legs out of bed. 'Let's go for lunch somewhere later, shall we?'

I could see him deliberately not acknowledging my sheepish embarrassment, and blessed him for it – if it *had* just been sheepish embarrassment, his tactful response would have gone some way towards alleviating it. But sitting in the bedroom and hearing him start to brush his teeth, I realised that his down-to-earth scepticism had inspired a sharp rise of regret; I'd *wanted* to believe Rebecca Fisher had lived in this village, to believe in anything that could distract my mind from the prospect of tomorrow morning.

36

5

I was sure to get used to these new surroundings, I told myself determinedly. It would be only a matter of time before everything around me took on the comfortable texture of familiarity. In that second week, while Carl was at work, I tried to bond with number four Ploughman's Lane as I would have done with any major purchase – an expensive winter coat, a new computer – studying it from all angles in a mirror or poring over an inch-thick manual, trying to reassure myself that I *did* really like it, I hadn't made a terrible mistake in a moment of consumer madness.

When Carl was at home, everything was as pleasant as it had been the previous week; his delight in his new job made everything comfortable and straightforward, we talked and joked and hugged as we'd done back in Reading. But, when the mornings came, the sound of his engine starting outside changed everything, and the rooms around me became faintly disturbing all over again. Not hostile, or threatening. Just *other*.

Perhaps it was only when Carl was at work that I had the time or inclination to analyse its atmosphere. But I thought there was more to it than that. The house seemed to expand and intensify in the strangeness of unaccustomed solitude; it felt too well-attuned to quiet mornings, to chilly sunlight and hours that lasted slightly too long. In as much as I'd noticed the walls at all, I'd thought them pure even-painted white, but when I came to look at them more closely, I saw that they had a slightly mottled look, random, wavery, almost untraceable patterns like the faint reflection of water. It wasn't just the bathroom, I realised; the whole house had the smell and taste of age, unforgeable as old parchment bound in crumbling leather, the half-recognised understanding that generations had lived here before us.

For all the thickness of its walls, the house seemed to actively deflect heat. In the mornings, it felt like a luke-warm bath on an equally tepid spring day. No matter how bright the day was outside, its shadows always looked a little too deep. It was a beautiful home in its own right, the country retreat of many urbanites' dreams; endlessly I reminded myself of the fact, told myself how lucky we'd been to get it at all. Still, as the slow days passed, my misgivings grew worse rather than better, and a horrible feeling of wrongness began to accompany the shrilling of the alarm clock. Homesickness for Reading sank into me with rusty metal teeth, minutiae of my life there taking on the golden shades of nostalgia. *This is never going to feel like home*, I thought starkly, *moving here was a terrible mistake, it's all wrong . . .*

Endless quiet, interchangeable days, punctuated by housework. I always shopped at the Asda on the outskirts of Wareham, driving there and back just to get out of the village for an hour or so. I didn't see any more of Liz next door, and, in my mind, she seemed more like a stranger than when we'd first met – now I knew about the ornaments and daughters and air of self-righteousness, she didn't feel like someone I could just pop round and visit without remaining constantly on guard. Even in the depths of homesickness, the sight of her little powder-blue Fiat outside didn't tempt me in the slightest. I desperately missed the company of people my own age, and people at work who hadn't seemed particularly important at the time. Above everyone else, I missed Petra.

During the daytime, she became my only real point of contact with the outside world. In Carl's new job, he wasn't able to email freely, and even when he had been, caution had edited his replies down to a four-line maximum. Petra had always been cheerfully indifferent to unwritten company rules governing personal correspondence, and I'd received the occasional epic from her in the past. Ironically, however, she seemed far busier than usual during those weeks – the long, determinedly cheerful emails I composed from the computer in the spare room were always answered by short, apologetic paragraphs littered with strangers' names, signed off with an extravagance of Xs as if in mitigation. It had always been the worst thing about Petra, if you could call something so integral to her entire character *worst* – the way her life was like a wildly popular, constantly-packed restaurant, leaving you permanently unsure whether you were sitting at the top table or in Siberia.

It was a ridiculous thing to worry about, the petty possessiveness of a primary-school playground, but everything around me seemed to encourage it. I had the radio or CD player on most of the time; but, in a funny sort of way, that only seemed to underline the dead silence pressing in beyond the windows, the absolute absence of other life and movement. An atmosphere where you could feel your mind turning restlessly in on itself, gnawing at its own tail for the sake of something to do.

While I tried to paper over my deepening misgivings about this place, it was inevitable that Carl would notice them. At first, I responded to his concerned questions evasively: I was just missing Reading a bit, I'd be all right soon. Acknowledging the way I really felt seemed unthinkable. We were here now, the mortgage in place, the phone connected, the carpets laid. It was far too late to sit down with him, confess I'd made a terrible mistake, explain I'd only be happy if we could somehow move back, away.

Soon, however, the pressure of private anxiety became too much for me to bear. Three weeks after we'd moved in, I knew I'd have to share at least some of it with him.

'Carl,' I said, when we were sitting in the living room after dinner, 'I never wanted to say this. But this place – it's really getting me down.'

He looked at me, startled. On the shelf behind him, the faux-Tiffany lamp tinted the dark room with rosy, baroque, antique-shop light. I forced myself to continue.

'I just kept hoping it would get better, but it hasn't done, at all. If anything, it's getting worse. I'm missing Reading so badly. I feel so *isolated*, out here.'

'Hey, come on.' He leant forward, elbows on knees, looking shaken, like a man who'd received shocking news unexpectedly, and was trying very hard to present a calm face to the world. 'We haven't been here a month – you can't judge yet. It's bound to feel a bit strange, at first.'

'Not *this* strange. I had no idea what it was going to be like out here, when I was alone all day.' I felt awkwardly aware that I was describing an insoluble problem and, more than that, making it his problem too. 'I know there's nothing you can do about it, I know it's not your fault – I *know* we can't just up sticks again; this is home now. It just really scares me to think it's always going to be like this. It's so quiet when you're not here. There's nothing to *do*.'

'Well, that's it, isn't it?' I saw relief dawn rapidly in his eyes, as if a brand new factor had entered the equation, instantly reducing it from postgraduate level to a five-point question on a GCSE paper. 'You're just bored, Annie. I'm not at all surprised – I know you've been missing work, it must be a real culture shock for you. But that's all it is. It's not this place that's upsetting you; you just need a new interest.'

I wasn't a hundred per cent sure that I believed him, but I wanted to so badly, I told myself I did. 'You really think so?'

'I know so. It's perfectly natural – you must be desperate for something to do.' The relief in his face had given way to an expression I recognised from a number of small emergencies – a power cut, a leaking pipe – eyes slightly narrowed, forehead creased, giving practical thought to a practical problem. 'Why don't you get to know some of the other people in the village? So far you've only really talked to the woman next door. No wonder you're getting a bit lonely.'

'That's a good idea.' I spoke cautiously, but felt anything but cautious – a kind of reckless optimism was beginning to take hold of me; I might not have made a mistake in moving here, this could feel like home after all. 'Maybe I could get Liz to introduce me to a few people. She's not really on my wavelength herself, but you never know, she might have some friends who are.'

'And you could spend more time in the village. Go to the local shop instead of Asda. Get involved in whatever it is people do round here. Get your face known.' He grinned. 'It's a lovely face. It's a shame to hide it away here all day.'

I smiled, suddenly wishing I'd raised this subject two days or two weeks ago. Vast obstacles began to look petty and ridiculous, my lonely exile in this house entirely self-imposed. 'I'm going to start thinking positive,' I said decisively. '*Christ*, I've been depressing. I must have been driving you up the wall.'

'You'd never do that,' he said, then, laughing at my quizzical expression and raised eyebrows, 'well, maybe a bit . . .' And I laughed with him, worries driven away by cheerful togetherness, looking forward to tomorrow for the first time in a fortnight.

When he'd left for work the following morning, I got up as soon as the front door had closed behind him, ran myself a bath, looking out at the trees extending over the horizon. I was amazed all over again by how different the world seemed, how a single conversation had changed the feel of everything around me. I hadn't embarked on a prison sentence in this house, but a whole new life; there were new people to meet, events to be part of, things to discover. Overcoming my fear of making first moves seemed a small price to pay in exchange for this new happiness.

Of course, I was well aware that this fear could never be permanently overcome, but I was more than willing to struggle laboriously past it until strangers' faces started to look familiar. After I'd washed and dressed, I decided to walk down to Abbots Newton Stores and get a few groceries we needed. Fresh optimism suddenly lent unexpected warmth and vivacity to my mental picture of that odd little shop – made it look like a hive of placid activity and *Archers*-esque gossip, a place to exchange casual pleasantries with the neighbours.

My walk there passed quickly, and when I stepped into the shadows under the jangling bell, the overcrowded look of everything was exactly as I remembered it. I expected to see the teenage girl named Julie, but there was no sign of her. The woman behind the till looked about sixty, with a wiry thatch of white hair and a squashed-in, bulldoggish face.

'Morning,' she said, as I came in. 'Lovely day, ain't it?'

She had a soft, gruff voice, a manner of ardent no-nonsense sociability. If I could talk to anyone in this village, I told myself, I could probably talk to her. 'Gorgeous,' I replied, then, steeling myself to continue, 'the weather's been lovely ever since I came here. My husband and I moved in a few weeks ago, but we haven't really met anyone else in the village, yet.'

'Oh, you will. It's a friendly sort of place, by and large – I should know, I've lived here most of my life. Welcome to Abbots Newton, love. I'm Maureen Evans.'

'I'm Anna Howell,' I said. 'Pleased to meet you. We live on Ploughman's Lane now, next door to Liz Grey.'

'Oh yeah?' A shrewd glint to Maureen's deep-set dark eyes, a new note of confidence in the voice. 'Suppose you'll have heard all about *her*, then.'

I looked at her, startled. 'Liz?'

'Oh, not *Liz*, love. Rebecca Fisher.'

'Well,' I said confused, 'I've heard a couple of things. But I thought it was probably just . . .' I was about to say *silly gossip*, and cast around for other, less offensive words without success. 'Well, nothing much.'

'Reckon you were wrong there.' A brief pause before she spoke again. 'Nothing much, my eye. Lived here all my life, I have, and I've never known anything like it.'

Her tone had the unmistakable edge of gossip – a ghoulish prurience that stopped just short of malice. 'Used to call in to buy her bits and pieces, she did. Called herself Geraldine. I thought she was a bit quiet at the time, not one to stay for a natter. But I didn't think there was anything *wrong* with her. Well, you wouldn't, would you? Not in a little place like this.'

43

In the half-light, there was something fascinating about that voice. I spoke slightly more sharply than I'd meant to, as if to break the spell. 'How do you know there *was* something wrong with her?'

'I was just coming to that, dear.' At first, she sounded slightly irritated, then continued in the same hushed tones. 'I heard on the grapevine she'd started getting anonymous letters. Nasty ones, too. Didn't know nothing more than that, at the time. Well, I can imagine she didn't want word getting out about what they said. Don't expect she'd have told nobody that, then. Only not long after, when she got home from Wareham, someone'd smashed all her windows in. Every last one. Her next-door neighbour was at work and all, nobody had heard a thing. She was hysterical, got the police round straight away.

'My son-in-law's with the local constabulary – he didn't get called out that day but he heard all about it from the ones who did. There were notes tied round the rocks they smashed her windows with, you see, and this time, she showed the police what they said. Suppose she was too scared not to, in case they could help.'

'What did they say? The notes?'

'Ooh, they were frightening. All cut out of newspaper letters, they were, like something off the telly.' A moment's pause for effect, an indrawn breath recalling shock. '*Get out Rebecca Fisher*, that was one of them. And one saying, *We know what you did*. And there was three all said the same thing: *This is your last warning*.

'Now, we all know there's no smoke without fire, but the police can't think like that, not when they don't know for sure. They did their best to get to the bottom of it, but with the best will in the world, there wasn't much they could do. No fingerprints on the notes at all, not one. And

44

nobody to see a thing, out there in the middle of nowhere. Makes this place look like Piccadilly Circus.'

'So what happened?'

'Well, that's just it. All I know is, she got her windows mended, and she never bothered the police again. She'd never talked to anyone round here much, and you can imagine how it was after that. Even if she'd been the friendly sort, there's plenty wouldn't have given her the time of day. Nobody heard another peep out of her. Next thing anyone knows, her house is on the market. And she's gone not six weeks later.'

'So whoever they were, they didn't stop.' I spoke slowly, without thinking. 'They threatened her again, and she didn't trust the police to protect her.'

'Knew she didn't have a leg to stand on, more like.' Maureen's voice was at once cosy and utterly judgemental. 'Wouldn't waste your sympathy on the likes of her. Someone found out who she was and what she did, and good riddance. I remember reading about it in the papers when I was first married, and a horrible story it was as well. I don't care what these social workers say. There's no two ways about it – evil people don't change their ways.'

Sudden suspicion sparked in my mind. 'How long ago did all this happen?'

'Don't you know?' For the first time in the conversation, Maureen looked ill-at-ease. 'Oh, I'm sorry, love. I thought you must.'

'Know what?'

'It was right before you moved in,' she said gently. 'You bought her house, you know. You bought Rebecca Fisher's house.'

6

As I left the shop and started walking, I was barely conscious of my surroundings. I could have passed anything or anyone, and wouldn't even have registered their presence. Cold, bright shock was beginning to fade around something altogether more unsettling; the implications of what Maureen had told me started to unwind in my thoughts.

I remembered the way I'd felt when I'd overheard the teenage girl and her boyfriend discussing the same subject – how superficially interested, how essentially indifferent. Now, my feelings had changed out of all recognition. This new revelation felt as vertiginous as a camera zooming down hundreds of feet in a split-second, from an aerial overview of a village to a close-up shot of number four Ploughman's Lane. The reassurance of distance had been snatched abruptly away. Rebecca Fisher had lived here, after all. *And she'd lived in our house.*

My imagination showed me a sheaf of ancient news cuttings – yellowed pages faded almost to the point of illegibility. Only some of the horror announced itself clearly, random words – MURDER, EVIL, MONSTER – driving home something that was almost too huge to comprehend. The hand that had wielded that knife more than thirty years ago opening the cutlery drawer in our kitchen. Turning on the taps in the bathroom. Reaching into the built-in wardrobe that now contained my clothes and Carl's, as its owner thought about her past, remembered those notorious events . . .

Fresh shock, as I realised we'd met her. That March, she'd shown us round the house herself. She'd been somewhere in her mid to late forties. She'd called herself Miss Hughes.

It was as if I'd carelessly tossed those memories into some internal dustbin, knowing I'd never need them again. I found myself struggling to retrieve them, wishing I'd preserved them with greater care. Rediscovering a woman who'd talked a little too quickly and nervously for a listener's comfort, whose every word and gesture had reflected what the estate agent had told us – she was keen to sell the house, was offering a heavily reduced price in exchange for a quick sale. A vague ghost-image of her face came back to me, and I found myself juxtaposing it with another; a face spelt out in grainy black-and-white newsprint dots, serene, angelic, notorious.

She hadn't worn well over thirty-three years; the fair hair turned dry and rough-looking, the pale eyes blood-shot. The slight build had grown scrawny with age. But it had been Rebecca Fisher. There was no doubt at all.

As the white house appeared in the distance, my attention turned abruptly inside out – there was nothing in the world but the scene ahead. That old house and its low-ceilinged rooms that had the faint tarnish of history, of lives and events that had taken place there long ago. And with cold crawling certainty, I understood there'd been more to that feeling that I'd realised – a ten-year-old killer had grown up and come to live there, had been driven out in fear of her life.

The front door creaked slowly shut behind me. The hallway felt even chillier than usual. As always, there were too many shadows. They seemed more sinister, reminding

47

me who else had seen them, who would have let herself in just as I'd done, who might have . . .

Stop it, I told myself sharply, and went into the kitchen to put the kettle on. But my thoughts kept turning back to a case I'd read about in passing, that I'd never dreamed I'd come to associate with my own life.

It had been her best friend, I remembered, that she'd stabbed to death all those years ago. What had the girl's name been? Emma? Elaine? Something along those lines. I found it inexplicably appalling to realise I hadn't even paid much attention at the time – it had just been an article about an old crime used to fill up space on a slow news day, like a TV repeat of an ancient sitcom. Anything could have distracted me from reading it, then. If a phone call had come for me halfway through, I'd have put it to one side and forgotten it existed.

But she lived here, I thought. I turned away from the kettle as it boiled, moved restlessly into the big, bare-walled living room. The oak beams that ran the full length of its ceiling made everything we'd brought with us from Reading look soulless, out of place. Our furniture had been bought to complement altogether smaller rooms, where everything encouraged newness and modernity and space. For the first time, I noticed how wrong it looked in this context, like a hastily-set-up camp in an empty house, as if we didn't belong here and could be driven out in the middle of the night, carrying our belongings in a few bulky bags.

A haunted feeling that I'd have laughed at mere hours ago. Rebecca Fisher's name kept repeating in the back of my mind, where a dark red light had snapped on above her image. And I realised how little I really knew about the previous owner of this place, the nervous householder who'd watched us a little too closely as she'd followed us round. The murderess.

Upstairs, the spare room faced onto the back garden as the bathroom did, and shared its odd breath of dank-edged age. It was easily the least prepossessing room in the house, and its few items of furniture had been placed rather than arranged – the narrow single bed, the rickety table beside it. Built-in cupboards provided extra storage space we didn't need. By the window, a self-assembly workstation housed the computer I'd written my first novel on and now used for nothing but emailing Petra, along with a printer, and an elderly fax machine of Carl's that he hadn't touched in over a year.

The computer took some time to start up, as ever. I sat through its endless, bewildering warm-up processes as patiently and uncomprehendingly as a savage watching a witch-doctor's incantations. When it was up and running, I went straight into Google Advanced Search. Under *Exact Phrase*, I typed in *Rebecca Fisher*. I entered, and waited.

www.eastlancashireonline.co.uk

TEASFORD – HOME OF THE UNEXPECTED
By WILLIAM HODGE

If you were to mention the East Lancashire town of Teasford to the average person in the UK, he or she would probably link it at once with a single horrific event – that, of course, being the notorious Rebecca Fisher case of 1969. It is sad that, even today, its unwelcoming public image remains unchanged. Over the course of the last thirty-three years, Teasford has become a very different place, and most people have completely the wrong idea about it.

It is true that, at the time it was most infamous, Teasford was very much the bleak town that the national newspapers described. The mining industry had been its main source of employment and prosperity throughout the first half of the twentieth century. However, this had been in a steady state of decline for some time, and Teasford's last remaining pit had closed in 1967. Since then, unemployment and deprivation in the area had increased dramatically. By 1969, the town's only major employer was the textiles factory owned by Dennis Fisher, who was of course Rebecca's adoptive father. In spite of the way newspapers have described it, it was not at all coincidental or surprising that Eleanor Corbett's own mother had worked here since 1965. As a widow with seven daughters to feed, Eileen Corbett would have had little choice.

Increasing poverty in Teasford naturally led to an influx of petty crime, most notably burglaries and prostitution, but it was far from the hostile environment people imagine. In character, it was surprisingly friendly and neighbourly, summarising all the good and bad points traditionally associated with the region. Families were large and close-knit, and the safety of young children and elderly people seemed guaranteed. While financial deprivation was immense, poor families had nothing to fear from their neighbours, and very few of these people would ever lock their doors in the daytime. This side of the town's character could be seen most clearly in the large network of post-war terraces adjoining the railway station, which remain to this very day (those familiar with the Rebecca Fisher case may well remember that Eleanor Corbett had grown up in this area herself.)

Today, however, any visitor to Teasford would see at once how dramatically it has changed. The textiles factory has been closed for more than twenty years, and a host of new employers have sprung up to take its place; an industrial park on its outskirts is home to several large call centres and an electrical goods manufacturer. Further regeneration can be seen in the modern housing estates which have sprung up around the town over the last twenty years. In 2003, far from being an unemployed miner, the average Teasford citizen is likely to work in a bank or an office, to live in a large and pleasant home and to shop in the town centre's branch of Sainsbury's. Grimy pubs have been replaced by the likes of the Rat and Parrot, and when you walk around the town, you are struck by how dramatically it has escaped from its deprived legacy.

It is undeniable that the tragic events of 1969 could have taken place just as easily anywhere else in Britain. With that in mind, it is deeply regrettable that they continue to cast such a long shadow in people's memories. Sadly, however, Rebecca Fisher remains Teasford's most famous daughter, and it is likely that her memory will alter perceptions of this town for some considerable time to come.

www.guardianonline.com

WITHOUT PREJUDICE
How a landmark ruling from 1969 may have many things to teach us about the nature of rehabilitation

ISABEL MANSFIELD
Sunday 20 April 2002

The phrase 'secret identity' has the unmistakable feel of John Grisham territory; one is instantly reminded of Mafia informants in the United States, treacherous spear-carriers exchanging information for a lifetime of guaranteed safety. With that in mind, it would appear a highly dubious and even immoral practice, which should surely be frowned on in any right-thinking society. All the more surprising, then, that it should have occurred in this very country more than twenty years ago, and that – much to the barely-veiled disappointment of the tabloid press – its outcome has been entirely successful.

When the notorious Rebecca Fisher case of 1969 was on every front page and news bulletin, the rise of public hatred for its central figure was startling and virtually unprecedented. It undoubtedly had as much to do with Fisher's appearance and status as with her age and the reality of her crime; the hackneyed phrase *pure evil* becomes far easier to use when neither financial nor social deprivation can be cited as mitigating factors. Nonetheless, in the years following her incarceration, this unsettling mood of mob fury towards her showed little, if any, sign of abating. It was to guarantee Fisher's safety following her eventual release that Edward Clarke, then Home Secretary, passed the landmark ruling ensuring her lifelong anonymity, stating that the issues involved hinged 'on almost unique circumstances'.

Inevitably, the details remain heavily shadowed to this day, and the sheer intricacy of the work involved again turns the mind to Hollywood thrillers; documents from birth certificates to National Insurance numbers have been altered, and those involved in the process legally bound to the utmost secrecy. The facts, however, remain simple enough for any child to grasp. Subject, of course, to her continuing good behaviour – a second violent offence would render the ruling instantly null and void – Rebecca Fisher was released and is now living as a completely different person.

Would justice have been better served if this notorious young woman had been released, under her own name, into a climate of violent hostility? To any sensible human being, the question answers itself at once. This is why I believe that Clarke's landmark ruling lends fresh depth and relevance to the concept of rehabilitation – and, on a more emotive level, that of redemption. As Fisher's story demonstrates, there exists a realistic and viable alternative to the mob's unspoken mantra of 'Give a dog a bad name, and lynch him'.

7

Carl got home from work at about seven thirty. 'Hi, Annie,' he called from the hallway. 'Smells good. What's cooking?'

'Poached salmon fillets in milk. I'm doing them with asparagus.' I stepped out of the kitchen, smiling. 'I thought we should have something a bit special tonight. Looks like a celebration's in order.'

He looked at me, frowning slightly – a formal, earnest-eyed figure, still in his work suit and work mode. 'How come?'

'Something wonderful's happened. I can't quite believe it myself.' I felt giddy, as I had done all afternoon, oddly weightless and a little unreal, as if I'd just stepped off the world's biggest, fastest fairground ride. 'I'm inspired again. I've got an idea for my second novel.'

A few seconds' dubious silence. I could see he was trying his hardest to look pleased for me, but not really understanding the importance of my news at all; privately bemused. 'Oh, I know you don't get it, but it's *fantastic* – I can't describe how good it feels to be inspired again when I'd started thinking I never would be. And it's so ironic how it all started – it's a terrible story, I should be horrified by it – I feel like a vulture, I'm quite ashamed of myself—'

The words came out with breathless, feverish, almost hysterical hilarity; I heard that note in my own voice as I saw it reflected in his face, his look of carefully veiled caution. 'Hey, slow down, slow *down*,' he said. 'What story are you talking about?'

'Well . . .' Everything about my body language was jittery, electric. I sat down, knowing it was the only way I could stay still, and made a huge effort to speak more slowly, more calmly. 'I went to Abbots Newton Stores again. Got talking to the woman who works there. Carl, Rebecca Fisher *did* live here. She was the woman who showed us round this house.'

His expression had become wary, doubt gathering in his eyes. I hated to see it there, and ploughed on with a zealot's determination. 'It's true – she knew all about it, there's no question she knew what she was talking about. She seemed like the kind of village gossip who knows everything about everyone. When Rebecca Fisher lived here, someone found out who she was and started trying to drive her out – she got anonymous letters and all her windows were broken. That's why she had to leave as soon as she could; *that's* why this house was such a bargain.'

I watched him, and was overwhelmingly relieved to see him begin to believe me. 'How did she know all about this?' he asked, but it was just a question now, carrying no undertow of suspicion. 'The woman in the shop?'

'Her son-in-law's with Wareham police. Rebecca Fisher called them out when she saw what had happened to her windows. Apparently, there was nothing they could do. She put this house on the market soon after. I thought she seemed jumpy when she first showed us round here, didn't you?'

'Maybe a bit on the nervous side. But there's nothing so unusual about that.' He spoke absently, and I sensed ninety-nine percent of his mind focused elsewhere. 'It doesn't bother me if she used to live here, and if all that really happened – you know me, I'm not that imaginative.

I'd have thought it would scare the hell out of *you*, though. What's all this about a new inspiration?'

'Well, when I got home from the shop, I was a bit freaked out. I thought I'd like to find out a bit more about the original case, get some idea of what she'd really been like. I looked her up on Google, did some surfing. Most of it was pretty predictable, just rehashing what I knew already. But a couple of the articles really got me thinking. About where she grew up, and that whole secret identity thing. They just ... sparked something off in my imagination. It's terrible, I know, but I couldn't help realising it would make an *incredible* basis for a thriller.'

Even now, guilt was fighting a valiant but doomed battle against elation. In the brief silence that followed, I thought I could see condemnation in his eyes, and spoke defensively. 'It won't be exploitative, it'll be a serious book. A good story, but serious. And it won't be based all that closely on the real case. Just loosely. Inspired by.'

While I was still trying to sound calm and rational, I could feel my voice picking up speed. 'I couldn't think of anything else all afternoon. In the end, I just had to get some notes down. Okay. My idea. A woman's released from prison with a whole new identity, settles down in the middle of nowhere; everyone just takes it on trust she's who she says she is. Gets a job, a husband – even he doesn't know a thing, and she'd never dreamed of telling him because she loves him too much, is scared he'd be appalled and leave her. Well, time passes and she's got a whole new life; she's a happy fifty-year-old woman with a family of her own. Then someone arrives in the village. Someone who knew her in prison. They start blackmailing her.' Ahead of that, there was nothing in my mind but blank white space, a cursor blinking at the top of an empty screen. I watched Carl's face closely. 'That's all I know so far. What do you think?'

'Jesus,' he said quietly. 'I think you've really hit on something, Annie. That sounds like it could make a great book.'

A huge wave of relief swept over me. I had been dreading polite, awkward distaste, feared presenting a treasure I thought I could retire on and finding it valued as worthless. 'I hope so,' I said. 'And there's something else. I want to write it all in the first person, from the point of view of the woman herself. My Rebecca Fisher character. Of course, she won't *be* Rebecca Fisher, she'll just be . . .'

'Loosely based on her. I know.' He smiled. 'It'll be tough doing it that way, though, won't it? I'm no writer, but I'm pretty sure you've never hung out with any notorious killers.'

'Tell me about it. I'm starting to wish I had done – maybe then I'd have some idea of how to bring one to life. I know we met Rebecca Fisher, but it didn't feel like meeting her at all.' Inspiration gnawed restlessly and my forehead corrugated in thought. 'I'll have to find some way around that; it must be possible. I've sent off for a book about her, from the internet. Maybe I'll ask around the village, too, see what people thought of her, try and get some kind of feel for her personality. What someone who'd do that might really be like, when you got to know them. *Someone* round here must have known her to talk to, it stands to reason.'

'Well, best of luck. Looks like you've had a pretty productive day. I think it's great you've got a new idea at last. Especially when it's such a good one.' Enthusiastic as he sounded, his voice had an edge of finality. 'Call me a philistine bastard for changing the subject like this, but

I'm starving to death now. Want me to put the asparagus on?'

Over dinner, he ate heartily, but I had no appetite whatsoever – I felt like a shaken-up Coke can, thoughts fizzing and bubbling inside me. The conversation moved to his brother's imminent birthday, whether I had any ideas regarding a suitable present, and various people he worked with. With the novel burning a hole in my mind, every other subject held all the interest of a bowling score, but I tried my best to look and sound as though I was paying full attention. We'd discussed the new idea for ages, and I couldn't drag the subject back out again tonight; deep down, I knew he didn't really appreciate how much it meant to me.

That night, I found it impossible to get to sleep for some hours. By midnight, Carl was snoring gently and rhythmically, and I lay beside him, mind teeming. I realised I hadn't been entirely honest with him regarding my feelings – not because I'd wanted to mislead him, but because I hadn't wanted to acknowledge the full truth to myself. While I'd described the bright, dizzy joy of inspiration, I could feel something moving behind it: the near-superstitious horror I'd experienced walking back from the shop, slowly blending into fascination.

The thrill of finally having a new idea. The unease of knowing where it came from. As the first flickers of characters and sub-plots began to move through my mind, these two emotions came together in the dark and fused into something I couldn't put a name to; squirming, treacherous, troubling.

I woke earlier than usual the following morning – Carl was still fast asleep, and the bedside clock told me it had just gone six. Normally, I'd never have dreamed of getting up at such a time. Now, however, I found I couldn't stop myself.

I edged out of bed, not disturbing him, and went downstairs. Curtains and blinds were drawn throughout the house, and everything around me had a desolate feel, chilly and grey as cold ash. When I opened the blinds in the kitchen, the sudden flood of sunlight was welcome – tentative and tepid, but sunlight just the same.

For long seconds, I stood there looking out into the slightly overgrown back garden and the dense woods beyond it. There was something hypnotic about all that freshly minted emptiness, and I felt as if I were entirely alone in the house. I wasn't used to the way the light looked at this hour, and its unfamiliarity lent everything a dreamlike quality. It occurred to me that Rebecca Fisher might have come down here this early herself, after the anonymous threats had begun; that she'd stood in this spot, at once restless and purposeless, unable to linger in bed as I'd been. I remembered the dog collar we'd found in our first week here, the pet we hadn't seen any sign of when she'd shown us around in March. I had a mental picture of it watching her incuriously from the corner, by the door, as she stood and remembered why she was hated . . .

I shivered in the early-morning chill, and forced myself to move away from the view. Making strong black coffee, I lit a cigarette and sat down at the table with a pad of A4 and a biro. Deliberately, I turned my attention away from the echoes that lingered on the air, towards the facts alone; the drama, the horror, the things that could easily be translated into fiction.

As it happened, it was easier than I could have hoped – the bare plot outline that had come to me yesterday was developing at an almost frightening speed, and fresh details began to unwind as I scrawled down first-stage notes. A child murderess who'd built a whole new life for herself under an assumed identity, a happy, respectable life as a pillar of village society. And her politely, implacably blackmailing nemesis – a retired female police officer now fallen on hard times, a chance sighting in the local shop sparking sudden recognition . . .

I don't think anyone else would have been able to decipher my handwriting. It had degenerated into a tiny, erratic scrawl, as if someone else was dictating at a hundred miles an hour and I was struggling to catch each word without the aid of shorthand. I was still scribbling furiously when Carl's voice came from behind me.

'Annie? What the hell are you up to?'

I turned, startled as if caught in some shameful or criminal activity. He was standing in the doorway, tousle-haired and dressing gowned.

'Just thought I'd make a start on the writing,' I said. 'Well, on the notes, anyway. The actual writing's a long way off, yet.' I struggled to sound casual, as if I'd been driven down by mild peckishness rather than starvation. I was well aware I wasn't making a very good job of it.

'I've never known you get up this early when you didn't have to,' he said cautiously. 'It's only just gone ten to seven. How long have you been down here?'

Over three quarters of an hour – the realisation startled me badly. I'd had no idea of how quickly the time had passed. 'About ten minutes or so,' I said quickly. 'I don't know, I just wanted to get something down on paper.'

'That's dedication.' He smiled. In his eyes, I saw my actions become characteristic of that charmingly foreign country Artistic Temperament, rather than the bleak and alien wastelands of Strange Behaviour. 'I wondered where you'd got to when I woke up a few minutes ago. Didn't break the flow too badly, did I?'

'Don't worry about it. I'll be able to pick up where I left off.' I closed and bolted a heavy door against the clamouring ideas. 'Want some coffee?'

'Thanks, but no thanks. Think I'll go and have a shower. I'll leave you to it – don't work too hard.'

As I heard him moving around upstairs, I tried to plunge back into the logistics of the plot, but when he'd finally left for work I was dismayed to feel the high-pressure jet of ideas slow to a trickle, and threaten to dry up completely. It was the house, I realised; in his absence it became somehow oppressive, distracting, reminding me how little I knew about the woman who'd inspired my shadowy central character. A nervous middle-aged woman who'd owned a dog and left its collar behind. A woman with bloodshot pale eyes and greying fair hair tied indifferently back in a ponytail. A woman whose personality and emotions and motivation were entirely hidden from me. A stranger . . .

My train of thought was derailed by the sound of the back door creaking open. Glancing round, I saw Liz's cat Socks poised in the doorway with the politely autocratic air of a duke waiting to be seated at the Savoy. The sight obscurely cheered me; I couldn't help smiling as I rose from my seat. 'Hello, puss,' I said. 'What's the matter, Liz at work? Come on – I'll get you some milk.'

I filled a saucer and set it down by the table. It was fine to have him here during the daytime; it was only the immediate presence of cats or dogs that started Carl sneezing. Socks glanced up at me with more acknowledgement than gratitude before lapping the milk up briskly. Then he shook a few drops off his whiskers and padded over to a broad square of sunlight on the underfoot tiles, where he curled up in its absolute centre, his attitude midway between sunbathing and sleeping.

Realising that the new visitor wasn't going to require a lot more attention, I sat back down to the notes, absent-mindedly lighting another cigarette. My earlier misgivings deepened as I looked at what I'd written earlier. A crucial absence stared out at me from each page, made the broad outline of this long-awaited new idea two-dimensional, unsatisfactory.

Some time later, I was startled by a second noise from the back door, this time a brisk, playful *tippety-tap*. Rising to get it, I saw Liz through the window, brown hair escaping from its bun in flyaway wisps. Untidiness normally brought with it a reassuring air of vulnerability, but in her case it seemed to imply the exact opposite, a woman too busy and confident and practical to care about any element of grooming other than cleanliness. Even her face reflected that; an unselfconsciously weather-beaten look said that she'd never worn any make-up beyond the occasional smudge of lipstick, and that she'd never wanted to.

'Hello, dear,' she said cheerfully, stepping in. 'Sorry to be a pest, but I was wondering if you'd seen— oh, there he is. I got back from the library a few minutes ago, and wondered where he'd got to. I do hope he hasn't been a nuisance.'

'Oh, not at all,' I said quickly. 'It's been nice having him around.'

'Really, dear, just shoo him away if he bothers you, there's no need to be embarrassed about it. He's only after more food, as if he didn't get enough at home. He can be a greedy little thing sometimes.' She smiled, looking affectionately down at Socks, then her gaze moved to the table, the scrawled-on pad of A4 beside the half-full ashtray. 'Oh dear, I didn't interrupt you, did I? Were you writing a letter?'

I remembered I hadn't told her about my writing, and decided that this wouldn't be a good time to do so. I had absolutely no wish to share my new idea and have it met by blank, rather wary incomprehension – everything I'd seen of her told me she'd consider it in extremely bad taste, if not actively morbid. 'That's right,' I said. 'To an old friend in Reading. I thought it'd be nice to keep in touch.'

'That is nice. I always think the telephone isn't quite the same – I don't care how many people say it's more convenient these days. My mother always used to say, nobody ever kept a nice telephone call.'

A brief and rather awkward pause. She was the kind of woman who it was decidedly stressful to receive an unexpected visit from; I was aware of her discreet but total alertness to domestic detail, tried not to wonder what she was privately disapproving of behind that polite social smile. The ashtray seemed the most obvious culprit, and I found myself thanking God there wasn't a half-empty wine glass on the table.

'Well, I'd better be off then, Anna,' she said. 'I'm sure I'll see you soon.'

She bent down and scooped up Socks with small hands that looked surprisingly unspoiled by cooking and gardening and other placid semi-rural pursuits. Her wedding and engagement rings caught the light, sun glinting off the thin gold band and dancing across the square-cut emerald conventionally set in diamonds. As she carried the big ginger cat over to the front door, something seemed to occur to her, and she turned back.

'Would you like to pop over in half an hour or so, dear? A couple of my friends are coming round for a cup of tea and a chat. Helen, who you saw when you first moved in, and another lady called Muriel. I'm sure it would be nice for you to meet them properly. I wouldn't dream of intruding, but you must be getting awfully lonely on your own here.'

Extraordinary, how much could change in less than twenty-four hours. This time yesterday, I'd have agreed joyfully in the hope of meeting new people, making new friends. Today, my enthusiasm was driven by something else entirely. One or more of them must have known Rebecca Fisher, I thought – must, at the very least, have spoken to her more than once.

'I'd love to,' I said. 'Thanks very much. I'll see you then.'

8

'So where were you living before, Anna?' asked Muriel.

The four of us were sitting round Liz's kitchen table over carrot cake and Earl Grey. As the youngest person present by at least fifteen years, I experienced a distinct self-consciousness, an outsider's feeling I was far too familiar with. There was something dutiful about their interest and my own smiling, polite replies. It was like visiting distant aunts for the first time in years. 'Reading,' I said. 'We were there quite a while.'

'That must have been very nice. My eldest daughter lives quite near there, you know. In Basingstoke.' Muriel was almost a caricature of a nervous fiftysomething widow who'd led a quiet and sheltered life: she spoke very fast, in a high fluting voice whose every cadence expressed vague uncertainty and anxiety to please. 'I went to visit her there once, nearly two years ago – the time does fly, doesn't it? I was rather worried, to be honest, even with my son-in-law in the house. There seemed to be an awful lot of crime in the area.'

'It's the same everywhere, these days,' said Helen, apparently to Liz and Muriel only. 'Not the same as when we were young.'

Up until now, she'd hardly spoken. Her voice was quiet and flat and somehow heavy, the opposite of Muriel's in every way. On our first meeting, it hadn't even occurred to me that she was attractive; her manner had combined with her clothes to deny any hint of that – the crisply ironed high-necked shirt, the fair hair pulled back in a pin-neat bun, the brusque, unemotional greeting to the new neighbour. Watching her more closely, I was startled to realise how good her bone structure and complexion really were. She was big without being at all fat, just built very slightly above normal scale. Her movements were as devoid of grace as they were of clumsiness – she didn't seem to have the self-consciousness necessary for either. 'We never used to *hear* about crime,' she went on, 'not when I was a girl.'

'Well, there's always been some, I dare say,' Liz said amiably. 'Even in some of the nicest places. It's an awful shame, when you come to think of it.'

Out of nowhere, I spotted a golden opportunity to take the subject where I most wanted it to go, a casual side-turning off the conversation rather than a brake-squealing change of direction. 'Even here,' I said, trying to sound as matter-of-fact as possible. 'You know, I heard yesterday that Rebecca Fisher lived next door, before we moved in.'

A brief moment's silence as the three of them glanced at each other quickly, and I was struck again by the almost cartoonish contrast between Muriel and Helen, the former tiny and anxiously animated, the latter the exact opposite. I observed Liz existing at some point between them, as if overseeing proceedings. Perhaps it was simply because she alone was on home ground, but the things that distanced me most from her had never been more in evidence – she was comfortably at the centre of her domestic world, a woman who'd never known what *outside* meant. 'Well . . . I suppose you had to know sooner or later, dear,' she said reluctantly. 'I expect you heard from Maureen in the shop. She's such a dreadful gossip.'

'I did,' I said. 'I must say, it came as a bit of a surprise.'

They all watched me for several seconds, faces betraying varying degrees of uncertainty; Liz spoke again at last. 'I'm sorry you had to find out like that,' she said quietly. 'Perhaps I should have told you myself. The thing is . . . I didn't think you'd want to know. I thought it would just upset you for no reason.'

'I don't mind. I'm not frightened – why should I be?' I remembered the way I'd felt walking back from the shop yesterday, the unfolding sense of hypnosis as the front door closed behind me. As if to hold those images at bay, I found myself speaking with Carl's earnest-eyed pragmatism. 'I'm not, you know, superstitious like that. I don't mind *who* used to live in the house, or what happened there.'

'You must have nerves of steel, Anna, you really must.' Muriel sounded awed. 'If I found out something like that about my little cottage, I'd move the very next day, I'd simply have to. It was terribly frightening, when all of that was happening – when I found out, I didn't sleep properly for *weeks*.'

'Don't expect she'd have done you any harm. Not these days.' At first Helen sounded dismissive, then judgemental. 'Still, it's a scandal they let her out at all. Good thing she finally got what was coming to her, or almost – you know about that, I suppose?'

She addressed me abruptly: I couldn't help but find her manner a little intimidating, casting me in the role of an unreliable witness facing an expert cross-examiner. I relayed in brief what I'd heard from Maureen Evans – the anonymous notes, the broken windows, the abrupt departure. When I'd finished, their expressions said that I'd been told the full story. I could sense both Muriel and Liz wondering what they should say, how they could reassure without actively lying.

'It was such a terrible thing to happen,' Muriel said hesitantly, at last. 'I can't help thinking she might not even have been who they said she was – whoever it was that did those awful things to her. It could just have been a dreadful mistake of some sort.'

'Don't be ridiculous, Muriel. Why would anyone go to all that trouble, unless they knew for sure?' Helen's voice was brisk and impatient. 'Myself, I'm just glad to know she's gone. Thank God for small mercies.'

I racked my brains to find further questions before this subject drifted away. 'Did any of you have anything much to do with her while she lived here?'

'Well, she wasn't here for long – no more than two months or so, if that,' said Liz. I looked at her, startled. 'It all happened so soon after she moved in, none of us really had a chance to get to know her. I invited her in for a cup of tea one afternoon, come to think of it.'

I saw Muriel's little *moue* of recollected horror from the corner of my eye, but my full attention was focused on Liz, her unexpected key to my central character. 'What did you think of her?'

'She seemed rather shy. Reserved. Perfectly normal, apart from that. I must say, I didn't really take to her, although I daresay that's just hindsight.' Across the table, Liz looked thoughtful. 'I don't think she made any friends around the village, before it all started.'

'What about that vet, Liz?' Muriel asked timidly. 'That Mr Wheeler?'

'Goodness, I forgot all about that. She had a little dog, a sort of terrier – I only saw it once or twice; she seemed to keep it inside towards the end. She must have taken it to Mr Wheeler soon after she moved in, and got to know him that way. I saw him coming and going next door quite often. Of course, I recognised him – there's only one vet's practice round here, in Wareham. He certainly spent a lot of time next door while she was living here. To be honest, I couldn't help but wonder if there was something going on between them.'

'Of course there was.' If Liz had spoken with casual acceptance of the idea, Helen had never sounded chillier or more judgemental. 'I saw them walking together in the village, more than once. A disgrace, I call it – that man hadn't been divorced for a year, at the time. I wouldn't be at all surprised if *she'd* had something to do with that. For all we know, they'd been carrying on for months before she arrived here.'

I'd rarely felt as ill-at-ease with a stranger as I did with Helen, but sheer surprise overcame that for a second and I spoke as frankly and impulsively as I would have done to Petra or Carl. 'You can't *know* that. It sounds harmless enough to me. What's so terrible about it?'

'I suppose young people don't have quite the same moral standards, these days.' There was no trace of irony in her voice, and her smile was thin, perfunctory, sunless. 'Even if he hadn't been so recently divorced, the woman was Rebecca Fisher – what sort of man would want anything to do with someone like that?'

I didn't say anything else, forced myself to nod earnestly; we'd never understand each other, I realised. On any given topic, the two of us would be poles apart. It was a relief when Liz spoke again, and I had an excuse to look at her instead. 'Well, that's all water under the bridge now, thank goodness. Would anyone like some more tea?'

It seemed that the vague shape of Rebecca Fisher was disappearing over the horizon. Inevitably, the conversation moved on to other, less controversial people and events in the village but, while I listened and nodded politely, most of my mind was somewhere else, lost deep in thought. Remembering the studded collar in the kitchen cupboard again, I found myself wondering whether Rebecca had liked all animals, or just dogs; if she'd been the sentimental, adoring kind of pet owner, or the brisk, no-nonsense type who behaved more like a practical, responsible, undemonstrative parent. As the three different voices flowed on and on around me, I realised that I didn't have a clue, felt my mind like an ancient computer overloaded with conflicting data, monitor blinking a random infinity of symbols that meant nothing.

When I let myself into the house through the back door, it had just gone half-three in the afternoon. A faint hint of stale smoke and ash hung on the still air, and the silence seemed heavier and more ambiguous than it had done earlier. I opened the windows and put the radio on, thinking back to Liz and Helen and Muriel – how they'd told me things, without really telling me anything.

Extraordinary, I thought, how three completely different women could all be so paralysingly unobservant. They'd *seen* Rebecca Fisher, lived alongside her, and Liz had even chatted to her over a nice cup of tea. Thinking about that meeting, I found I could visualise it only too clearly. The big, prosperously crowded kitchen and ginger biscuits at the table, small-talk about how difficult it was to move house, and what the village was like, and nothing in the world that really mattered. Even knowing what she did now, I didn't think Liz would look back and kick herself for not asking and noticing more, didn't think she'd even find herself replaying that mental footage from time to time, alert to small details she might have missed. Rebecca Fisher had been *pure evil*, and then she'd been *perfectly normal*, and that was all there was to the situation – straightforward as two plus two equalling four; only an idiot could possibly argue.

But there was far more to her than that, I thought. There had to be. Everything around me hinted mockingly at the three-dimensional reality of the woman, the too-beautiful child who'd stabbed her best friend to death. It frustrated me beyond words to feel the truth of her life hidden away from me – my new idea was entirely dependent on its central character, and only Rebecca Fisher could breathe life into it. And there was something else there, too, that I barely acknowledged to myself: alone in this house, I found it deeply disturbing not to know what it had contained before, what secret rooms and byways had existed in its previous owner's mind.

Abruptly I hurried into the living room, towards the Yellow Pages under the telephone table. As Liz had said, there was only one vet's practice listed for Wareham. I dialled the number quickly, before I could think better of it. The ringing tone began down the line. My heartbeat quickened.

'Wareham Veterinary Surgery. Can I help you?'

A female voice, simultaneously kindly and harassed – I could hear another phone ringing faintly in the background. 'Oh, hello,' I said, trying very hard to sound confident. 'Is there any chance I could talk to Mr Wheeler?'

'I'm afraid he's in surgery at the moment. Can *I* help you at all?'

Damn – but I knew it would be the same story tomorrow, or this time next week, and there was nothing I could do but tell the truth. 'Well, I hope so,' I said. 'This might sound like a weird thing to ask, but I'm researching a novel at the moment – I've had one published before, called *A Deeper Darkness.* My name's Anna Jeffreys.'

Silence down the line. I pressed on, struggling for the right note of brisk professionalism. 'I was wondering if I might be able to talk to him. I wouldn't take up much of his time, just fifteen minutes or so. Any time that's convenient, of course. I'd be very grateful.'

'Well, it doesn't sound as if it should be much of a problem . . .' I couldn't help being faintly amused by the new note of surprised near-awe in her voice, as if I'd rung up from Miramax inviting the vet in for a screen test. 'If you leave your number, I'll pass it on to him when he's free. I'm sure he'd be only too happy to help.'

'Thanks a lot,' I said. 'That's great.'

After I'd given her my number, I went back into the kitchen, where I lit another cigarette and unearthed the notes I'd written earlier. Now I could see some clear way into the centre of this novel, I rediscovered the fascination with them that I'd experienced first thing that morning.

Maybe three quarters of an hour after I'd sat down, the phone shrilled in the hallway and, putting my pen down, I hurried to answer it.

'Hello?'

'Hello, is that Anna Jeffreys?' It was a quiet, level male voice, pleasant and unemotional in equal measure – a voice you could trust to care about your pets in the same low-key way its owner would care about his own.

'Speaking.'

'This is Colin Wheeler. I got the message you left at reception earlier, and thought I'd give you a ring. I must say, I was a bit surprised – couldn't help thinking you must be after a different man.'

'Not at all, I've definitely got the right person.' Despite myself, I was startled by how easy this conversation felt. I'd expected it to be uphill all the way, but it was like talking to an old friend. 'As I said earlier, I'm researching my second novel, and wondered if you'd mind if I came in

72

and talked to you for ten minutes or so. Whenever it suits you – I understand you must be busy.'

'Well, that's the life of a local vet for you. I never thought anyone would want to *write* about it, though. What sort of thing would you like to find out?'

Actually, I was interested in finding out about Rebecca Fisher and what she was really like— the words were almost out of my mouth before I realised they'd be a mistake. It was too easy to imagine his quick knee-jerk response: *Oh, I can tell you that now, she was very nice, much like anyone else –* leaving me with no polite option but *Thanks very much, bye.* He had known her, perhaps even loved her, and I instinctively sensed that I'd be able to find out far more face to face.

'Oh, just this and that,' I said quickly, 'nothing to worry about. When do you think would be a good time for me to come in?'

We agreed that I'd visit him on Friday at twelve noon. I thanked him very much and hung up. Back in the kitchen, I made a few more notes before starting on dinner and waiting for Carl to come home.

9

Carl had never really understood how uncomfortable I'd been telling people about my writing – or, perhaps more accurately, he'd never understood why I felt that way. Impossible to explain that it felt too private to easily share with indifferent near-strangers, that I'd only let it be known at work after an overheard phone-call from my agent left me with little choice in the matter; on holiday, meeting new people beside Carl, I'd always say I worked as a PR officer for my local council and leave it at that. And I'd sense his guarded, slightly wary puzzlement throughout the rest of the encounter. *I don't know why you didn't just tell them, Annie,* he'd say later, *I really don't understand you, sometimes.* I hated the expression he always wore at those times – as if I was dragging him into an odd and slightly sinister conspiracy he wanted no part of.

He distrusted secrecy intensely. It was a key element of his personality, in some way seeming to hold the DNA blueprint for everything else about him – the career-minded pragmatism, the love of state-of-the-art technology and doing the right thing. Perhaps it was nurture as much as nature, the result of growing up in a household where everything was absolutely as it should be. Whatever the reason, he was as ill-at-ease with hidden things in his life as he would have been heading through Customs with a small bag of cocaine in his pocket; it was all-important to his peace of mind that people *could* look, if they wanted, and find nothing that shouldn't be there.

For that exact reason, I was very unwilling to tell him

about my conversation with Mr Wheeler and admit that, if I hadn't actually lied, I had at the very least colluded in a serious misapprehension. I knew only too well how he'd react, and how he'd interpret it. He'd see it as the worst possible thing: secrecy for its own sake, feverishly concealing an entirely inoffensive truth. It would turn his mind back to other things I'd told him about before we'd married, things he'd ended up telling his parents shortly afterwards. The more I thought about it, the more clear-cut the situation became. I couldn't possibly let him know about the vet.

It didn't matter, I told myself; my imminent visit to the Wareham surgery was no more important than dozens of things he did at work every day and I never knew about; his tales from the office generally involved nothing more personal than a joke someone had emailed round or the too-ambitious sales targets Head Office had set for next season. At the same time, though, I was well aware that it *was* more important and that I was lying to myself. Every evening, I felt it burning in my mind, and tried to pretend it wasn't there. And I could feel him comfortably attributing my preoccupation to the broad outline of *the novel*; of course I was thinking about it a lot at the moment, but soon it would lose the urgency of novelty and I'd be able to settle down again.

During the day, I spent most of my time making notes in the kitchen, at once unnerved by the feeling of solitude here and intrigued by it – a multi-layered sensation that was practically impossible to rationalise. Socks came round occasionally when Liz was at work. His presence never failed to dilute the tension with easy domesticity – nothing could be further removed from the darkness of Rebecca Fisher than an amiable ginger cat in search of milk and companionship. The reassurance of knowing there was something else alive in here, purring in a square of sunlight, lapsing into feline dreams.

Intense restlessness for Friday, impatience, the time seeming to pass too slowly. My thoughts obsessively circled the place where Rebecca's character should have been, knowing there was nothing there but empty space, returning every few minutes just to make sure she hadn't miraculously sprung into fully-formed life. And as they came back, they always passed directly over other things; the quiet tensions of the house I'd grown up in, and that endless terrifying autumn somewhere else, and the places I was in most agony never to return to.

I'd expected the practice on the outskirts of Wareham to be virtually deserted on a weekday lunchtime – from what I'd seen of the town so far, it seemed a safe enough bet. But when I came in at quarter to twelve on Friday, I was surprised by how busy it was. The rows of plastic chairs in reception were crowded with owners bearing animals; I counted three cats, four dogs and something unidentifiable in a cage. A couple of little kids ran around shrieking, drawing irritable glances from everyone but their mother. The phone rang incessantly, even as the harrassed-looking receptionist spoke quickly and purposefully into another line.

'So I'll book you in for Monday the twentieth,' she was saying. 'See you then, Bye.' She looked up as I approached, with the air of an efficient woman trying to do far too many things at once. 'Can I help you?'

I'd expected to feel awkward and slightly embarrassed, and I did – I forced myself to speak with a semblance of confidence. 'I rang up on Tuesday. My name's Anna Jeffreys. I arranged to talk to Mr Wheeler for ten minutes or so this afternoon.'

'Oh, you're the writer. He told me about that – it's not often he gets interviewed.' The phone's relentless shrilling had become impossible to ignore. 'If you take a seat, I'll call you when he's free,' she said, then, 'hello, Wareham Veterinary Surgery?'

I sat beside an elderly lady with a Yorkshire terrier on her knee, and waited. The walls were covered with posters, and I scanned them as the minutes passed. *PetPlan Insurance. Wareham Cattery.* 'Miss Jeffreys?' the receptionist called at last. 'If you'd like to go through.'

Mr Wheeler turned out to be a tall man in his early forties, with receding brown hair and a kindly, mournful, bloodhoundish face. He was dressed in a white coat, all amiability as I came into the small, functional consulting room. He seemed every bit as approachable as he had done over the phone, and I couldn't help but wonder what had drawn him to Rebecca Fisher.

'You must be Anna Jeffreys,' he said. 'Pleased to meet you.'

We shook hands, and he gestured for me to take the single plastic chair. 'It was quite a surprise to hear from you,' he went on. 'I had no idea we had any writers in the area.'

'Well, I only moved in recently.' I had a sudden mental image of word somehow filtering back to Liz, Helen, Muriel and Maureen, the soul-destroying references to my book's apparent absence from bookshops picking up where they'd left off in Reading. It was the very last thing I wanted, I realised, and I was prepared to sound more than a little eccentric to try and stop that happening. 'I'd really appreciate it if you kept it to yourself – I haven't really told anyone else round here.'

'That's very modest of you.' It was a habitual misinterpretation, and one I had no real urge to explain

77

further. He carried on pleasantly. 'So where are you living now?'

'Abotts Newton. Four Ploughman's Lane.' Seeing the recognition and surprise dawning in his eyes, I forced myself to continue. 'Actually, I'm afraid I might have misled you a bit, about what I wanted to find out. To be honest, I really wanted to discuss Rebecca Fisher – I heard she'd lived in our house, before we moved in. Someone mentioned that you'd known her, and I wondered if you'd be able to tell me a bit about what she was like. I . . .'

My words tailed off uneasily – in the space of a few seconds, his face seemed to have changed completely. 'I'm sorry,' I said, bewildered. 'Did I say something to upset you?'

'Not at all.' But his voice was completely different too, cold and taut, trembling just below the surface with something that almost sounded like hatred. 'I'm very glad that the village ghouls have found a more imaginative way of approaching me at last. You know, they normally just stop me on the street, and ask, *Was it really true you knew her? Isn't it a mercy she's gone now?*' His voice rose to a savage, pitch-perfect imitation of a gossipy old woman, cracked and quavery. 'I never knew any of them would have the brains to dream up a story like yours, researching a novel – congratulations, that's very clever. You know, I honestly believed you, at first.'

'I'm sorry.' My own voice seemed to be coming from a long way off. 'I don't know what you—'

'You know, I'd have thought you were all tired of hounding her by now. But obviously it's not enough, even after she's been forced out of her own home. Even after her little dog was killed to make her leave. Want to know the full story, do you? If I could sense something evil about her? If I recognised her from the old photograph?' A kindly bloodhound of a man, I'd thought him – now he faced me, snarling. 'If you want to see evil in that bloody village, look at your neighbours, who watched that woman reduced to a gibbering wreck without lifting a finger. Or look at yourself, gloating over the details. I'm going to have to ask you to leave.'

'Honestly, you've got the wrong idea—' but it was token resistance only – I was getting up and backing away as I spoke. 'If I could just explain—'

'*Goodbye*, Miss Jeffreys.'

There was nothing I could do but leave, heading back out through the crowded reception, deeply shaken, cursing myself over and over again for screwing up so badly. If I'd only begun in a different way, if I could only step back in time and rephrase my opening words ... but I knew perfectly well there was no point thinking about it. I'd lost my chance for good. It didn't take an author's sensitivity to realise he'd be less than happy to get a follow-up call from me in the near future, attempting to clarify my motives.

Remembering how his face had changed, a small, involuntary shiver ran up the back of my neck. It was as if an unexpected cloud had passed across the sun, and the world around me seemed to darken in some tiny but unmissable way. She'd been his friend and possibly his lover, I told myself, it was only natural that he'd want to protect her. I couldn't help but wonder how Rebecca Fisher could inspire such loyalty – how anyone could describe what had happened as an appalling violation, when the rest of the world seemed to perceive it as nothing more than rough justice.

Of course, he'd known something nobody else had, not even Maureen from the shop. As I drove, his voice came back to me along with the abandoned collar from the cupboard: *Even after her little dog was killed to make her leave.* Everything in his recollected tone expressed naked hatred for the others in the village – and, while it disturbed me to acknowledge it to myself, an apparently newborn hatred for *me*.

My own distress embarrassed me intensely – he was only a country vet, after all. It wasn't as if I'd just made an enemy of a Sicilian Mafia boss. Turning the radio on and up, I sought out cheerful chart tracks to flush the worry away; banal rhymes expressing slick stock emotions, bouncy music that denied the very existence of dark corners.

10

Approached from Wareham, Ploughman's Lane strayed off a very minor road and up a steep, fair-sized hill – driving up it, you could see nothing at the top but empty blue sky and a few chalky smudges of cloud, and the view gave you the alarming optical illusion that you were about to speed off the edge of the world. Then, when you crested it and were heading into green, leafy, picturesque depths, my own and Liz's houses became clearly visible in the middle distance, on the left-hand side of the road – the only man-made structures the eye could see before another, gentler hill rose to cut off the view.

As they came into sight again, I was abruptly reminded of how different my mood had been as I'd set out earlier. Then it had been all optimism, was now all uncertainty. I wished I'd never gone into Wareham at all. Suddenly, I felt a kind of craving for the comfortable certainties of Liz's kitchen, cups of tea and reassuring chit-chat delaying solitude and worry in an empty house. But long before I'd turned into our driveway, I knew it wasn't going to happen. The one time I really wanted to see her little powder-blue Fiat parked outside, it wasn't there.

My thoughts and her absence made the silence seem more oppressive than ever before. I supposed that Socks must be next door somewhere, but it felt as if there was nothing and nobody for miles around. As I got out of the car and walked towards the front door, my footsteps sounded louder than usual. In this absolute stillness, the unexpected chirruping of a single grasshopper would have made me jump.

I let myself in. The hallway was cool and stale-smelling, as though there'd been nobody here for weeks. Deep inside, my conversation with Mr Wheeler kept repeating and repeating, caught on some nightmarish mental tape-loop – I kept listening to his side of it, trying my hardest to hear prosaic irritation. Unable to hear anything but cold loathing mixed with fury. There was something terrifying about the thought that a virtual stranger hated you that much, and there was nothing you could say or do to change their mind, that a person you didn't know at all might actively wish you harm. Especially when you'd told them where you lived. Of course, he'd remember – it had been Rebecca's address, he'd been here himself. At some point in the not-so-distant past, he must have stood in this very hallway, must know the layout of this house as well as that of his own.

I told myself I was being melodramatic, over-imaginative. He'd certainly been angry, but I had no possible reason to fear reprisals. But rational or not, my tension wasn't going anywhere. The second it started to retreat, Mr Wheeler's furious eyes flashed in my mind and brought it rushing straight back. I had a sudden need for a comforting, familiar voice, but I couldn't tell Carl about this turn of events; he had no idea that I'd gone to see the vet in the first place. Checking my watch, I saw it was only one thirty and there was a good chance that Petra would be on her lunch break. I got her mobile number from the little book by the living room phone and dialled, praying she wouldn't have absent-mindedly switched it off.

She hadn't – I heard her answer on the fifth or sixth ring, blessedly cheerful and outgoing and herself. 'Hello?'

'Hi, Petra, it's me,' I said. 'Haven't called at a bad time, have I?'

'*Anna* – good to hear from you! No, it's fine, I'm free to talk. I was just having a sandwich in the office.' I tried to imagine where she was sitting as if I could somehow transport myself there, vague background noise down the line lending details to the scene: Boots sandwiches and Diet Coke on an overcrowded desk, distant telephones and colleagues' voices in an untidily, unglamorously open-plan office. 'How's it going?'

'Not bad,' I said, 'not bad at all. I've got an idea for a new novel – you were right, Dorset *did* inspire me.'

'Congratulations, that's terrific!' I was worried she'd ask further and drag Rebecca Fisher into this conversation, but she didn't – carried on with the vicarious wonderment that was the nearest she ever came to envy. 'It must be gorgeous there now, where you're living. The weather's so beautiful, but it's like an oven in this bloody office. Jim and Dan are talking about getting a petition up for better air-conditioning. Jim said you wouldn't be allowed to keep chickens in this heat – well, not unless you were cooking them.'

I'd rung up in the hope that she'd distract me from the morning's events, but they were expanding to block out the light, and I realised I'd have to share them. 'Well, it's not that idyllic here,' I admitted unwillingly. 'I've had a nightmare morning. I went to visit this vet who lives nearby, thought he could help me with a bit of research for the book. Anyway, he got the wrong end of the stick, thought I was just being nosy – I didn't even have a chance to explain. He sent me off with a flea in my ear.'

The phrases and tone were all wrong, entirely misleading, but there seemed no way to accurately describe that meeting without using Edgar Allen Poe words surreal in

83

the context of a pleasant lunchtime chat – *fury, hatred, terror.* Down the line, her easy incomprehension came across clearly. 'That's a bummer – what a paranoid *git.* Don't worry about it, Anna. You can find out what you want to know from someone else, can't you?'

'Well,' I said, 'I hope so.'

'I bet you can. Why don't you try the British Library? It's supposed to have every book in the world, or something. By the way, now you've settled in and all, you're going to have to invite me down soon – I *really* need a break from Reading.'

'That'd be terrific.' I spoke a little too gratefully; of all the people in the world apart from Carl, she'd be able to distract me from this new worry, if not dispel it entirely. 'What about this coming weekend? Tomorrow?'

Only wild optimism could have made me even hope that she'd be free so soon – her regretful little noise down the line told me I should have known far better. 'I'm really sorry, but I'm *massively* busy this weekend. I'm going shopping in London with Jenny tomorrow, and then there's a big night out planned with Jim and Louise and that lot. And – oh, Christ – next weekend it's my eldest brother's wedding. I can't exactly miss *that.*'

It was a predictable disappointment, but in this sunny, silent room, I felt it too keenly – a fortnight alone with a worry I couldn't tell Carl anything about. 'Well,' I said, trying my hardest to sound amused and untroubled, 'how about the weekend after *that*?'

'That sounds cool – no it doesn't, *bollocks*, Melanie's party's that Saturday, and I've already promised to go. Tell you what. The weekend after *that*, the second weekend in July. I'm definitely free then. Tell me you are, too.'

I had a childish and momentary impulse to invent some big social occasion of my own, an impulse that, even in

Reading, had been far from unknown when booking nights out with Petra – but I knew it was ridiculous, there was no point. It wouldn't even irritate her; she'd just sympathise before deferring indefinitely. 'I can,' I said, 'it's a date. I'll let Carl know tonight.'

'And I'll put it in my diary.' We laughed. 'Listen, I've got to run – just got an urgent email, a *work* email. Say hi to Carl from me, won't you?'

'Sure thing,' I said, then, with an urge to prolong this conversation, 'I'll give him your love. He's still really enjoying his new job – *and* his new car.'

'Good for him. I'll give you a ring soon, anyway. Bye for now.'

My tenuous link with the outside world was instantly severed. A flat, dead buzz ran on and on in my ear for several seconds before I put the phone down. Inexorably, the silence closed back in around me, and with it came the memories of Mr Wheeler snarling in a sterile consulting room, loyalty and loathing and bitterness in every line of his face. I wondered what he was doing right now, and whether he was thinking of me.

I thought he was.

Sometimes, worry can prevent you from concentrating on work. At other times, it can do the exact opposite, driving you to seek out anything else just to take your mind off it. Following that horrible confrontation in Wareham, it seemed that only thoughts of the novel could distract me from niggling, gnawing anxiety. And *thinking* about the novel was nowhere near enough. There had to be another way into this elusive central character, I told myself, and remembered what Petra had said about the British Library. In the shadows of the spare room, I sat down at the computer and began a long and superficially tedious hike through the less colourful regions of the internet.

When Carl got home from work that evening, I was just making a start on dinner. After he'd changed into jeans and a T-shirt, he joined me in chopping and dicing and peeling at the kitchen counter.

'So how's your day been?' he asked casually. 'Find out any more vital facts for the book?'

More than anything, I wanted to tell him about what had really happened, leaving out none of the raw emotion that had startled me so badly. I longed to know how he'd interpret it, whether he'd see it as a reasonable cause for alarm or as something to dismiss with a flip comment and a smile. But I knew I'd effectively gagged myself on the subject, that telling him now would create far more problems that it would solve. 'Well, in a way,' I said. 'I called Petra earlier, and we were talking about it. She mentioned the British Library. When I looked it up on the net earlier, it looked like it could really help me – there's a separate branch of it, a newspaper library that's got copies of every paper since God knows when. It's got to have the original news stories about Rebecca. Of course, it's in London, but that's not such a big deal. I thought I'd get the train down there on Monday, have a look round. I checked the times, and it's only about four and a half hours each way.'

'That's a good idea,' he said amiably. 'You might find something interesting. How is Petra, anyway?'

'Oh, she's fine. Busy as ever. I hope you don't mind, but I've invited her to stay on the second weekend in July. She said she'd like to see the place for herself.'

'I don't mind at all; it'll be good to see her again. Good for you, too. I know she's your best mate, you must be missing her a bit.'

A few moments of companionable peace in which I could almost forget my new anxiety existed. We stood side by side at the counter, him chopping carrots, me peeling potatoes. The radio was on quietly in the background and, beyond the window, golden summer evening was gradually fading into a rich, glorious, spectacular sunset.

'Seems like it's been a bit of a social day for both of us,' he said at last. 'I was talking to the manager of the Poole store this afternoon – Jim Miller, you know, I've told you about him before. Anyway, I mentioned having him and his wife round for dinner next weekend, but I thought I'd better check with you before arranging anything specific.'

In all honestly, I had no interest whatsoever in dinner-party small-talk with strangers – the bright light of this new idea had shown my loneliness up for what it really was: boredom, restlessness, and worry that I'd never write another book in my life. But he'd greeted Petra's visit so enthusiastically that it seemed unkind and selfish to say so; Petra was far more my friend than Carl's. 'I don't mind at all,' I said, 'it sounds great. Invite them round whenever – it'll be nice to meet them.'

'I thought you could do with a couple of new faces.' He smiled. 'Jim's wife's a nurse in Poole Hospital. I think she's about your age – she could probably introduce you to some more people, if you got to know her. Whoever her friends are, they've got to be a bit livelier than the old dears around here.'

It wasn't exactly age that was the issue, I knew. I wouldn't have found Helen any easier to talk to if we'd been eighteen-year-old students sharing a house in Reading. Still, I could sense his good-natured desire to make me a part of things during the daytime, as he was himself – he'd have the office, I'd have an accessible network of friends to chat with – and, while I knew it was misguided, it was too earnest to brush irritably aside with a quick *no thanks*. 'That's a good idea,' I said. 'Well, I'll look forward to meeting her. To meeting both of them.'

Over dinner, my thoughts kept coming back to the newspaper library. While I was well aware it meant about as much to him as his monthly sales targets did to me, I couldn't help mentioning it again. 'I do hope I can find something. On Monday, I mean. There's got to be something there that tells me a bit more about Rebecca – don't you think?'

'Well, I expect so. To be honest, I don't know much about it.' His serious, rather puzzled expression creased into an unexpected smile. 'You know, it's funny to hear you talk about her like that – you sound as if you're on first-name terms with each other. As if she's an old friend.'

I laughed, but felt jolted; his words seemed to reflect some essential but subtly disturbing shift in my approach to her: she wasn't *the notorious Rebecca Fisher* any more, but a woman I desperately needed to understand. 'That's the whole problem,' I said. 'I don't know her from Adam. Not yet.'

11

On Monday I got the train to Waterloo station and then the tube. When I emerged at Colindale, the newspaper library caught my eye at once, a vast building that looked badly out of proportion with the small houses and scrubby patches of grass surrounding it. I crossed the road towards it, and went in.

Once inside, through an odd, faint smell of chlorine, past an ancient-looking cloakroom, I followed the signs upstairs, where the library itself was a hive of near-silent activity. The internet had told me that I'd need ID, and I presented my passport to the pallid young man behind the main desk. 'If you'd like to fill out this form . . .' he said, passing one to me. I scrawled perfunctory details of name and address and phone number as he spoke again. 'You been here before?'

'It's my first time,' I said. 'I'm doing some research for a novel.'

Even here, it seemed to come out as a confession rather than a fact, but he didn't seem surprised, or even particularly interested. 'What sort of thing are you looking for?'

'The original articles about a case.' His expression clearly asked *which one*, and overcame my fear of seeming morbid. 'The Rebecca Fisher case – you've probably heard of it. It would have been in all the papers in 1969, during the summer.'

I finished completing the form and passed it back across the desk to him. Putting it on a stack of them, he stepped out from behind the desk. 'Follow me,' he said, 'I'll show you how to look things up in here.'

We headed into a slightly smaller room, lined with a bafflingly endless series of leather-bound volumes. A few people sat consulting them at desks. 'Just find the reference book from the year you want,' he said, 'then the name you're after. It'll have page and paragraph references – take a note of them. After that, just go into the room through there, and find the box of microfilm from the right month and year. Then you can load it and keep an eye on the page numbers, till ...'

It was like asking for directions, and finding them so complicated you lost track after the first few seconds. I nodded, and struggled to look as if he hadn't lost me completely somewhere during his second sentence. At last he finished speaking. 'Well, if you need any more help, I'll just be at the desk,' he said. 'I hope you find what you're after.'

In the event, I did, more from trial and error than any feel for the system. Roughly an hour later, I was entering the microfilm room, hunting down the box marked *July 1969* from a selection that lent new meaning to the concept of infinity. Beyond them the room was very dark, and if I'd closed my eyes, I'd have been convinced it was both completely deserted and filled with unattended machinery – tiny repetitive clicks and whizzes came from all sides, occasional discordant clacking noises that said they almost certainly shouldn't sound like that. But I saw that nearly all of the alcoves by the microfilm machines were occupied; silent people intent on the projected, luminous pages in front of them, the noises coming as they loaded and unloaded film, and scrolled along their findings.

I sat down at one by the far wall, where a tiny, high-set window slanted a distracting streak of sunlight across the desk. Printed directions told me how to load the film, and I followed them carefully. A page of ancient newspaper snapped into sudden light. Turning the dial to move on from it, I watched the July of 1969 speed across the screen in front of me; births, deaths and marriages, politics, celebrities, crimes.

The projected paper was the colour of old ivory, and something about the print looked archaic to a point where I had to double-check the date – it looked as if it might have come from the 1920s, but was from 1969 just the same. For some reason, the ads particularly caught my attention, ads that would be ultra-ironic today. *Buy tinned peaches*, I read, above the blurred photo of a brand-named can, *they're delicious!* The whole journalistic tone had been different then, too. For the first time, I realised how life had changed since Rebecca Fisher first leapt into the horrified public eye. Back then the world had been a very different place.

East Lancashire Morning Star, 19 July 1969

LOCAL GIRL VANISHES
'She went to get her skipping rope' say friends

A nine-year-old Teasford schoolgirl was yesterday reported missing by her mother. Eleanor Corbett, a pupil at St Anthony's Primary School, was on her summer holidays and had gone out in the morning with a group of friends. She left them at roughly ten thirty a.m., saying that she was going to fetch her skipping rope and would return soon. Since then, Eleanor has not been seen.

As a widespread search begins across the area, her distraught mother is appealing for information.

'When she didn't come home for dinner, I thought she must be at a friend's house,' Mrs Eileen Corbett said. 'I went to ask some of them if they knew where she was. They said they thought she'd been at home all day, and that they hadn't seen her since the morning.'

Fighting to hold back tears, she went on to beg witnesses to come forward.

'Someone must have seen where Eleanor went to,' Mrs Corbett said. 'She wasn't the kind of girl who'd wander off on her own, and everyone knows her around here. If you saw her walking along with someone that morning, please let us know, so we can find her. Her sisters are all worried sick, and so am I.'

Eleanor Corbett is described as noticeably small and slight for her age, with curly brown hair, freckles and hazel eyes. At the time of her disappearance, she was wearing a flower-patterned knee-length skirt, a short-sleeved pale blue shirt and white sandals.

'We are doing everything in our power to look for Eleanor,' Detective Inspector William Harris told us. 'Many local residents have kindly volunteered to help us in our search. We are currently conducting a thorough door-to-door investigation.

'All of us pray that she will be found soon, and that there will be a simple explanation for her disappearance after all.'

The Times, 21 July 1969

CONCERNS GROW OVER MISSING CHILD

An East Lancashire schoolgirl reported missing three days ago has still not been found. Eleanor Corbett, aged 9, was last sighted on the morning of 18 July, walking alone in the direction of her residence.

As local residents become increasingly concerned, the police have stated that they are taking every possible measure to find her, and are currently following several leads.

The search continues.

The Sun, 22 July 1969

SCHOOLGIRL FOUND IN HORROR DISCOVERY

The mutilated body of missing Lancashire schoolgirl Eleanor Corbett was discovered late last night, in a derelict house on the outskirts of her home town.

Police were dispatched to the location after an unexpected witness came forward with information. The young woman, who cannot be named, had been with an illicit boyfriend when they had seen Eleanor entering the building on the day of her disappearance. Unable to explain her presence in that area to her parents, the witness had been afraid to volunteer her information at an earlier stage.

Officers present at the scene described their discovery as 'horrific'. The nine-year-old had been stabbed more than thirty times in an attack 'of savage ferocity'.

'In the room where we found Eleanor's body, there were clear signs of previous habitation,' one officer told us. 'From the evidence, it would appear that Eleanor had been there several times before, almost certainly with other children. We are currently in the process of questioning her friends, in the hope that they might be able to cast new light on this tragedy.'

Her distraught mother, Mrs Eileen Corbett, said she was 'shocked and devastated'.

'None of us can believe this has really happened,' she said. 'Eleanor was the sweetest little girl you could hope to meet, and she didn't have an enemy in the world. We can't imagine what kind of monster could possibly have done this to her.'

REBECCA'S FORGOTTEN VICTIMS
By Alice Young

Upon meeting Mrs Eileen Corbett, you have the instant impression of warmth, practicality and strength. In her early sixties and widowed for almost twenty years, she is the picture of a kindly Northern matriarch who has endured many hardships without complaining, and protected her family throughout.

But there is a tragedy in Eileen's past that few could possibly guess at. Twelve years ago, her beloved youngest child was brutally murdered by angel-faced psychopath Rebecca Fisher. On the eve of the monster's rumoured release into society, Eileen has bravely decided to break her silence and speak of a bitterness she is unable to deny.

'When I first heard about her being released with a whole new identity, I honestly couldn't believe what I was hearing,' Eileen tells me, her face hardening. 'When I think of her coming to live in an ordinary street and nobody even knowing her real name, it chills my blood. Almost as much as it does to think that I had her in my house, and thought of her as Eleanor's friend.'

Eleanor Corbett met Rebecca Fisher when they were both pupils at St Anthony's, which then as now was the Lancashire town of Teasford's only primary school. Although Rebecca was a year older and from a far more privileged background – by an eerie coincidence, her adoptive father owned the textiles factory where Eileen worked six days a week – the two schoolgirls rapidly became friends.

'She seemed such a sweet little girl,' Eileen remembers wistfully. 'She was very polite and well-behaved – so pretty, too, with long blonde hair and bright blue eyes. I honestly never had the slightest doubts about her, at first. In fact, I was glad Eleanor had found such a nice best friend.'

As the friendship progressed, however, events took a new and sinister turn. None of the five Corbett daughters received pocket money, but Eleanor would return from school with toys, sweets and other new belongings. 'Of course, I knew she'd never have stolen them – I'd brought all my girls up to know right from wrong,' Eileen says. 'When I asked her where they'd come from, she told me Rebecca gave them to her. At first I was quite offended, because it sounded like charity, but the more Eleanor talked about it, the more I realised that it wasn't charity at all. It looked as if Rebecca was trying to buy Eleanor's friendship.

'I remember about a month before Eleanor went missing, my eldest daughter Agnes was doing some cleaning upstairs when she came rushing down with this bracelet in her hand. She said that she'd found it under Eleanor's bed. Well, I was shocked. I don't know a great deal about jewellery, but even I could tell it was very expensive. When Eleanor came home and I had it out with her, she said Rebecca had given it to her as a present. Even though I believed her, I was still angry. I said no child would be allowed to give away a valuable piece of jewellery without their parents minding, no matter how rich they were, and that she should have known better than to accept it. Then I made her put her coat on, and we walked all the way to the Fishers' house to give it back.'

It was in no way surprising that the ten-year-old Rebecca had access to such an expensive item. Although she had been adopted, she was almost freakishly privileged by the standards of the time and place in which she lived. As well as being the wife of the wealthiest businessman in the area, her adoptive mother Rita had been a minor heiress in her own right, and the otherwise childless couple had showered gifts as well as affection on the daughter they'd always longed for. In an area of deprivation, where the majority of children wore hand-me-down clothes, Rebecca had a wardrobe to rival her elegant mother's. She owned more than twenty pairs of shoes and several pieces of jewellery that, like the bracelet Eileen had found, were both genuine and specifically designed for children.

On the surface, she appeared to be the perfect little girl – Eileen's favourable impression of her was echoed by every other adult in Teasford, including teachers at the school where she excelled academically. Nonetheless, there was a chilling side to her nature that these people never saw, a vicious temper combined with an obsessive desire to possess those she cared for. At Rebecca's trial, Eleanor's grieving schoolfriends described her unhealthy attachment to the younger girl. 'Rebecca just didn't seem to want anyone else,' a classmate of Eleanor's told the court. 'She clung to Eleanor all the time. I think she'd have liked it if they'd been the only two people in the world.'

As time passed, it became apparent that Rebecca demanded that same kind of obsessive, exclusive friendship from Eleanor herself. After going to increasingly desperate lengths in an attempt to buy this friendship, Rebecca finally stabbed Eleanor to death in a terrifying jealous fury, enraged that, despite her entreaties, Eleanor was continuing to see her other friends.

As Eileen describes her tragic daughter, I can see her fighting to hold back the tears. 'Eleanor was such a sweet, vivacious child. She made friends so easily, and loved meeting new people. There's not a day goes past that I don't think about her.'

Now, Eileen believes that her daughter's appalling fate should serve as a stark warning for prison services and the government alike.

'They're making a terrible mistake to let Rebecca out like

this,' she says flatly. 'Children don't change when they grow up, not really. Soon, nobody's going to know who she is – she could be their colleague or their neighbour or even their wife. But one of these days, she's going to show her true colours all over again. And the people who make these decisions are finally going to realise how wrong they were.'

12

I arrived at Waterloo three quarters of an hour before the train that would take me back to Wareham. I got a latte in one of the concourse coffee-shops and sat by the window, lighting a cigarette and watching the steady ebb and flow of milling strangers. It was quarter to five in the evening, and rich gold light flooded in through the station's glass ceiling, bathing the prosaic scene in an almost unearthly radiance. On the counter behind me, an ancient tape deck was playing Suzanne Vega, 'Marlene on the Wall'. It felt like a soundtrack, somehow, that sweet childish voice haunting the cappuccino-smelling shadows with something bittersweet and enigmatic; evocative of long journeys to unknown places, and contemplation.

My thoughts turned to the pages I'd photocopied in the microfilm room, first regarding them en masse, then focusing sharply on the *Daily Mail* interview with Eleanor's mother. Remembering its description of Rebecca's possessiveness made me feel much as I had done reading it for the first time – like a hard, unexpected pinch in a sensitive place. *I think she'd have liked it if they'd been the only two people in the world.* It was ridiculous, I knew, that it should disturb me to see a distinct element of my own mind reflected there; this was exactly what I'd been struggling to discover, a sense of empathy, a hidden alley into a ten-year-old killer's thoughts and feelings and self. But I'd anticipated slipping on her skin like a costume before stepping out onto the writing-stage, knowing her well enough to accurately impersonate, aware that I could take her off as soon as I put down the pen. It had never occurred to me that I might not *have* to act all the time, that some aspects of her character were intrinsic to my own.

And the reality of what she'd done all that time ago seemed to move a little closer; horror wasn't impersonal any more, it had begun to acquire a kind of face. A child who'd been small for her age, who'd had curly brown hair, who'd been loved and mourned and missed. Who'd put on white sandals and a flower-patterned knee-length skirt one morning, before leaving her house to play . . .

With a considerable effort, I forced myself back to the straightforward mundanities of research, mystical and enigmatic as Carl's monthly regional sales targets. St Anthony's Primary School might still be open for business, I told myself. Tomorrow morning I'd call directory enquiries and find out if it was listed. If so, I'd grit my teeth, dial the number and launch into an introductory spiel: Anna Jeffreys, one book published, WLTM anyone who'd known Rebecca or Eleanor, or who knew someone who'd ever known such. There had to be *someone*, I told myself.

After that, there was nothing prosaic left to think about – suddenly, the evening light seemed far too evocative. Even here, in this vast, impersonal, unlovely place that echoed with voices like the world's biggest swimming-pool, its power couldn't quite be denied. There wouldn't be any greyness as that light faded, just rosy-gold slowly darkening to black. The sight and feel of it reminded me of a home I hadn't been back to for over five years.

The kind of childhood memory that stays in your mind, inexplicably preserved while hundreds of others fade into nothing. An evening much like this one through the window in front of my desk, the tired-looking apple tree in the front garden edged with gold. An eleven-year-old self in shorts and T-shirt, intent on her first short story as her cat drowsed on her bed. And behind it all, the muted hint of voices from downstairs, voices I'd picked up the pen to block out. They'd be in the kitchen, as the evening came down. They'd be laughing together.

The following morning, Socks arrived shortly after Carl had left for work – as soon as I'd come downstairs I heard him mewing outside the back door and gave him his usual saucer of milk. By now, I was perfectly comfortable leaving him on his own in the kitchen, aware that his tastes ran far more to sunbathing than vandalism. Going into the living room, I phoned directory enquiries and got the number of St Anthony's Primary School, Teasford, East Lancashire.

I thought about waiting a while before ringing, but realised there was no point. I'd been thinking about this phone call all the way back from Waterloo and, if I was honest with myself, most of last night. It was ten past nine in the morning, the school would be open, and I was full of an overwhelming impatience for discovery.

While I was well aware that modern Teasford was much like anywhere else, part of me couldn't help envisioning a school straight out of D.H. Lawrence – neatly written alphabets on blackboards, smells of chalk and cabbage and disinfectant. But the voice that answered brought me back to the world I knew with a mixture of relief and disappointment: the chilly, harassed tones of school secretaries around the country. I explained who I was and what I wanted, trying to sound as confident and professional as I possibly could, sensing confusion and vague suspicion down the line before she spoke again.

'I'll put you through to the headmistress. She might be able to help.'

I didn't have a chance to thank her before I was plunged into dead silence, then a new voice spoke in my ear. 'Judith Davies.' I had the immediate impression of a blunt, no-nonsense fiftysomething, a woman in sensible brogues who didn't suffer fools gladly.

'Oh, good morning,' I said, with no idea how much she'd been told about me. 'My name's Anna Jeffreys, and I'm researching a novel about—'

'Rebecca Fisher. The school secretary told me.' She didn't seem in the least embarrassed about interrupting. 'Our most famous old girl, more's the pity. I must say, I thought all the interest in her died down decades ago.'

'Well, in a way, that's what gave me the idea. A lot of people don't know that much about it, and I thought it would make a great premise for a thriller.' A brief pause, into which I could read absolutely nothing. 'Do you think you might be able to help?'

A short, dry laugh. 'I can't promise anything scandalous. But yes, there are some things I could tell you.' If this had been a face to face interview, I guessed I would have seen her check her watch. 'I'm afraid I'm quite busy. I should have more time to discuss Rebecca at . . . shall we say one o'clock?'

'I'll phone you back then,' I said. 'Thanks a lot for your help.'

Off the phone, long hours extended ahead of me like dull scenery. Since going to the newspaper library, my notes had been entirely drained of interest – reality made my invented details look flat and unsatisfying. I tried to distract myself by doing some housework and putting a wash on, and was pegging it out on the line when I heard Liz's back door opening. 'Socks,' she called through it. 'Socks!'

'Sorry, Liz,' I called back, 'he's round here. Want to come and get him?'

'Certainly, dear. I'll be right over.'

She was, in about five minutes, bustling cheerfully through the back door. 'I was quite worried about the little thing,' she said. 'I came home just now, and couldn't find him anywhere. I've been at Muriel's house all morning – Helen was there, too. They both send their love, said they enjoyed meeting you very much.'

'It was good to meet them, as well,' I said quickly. 'They seemed nice.'

Liz smiled, a diplomatic, slightly conspiratorial smile that said she knew I wasn't telling the whole truth. 'Well, I know Helen can seem a bit funny sometimes, but she's very nice when you get to know her. And it's only to be expected, really ... she's had a hard life, poor thing.'

I was about to ask further, but Liz was going over to Socks, bending, scooping him up in her arms. 'I'd better get on, anyway, I should be making a start on the housework. Do let me know if he pops round again when I'm at home, won't you – just check and see if my car's there. He's such an old cat, it's quite a worry when I don't know where he is. I can't help fretting that something's happened to him.'

'Don't worry about it,' I said as she headed towards the back door. 'I will.'

When she'd gone, I found myself thinking about Helen, wondering exactly what her background was. She was virtually a stranger to me, but something about her interested and repelled me simultaneously. That air of chilly self-righteousness, that quiet, flat, emotionless voice. If it hadn't been for Rebecca, she'd have stayed in the foreground of my thoughts much longer; as it was, however, she was driven out in minutes, replaced by more immediate concerns. I thought of that girl from the ivory-coloured newspaper pages and their archaic-sounding world, standing in this kitchen just as I did, thinking, feeling, *alive*.

St Anthony's would have changed over the years, I thought, but it was still the same school. There must be some still-functioning links back to 1969, what people had thought of the name Rebecca Fisher when it had been no more notorious than my own. The girl she'd been then, adequately described, would give me the key to so much else – not just the ten-year-old killer, but the woman she could have become . . .

Pulling myself together with an effort, I went over to the back door and slammed it. Then I made a start on vacuuming the living room; trying not to sense the echoes its previous tenant had left, focusing my thoughts on the prosaic reality of one o'clock.

13

'I was just starting out as a teacher at the time it happened,' Judith Davies told me. 'I'd only been at this school for a year – my God, I was twenty-three years old. To think of that, now.' A short bark of laughter – I tried to join in.

'So you taught her class?'

'Not on a full-time basis. But I stood in for her teacher once, for two weeks. I must say, I was a lot less impressed with the famous Miss Fisher than most of my colleagues seemed to be.'

Was that truth, or hindsight? 'In what way?'

'Well, of course, the school's changed a good deal between then and now – the whole area has. But it was rather a snobbish place then.' Seeming to read my bewilderment, she carried on quickly, slightly impatiently. 'Oh, I don't mean wealthy, or privileged. Quite the opposite, in fact. Nearly every local parent with a say in the matter sent their children to a single-sex private school in the area – the girl's one was called St Anne's. Maybe that was why so many of the teachers were so snobbish. Tired of all the outbreaks of headlice and scabies and what have you; you'd be amazed what some of the children brought to school with them in those days.' A deep, world-weary sigh. 'They tended to treat Rebecca differently for just that reason. I never had any patience with that. As far as I was concerned, she was just the same as any of the others.'

'They treated her differently because she was well-off?'

'Her parents were *extremely* well-off. In a completely different class from most of the others. Even I sometimes wondered why she wasn't at St Anne's – it was impossible not to. From the little I saw of her parents, they certainly didn't seem the type to hide their wealth.'

My cigarette was burning away to nothing in the ashtray beside me. I took a deep, quick drag before speaking again. 'Perhaps she was thrown out of St Anne's. Expelled.'

'She joined St Anthony's at the age of six. No school in the area took children younger than that.' I scribbled down a short note on my pad of A4. 'Rather a mystery, isn't it? You should have seen the sort of things she wore to school. Ridiculous things to give a child.'

'What sort of things?'

'Oh, the sort of thing children seem to wear all the time these days. But I can't tell you how bizarre they seemed then. Little gold earrings and velvet hair-bows, little high heels like a grown-up woman's. Her mother sent her to school dressed up like a china doll. Of course, it was totally against school regulations. But as far as the other teachers were concerned, they simply didn't seem to apply to her.'

A china doll. I seemed to be hearing about one, some-how – there was an odd unreality about the description. In Judith's words, I sensed a character as essentially fictional as the beautiful, sinister Child of the Damned I'd read about in that *Daily Mail* article; I struggled to find some detail that would make the picture come alive, give human detail to a competently drawn cartoon-girl. 'Did she ever take advantage of that at all?' I asked. 'Break other rules?'

'Far from it. If it wasn't for her clothes, I'd hardly have noticed her at all. A very colourless sort of child, I always thought. Insipid. Obedient.' She laughed. 'In all fairness, a lot of teachers love children like that, rich parents or not. I was never one of them. I always preferred the ones with a bit more get-up-and-go.'

'But she was intelligent?'

'I wouldn't go that far. You'd be surprised how many children can be competent at primary-school level – it's really just a matter of neat handwriting and a reasonable memory. No, she was the very last child I'd have expected to become notorious. In terms of her personality, I'd have said there were dozens of girls just like her, in every primary school in Britain.'

I had a clear mental picture of the sort of little girl she was describing, a type I recognised from my own primary school days, the sort who worried about colouring-pens running out, and flinched old-maidishly from any activity more controversial than skipping. It couldn't have been further removed from everything I'd read about Rebecca. 'So she blended in well?' I asked. 'She was a part of things?'

'In what way?'

'With her classmates. In the playground. You know.'

'To be honest, I can't say I ever noticed. I've never had time for teachers who get involved with eight- or nine-year-olds' social lives – who's best friends with who, and who's not talking to who, and who we should have a quiet word with for not inviting so-and-so to their birthday party.' She spoke frankly and dismissively. 'Unless a child's being physically threatened, I've always believed they should be left to sort things out on their own. What they do outside the classroom is their own affair, as long as they don't break any rules, of course.'

I struggled not to let my mounting frustration show in my voice. 'Well, what about in the classroom? Did you feel she was in the middle of a group? Or did she seem more isolated?'

'I'm afraid it never occurred to me to think about it.

She never seemed particularly unhappy, as far as I can remember.' The short silence had an unmistakable edge of finality. 'Well, I'm afraid that's very much all I know about her. I hope it's been of some use to you.'

'You've been very helpful. Thanks a lot for your time.' I felt deeply disappointed, and my next words sounded more perfunctory than purposeful. 'If I could just ask – do you know anyone else I might be able to talk to? Any of your colleagues who were there at the time?'

'Nobody who still teaches here. But there is an ex-colleague. Her name's Miss Watson, Miss Annette Watson.' Judith's voice was businesslike. 'She was Rebecca's teacher for a year. She retired three years ago, to Bournemouth.'

'That's near me. I live in Dorset, too,' I said quickly. 'If you know how to get in touch with her, do you think you could pass on my phone number?'

'Well, I can certainly do that. I must say, I'm not sure she'll want to go over it again, after all this time. But there's no harm in trying.'

The aftermath of that phone call brought a profound sense of anticlimax. It was as if the newspaper library had brought my appetite raging up, and the promised meal had never arrived. I'd felt much the same way following my conversation with Liz, Helen and Muriel, but this time, frustration and disappointment seemed a hundred times worse. It stood to reason that the adult Rebecca would go out of her way to seem colourless and *perfectly normal*, so perhaps they couldn't be blamed for noticing so little. But Judith Davies was a completely different matter. Rebecca hadn't needed to wear a mask in those days; there was no possible reason why she'd have had to hide her true self that skilfully. She'd killed her best friend

107

at the age of ten, and her former teacher could have been describing virtually any well-behaved little girl in Britain.

In the days that followed, the other teacher Judith Davies had mentioned began to feel like a lifeline, a last resort. Whenever I was in the house, part of me was alert and waiting for an unexpected phone call, an unknown woman's voice on the line. It was, I knew, ridiculous; there must be other people I could track down, and the book I'd bought online should arrive soon. But I worried there'd be nobody to find, and made a shrewd guess that the book in question would contain nothing but crude half-truths polished up into high-gloss clichés. A morbid, fretful little voice spoke up inside me rather too often, warning that there might be no way into this novel after all, that I'd had a distant glimpse of an apparently accessible paradise only to get a little closer and find eight-foot gates uncompromisingly padlocked.

But there was something else. Something I didn't care to look at too closely: my hunger to find out more about Rebecca wasn't just about the book, not any more. The article from the *Daily Mail* had revealed a too-sharp parallel between her mind and my own; it had taken root in my thoughts, and demanded to be torn out. I wanted to know her true character so I could look back at this irrational unease and laugh at myself. Possessiveness was a common enough characteristic, and Rebecca's had been created by entirely different circumstances. Beyond our ownership of this house, we had nothing in common at all.

It seemed that I sensed her presence there more and more strongly, that week. When I came back from the shops in the afternoon and the heavy front door creaked shut behind me, the rooms looked alien for a second, as if I was trespassing in someone else's home. And in those moments, I had the distinct feeling that the real owner had left a very short time ago, and that she'd let herself out through the back door mere minutes before I'd entered.

That feeling always vanished when Carl came home in the evenings; its charged, haunted quality couldn't possibly coexist with his good humour, his practicality, his incidental tales from the office. It was as if the sound of his car outside flicked a hundred-watt light on in a darkened room, showing the monsters lurking in shadow for the prosaic furnishings they really were.

'I saw Jim at work today,' he said on Thursday night. 'Him and his wife can't do this Saturday night, but I've invited them over for dinner on Sunday – is that okay with you?'

We were sitting in the kitchen over our evening meal, and his voice came unexpectedly to disturb a lengthy pause – I'd been thinking about Rebecca and the living room phone simultaneously, and pulled myself back with an effort. 'Fine,' I said. 'That's fine.'

'You don't sound very enthusiastic about it.' Laying his knife and fork down, he looked at me closely. 'Ever since you came back from that library, it seems like you've been on another planet, Annie. What's the matter?'

'Nothing's the matter. Not really.' My reaction to that *Daily Mail* article felt as impossible to share as an intensely personal, disturbing dream – at best it would make me look ridiculous, at worst, something I didn't like to think about. 'I'm just a bit preoccupied, I suppose. With the book and everything. With the research.'

I could see him trying to look supportive, but instead looking slightly worried. He was obviously about to say something when the phone shrilled through the half-open doorway, and I jumped up from my seat. 'I'll get it,' I said quickly, 'I think it's for me.' Hurrying into the living room, I took a deep breath before answering, composing myself to speak professionally to a stranger. 'Hello?'

'Hi.' Disappointment hit me hard – it *was* a stranger, but a male one. 'Can I speak to Carl, please?'

'Certainly, I'll go and get him.' I went back into the kitchen, trying my hardest to look untroubled. 'It's for you.'

A last frowning, concerned glance at me, and he was leaving the room himself. I overheard snippets of brief and businesslike conversation, the kind that only men seem to have. 'Sure,' he said, 'not a problem. I'll bring it in tomorrow morning. See you then.' He hung up. When he reached the kitchen doorway, he stopped and stared at me for several seconds, with an odd mixture of puzzlement, exasperation and concern.

'*A bit preoccupied?* When the phone rang just then, I thought you were about to have a bloody heart attack. Annie, you really need to relax.'

'I *can't*. I'm still waiting to hear from that woman, the one who taught Rebecca – you know, I told you about her the other night. The headmistress told me she'd give her my number.' His incomprehension suddenly infuriated me. 'It's *important*,' I said hotly. 'She's got to call. She's just *got* to.'

'She hasn't *got* to do a damn thing. She's a free agent. Maybe she doesn't want to go over it all again, wants to forget she ever taught that kid in the first place.' Seeing my stricken expression, his own softened slightly and he came over to the table and sat down. 'I'm sorry, Annie, I know it's important to you. But you're taking all this a bit too seriously – it's research for your novel, not life and death.'

'I know.' But I spoke to conciliate only; in the most literal sense it was, or at least had once been, exactly that. 'Look, I'm sorry. But I just can't wait to make a start on this idea. You can understand that, can't you?'

'I suppose.' He smiled as if against his will, and I watched the inexorable return of seriousness. 'But there are other things in the world, you know – this book's not the be-all and end-all, you've written one, you've proved you can do it. If you start having too much trouble with this one, just give it up. Nobody's going to hold it against you.'

I would. The words rose in my throat; I forced them back down. 'And then what?' I asked. 'Fun-filled days at the WI?'

'Well, *that* can wait a few years. Or a few decades.' We laughed. 'But come on, Annie, I'm making good money now, we've got a nice house. You know, this would be a great place to start a family. From the sound of it, a baby would be a lot less trouble than a book.'

It was a subject we'd never really discussed at all seriously before. I struggled to suppress my instinctive rise of panic, to speak with warm, sweet rationality. 'Look, Carl – I'm really not ready for all that yet. There's plenty of time.'

'You know I'm happy to wait.' His voice was slightly but unmissably defensive. 'I just think it'd be good for *you*.'

'It *wouldn't*.' The last word came out a little too strongly. 'I'm not having a child I don't want in the hope I'll get to like the idea, that I'll feel different when it's born. I've been there myself, you know that – you don't understand how it feels, growing up that way.'

I felt his surprise at the same time as I felt my own – it was something we rarely talked about, the kind of subject that dominated a three-hour heart-to-heart before being placed tactfully out of sight. 'You wouldn't be like that, Annie,' he said quietly. 'You'd try.'

'My mother *tried*. All the time. It didn't make any

difference. In fact, it made things worse.' A moment's pause as I struggled to move this conversation away from my childhood, back to us. 'I want kids as much as you do. There's going to be a time for them. It's just not now.'

For several seconds, neither of us spoke; while I was very pleased that the matter had been brought out into the open at last, the silence was heavy and awkward. Unexpectedly, the phone shrilled again in the living room, and my relief at the interruption almost overcame the sharp rise of hope. 'Okay, okay, I'm not moving a muscle,' I said, 'I'm totally relaxed. *You* get it, if you like.'

With a slightly distracted smile, he got up and left the room. 'Sure,' I heard him saying, 'I'll just get her.' Then he was coming back in, expression part-pleased, part-cautious. 'For you,' he said. 'I think it's that teacher of yours.'

Delight, apprehension that he might be wrong – with his eyes on me, I found myself trying to conceal both. In the living room's Tiffany-shaded half-light, I lifted the receiver from the table and prepared myself for disappointment. 'Hello?'

'Oh, good evening. Is that Anna Jeffreys?'

My writing name. My heart jumped. 'Speaking.'

'This is Annette Watson. Judith gave me your number this morning.' There was something vague and kindly and approachable about the elderly female voice – it seemed expressly designed for pleasant chit-chat over a sweet sherry. 'I hear you're writing a novel about Rebecca Fisher.'

'Well, *based* on Rebecca Fisher. Based on the whole case, really.' That memorable experience with Mr Wheeler made me wary of half-truths, and I spoke carefully. 'I was hoping you could give me some background on her character.'

'Oh, I'd be more than happy to help. I always felt there was more to be said about that little girl – I'm delighted a writer feels the same way. She wasn't at all what you'd have imagined from the newspapers, you know. When I read them all those years ago, they could have been talking about a different person.'

'That was the impression I had,' I said slowly. 'When would be a convenient time for us to talk for an hour or so? I can come and visit you in Bournemouth – I'm based near Wareham.'

'I'm free most of the time, to be honest. One of the best things about being retired, I suppose. What about this Saturday, if that's not too soon for you?'

She gave me her address, and we agreed that I'd come round at half-eleven in the morning. As I replaced the receiver and came back into the kitchen, everything else was virtually forgotten – Mr Wheeler, the conversation I'd just had with Carl, even the novel – it was as if I'd walked out carrying two heavy suitcases and returned empty-handed. 'You were right,' I said, sitting back down. 'It was her. Annette Watson.'

'That's great.' I could see him trying to look as pleased as I did. 'You going to speak to her face to face?'

'On Saturday. I hope you don't mind, but when she mentioned a date so soon, I couldn't help jumping at it. It shouldn't take long, she only lives in Bournemouth. I'll probably be home by two or so.'

'It doesn't matter. Don't worry about it.' The fake-pleased look had faded, leaving the doubt more visible than ever. 'You know, I can't help thinking you might be pinning too much hope on this woman. What makes you think she's going to be any more help than that headmistress was?'

Because she had to be, because she was the only lead I

had, but luckily there was more to it than that. Judith Davies' very voice should have alerted me to her impatience with the nuances of child psychology, but Miss Watson's had been entirely different; she sounded like the kind of woman who listened. 'I just think she will,' I said unwillingly. 'From what she said, she knew Rebecca pretty well. It sounds as though the case was quite important to her.'

'Probably not as important as it is to you.' I could tell he was joking, and that he wasn't. 'I think it's becoming a bigger deal to you than it was to Rebecca herself. It all happened more than thirty years ago, Annie. Why go digging it all up again now?'

'To write the novel. Why else?' I gathered self-interest around myself like a protective, concealing cloak – the dark corners of fascination didn't exist, just clean, bright, open research. 'Honestly, Carl, you don't have to worry. I just need to get some kind of handle on her character. I'm obsessed with this new novel, not with *her*.'

He looked at me for long and searching seconds; what he saw appeared to reassure him, and I sensed an unpleasant suspicion backing rapidly away in his mind. 'Well,' he said at last, 'if you say so. Anyway, 24's about to start – shall we go and watch it?'

The rest of the evening was spent in the calm, shallow waters of neutral territory, and we didn't talk again about anything that mattered much to either of us. But after he'd gone to sleep that night, I felt the currents deepening and strengthening around me. Rebecca Fisher and Eleanor Corbett crept out from where they'd been hiding, along with my imagined picture of Miss Watson, and the three of them seemed to blur together, expanding till they filled my mind. The night was as it always was here, a kind of darkness you simply didn't get in towns or cities – no streetlights outside or car headlights passing, or even the tiny hint of light filtering in from the porch of a distant house. This was power-cut darkness, thick as Indian ink.

It was then that the cry came, out of nowhere – a sharp, shrill, inhuman cry, a sound of pain. I couldn't tell whether it had come from next door or outside, and sat bolt upright, heartbeat pounding in my ears. For some minutes, I listened intently, but there was no other sound; the dead, black emptiness had closed over the cry like deep water over a dropped weight, and might never have been disturbed at all.

Finally, I lay back down. *It was probably an owl or something,* I imagined Carl saying to me. *Just sleep, Annie. Sleep.*

14

The following morning, I got up shortly after Carl did, limbs heavy with the kind of exhaustion that felt more like a whole-body migraine than simple lack of sleep; that horrible banshee-like noise had had much the same effect on my nervous system as a jug of industrial-strength filter coffee, and I hadn't drifted off till past two a.m. Still, I didn't feel remotely like sleeping now. Sweet, fresh summer pulled at me through the window, the kind of picture-postcard morning you could only quite believe in when you saw it for yourself. Not a day to try and chase elusive dreams in a heavily-curtained bedroom, a day to be outside and to be part of.

Before Carl left for work, I wanted to tell him about that noise, but something stopped me. I remembered his concern of yesterday evening, which I'd only been able to get rid of with a direct lie. Instinct told me he'd be less than thrilled to hear I'd lain up half the night, building morbid fears around a cry that could quite easily have come from a mating fox. After the front door had closed behind him, I tried to forget about it myself, and thought about driving into Poole town centre later in the day, the few small things I had to buy becoming convenient excuses for a long, refreshing drive and an afternoon's cheerful activity.

I got my newspaper library print-outs down from the spare room. Sitting down at the kitchen table, I lit a cigarette and started reading through them as if for the first time.

I'd left the back door open to let the breeze in and the smoke out, and a flicker in the corner of my eye announced that Socks was padding through. I turned, smiling, then felt the smile dissolve on my lips. His right eye was filmed over with a blood-red glaze and heavily crusted round the edges, horribly sore-looking, painful even to look at.

'What have you been up to, puss?' Jumping up from my seat, I reached out impulsively to stroke him but he backed away slightly. 'Looks like you've been in the wars a bit – come on, I'll get you some milk.'

I did, then remembered what Liz had said about letting her know if he came round. Her car was outside, so I walked out of the back door, and saw her own was slightly ajar. 'Liz,' I called. '*Liz.*'

She stepped out. 'Hello, dear – what is it?'

'I just thought I'd let you know Socks is round here,' I said. 'In case you wondered where he was.' She came into our kitchen a few minutes later, politely accepting my offer of a cup of tea. 'By the way,' I said as she sat down, 'what's the matter with his eye?'

'I've no idea.' She frowned. 'I put him out for the night as right as rain, and when I came down this morning – well, you can see for yourself. I suppose he must have been fighting.'

The agonised cry I'd heard in bed came back to me. Now I came to think of it, it could very easily have been made by a cat, but hadn't sounded at all like two of them fighting. Still, I didn't want to alarm her over nothing, and forced myself to speak with brisk, pragmatic sympathy. 'That's probably it. Looks like he lost, poor old Socks.'

'It's not like him at all. I've never known him get into a fight all the time I've had him.' Her expression was thoughtful and preoccupied – she spoke almost to herself.

117

'I do hope it's going to clear up on its own. But if it hasn't got better in a few days or so, I'll really have to take him to the vet.'

A momentary image of Mr Wheeler flashed in the back of my mind. I remembered what he'd said about Rebecca's dog being killed, and couldn't quite understand the nature of my sudden unease.

I realised Liz was looking at me strangely. 'What's the matter, dear? You've gone quite pale.'

'Oh, it's nothing. It doesn't matter.' I noticed the kettle had boiled. 'Anyway, do you want milk and sugar?'

At the kitchen table, we made perfunctory small-talk over our mugs, but I could tell that Liz was very distracted; her eyes kept straying over to the sunny corner where Socks lay, curled up hedgehog-like as though in self-defence. We discussed a recent letter from her elder daughter and my imminent dinner party, until the tea was finished, and there wasn't anything much left to say.

'Can I leave him with you for a while, Anna?' she asked, as she rose from her seat. 'He's been awfully jumpy all morning, poor little thing, and he looks so comfortable there. I'm sure he'll come home when he's ready.'

'That's fine.' Her obvious worry made her seem somehow more human than her habitual smiling composure, and I felt a kind of empathy with her that I'd never felt before. 'Don't worry about him. Cats are tough as old boots.'

When she'd gone, my gaze travelled restlessly around the room before settling on Socks. He was, I realised, sleeping in front of the cupboard where I'd found that studded leather collar. The malaise came drifting back: Rebecca's dog had been killed to make her leave, Socks had been injured while I was looking after him on a regular basis – the merest hint of a parallel between Rebecca's life here and my own . . .

But that was ridiculous, I told myself sharply. Socks wasn't badly hurt, and wasn't even my cat. He'd simply disturbed a sleeping badger or something last night; there was no mystery or menace about the situation. Pulling out the library photocopies I'd tucked away before Liz came in, I hurried gratefully back to something I could understand. Tomorrow morning, I thought, I'd be interviewing Miss Watson, but behind that comforting idea came something else – barely audible in my head, as if filtering thinly through glass – a desperate shriek of pain in a summer night.

Driving into Bournemouth the following day was like driving into the heart of summer – all space and greenery, fresh air and bright colours – and I could understand why so many people chose to retire here. I eventually found Miss Watson's apartment block down a quiet, tree-lined street; a large, modern, surprisingly soulless building that didn't seem to go with its surroundings. At the intricate intercom system by the double doors, I pressed the button marked with her name.

The voice I'd heard on the phone crackled through the speaker at once. 'Hello?'

'Hi, Miss Watson? It's Anna Jeffreys.'

'Come on up, Miss Jeffreys. I'm on the first floor, Flat twelve.'

Inside, the apartment block had an institutional feel, neat and spotless as only anonymous places can be – there was nothing in the hallways that could be broken, or stolen, or enjoyed. I got the lift up to the first floor and knocked on Miss Watson's door.

'Oh, hello, Miss Jeffreys. Do come in.'

I followed her into a small flat that was as untidily personal as the rest of the block wasn't. Its owner suited it perfectly: a small, birdlike woman in her late sixties, with a lot of floury face powder and wispy grey hair. 'Please,' I said, 'call me Anna.'

'And you can call me Annette.' We stepped into a tiny, sunny living room crowded with furniture and photographs. An archway led to the kitchen. 'Would you like some tea?'

'I'd love some. White with no sugar, please.'

She went into the kitchen and put the kettle on while I sat down on a cushion-strewn chair, fumbling for small-talk. 'It looks a lovely place to live, Bournemouth. I'm quite new to the area – only moved to Abbots Newton a few months ago.'

'Oh, Dorset is lovely. I've lived here nearly three years, ever since I retired from St Anthony's.'

'You stayed there all that time?'

'That's right. A lot of the teachers there do. It's a nice place to work, if you like a quiet life. Next to nothing ever happened in all the years I was there – except for Rebecca, of course.' She gave a small, rueful laugh. 'It came as an awful shock to all of us, what she did. It was so unexpected.'

'I can imagine.' She came back over with two cups of tea on a tray and I took mine, thanked her. 'How long did you know her for?'

'Ever since she came to school at the age of six. Well, of course, I didn't really *know* her to start with, she was just another face in the crowd. But then I was her class teacher in Junior Three. She must have been nine years old, at the time.'

All possible questions suddenly dovetailed into a single

one, simple and complex beyond belief. 'What did you think of her?'

Annette sighed. 'It's a terrible thing to say, now she's so notorious; it makes me seem an awfully bad judge of character. But I liked her very much, and felt sorry for her. She seemed such a sweet, gentle sort of child, not particularly clever but very hardworking, very conscientious, as though she was frightened of getting things wrong. And terribly lonely. When I'd been teaching her for a month, I thought she was one of the loneliest little girls I'd ever seen.'

It wasn't just a different angle on what I'd learned already, it was a completely different picture. I sat bolt upright, intent. 'In what way?'

'Well, you'd have needed to know Teasford at the time to understand, I suppose. It's very different these days, but back then it was such an enclosed little world – nearly all the other children at St Anthony's had grown up in the same streets, knew each other's parents. Rebecca didn't have any of that. She was a stranger to all of them when she joined.'

'And she didn't blend in later?'

'Not at all. It wasn't the way you might think – a stuck-up little madam not wanting to mix with the others, thinking she was better than them because her parents were rich. She was just very shy. She must have felt like an outsider there, coming from a totally different background. I couldn't help wondering why she wasn't at a private school instead. Her parents could certainly have afforded the fees.'

I remembered Judith saying much the same thing; the huge difference between the two women implied that the question had occurred to every teacher who'd worked there.

Annette sipped at her tea before speaking again. 'I suppose, in a way, Rebecca was my favourite pupil in that class. But not as the papers might have thought, if they'd known. I can imagine only too well how they'd have described it: that she manipulated me with her sinister charisma, some awful nonsense like that.' She sighed deeply. 'Goodness, if she'd been anything like the little girl *they* described, I'd have been scared to go anywhere near her.'

'So she never showed any signs of, well, what she was capable of, before?'

Annette bit her lip, and there was a long silence. 'Perhaps she did,' she said at last. 'To be honest, I like to think she didn't do *that*, even now. I really don't want to think how unfair I might have been – it's horrible to remember.'

My attention was focused on her completely. 'What happened?'

'Well, it started in the summer term, about a year before they found Eleanor's body – almost exactly a year, come to think of it. It was the last day of term. The class pet was a hamster called Toffee, and I asked who'd like to look after him in the holidays. Nearly all the girls put their hands up, but I knew most of them couldn't be trusted to take proper care of him – they never volunteered to feed him or clean his cage out during term time. Rebecca always did. She treated him like her own pet even in the classroom, so I told her she could take him for the summer.

'At the start of the autumn term, she brought him back as right as rain. I remember thanking her for it, telling the rest of the class that we'd all have to start looking after him again, now. I didn't think anything much of it at the time.

'A couple of weeks later, I was walking back to the

classroom at lunchtime to finish off some marking, when a classmate of Rebecca's called Peggy Jones came racing up to me. I couldn't get any sense from her at first, she was so out of breath. She finally said she'd just been going back to the classroom to get something, when she'd seen Rebecca through the glass door panel. She said that Rebecca'd been at Toffee's cage, and she'd looked like she was wringing his neck.

'Well, I hurried in with Peggy following behind, and Rebecca was still standing at the cage, crying as if her heart would break. She was nearly hysterical. She said she'd come in to feed Toffee and someone had killed him. It looked like they'd broken his neck.' Annette took a long, deep breath. 'I still can't quite believe she did it. If you'd seen her, I'm sure you'd feel the same way. I'd never seen her so upset about anything, and I knew how fond she'd been of the little thing.

'Anyway, I was absolutely convinced that it had been a spiteful trick of Peggy's. I'd never warmed to that girl. She was part of a nasty little group who'd often been in trouble for bullying other children – Rebecca was one of their victims; I knew they called her a goody-goody and a snob and things like that. I knew she'd been keen to look after Toffee in the summer holidays, too. It looked like the meanest kind of jealousy, and the cruellest kind of trick. To try and put the blame on Rebecca. I was absolutely furious with her. I took her to the headmistress's office then and there.

'Well, the headmistress called Peggy's parents in, and she was suspended for two weeks. She kept on saying it hadn't been anything to do with her, but you can imagine how plausible *that* sounded – she'd lied about all sorts of things before, whenever she'd been in trouble. Which was often.' She broke off for a second or two, looking troubled. 'I'd have blamed anyone in that class, before Rebecca. I still can't think she'd have done anything to hurt Toffee. At lunchtimes and things, when the other children were all playing outside, I'd often come in to the classroom and find her fussing round his cage. It was sweet, but ... it was sad, as well. As if that hamster was her only friend.'

'What about Eleanor Corbett?' I asked.

'It was that autumn term I started noticing the two of them together, come to think of it. After Toffee was dead. Rebecca never helped out with the new class pet, a white mouse it was – it was as if she was scared of coming too close to it.' Her expression was thoughtful. 'I saw her and Eleanor in the playground a lot. At the time – God help me – I thought it was a good thing for Rebecca, that it might bring her out of herself a little.'

'Did you know Eleanor at all?'

Annette nodded. 'She was in the year below Rebecca's. I taught her in the spring term and summer term of nineteen sixty-nine. The last terms she ever lived through, come to think of it.' A brief and awkward silence. 'I can't say she was one of the more memorable children in the class. If it hadn't been for her friendship with Rebecca, I'm not sure I'd remember her at all.'

'But as it is?'

'Well, she wasn't anywhere near as pretty as Rebecca, but she was a sweet-looking little thing. Tiny for her age. I don't think she was terribly bright, but she seemed a nice enough girl.' Annette paused, obviously remembering. 'Very shabby. There were a lot of large, poor families in Teasford then, but even so, the Corbetts stood out. I think there were six daughters, or something like that.'

'Did she get on with the others in her year, before she met Rebecca?'

'It looked more like tagging along than being in the middle of things. Still, I'd say she was accepted. She was very much less of an outsider there than Rebecca was. Anyway, soon you only ever saw the two of them together. I got the impression that Rebecca was quite possessive of her.'

'Did that strike you as being at all sinister? At the time?'

'Well, during that final summer term – when I was teaching Eleanor's class – I must say, it began to. When the bell rang at the end of lessons, Rebecca was always waiting outside the classroom, almost *snatching* Eleanor away from her classmates. It seemed . . . almost obsessive. It worried me a little.' A brief and humourless laugh. 'Of course, at the time, I had no idea what there was to worry about. None of us did.'

'Did Eleanor seem scared by it herself?'

'It's hard to tell, really. She certainly seemed to be hiding something – she behaved more secretively that term, somehow. But that could well be hindsight.' Annette looked earnest, meditative, slightly sad. 'There was never an awful lot of interest in Eleanor, even after she was killed. The media seemed to see her as . . . as just a crime committed by Rebecca.'

'I don't think I've ever seen a photo of her, come to think of it.'

'There were next to none in the papers, even when the case was headline news. All you ever saw was that famous one of Rebecca, the head-and-shoulders shot where she's wearing school uniform.' Something seemed to occur to her. 'Hold on. I'll be back in a minute.'

Annette hurried out of the room. When she came back in, she was carrying a foot-long photograph, mounted on thick, age-darkened cream card.

'I always got a copy of the annual school photo. I've

thrown most of them away, over the years.' Her smile was slightly embarrassed. 'You'll probably think I'm morbid, but I could never quite throw *this* one away. It was taken on the last day of the summer term, in 1969, about a month before they found poor little Eleanor in that house.'

Annette handed it to me, stood beside me as I looked. Sharp, well-defined black-and-white showed neat rows of schoolchildren, crisp white shirts and fixed smiles at the camera, open, cloudless sky behind them. 'That's me, there,' she said, pointing to a pretty, young, dark-haired woman sitting on the left-hand side of the front row, 'and ... let's see, now ... where's Eleanor ...?' Her finger navigated the sea of faces, then stopped dead. 'That's her.'

The photograph showed a tiny, sweet-faced girl with freckles and curly hair in pigtails. I looked closely for several seconds. 'What about Rebecca?'

Annette's finger strayed to the right, up two rows. 'There she is.'

It was indescribably strange, seeing that face in such a mundane setting, far removed from stark newsprint dots on the front pages of ancient newspapers, one of maybe a hundred children smiling for a harassed photographer on a sunny afternoon. Fascination unfolded deep inside me as I looked; I was very aware of Annette watching me, well-meaning but off-putting just the same.

'I don't suppose I could borrow that for a few days, could I?' I asked quickly. 'I'd send it back to you in no time. I'd just like to get it copied.'

I was expecting her to say no – I wanted it so badly, I was superstitiously convinced that she would – but she didn't even seem doubtful. 'Well, certainly, Anna. I hope it inspires you.'

I felt almost dizzy with the weight of fresh knowledge,

and struggled to think of some remark to make. 'I think that's all I wanted to know,' I said at last. 'Thank you very much. You've been fantastically helpful.'

'I've certainly told you all I know,' she said, smiling. 'If there's more you need to find out, there are an awful lot of people who knew Rebecca still living in Teasford. I'm sure a lot of them knew her better than I did.'

'I'd be glad of any information I could get. I don't suppose you know anyone I could talk to?'

'Come to think of it, my eldest niece was in the class above Rebecca's. We're very close, and I know she'd be happy to talk to you. Of course, I wouldn't give her number to just anyone, but I can tell you're trustworthy. Her name's Melanie. Melanie Cook. She and her husband both work during the day, so it's probably best to call after seven or so.'

'That's great.' She went over to the notepad by the phone and wrote down a number for me. 'Honestly,' I said, folding it into my wallet, 'I can't thank you enough.'

'Don't worry about it, Anna. Come to think of it, you could also try looking for Eleanor's sisters – I don't know any of them well, but I'm sure they all stayed in the area. The eldest, Agnes, got married the year before I retired, to a Mr Og.' I jotted it down. 'Easier to find in the phone book than Corbett, I should think.'

She paused for a moment, and her expression clouded over, as though she was regretting the past rather than simply recalling it. 'I hope it does help you. It's probably silly, but I hope someone can understand what Rebecca was really like, even if it's just for the sake of writing a novel. The media changed her into a different person. There was something frightening about that, I always thought. As if they were making sure she'd always be a stranger to everyone.'

Her shoulders rose and fell, and she started walking out of the living room. I followed her.

'I suppose she always will be, now,' I said. 'With the secret identity and everything.'

'That always felt wrong to me. Not because it was too good for her, quite the opposite – because it meant she'd always have to be someone else. She'd be in disguise for the rest of her life. It's sad, in a way, I think she was always hiding her real feelings at school as well. Looking back, I don't think any of us understood her, not properly.'

We were by the door at the end of the narrow, crowded, slightly too hot hallway now, and her hand reached for the doorknob.

'Eleanor did,' I said quietly. 'At least at the end.'

'Yes, of course – poor Eleanor.' She looked suddenly guilty, and older. 'But it's so easy to forget about her, isn't it? Rebecca was always so much more newsworthy.'

15

The drive back from Bournemouth passed on autopilot; while something kept me obeying the rules of the road, I was almost oblivious to my scenery. Miss Watson's Rebecca was as different from the *Daily Mail*'s sinister prodigy as she was from Judith Davies' blandly identikit primary-school girl. Nothing could relate the emerging picture to a recognisable stereotype: sweet-natured, lonely, vicious, possessive, well-behaved, manipulative and *pure evil*. Fresh details and truths seemed to make her more enigmatic than ever.

I couldn't help wondering what I'd have thought if I'd been at St Anthony's in 1969, observing the events of that summer term first-hand – whether I'd have liked Rebecca, whether I'd have liked Eleanor. The photograph Annette Watson had given me rested face-up on the passenger seat, a constant presence on the outskirts of my vision. I kept trying to imagine that frozen split-second of history continuing in real time – the photographer's brisk cry of *that's enough, thank you, everyone*, the neat rows disintegrating as friends rejoined friends and giggling groups returned in the direction of classrooms. I wondered whether Eleanor had walked back with Rebecca, and how it had been between them on that bright afternoon; whether Eleanor was beginning to have certain misgivings about Rebecca's devotion, whether Rebecca had any idea she was going to kill the girl beside her in a month's time.

And, thinking of the murdered girl, I felt an obscure species of guilt. How little I'd cared about her reality at first. How accurate Miss Watson's parting words to me had been.

Passing through Wareham, I parked near the little town centre and walked the rest of the way there. In the Saturday lunchtime sun, the narrow streets crawled with human traffic, and I joined a short queue at the Supasnaps till. I was told that my version of Miss Watson's photo would be ready first thing on Monday.

I was heading back towards the car when I saw the library come into view across the narrow, empty road. I hardly ever came through this part of Wareham, and it was the first time I'd ever really noticed Liz's workplace, a squat and vaguely churchlike stone building, its heavy, institutional double doors standing wide open. Suddenly, it occurred to me that it would be a good idea to look up Agnes Og's phone number as soon as possible, and I crossed towards the library, wondering if I'd see Liz.

Inside, a dark-haired woman in her early thirties sat behind the returns desk, reading intently. There was no sign of anyone else, and golden sunlight filtered in through high windows, slanting over tall, old-fashioned wooden shelves, giving everything a dusty, sleepy look. I quickly found the phone book for Lancashire and sat down with it at a side table, getting my notepad and pen out of my bag before flicking through it.

Three Ogs, only one listed for Teasford. I was copying down the number when a shadow fell over the table. At the same time, the voice came unexpectedly from behind my shoulder. 'Hello, Anna. What are you doing here?'

Apprehension hit me a split-second before conscious recognition – that flat and oddly unmusical voice, quiet, accentless. I turned in my seat. Helen was as neatly and plainly dressed as ever, her face entirely expressionless. It occurred to me that there was something almost guilty in my movements. I'd never like this woman, I realised; her very presence put me on edge.

'Just trying to track down an old friend's number.' I found myself shielding the open directory pages with my forearm, trying to make it look like a casual movement. I had no wish to announce that I was finding out about Rebecca, and, for all I knew, she might be familiar enough with the case for a glimpse of the word *Teasford* to trigger instant recognition. 'I thought Liz might be here today. Is she?'

Helen shook her head; she didn't say anything, but showed no sign of leaving. An oppressive silence seemed to surround her. I couldn't tell if she was aware of its existence, whether she was consciously intimidating, or simply oblivious to other people's feelings and thoughts. She had pale blue eyes with a deep frown-line between them, and it gave her a permanently intent, suspicious look. She might have been studying a bank note she suspected of being forged.

'Lancashire?' With a rise of panic, I saw that she was reading the directory over my shoulder, looking at the heading above the names and addresses and numbers. 'That's a long way away, isn't it?'

I couldn't think of a single thing to say, and nodded. Around us, the sleepy, dusty-looking little library was far too quiet.

Finally, she spoke again. 'I'll be getting on,' she said. 'Goodbye, Anna. I'm sure I'll see you soon.'

It sounded more like a threat than an amiable parting remark. As she walked away, I felt an intense rush of relief. I had no idea how anyone could like that woman, or feel remotely comfortable in her presence; we'd met each other three times, and she seemed inexplicably more disturbing than anyone I'd ever known. Although I'd already copied down Agnes Og's number, I waited till she'd vanished through the open double doors before rising from the table, replacing the pad and paper in my bag, the phone book on the shelf. Then I was walking past the main desk, stepping out into heat and dazzling sunlight towards the parked Mazda, and home.

Carl's car wasn't outside as I crested the hill that led down to our house. As I let myself in, the door between the hallway and kitchen was open, and the conspicuously folded note on the table drew my attention at once. Picking it up, I saw a few quickly jotted lines in Carl's angular but clearly legible writing. *Annie – thought I'd go into Wareham to pick up new strimmer. Back about 3 – Cx.* Checking my watch, I saw it was coming up to two o'clock now. I had a feeling he'd written the note no more than ten minutes ago, that we'd only missed passing each other because he'd taken a different route into town.

I couldn't think of anything to do till he came back and feared the return of nonspecific worry. I held an image of Socks' wounded eye at bay while focusing hard on Miss Watson. I took out the number she'd given me. *Carl won't be back for at least an hour*, I thought as I dialled, *I've got plenty of time.* And something in the tone of that thought brought alarm – it seemed that research itself was becoming an all-important secret I had to keep from him, like my meeting with Mr Wheeler, and the cry I'd heard in the night.

Melanie Cook answered the phone herself. Annette had called her as soon as I'd left her flat, and I was relieved that she'd made nine-tenths of my lead-in speech unnecessary. Melanie's personality came across clearly and favourably, a pleasant, brisk home-maker in early middle age. She would, she said, be happy to spare an hour or so of her time; she'd been aware of both Rebecca Fisher and Eleanor Corbett at school, although she hadn't known either well. She invited me to visit her at home the following Saturday, preferably in the afternoon.

While she seemed to think I lived far closer to Teasford than was actually the case, a second's thought was enough to stop me demurring and offering to conduct the whole interview over the phone. Partly, I sensed I could find out much more from her in person, but I also longed to see the streets where it had all begun, the backdrop to national headlines. I acquiesced gratefully, jotted down the address and told her I'd come round at about two o'clock.

Off the phone, I lugged the Hoover upstairs and started vacuuming the upstairs rooms, more for the sake of something to do than because anything really needed doing. I kept thinking about calling Agnes Og. The prospect was intimidating. The murdered girl hadn't been a casual acquaintance to *her*, but an adored youngest sister; I imagined her greeting my request for an interview with fury, slamming the phone down in my ear. Seeing me as an opportunistic hack keen to cash in on real-life tragedy, indifferent to the fact that Eleanor Corbett had been loved.

I was edging round the dressing table by the main bedroom window, when something beyond it caught my eye. I turned the Hoover off and looked out, frowning. Where the road met the turn-off of our driveway, a car had been parked, an elderly off-white Ford that I'd never seen before. And there was someone standing beside it, looking up at this house. A man. Mr Wheeler.

Involuntarily, I took a step back – I wasn't sure why I didn't want him to see me framed in the net-curtainless window, but I didn't. Still, I could see him quite clearly. He wasn't moving, or doing anything at all. Just standing and looking, an odd expression on his long bloodhound's face. Sad. Reflective. Bitter.

Then, abruptly, he turned away. I saw him getting back into his car, starting the engine. In a matter of seconds, he was gone.

I stood where I was for some time, staring out into the empty front garden and the deserted road beyond it. Wondering over and over again what on earth he could have wanted. For the first time in over a week, I found myself recalling specific details of our interview, the way his face had changed and how furious he'd been. And I remembered how familiar this house must be to him, how he might know it almost as well as I did; the slight creak on the top stair, the chilly edge to the air in the bathroom, the myriad elements of its personality that recalled Rebecca Fisher.

His friend Rebecca Fisher, I thought, and turned the Hoover back on, trying and failing to move my mind away from what I'd just seen.

Carl got home shortly afterwards, lugging the boxed-up new strimmer we needed. As I came downstairs, he was setting it down by the kitchen counter. 'So how'd it go with the teacher?' he asked. 'Find out anything useful?'

Of course, I couldn't tell him about that inexplicable sighting of Mr Wheeler. I struggled to speak cheerfully and calmly, as if trying to convince myself there was nothing to worry about. 'It went well,' I said, 'really well. I think I found out quite a lot.'

'That's great. I'm pleased for you.'

A couple of seconds passed without further comment. There'd be a better time to tell him about Melanie and Agnes Og and Teasford, I decided. A eulogy to unfolding intrigue would only drive a wedge between us.

'Oh yeah,' he said, 'I was thinking, we'd better start

giving some thought to the dinner with Jim and his wife tomorrow night. Have you had any ideas about the menu?'

The last two words came out in a parody of a maitre d's supercilious Franglais, and I smiled. In the kitchen's afternoon sunlight, we discussed tuna steaks and lemon sorbet, what we had in the freezer, what we could get from Asda tomorrow morning. The cheery, companionable normality of it all overcame me, reminding me of all the things he didn't know about.

16

Carl's colleague Jim and his wife Tina were in their late twenties. He was dark and heavy-set with a lot of aftershave and a big white PR smile; she was petite, with short fair hair and the manner of an experienced customer services rep. They were pleasant enough, but something about them said I could know them for fifteen years and still see them as strangers – it was as if we emitted opposing currents, keeping each other at a constant distance.

'I meant to ask earlier, Anna,' said Tina. 'What do you do for a living?'

It was coming up to nine o'clock, and her voice rose behind me as I took the dinner out of the oven. I'd left the back door half-open to get rid of the cooking smells. Passing it en route to the kitchen table, I felt a brief waft of cool night air, glimpsed rosy, enigmatic shadows giving way to solid black beyond the furthest reach of the house lights. 'I used to work for Reading Council before we moved,' I said. 'These days . . . I suppose I'm a housewife.'

'Oh, come on, Annie, you don't have to be so modest.' It was Carl who spoke. I darted him a warning look, but he was speaking to the others at the table. 'Anna's a writer. She had her first novel published last year.'

'Well, yes, but it hasn't done very well. You probably won't be able to find it anywhere.' Most maddening of all was the way I always had to say that, voluntarily surrender the truth rather than be mugged for it. 'I haven't made much money out of it, I'm afraid.'

'Oh, I suppose that's not everything,' said Jim, but his former expression of avid interest had instantly turned to disappointment. 'What sort of books do you write, if you don't mind me asking?'

'My first was a sort of thriller called *A Deeper Darkness*. I'm working on another thriller right now.' I felt guarded and wary at the prospect of revealing my idea to these virtual strangers – it meant too much to me, inspired a kind of fierce, protective love. 'It's about ... well, it's loosely based on Rebecca Fisher. You know. From the Sixties.'

'Doesn't ring a bell,' said Tina, frowning.

'Oh, you must have heard of her,' said Jim. 'Little kid who killed her mate. What was she, eight years old?'

'Ten,' I said.

'How awful,' said Tina. 'What *can* you write about someone like that?'

'Sounds like pretty gruesome stuff,' said Jim, laughing. 'Pure evil, that kid was.'

The infinite intricacies of personality and circumstance suddenly bewildered me more than ever, and I felt Rebecca's character slipping through my fingers like mist. 'You really think so?' I asked.

Jim just laughed. I was very aware of the night beyond this bright, warm kitchen, the things outside that rustled in the dark.

'No, really,' I said. '*Do* you?'

'Oh, come on, Anna. What else can you call a kid like that?' He was all well-tanned, good-natured certainty, tucking into his meal with gusto. 'I thought my brother's kids were little horrors. Compared to that one, they're saints.'

The casual conviction that murder belonged nowhere but a television screen, some slick Sunday night drama – it was in his eyes, and Tina's, and even Carl's. Only I seemed to understand Rebecca's reality. It occurred to me again that she might have eaten in this very kitchen, and my initial inspiration flared more brightly than ever – out of nowhere, I wanted them to see its potential as I did.

'After she was released, you could have *known* her,' I said urgently. 'You could have *worked* with her, and you'd have thought she was just like anyone else. You wouldn't have thought she was pure evil, or any of that newspaper bullshit. Just an ordinary, middle-aged woman doing her best. And, what's fascinating – after all that time, how do you know she wasn't?'

Silence fell like a lead weight from a tenth-floor window. I could see in their eyes that I'd sounded too passionate – that normal, sane, well-balanced people weren't supposed to care that deeply about anything that didn't directly affect their family's wellbeing or their bank balance. I felt Carl's embarrassment at the same time as I felt my own. 'Well, that's what I'm writing about, anyway,' I finished lamely. 'Anyone want some more potatoes?'

I said very little for the rest of that evening, aware of a new and dubious mistrust emanating from their direction. It couldn't help reminding me a little of Carl's parents, how awkward I'd felt around them since he'd told them things I'd told him in confidence. As soon as we'd waved Jim and Tina off at the door and closed it behind us, I turned to him with some irritation.

'Carl, you *know* I hate talking about my writing. Why did you have to go and mention it?'

'Jesus, why does it always have to be such a secret? I thought it was something to be proud of.' His expression suddenly matched mine for annoyance, bordering on exasperation. 'What have you got against them, anyway?'

'I haven't got anything against them, it's not about

them. I haven't even told Liz next door yet – you know that.'

'Well, it seemed like it was about them. You hardly said a word to either Jim or Tina after dinner.'

Something both patronising and critical in his voice infuriated me, and I spoke hotly. 'That's because they kept looking at me like I had two bloody heads! Ever since I talked about Rebecca Fisher.'

'Do you blame them?' I stared at him, hurt, shocked. 'I mean, think about it rationally, Anna – it's pretty morbid. It's not that I mind you doing it, but—'

'Oh, *thank* you. You don't mind me doing it. That makes all the difference. I'd never have *dreamed* of doing it without your permission.'

Turning away from him, I walked into the living room, anger hammering at my temples. Only the Tiffany-style lamp was on, and its thin glow turned the furniture in the corners of the room into dark, indistinct shapes, throwing a corona of multicoloured fairground light over the sofa and armchairs. Sitting down on one, I looked fixedly at the opposite wall as he came in. Heavy silence pressed in on us before he spoke again, his voice conciliatory.

'Come on, Annie, let's not argue about it. It seems like we're spending half our time bickering about this research of yours, lately.' I saw his face change suddenly, become both practical and impulsive. 'Tell you what. Let's get away from it all somewhere, next weekend. How about going to Paris? We can book the hotel and everything tomorrow, get the Eurostar from Waterloo on Saturday morning, and—'

'Oh, God.' From feeling completely in the right, I went straight to feeling completely in the wrong. I'd meant to tell him about my plans earlier that day, had kept thinking a more convenient time would present itself. 'I'm really sorry, I meant to tell you yesterday but I completely forgot. I'm going to Teasford next Saturday. I'll have to leave at about seven in the morning. I'm interviewing someone who knew Rebecca.'

He looked at me for some time, disappointment and confusion fighting for supremacy in his expression. 'Can't you interview them over the phone, instead?'

'*No.*' Suddenly, I was as defensive as though he could forcibly stop me from going, and I spoke with the urgency of a woman fighting her own defence from the dock. 'Carl, I've *got* to go. It won't be the same otherwise, it won't be any good. I just have to see Teasford for myself.'

'So why not go during the week? I mean Jesus, Saturdays and Sundays are the only time we really have to do things together.'

'Look, I've *said* I'm sorry. But I've arranged it now – it's all set. It's no big deal, is it? There's always the weekend after.'

'There isn't.' He sounded hurt, and almost childishly sullen. 'The weekend after, Petra's coming down.'

'Well, the weekend after *that*, then. What's the problem?' I felt guilt rapidly draining away around annoyance; he was backing me into a corner. 'You don't have to act like such a bloody martyr, Carl. I'm going for a *day*, not a month.'

It wasn't what I'd said, but how I'd said it. The atmosphere was suddenly electric with implications: his apparent indifference to something toweringly important in my life, and the fact that Rebecca meant infinitely more to me than a romantic weekend together. There was a long silence, subtly and mutually damning.

'Well, we'd better get to bed, anyway,' he said quietly. 'I'll turn everything off down here.'

I went up to the bathroom, flicking the light on and

closing the door behind me before leaning back against it, exhaling deeply. On one hand, I knew I should have told Carl about Teasford sooner; on the other, I was aware that he'd overreacted in grand style. It was one Saturday in our lives, and I'd known about the impending trip only yesterday. But our argument hadn't really been about that at all. If I'd arranged to go anywhere else on earth that day, it wouldn't have mattered so much, even if he'd already made other plans for us, and I'd left it to the very last minute to tell him I'd be otherwise occupied.

That was the worst thing – knowing that he was worried as much as angry, that most of his apparent irritation had acted as a smokescreen to conceal that. It cast me in a clear-cut role, an inconsiderate wife with a silly interest, a straightforward sitcom situation that was annoying rather than disturbing. I could sense him trying not to think about other things, things that frightened him because he couldn't relate them to anything he'd ever known at first-hand. For a long time, I'd understood his inability to find a satisfactory place for them in his neat mental filing-cabinet, and knew that, by now, he'd uneasily stuffed them away in a seldom-used drawer marked *Oddities*.

He was, I realised, distrustful of my research and everything relating to it because it came so hot on the heels of our move here. I imagined him drawing parallels between my past and my present: then, as now, I'd been uprooted from what I knew, was living in an entirely alien environment. Imagined him thinking that a similar situation could only too easily lead to similar consequences. The idea brought a rise of incoherent frustration close to fury. He knew nothing about that time beyond what I'd told him, and it had been impossible to describe its true taste and texture out loud – *then* and *now* had nothing in common whatsoever.

A million light-years away from a home that had never really felt like home, and more afraid than I'd ever been in my life – as if every possible link with familiarity had been slashed straight through, leaving me adrift. In place of the colourful new life I'd longed for since childhood, an empty grey ocean extending to the horizon on all sides. Closing my eyes, the small, impersonal room I'd lived in then came back to me in dense and paranoiac detail; I remembered the way it had been as the evenings came down there, and how the tiniest noise could set my heart hammering at breakneck speed, and what it meant to be alone in a world far bigger than you'd imagined, feeling your mind beginning to buckle.

But Carl would never understand all that. I knew it perfectly well. In an odd sort of way, it was why I loved him.

When I woke up the following morning, the clock by the bed told me it had just gone half-seven. I could hear Carl having a shower. As I yawned and stretched, I was aware of nothing but a vague sense of wrongness, then it contracted to ultra-sharp focus as I remembered the row we'd had last night. It hadn't really ended at all, I realised. We'd exchanged brief, formal, carefully polite *goodnights* before I'd drifted into troubled sleep.

There was something terrible about serious arguments that carried over into the following morning, as if there was no knowing when, or even *if* they would end. I prayed he'd be as keen to make up as I was, and waited for him to return from the bathroom with some trepidation. As he stepped in, it was as if strong hands had been holding my heart down and suddenly let go – his slightly sheepish expression told me he felt exactly the same as I did. *Let's just forget it ever happened,* his eyes said. *Put it down to too much wine, or whatever . . .*

'Listen, I was thinking,' he said as he got dressed. 'How about going to Poole Tower Park next Sunday – I hear there's a ten-screen cinema there. We can go and see a film in the afternoon then drive somewhere for dinner. Even if you are going to Teasford next weekend, it doesn't have to be a complete write-off.'

'That sounds great. Good idea.' I went over and kissed him with a mixture of relief and heartfelt gratitude. 'There's bound to be something decent on. I can't wait.'

A buoyant and inviolate good humour lingered even after he'd gone to work, a feeling of reprieve that made the world a brighter place; last night's row had seemed the kind that was far deeper and more serious than it looked, but had been the exact opposite. Even my research took on a more reassuring edge; no Byzantine labyrinth but a practical timetable of necessary activities. Later on that day, I'd pick up my copy of Miss Watson's photograph, and send the original back to her with a thank-you note. Then, when I came home, I'd give serious thought to ringing Agnes Og. I would, I told myself, simply have to grit my teeth and dial her number – it seemed the kind of thing that it was only too easy to put off and off and off till you'd forgotten all about it.

Downstairs, I was putting the kettle on and gazing out when something caught my eye. Opening the window, I leant out into the chilly morning air to look more closely. There was something lying on our garden path, maybe four metres away from the back door. My first thought was that a top or something had blown off the line; a second later, as my eyes caught patterns of light and shade and defined the texture of dew-damp fur, I realised it must be a dead fox cub. It was only when I'd opened the door and taken my first uncertain step towards it that I realised I was looking at Socks.

17

It was a long time before Liz answered my knock at her back door. I'd obviously got her out of bed. In her quilted pink dressing-gown, she looked smaller and younger and somehow different – her hair was pulled back in a loose ponytail with random wisps escaping, her face shiny from recent sleep, her eyes confused. The kitchen behind her seemed designed for the Liz I knew, that unflappable Women's Institute stalwart. Now she looked out of place in front of the shelves of cookery books, the crowded spice-racks, the myriad small details that made up a scene of domesticity.

'Anna? You look as white as a sheet! What's the matter, dear?'

A long pause, in which I realised there was no nice or gentle way to break the news. 'I'm sorry, Liz,' I said. 'It's Socks. He's dead.'

'Oh, my God.' She took a step back. 'Are you sure?'

I was as certain of it as I'd ever been of anything, but could only nod. 'He's in my garden,' I said. 'I saw him as soon as I opened the door.'

Then she was hurrying down her own garden path, crossing to mine. I followed her, unsure what else to do.

'Where is he?' she asked.

But I didn't need to say anything – she'd just seen him. She approached, bent down, reached out to touch him.

'Socks?' she said, shaking him as if to wake him up. '*Socks?*'

'Liz,' I began, but she didn't seem to hear me.

A few seconds passed in virtual silence, and a flock of birds took off from the roof. Liz stood up again. 'You're right,' she said haltingly. 'He's . . . *dead*—'

As I watched, her face crumpled into noisy, unself-conscious tears. Aghast, I tried to comfort her, having no idea what I was supposed to do in this situation. 'Liz. Come on, Liz.' I put an arm round her shoulder gingerly, even now feeling intrusive, potentially unwanted. 'Look, come on in. I'll put the kettle on.'

In her current state, I could have led her off a cliff and she wouldn't have noticed. I took her arm, guided her into the kitchen and over to the table like a sleepwalker. She sat wordlessly, and I went to the kettle at the counter, filled it from the tap, plugged it in. With my back to her, I thought she'd stopped crying, but when I turned, there were silent tears running down her face, squeezing out from between her closed eyelids. In her dressing-gown, she looked desolate, virtually unrecognisable.

'He was an old cat, of course.' She spoke quietly at last, in a tear-clogged voice. I put a cup of tea down in front of her, but she didn't seem to notice it. 'Nearly thirteen. I got him from the rescue centre when he was all of seven years old; it seemed such a shame nobody else wanted him. Everyone else just wanted the kittens. Poor little Socks.' She took a convulsive breath. 'Still, even though he was old, it's such an awful thing to happen. He seemed so healthy. In all the time I had him, all he ever had wrong with him was that funny eye . . . and even that was starting to get better . . .'

Picking the cup of tea up, she took a sip. When she spoke again, she sounded a little more like her old self. 'I suppose it had to happen some time. At least it looks like he didn't suffer. After I put him out last night, his heart must just have given out, or something . . .'

Silence again. I watched Liz sip at her tea. The morning had taken on the feel of an ominous dream that could turn into a nightmare at any second.

'I don't suppose you'd help me bury him, would you, dear?' she asked. 'I can manage the digging on my own. To be honest, I could just do with the company.'

So at quarter past eight, we buried Socks in Liz's back garden, under the shade of an apple tree. There was no attempt at even a makeshift service – Liz just dug, I just stood there. She'd wrapped Socks in a fluffy white blanket as a shroud, had changed quickly into trousers and a sweater that looked far too heavy for the time of year. She still looked as indefinably unlike herself as she'd done earlier. 'Poor little Socks,' she said quietly, lowering the small shape into the hole. 'I did care about him, you know. You might think it's silly, but I really loved the little thing.'

'I don't think it's silly at all. I had a cat when I was younger, called Tinkerbell. It's an awful name, but I chose it. I thought it sounded pretty, at the time.' The memory brought too much baggage with it, this quiet morning – eight years old and coming home from primary school, little black-and-white Tinkerbell the only reassuring presence in the house. 'She died when I was twelve. I was heartbroken. It felt like—'

Losing my only friend was what I wanted to say, but I bit down on that hard. It was nothing but the truth, and maybe that was why I felt so unwilling to share it. 'It felt like growing up,' I said. 'I'd had her since I was six.'

The words fell away into the awkward, oppressive silence of mourning, and the first shovels of earth went into the hole, concealing the white blanket. The grave was filled. Liz took a step back from it, shovel in hand.

'What's the time, dear?' she asked, unexpectedly.

147

I glanced at my watch. 'Nearly quarter to nine.'

'Oh, dear. I'm supposed to be at work for ten. Thank you so much, you've been such a comfort – but I'd better get a move on. I'm going to be late.'

'You're going into work? Today?'

'I think it's best if I'm busy. I couldn't stand sitting at home on my own all day, thinking about him. It's going to be bad enough when I come home.'

'I'll stay with you,' I said quickly. 'If you like.'

'That's sweet of you, dear – but really, I wouldn't dream of it. I'll be fine at work. I'll have other things to do.'

Back at home, I sat in the living room, keeping an eye out for movement beyond the window. At last I saw her heading out to her parked car, dressed in a long flowered skirt and faded T-shirt, looking like the woman I'd first seen in the front garden. Her untidiness had become something comfortable again, implying a woman who was too busy baking cakes and growing roses to pay attention to silly things like lipstick. Still, I felt I'd seen another side to her, something beyond the middle-aged platitudes and generic amiability; it had never occurred to me that she might be vulnerable at any level, that the death of her pet would inspire any reaction beyond the conventional degree of regret and a few neat little tears. As I watched her getting in behind the wheel, I found myself wondering if she'd be all right, and remembering how devastated she'd seemed.

I heard her engine starting. It was as if amazement and sympathy had hypnotised me for the past hour or so, and the sound snapped me out of a trance. It all came rushing back to me in the silence of the living room: the frozen image of Socks lying dead, the moment of stark realisation. And I had exactly the same sensation that I'd had then – as if I'd been alone and daydreaming in a Muzaktinkling lift, before the lights shorted out in a split-second's explosive pop, and the floor plummeted down under my feet.

They'd killed Rebecca's dog to make her leave, Mr Wheeler had told me. And, in that moment, I'd seen the version of myself that *he* saw – the living embodiment of callous, prurient gossip, a convenient focus for all his suppressed rage. A village was too faceless to hate in that way. Too impossible to retaliate against.

I stood in the living room and looked out, aware of nothing beyond my own mounting terror. *An eye for an eye*, I thought. I'd been looking after Socks on an almost daily basis; in a way he'd been my pet as well as Liz's. I remembered Mr Wheeler standing by his parked car on Saturday, looking up at the house. It dawned on me that he could have done that on any number of occasions without my being aware of it – that he could have watched the back door as well, camouflaged in the woods beyond the garden. Could have seen Socks, coming in and out . . .

He could have injured and killed Socks himself. He could have seen it as a kind of twisted justice: a cat's wounded eye and execution in exchange for a dog's untimely demise . . .

I told myself that I was being ridiculously paranoid – he was a *vet*, the very last person who'd harm an animal. But I couldn't help thinking that his anger against me might run deep enough to obliterate kindness, or ethics, or perspective. That he could have been indifferent to Socks' life, simply because he'd seen the cat as mine.

It was, to say the least, a coincidence. Two dead pets at number four Ploughman's Lane in less than six months. And it wasn't as if Liz and I had conducted an expert postmortem on Socks' corpse. If he'd been poisoned, or strangled, or suffocated—

I tried to stem the flow of new fear, forcing cold practicalities down on it as hard as I could. Too-coincidental as Socks' death seemed, coincidences did happen – old cats did die, and their hearts could suddenly give out on someone's garden path as easily as anywhere else. But for all my deliberate attempts to reassure myself, my worries only intensified as the minutes passed. The empty rooms pressed in around me, there were too many shadows, the faint chill on the air was too pronounced. And I had an infinitely disturbing feeling that I wasn't alone here at all, a fleeting sensation that I was being watched.

If there was one good thing about this disquiet, it made any activity at all look more attractive than idle, solitary reflection, and at last, it did what very little else could have compelled me to do. It drove me towards the piece of A4 with Agnes Og's number written on it. Sitting down on the sofa, I picked up the phone and dialled. Suddenly, it had become actively reassuring to have something else to worry about, something straightforward and understand-able – maybe she'd scream at me down the line, maybe she'd hang up on me, maybe she wouldn't even be there. Whatever the immediate future held, it was certainly the lesser of two evils.

The phone rang for some time before a woman answered it abruptly. 'Yeah?'

'Excuse me, I was wondering if I could speak to Mrs Agnes Og?'

'You're speaking to her. What do you want?'

In her voice, there were none of the affectations you got used to hearing over the phone, the deliberate theatrical rises and falls implying curiosity, or goodwill, or pleasure.

It could have been because she didn't know who I was, but something about her tone said she'd have spoken in the same way to a close relative. While I couldn't warm to it at all, it reassured me; it was dour, practical and emotionless, and I couldn't imagine its owner dissolving into tears or hysterics when she found out what I wanted. 'Oh, good morning, Mrs Og,' I said. 'My name's Anna Jeffreys, and I'm a writer.'

Silence, betraying nothing. I saw the huge obstacle looming ahead, tensed myself to jump over it. 'I'm very sorry to bother you, but I wondered if you could help me,' I went on quickly. 'I'm researching a novel – a thriller – that's loosely based on the Rebecca Fisher case. I'm going to be in Teasford this coming Saturday, and I was hoping you could spare half an hour or so to answer a few questions.'

'Where'd you get this number from?'

Instantly, she sounded narrow-eyed and suspicious. With a sinking feeling in the pit of my stomach, I explained as best I could about Miss Watson, and what she'd told me. 'I honestly don't mean to intrude,' I finished, 'and I don't mean to exploit your sister's memory. But I'd be very grateful for anything you could tell me.'

'Well, suppose there's no harm in it. Don't know what you want to hear, mind.' Amazement and relief overcame me as she spoke – her tone had become indifferent again, unsurprised and impersonal. 'Wasn't like I was friends with the little cow at school. All I knew of her was what I knew from poor Eleanor.'

The last two words came out without emotion or emphasis, as a single name, the way you'd say *Mary Anne, Sarah Jane*. She sounded entirely untroubled by it, and I

151

couldn't help wondering how much of her sister's memory still remained to her.

'Thanks very much,' I said. 'Listen, I don't know the area at all well. I don't suppose you know anywhere we could meet up to talk?'

She'd been so instantly defensive of her phone number, I automatically assumed she'd name a cafe or a pub, but she didn't even hesitate. 'Come round my house, I suppose. We're number forty-three Harris Road, me and my husband.'

I took down the address, and she gave directions parsimoniously, as if I should know already. 'Well,' I said at last, 'I'll see you at one o'clock, on Saturday.'

'All right. Bye.'

She hung up. Frowning at the receiver in my hand, I followed suit. I found myself thinking back to the *Daily Mail* article I'd read in the newspaper library, and the picture it had given of Eileen Corbett – the kindly Northern matriarch, a lovable figure straight out of a Catherine Cookson mini-series. Irrationally, I'd imagined that her eldest daughter would resemble her intensely. Then it dawned on me that perhaps she *did*; there'd been absolutely no doubt where the journalist's sympathies lay, and the more charming the bereaved mother appeared, the more indefensible the *angel-faced psychopath* would be. I found myself wondering what else could have been exaggerated, and underplayed, and even ignored completely.

I walked into the kitchen aimlessly. A large bluebottle had somehow got trapped in here, battering itself against the window and swooping erratically round the room. Its frantic buzz was deafening, and I opened the window to let it out. It flew away almost at once, dwindling to a tiny speck and then vanishing. As it did, its background

suddenly became the sole focal point of my attention –
those dense, dark-green woods extending into the hazy
distance; woods that, at night, could conceal anyone,
anything.

18

While I desperately wanted to tell Carl about the events of that morning, I couldn't explain their full importance. Taken out of context, Socks' death was nothing out of the ordinary – its ominous undercurrents came directly from Mr Wheeler's anger and the cry I'd heard in the night. The two things he knew nothing about. It had started out as such a straightforward decision, my unwillingness to let him know about my trip to the vet's, but suddenly, I could feel secrets and fears tangling up into the kind of knot that even the nimblest of fingers couldn't undo.

I couldn't go back now – God knows how he'd interpret this backlog of unnerving truths. If nothing else convinced him that this research was affecting my state of mind, that certainly would. Still, when he got in from work that night, I knew I couldn't just ignore the subject either, and, as we sat together in the living room before dinner, I broached it carefully.

'Something sad happened today, you know – Liz's cat died. I found him on our back path this morning.' I watched him carefully, trying to see if it struck him as odd in any way. Apparently it didn't – he just looked startled and politely concerned. 'She was really upset,' I went on. 'I helped her bury him in her back garden.'

'That's a shame. Poor old Liz.' Carl spoke in the tone most people reserved for near-strangers' sorrows, at once sympathetic and essentially untroubled. 'What happened? Did a fox or something get it?'

'*Him*,' I corrected automatically, then, 'no, nothing like

that. He just ... died. Liz said he was getting on a bit, mind you – apparently, he was thirteen.'

'That's ancient for a cat, isn't it?'

'Pretty old.' A brief pause fell, heavy with one-sided anxiety. I couldn't quite stop myself speaking again. 'It seems ... horrible, somehow. That he died on our back path. I know it sounds silly, but I can't help wishing I'd found him somewhere else.'

Carl looked frankly bewildered. 'Why?'

'Oh ... I don't know,' I said unwillingly. 'It just seems like bad luck, in a way.'

'Jesus, Annie. You're not normally that superstitious.' He smiled. 'You know, you're supposed to worry about black cats crossing your path, not ginger ones *dying* on it.'

After that, there was nothing more I could say without saying far too much. The subject drifted rapidly away, and we didn't refer to it again. But not being able to share my concerns seemed to make them worse than ever. Over the next few days, they lingered like unwelcome house-guests who showed no signs of ever going home – sometimes I could almost forget they existed, but at other times, I'd enter a room to find them confronting me. Whether they were visible or not, they were always *there*, and I could find no possible way of driving them out.

Occasionally, during the daytime, I thought about calling Petra and telling her all about it, but a few minutes' thought was always enough to stop me. Everything about the subject demanded privacy and time, and she had neither. I'd confide in her, I told myself, the weekend after next. She'd be coming down soon; I wouldn't be alone with these worries much longer.

It was a very quiet week for me, and a very strange one. Socks' absence seemed far more glaringly obvious than his presence had ever done, and several times I found myself longing for his discreet self-absorption in a sunny corner of the kitchen. Liz was out almost constantly, and I guessed she was taking on extra hours to distract her from bereavement. On the rare occasions we saw each other, we exchanged smiling, perfunctory greetings and goodbyes that tactfully denied any knowledge of her sadness. She seemed to have reverted to her old self at once, the self I couldn't really empathise with, or relate to, or confide in. I observed her bustling briskly through a world devoid of darkness, a hundred miles away.

And I found myself turning to Rebecca Fisher with a kind of desperation, as if she and she alone could distract me from everything else. The school photograph pulled at me too often, drawing me up to the spare room where I'd put the copy I'd collected from Supasnaps in a folder with my internet print-outs. At the desk, I saw her face leap out from a sea of others, as if some advanced computer trickery made it the only pin-sharp detail in an amorphous grey-white blur. *Who were you?* I'd think. *Who are you now?* And, as I thought about them, they seemed to become the only questions that really mattered. I kept thinking about Teasford, longing for Saturday to arrive.

19

The Teasford of my imagination was an oddly unreal and cartoonish sort of place, drawn and coloured in by the article I'd read about it online. From the sudden sea-change it had described – a transformation from cloth-capped purgatory to yuppie Utopia – I'd envisioned a scaled-up Ideal Home exhibition, all newness and offices and upmarket pubs, with nothing in evidence that predated 1985. During my train journey from Bourne-mouth, I became convinced that I'd step off into a state-of-the-art little station, all gleaming glass and plastic; the past would have been scrubbed away with meticulous care, and there'd be no hint of the place it had been long ago.

So when I finally emerged at Teasford station, I was oddly relieved to find that wasn't the case at all. It was a dingy old three-platformed affair with dank brick walls the colour of old blood, that looked as if it could have been built at any time in the past hundred years. The closed-in waiting-room I passed on the platform was heavily scarred with graffiti, and looked as wholesome and enticing as an abandoned mattress in a skip. Out of the station, I emerged into fresh sunlight, checked my watch and extracted the directions Agnes Og had given me.

She lived too near the station to necessitate a taxi, and I started walking in what I hoped was the right direction. For some time, I was convinced I'd never find her house; rows and rows of identical-looking terraces extended endlessly, mazelike, confusing. Each row faced another as if in a mirror, across a narrow strip of road – dark red-brick houses with green-painted front doors, one ground-floor window and two first-floor windows each. The streets were very quiet. At last, to my relief, I saw Harris Road, and crossed the street towards it.

Finding her house number quickly, I knocked at the door and waited for some time. I'd started to wonder whether she'd forgotten about me and gone out, when the door opened at last.

'You must be Anna Jeffreys.' It was the same flat, uninflected voice I'd heard on the phone. A large, pallid woman with lank red hair faced me, without apparent interest. 'Suppose you'd best come in.'

Through the front door, I stepped directly into a sweltering living room – a battered leatherette three-piece suite, intricate ornaments arranged above an electric fire, a recent-looking wedding photo framed in the centre of them. The TV that dominated the room was showing a garish daytime quiz show, at roughly the same volume as a normal conversation. Agnes made no move to turn it off, or even down. She sat. I sat across from her.

'Well, it's nice to meet you at last.' She didn't say anything and I began to feel intensely awkward. 'If I could just start off by asking – did you and Eleanor grow up round here?'

The clumsiness of that question made my cheeks burn – of course, Eleanor Corbett had never *grown up* – but Agnes didn't seem to notice. 'Yeah. Just round the corner, in Churchill Street. I stayed there with Mum up till two years ago. She was ill, you know. I couldn't get married to my boyfriend Dave till she died.'

It was hard to know what, if any, reaction she wanted. My expression flickered uneasily between sympathy and congratulations. 'What about your other sisters?' I asked. 'Did they all move out?'

'Yeah. Soon as they could, really. Even after poor Eleanor died, the house was too crowded. It was just the same size as this one, we was always getting in each other's way. You wouldn't believe what it was like when we was kids. When there was *five* of us.'

Despite myself, I was jolted by the ease with which she alluded to her sister's death. There was no sentimentality in her voice, just a matter-of-fact nod to the reality of murder. There seemed no way I could move the conversation directly to Rebecca. 'Have you got any photos of her?' I asked. 'Eleanor?'

'Yeah. Got photos of all of us.' I thought I was going to have to ask if I could see them, but then she rose from her chair. 'I always keep photos. Got a whole album of me and Dave's wedding snaps.'

She went over to a nearby drawer, got out an album bound in padded pink plastic. Peeling gold letters on the front spelt out *My Family* in flowing, sentimental script. She sat down beside me on the sofa, opening the album in her lap. 'We're all in this,' she said, and began showing me through the photographs.

It was the kind of slow, pedantically-detailed guided tour of strangers' faces that normally crawled by, but to me Agnes couldn't linger long enough on each picture. 'That's Mary and Pat going to their friend's birthday party,' she said. 'That's Bernadette when she was a baby.' The children looked uniformly nondescript, and it was hard to imagine there had ever been a clever one or a pretty one or a rebel – in the pictures, they were interchangeable as a litter of puppies, with Eleanor as the distinctive, oddly appealing runt. 'That's poor Eleanor when she was six,' said Agnes, 'her first school photo.'

An individual picture, the kind you posed for in a primary-school assembly hall like a criminal in a mugshot

– far more detailed than Annette's photo, or any of the others in this album. The murdered girl had been cute rather than pretty, the kind of cuteness that owed everything to extreme youth and small stature – the pronounced gap between her tiny front teeth intensified her resemblance to some small, appealing animal that Disney would make even more lovable on drawing-boards.

'She was a lovely little girl,' I said quietly.

'Yeah.' I had a strong sense that it had never occurred to her before. Far from seizing on it now, she let it drift away with an expression of vague incomprehension. 'Weren't that bright, mind. Reckon she was a bit backward, to be honest.'

'In what way?'

'In every way, really. Just slow. Couldn't hardly read or write, never mind do housework. All the rest of us was helping Mum out by the time we was seven or eight; poor Eleanor was almost ten when she died, and she still couldn't iron a shirt without burning a hole in it.'

Agnes closed the photograph album and set it aside absently. I tried not to show how startled and subtly horrified I was by her apparent lack of emotion. 'She was clumsy?' I asked.

'Dunno, really – she didn't normally trip up and break things and that. But she was useless round the house. More trouble than it was worth, letting her do a thing. Bernadette normally did her chores for her, even when she was old enough to do them herself. I was working by then, so I couldn't.'

'What was she like, apart from that?'

'Like I said, not that bright. Too easily led by the other kids, you know.' A brief pause, in which I saw her thinking deeply – her expression was that of an earnest student in an unexpectedly tough final exam. 'Like, she got done for nicking sweets from the corner shop when she was about seven. She was hanging around with a couple of older kids – course, they'd put her up to it. The lady from the shop knew Mum and come round to complain. The older kids just lied their way out of trouble, said they hadn't known nothing about it. But Mum knew poor Eleanor was telling the truth, she didn't have the brains to do anything else. She wasn't allowed to go round with those kids, after that. God knows what they'd have talked her into next.'

'Was she happy at school? Before she met Rebecca?'

'Dunno. Suppose so. She was always going out and playing with the other kids round here and that. Mind you, it all changed when she met that little cow. Rebecca this, Rebecca that. They acted like they was joined at the hip.'

I watched Agnes closely. 'Did Rebecca ever come to visit Eleanor at home, when you were there?'

'A few times. All she ever did was try and get poor Eleanor out of the house – didn't want nothing to do with the rest of us. Stuck-up little cow, like the rest of her family. You should have seen the way her mum looked, when she dropped her off here – like she had a bad smell under her nose. Drove this big flashy sports car, stuck out round here like a sore thumb. She was always tarted up to the nines even first thing in the morning. Looked just like Rebecca, she did.'

'But Rebecca was adopted, wasn't she?'

'Was she?' Indifference looked back at me, unsurprised, uninterested. 'Well, I dunno, then. She still looked like her.'

A slightly too-long silence. Suddenly, I was afraid she'd bring this interview to an arbitrary end, and searched my mind for another avenue of enquiry. 'I heard Rebecca

161

bought things for Eleanor, as if she was trying to buy her friendship. Did you ever see any of the presents at the time?'

'Oh, yeah. There was this gold bracelet once – I found it under poor Eleanor's bed, showed it to Mum. That started some trouble, all right. Mum went on and on at her asking her where she'd got it. When she said Rebecca'd give it to her, Mum made her put her coat on right away. Said the two of them would have to go straight round the Fishers' house and give it back, said no kid would be allowed to give away something like that.' It was a clear echo of that *Daily Mail* article, and was also the first time I'd heard Agnes laugh; her amusement seemed to come out of nowhere, for no reason. 'They didn't get back till hours later because it was such a long walk, but you should have seen Mum's face when they did. Never saw her so angry in my life. Face like thunder, told us all about it as soon as she'd got in the door.'

'What did she say?'

'Oh, all about Rebecca's mum. That stuck-up cow treating her like dirt and what have you. Rebecca's mum didn't even invite them in, just kept them on the doorstep like they was rubbish, and called Rebecca down from her room. Asked her if it was true she'd given her bracelet away. Course, Rebecca said it was, but her mum just snatched it back like poor Eleanor had *nicked* it, got really snotty, said her little girl wouldn't be giving anything else to our family if she had any say in it. Then she just sent them off with a flea in their ear. Mum was hopping mad about it for days.

'Well, she wasn't happy about Eleanor playing with Rebecca, not after that – said if we weren't good enough for Rebecca, then Rebecca wasn't good enough for us. But it was only a couple of weeks later that poor Eleanor went missing. She must have been meeting up with the little cow in spite of what Mum said. Like I said, she weren't that bright. Didn't seem to understand much of anything.'

I had a question burning a hole in my mind, but could find no diplomatic way of phrasing it, and finally realised it could only be asked outright. 'It sounds as though Rebecca was a very possessive kind of friend to Eleanor,' I said carefully. 'At the time, with the expensive presents and everything, didn't it strike any of you as being a bit sinister?'

'Not really. Me and Mum was working most of the time, Pat and Mary had boyfriends, Bernadette and the others just had their own mates. You know.' A brief pause, in which I observed an apparently uncharacteristic moment of insight – the essential coldness of the household she'd described, a group of indifferent strangers sharing bedrooms and blood-groups and nothing else. When she spoke again, there was an edge of defensiveness to her voice. 'I did tell her it weren't right once, it weren't normal to hang round with kids in different years, even kids from round here. But poor Eleanor didn't pay any attention.'

I became aware of the too-loud telly for the first time in some minutes; a middle-aged man in a bright purple suit was pulling faces and gesticulating wildly, to fits of canned laughter that had a slightly disturbing, hysterical edge. 'Well, I think that's all I need to know,' I said. 'Thanks a lot – you've been very helpful.'

I rose to my feet and she looked up. 'You going to send us a copy of your book, when it's done?'

'Sure,' I said. 'It's going to be quite some time, though – I'm just researching it at the moment.'

'But you'll mention my name in the credits and that?' I nodded. It was perhaps the first time I'd seen her smile without an edge of sullen, judgemental misanthropy. 'My mum talked to loads of journalists about poor Eleanor,' she said confidentially, 'kept a scrapbook of all the cuttings. She was in the *Daily Mail* once. Left it to me when she died – that's it, up there on the shelf.'

Curiosity rose inside me, but was instantly forced back – I couldn't get out of this claustrophobic little living room quickly enough, out of this woman's blank, spiteful, profoundly unnerving presence. 'I'm sure it's very interesting,' I said, taking a step backwards, towards the door. 'Thanks again. I'll let you know when my book finally comes out.'

There was no hiatus of hallway between living room and street, and I stepped straight out onto the pavement. As the door closed behind me, I couldn't help taking a deep breath, urgently in need of fresh air. There was something insidious, not in her possession of that scrapbook, but her naked pride in it; I imagined her reading through it and glorying in the sight of her family's names in print, not even recognising the vast gulf between the words in the cuttings and the reality she'd lived through. I thought of the rose-tinted Catherine Cookson idyll the *Daily Mail* had portrayed – the loving extended family, financial hardships counterbalanced by warmth and togetherness – and held the images up against the big, pale woman with the lank hair, her emotionless, dutiful references to *poor Eleanor*.

As I walked, a picture of the life Eleanor Corbett must have led back then slowly crept up on me. A mental image of these streets in 1969 became clearer, as I imagined how they'd look bare of bristling satellite dishes and phone lines. No river or open parks or trees or even front gardens to interrupt the monotony and give the senses space to

164

breathe, just red-brick terraces and narrow roads, occasional concreted-over yards that were either junk-filled or
empty. It occurred to me that Eleanor would have had no
reason to go beyond this area in the usual run of things,
except when she went to school. Even during weekends, I
expected she'd have stayed here. As the picture sharpened,
I felt a combination of claustrophobia and pity. The
network of empty streets took on the feel of a prison cell
with a single high window: seasons could change, years
could pass, and nothing would ever alter here but the
colour of the sky.

I could have got a taxi to Melanie Cook's house, but
preferred to walk – I had comprehensive directions and
plenty of time, and there was something inexplicably
reassuring about the gradual change in my scenery. The
relentless dictatorship of red-brick terraces began to
loosen its grip, and then was over completely. Down a
wide, tree-lined road on the outskirts of the town centre, I
passed a pub called the Golden Lion. Blackboards outside
promised toad-in-the-hole and cod and chips, reminding
me that I hadn't eaten all day. I sat in the sunshine on one
of the wooden benches outside, first with a diet coke, then
a ploughman's lunch, then a cigarette. As I was lighting it,
I saw a little group of seven- or eight-year-olds running
together across the road, shrieking happily. Their shrill
voices tumbled down the pavement like something blown
by the wind, and lingered a long time in the quiet distance.

20

Annette Watson, Judith Davies and East Lancashire Online had all told me that Teasford had changed dramatically over the years, but they hadn't told me *how*. I'd imagined it all evolving simultaneously, while, in reality, certain areas had raced ahead, leaving others far behind. If the post-war terraces near the railway station had been alive with bleak and petty history, the private housing estate where Melanie lived had the inviolate, pristine newness of a doll fresh out of its box on Christmas morning: well-tended lawns, twin coachlights on either side of front doors, adjoining garages. The interior of her house matched its atmosphere detail for detail; everything in the kitchen we sat in looked spotless, wipeable, apparently unused.

'We should have the house to ourselves for an hour or so,' she was saying over a cup of coffee. 'My husband's off watching the football with the boys and his dad – the boys are both primary-school-aged, so it's a bit more peaceful here without them.'

Melanie was a pleasant-looking brunette in her mid-forties, with a charm both impersonal and impossible to dislike – her manner was that of an efficient receptionist at a good hotel. 'Are they at St Anthony's themselves?' I asked. 'Your sons?'

'That's right. Of course, it's much better these days. I hardly recognise the old place when I do the school run. It used to be very run-down, and quite a lot smaller.'

'You knew Rebecca there,' I said, 'didn't you?'

'That's right – well, as I said on the phone, I didn't really *know* her. She was a year below me, but I think everyone knew who she was. She was a bit of a celebrity there, thanks to those parents of hers.' She frowned, correcting herself. 'Adoptive parents, anyway – I remember reading in the paper that she wasn't their real daughter. I was quite surprised I'd never known. I don't think anyone else at St Anthony's was adopted – you'd have thought word would have got around.'

'That is pretty strange,' I said thoughtfully. 'What did you think of her?'

'Not very much, to be honest. I don't mean I disliked her, just that she struck me as surprisingly ordinary. With a family like that, you'd have thought she'd be an arrogant, spoilt little princess, but she seemed just like any other quiet little girl, a bit shy, nobody's idea of a troublemaker. Lovely clothes and things, school uniform or not – her mother must have bought it all from some expensive shop miles away, it was far smarter than anyone else's – and of course, she was amazingly pretty. Apart from that ... God, I could kick myself for not noticing anything else ... I suppose she was a bit of a disappointment to all of us. I think we'd have quite liked to have an authentic rich bitch around the place – it would have made our schooldays much more interesting.'

She broke off for a second, looking thoughtful. 'It's funny. I only saw her father – her adoptive father – once, and he was an awful disappointment as well. I must have been eleven or so, and someone pointed him out to me, driving past. He was a sort of legend around the area, owning the big factory and everything. The way everyone talked about him, he was richer than Bill Gates. But from the little I saw of him, he looked much like anyone else. Glasses, dark hair. Ordinary sort of car.' She smiled. 'I remember being quite annoyed that he didn't have a chauffeur. Or even white hair, or a big cigar. Well, I suppose you live and learn.'

'Did you ever see her adoptive mother at all?'

'Oh, God, did I ever. She was definitely the colourful one in that family. You couldn't possibly *not* have noticed her when she came to pick Rebecca up from school – her husband's car might have been ordinary, but hers wasn't. She had this incredible two-seater sports thing, pillar-box red. I think it would look pretty good these days, but it must have cost a fortune back then. She certainly knew how to attract attention, that woman – not the good kind, either. She seemed to have a genius for rubbing people up the wrong way.'

'In what way?' I asked. 'What did she do?'

'Well, it was everything about her, really. I know how vague and annoying that must sound, but I don't know how else to put it.' Again, the thoughtful look, then I saw her face light up unexpectedly. 'Actually, I can think of a specific example. I heard about it from a friend's mother, who'd tried to strike up a conversation with her at the school gates one day. You'd really have had to know what my friend's mother was like; she couldn't *see* a stranger without launching into a heart-to-heart. Just as poor as most of us were, then, but she wouldn't have been a bit embarrassed to talk to the Queen herself.

'Anyway, she just said something complimentary about Rebecca's mother's new hairstyle, and they started talking politely enough, then Rebecca's mother said something about it being hard to keep her hair perfectly clean in the summer. Something like that, anyway. What I do remember is that she said *you people*, as in *I suppose you people don't worry so much about that*. My friend's mother remembered it word for word a year later, and still got angry whenever she mentioned it – "you people," she'd say, "bloody cheek." She said the most incredible thing was that Rebecca's mother said it quite blithely, as if she had no idea it might cause offence. Anyway, my friend's mother never spoke another word to her, after that – always said Mrs Fisher was a poisonous woman.

'Actually, I heard her and my own mother talking about Mrs Fisher, once. Well, *bitching* about her, really. They said she'd been the one with the money to begin with, and that was the only reason Dennis Fisher had married her. Called him a cold fish. Apparently, her own father had been a millionaire, or close to one – he'd owned a lot of coalmines round here, before they'd all closed down. Local boy made good, like the great Dennis Fisher himself.'

I couldn't help but be interested by the introduction of this new character, the *elegant mother* the *Daily Mail* had referred to so casually in passing. 'What did you think of Mrs Fisher yourself?'

'I can't say I ever spoke to her. I remember she had this very loud, very posh voice that really carried. *Nobody* talks like that unless they're the Duchess of Devonshire or something, and I knew she'd grown up near Teasford herself. There was something terribly artificial about it, trying really hard to project the right image. Everything about her was like that. The way she walked, the way she dressed. Even what she looked like.'

I remembered what Agnes had told me. 'I heard she looked a lot like Rebecca.'

'Whoever told you that must have needed their eyes testing. Mrs Fisher couldn't have looked like Rebecca in her wildest dreams.' Melanie's expression was frankly incredulous. 'Oh, she had lovely hair, she was always perfectly made-up, and as for her clothes – I don't think I ever saw her wearing an outfit that *Vogue* wouldn't have put on the cover. But her actual *looks* . . . there's no nice way to say this, but she looked like a man. Not a handsome one, either. Small eyes, big nose, heavy jaw. You certainly couldn't have called her attractive.' She broke off for a second, looking deep in thought. 'It was strange how all the things she could change about herself were so beautiful, and all the things she couldn't were anything but. I suppose these days she'd have plastic surgery – she certainly had the money, and anyone who spent that much time on their hair and make-up must have had the inclination – but back then it was totally unheard-of. Whoever told you she looked like Rebecca?'

'I interviewed someone else before I came here – one of Eleanor's sisters, Agnes. She was the one who said that.'

'That explains it. God, those Corbett sisters! I don't have anything to do with them these days, but one of them was in my class at St Anthony's. Bernadette, it was, but it might as well have been any of the others. They were all practically identical, apart from Eleanor.' Melanie sighed deeply. 'I suppose they were harmless; they certainly weren't troublemakers, or anything like that. But they were so *stupid*, it was depressing. They didn't seem to have a single original thought or sense of humour between the lot of them. I can quite believe *they'd* have thought Rebecca and Mrs Fisher looked alike. Both quite slim. Both well-dressed. And of course, they both had shiny blonde hair.'

Melanie's expression was one of comic but genuine exasperation. I found I could relate to it only too well. 'Did the others in your class think the same?' I asked. 'About the Corbett girls, I mean?'

'Oh, I think a few did. There were plenty of others who didn't seem to notice or care how *blank* they were – they'd grown up as near neighbours, and knew each other's families, so, the way they thought, the Corbett sisters had to be all right. But, to me, there was something infuriating about that family, just like nails down a blackboard. There was something – it sounds so nasty, but – *cow-like* about all of them. Except Eleanor, anyway. As I said, she wasn't quite like the others.'

'How was she different?'

'Oh, she just seemed to have a bit more life. Not necessarily in a good way, but I thought anything was better than those sisters of hers. She was two years below me, so I didn't know her at all well, but I can still remember her clearly. Before she fell in with Rebecca, she used to tag round after a group of kids in my class sometimes. I heard something about them stealing sweets together, but I don't know the details.' She smiled ruefully. 'I know it's wrong to speak ill of the dead, but that girl had the persistence of a door-to-door salesman. I heard the kids in my year telling her to go away in the playground sometimes, only, you know, a bit less politely. But she always came straight back. Finally, I think they just resigned themselves to putting up with her. Short of running away every time they saw her, there wasn't much else they could do.'

'It sounds like she was pretty annoying,' I said cautiously.

'I thought so. Oh, she was a sweet-looking little thing, even though she was always as shabby as Bernadette and the rest – but, in a funny sort of way, that made her even more annoying. Like a squeaky little cartoon hamster you just couldn't get rid of. I don't know, maybe she was lonely, wanted friends outside that awful family of hers. She certainly couldn't have found anyone much further removed from them than Rebecca Fisher.'

A long, mutually reflective silence extended for some seconds before the sound of the front door opening cut through it. Loud masculine voices filled the room unexpectedly, coming rapidly closer. 'You ought to come out with the kids more often, Dad,' said one, and another said, shyly and rather evasively, 'Well, that's as maybe.' Then the speakers were entering the kitchen: a red-faced man in his mid- to late-sixties, a fortysomething man who had to be Melanie's husband, a couple of little boys.

'Hello, kids,' said Melanie. 'Good game, was it?'

'Not bad.' It was the father who answered – both children were looking at me with a dubious and somehow dehumanising expression, as if I was a squirrel they'd found perched on the kitchen table. 'Wolves won, but it was a good day out.'

A brief silence, in which I saw that squirrel-look on the old man's face, too. I was about to introduce myself, when Melanie did. 'This is Anna Jeffreys, the writer I mentioned.'

'Oh, yeah. You're writing a book about Rebecca Fisher, aren't you?' Again, it was the father who spoke. I nodded, murmuring assent. 'Sounds interesting. Make a good book, that case would.'

'Thanks. I hope it will.' I had an idea that he thought I was writing a true-crime book, but had no impulse to set the record straight. Suddenly I felt very out of place here, as if I was intruding on a private family Saturday. 'I'd better be off, anyway,' I said quickly, 'I'll miss my train. Thanks very much – you've been a lot of help.'

'No trouble. Really.'

I rose from my seat, wondering how much else I'd have found out if our interview hadn't been terminated like this. I realised how unprofessional it would look to ring back tomorrow or the day after: *Excuse me, sorry to bother you again, but I just remembered I forgot to ask.* And I had no specific questions left to ask her, just the all-important details that you stumbled across while talking.

'Just one more thing,' I said. 'Would you mind telling your friends about my research? If any of them know anything about Rebecca or her parents, I'd really appreciate it if you'd give them my number.'

'Certainly,' said Melanie. 'I don't think I've got it.'

I smiled polite, relieved, embarrassed goodbyes at the strangers in the kitchen as I walked with Melanie into the hallway, where I wrote my number down on her telephone pad. 'It's really kind of you,' I said. 'I'd be glad of any information I could get.'

Out of the house, I checked my watch and saw with a shock that my convenient excuse had been very close to the truth – I was in genuine danger of missing my train, which left in half an hour. But even the real threat of being marooned here overnight couldn't make me go back to that family and interrupt their conversation with a request to call a taxi; the prospect dragged far too much of the past behind it. Hurrying back towards the town centre, sheer luck took me past a taxi rank, and I jumped in a cab, hoping like hell I didn't reach Teasford station just in time to see my train pulling out.

21

In the event, I caught the train with bare moments to spare and heard the guard's whistle shrilling as the doors swung shut behind me. I sat by a window, looking out at the changing scenery as it flew past. Bare fields. Industrial parks. Cars on distant motorways. Anonymity. The day's events replayed in my mind as if on fast-forward. There was so much more to discover, I realised; all I'd really found that day were more questions that needed to be answered. And I thought about the enigmatic Mrs Fisher, and her too-ordinary husband, and pitiful little Eleanor Corbett – that sweet, haunting, gap-toothed photograph in Agnes' album, the loveless emptiness of the world she'd inhabited.

Don't worry about them, I told myself, *all that matters is Rebecca*. But suddenly that felt wrong. It *was* all about Rebecca, every last detail. Nothing was irrelevant; the key to her true self could lie in any of it. Her best friend. Her classmates. Above all, her family . . .

My thoughts veered abruptly to Melanie's kitchen, the way I'd felt as the front door opened and the voices came pouring in. How I'd had to get out as quickly as possible, seeing them together and knowing I didn't belong here any more, embarrassingly aware that I was interrupting a family's pleasant Saturday afternoon of togetherness, laughter and in-jokes; knowing that my presence made everything self-conscious and subtly strained. It was far from the first time I'd had that feeling, and I knew perfectly well where it came from. It was irrational but only too explicable if you knew what to look for; a kind of nightmare flashback that took me straight back to my childhood home. Talking with my mother in the kitchen there, tasting the illusion of cheerful normality before the front door opened, and everything changed in an instant.

'It's such a relief things have all worked out so well for Kay,' I'd overheard my maternal grandmother telling a friend once. I'd been nine and at her house for the day; she'd thought I was out in the garden. 'We were so worried about her after she had Anna, even thought perhaps we should have let her have the abortion, like she wanted to at the time. Still, it just goes to show, you shouldn't jump to conclusions. Look how happy they all are, since she married that nice Bill . . .'

My mother's child by a previous relationship – on the surface, that description was as good as any. I had a stepfather, two half-sisters and one half-brother, nothing that would raise eyebrows in the street or jeers in the playground, nothing that plenty of other kids didn't have themselves. But when I observed or read about apparently similar family set-ups, they seemed to come from another world, a casual democracy of birth and circumstance, where all the children were equally loved and wanted by their parents. It couldn't have been further removed from my own life, growing up; my mother could try as hard as she liked to treat all her children the same, but she just wasn't that good an actress, and, when we were together as a family, it was painfully obvious to all of us where her real priorities lay. Sometimes I could feel the weight of her guilt, and it made me feel guilty myself. How hard she tried to bring me out of myself when we were alone together. How, when it was just the two of us, I could feel life changing tantalisingly into the way life ought to be.

'You shouldn't spend so much time up in your room,

all on your own, love. It's not right. I worry about you, sometimes. You don't have to be left out of things here. You know, your stepfather loves you very much, and—'

The front door opening. The sincerity in her eyes flickering, awkward, divided. My stepfather coming in with Tim and Emily and Louise, all laughing together. The tiny and unmissable change in atmosphere as they came into the kitchen and saw me at the table. Too polite to be dismay, too kindly to be rejection. Something elusive, virtually indefinable.

I was the difficulty in an easy life. The complication in a straightforward one. The only thing in a big, suburban, conventional family home that wasn't supposed to be there.

In the red corner, an unwanted and entirely uncharacteristic teenage pregnancy that only parental pressure had made Kay Jeffreys carry to term, then keep. Not even the offspring of a boyfriend, just an older boy whose attentions she'd been too flattered to turn down, who'd led her further than she'd ever been before one night, and hadn't wanted to know her next morning. The result of that one date, if you could call it a date, was a child nothing like her in looks, personality or anything else – a child who'd come close to destroying the placid, prosperous future she'd been heading towards from the day she was born. Stigmatised single-motherhood in the house she'd grown up in, neighbours gossiping, parents interfering in everything from feed times to brands of nappy. Undoubtedly the darkest years she'd ever lived through, years she'd look back on and shudder . . .

And, in the white corner, three planned and wanted children, products of the wonderful, unexpected marriage her parents had thought she'd never make with an illegitimate two-year-old in tow. Fathered by the man she

176

loved, nice, affectionate, conscientious Bill Arnold, who'd even been willing to take on another man's child for her sake, to try his best to be a good stepfather. Children whose looks and temperaments resembled one another's, his and hers in equal measure, whose early years she'd look back on with a comfortable, nostalgic smile. Children from the life she should have led uninterrupted, if only a moment's impressionable madness with the school heart-throb hadn't sent it veering in a different direction. If only she hadn't conceived me.

Three children who should have been there, versus one who certainly shouldn't. No matter how hard we all tried to pretend, there wasn't much equality about that. Far from being *my mother's child by a previous relationship*, I'd grown up feeling more like a child who'd been adopted, where one adoptive parent hadn't particularly wanted you in the first place, and the other had rapidly tired of the idea when it was too late to go back. Growing up in a stranger's home, trying to stay out of the way as much as possible, knowing that your very presence made things awkward . . .

Sitting and gazing out of the window, I thought about Rebecca, and how she'd been adopted herself. Found myself restlessly wondering how it had been for her; whether she'd felt that bone-deep isolation, whether the velvet hair-bows and gold jewellery had camouflaged an alienation akin to my own. As the train trundled into Dorset, I looked out at lush, undulating greenery bathed in early evening sunlight, beyond the faint ghost of my reflection in the glass. And, for a second, I saw Rebecca's face there in place of mine, that notorious photograph from front pages and true-crime books – the large, pale eyes, the delicate cameo features, and the enigmatic little half-smile that could have meant anything.

22

On Sunday, Carl and I drove to Poole Tower Park and watched an action thriller he'd proposed and I hadn't objected to. We held hands, shared popcorn, laughed and chatted as casually as we'd done in Reading. When the film was over, we went for dinner in a nearby restaurant. On the surface, everything between us was back to normal, and neither of us mentioned Rebecca's name all day.

Still, all the time, part of me was distracted by her. I could feel her mystery gnawing away in a distant corner of my mind, and struggled to ignore it. In a way, it was a relief when Monday morning came and Carl left for work, and I was free to acknowledge the extent of my growing fascination. It had become so heightened as to feel utterly personal, impossible to share. Especially now it was tied in with certain other things – Mr Wheeler, Socks' death – and lived so closely alongside my fears that it seemed to have caught their sickness.

It was easy to track down the number for East Lancashire Social Services, less so to be put through to their Children and Families division. After endless strangers had played pass-the-parcel with my call, an irritable-sounding woman came on the line. I asked her if they'd still have their area's adoption records from the 1960s, presented my credentials as a published author, and explained my interest in Rebecca Fisher. She sounded more than a little dubious, but didn't imply that my request was out of the question.

'If you'd like to call back in a few hours' time,' she said,

'I'll try and find out if we can help you.' I thanked her and hung up, then realised with some dismay that I hadn't asked for her name.

I went out into the back garden to take the washing in and saw Liz across the fence, wispy-haired and gardening-gloved, pruning the roses that ran up a trellis by her back wall. Looking round, she smiled, raising a hand in greeting. 'Hello, Anna. Isn't it a lovely morning? It's shaping up to be a beautiful summer – I'm sure the weather wasn't anywhere near this good last year.'

As always since Socks had died, I couldn't help wondering how much of her practical good humour was a show, whether, deep inside, she was as devastated as she'd been when we'd buried him. I had a momentary longing to reassure her that she didn't have to act, that seeing her true feelings wouldn't make me respect or like her any less. But social embarrassment stopped me, underscored by a humiliating sense of presumption. She certainly didn't need me as a confidante; she had family, friends, any number of people who were closer to her than I was. It was better to keep things on the surface, out in the sunlight, the peace.

'It's wonderful, isn't it?' I said. 'Think I'll come and sit out in the garden after I've brought the washing in.'

I did, about ten minutes later, having lugged a folded-down sun lounger out of the shed. I set it up nearby, alert for lurking spiders. Liz's voice drifted over the fence again.

'I haven't seen you for a while, dear – what have you been doing with yourself?'

'Oh, just this and that, really. You know.' Beyond the research I didn't want her to know about, there seemed to be nothing whatsoever to say. I racked my brain for something to give my life detail and colour in her mind, to stop it looking empty and dull. 'A friend of mine's coming to stay this weekend – my best friend, really. We were at university together in Reading, and we both got jobs there after graduating.'

'That is nice. I expect you're looking forward to seeing her again.' Liz spoke comfortably – she'd set her pruning shears aside and moved towards the fence to chat. 'Doing anything in particular, are you?'

'Nothing special. Just hanging out, really.' I was, I realised, looking forward to Petra's visit intensely – it coloured everything in my voice and manner, an honest enthusiasm I hadn't felt for anything but research in some time. 'I thought I'd show her round the village, but there's no set agenda. We'll just see how we feel at the time.'

'When's she coming down?'

'Early on Saturday morning. She'll be going home on Sunday evening.'

'That *is* a stroke of luck – I was going to invite you and your husband, but I'm more than happy for your friend to come as well. We're having a bring-and-bake sale at St Joseph's in Wareham on Saturday evening – it's a WI event, Helen and Muriel are going to be there. I'm sure you'd all enjoy yourselves.'

Damn it. I found myself wishing I'd invented a packed itinerary for the weekend, with every split-second accounted for.

'I know it's in a church hall, but it won't be at all *religious*,' Liz went on, 'not in a stuffy way, anyway. There's always wine and nibbles at our events, and the people are all very nice. Of course, I wouldn't expect you to stay long – it stands to reason you'll want to catch up in private, when you haven't seen each other for a while. But you're more than welcome to pop by.'

At first, cold duty had told me we'd have to put in a showing, but, as she spoke again, something altogether warmer and less grudging brought me to the same conclusion – she hadn't extended her invitation out of a conscious desire to ruin our weekend, she'd just thought we might like to go. 'That would be lovely,' I said, smiling. 'We'll look forward to it. What time does it start?'

'Half past five. You know where St Joseph's is, don't you, dear? It's just up the road from the library.' I nodded. 'I'll look forward to seeing you there,' she went on briskly. 'Better get back to my roses, anyway. I'll leave you to sunbathe in peace.'

Lying back full-length on the lounger, the curt *snip-snip* of her pruning shears across the fence sounded oddly clear and loud. The sky was a luminous field of pure blue, and shadows lay sharp, black and perfect on the grass. It was hard to believe that anything truly disturbing existed in the world on a day like this, with Liz's reassuringly solid and mundane presence in the next garden. As I closed my eyes, brightness seemed to filter through my eyelids as through paper. I reminded myself to call the council back at around three, setting an alarm clock in my mind.

My second attempt at reaching the Children and Families division was, if anything, even more torturous than my first had been. Bizarrely, I found myself put through to Housing, then Finance, then back to the central reception desk. At last I was greeted by a man who sounded as cheery as an enthusiastic youth worker. 'Children and Families. You're through to Nick Jones.'

I thought I'd have to go through the whole story again, but, as soon as I mentioned my name, he cut in. 'Say no more. A colleague told me about you earlier. You were interested in the Rebecca Fisher file, right?'

'That's right,' I said. 'Of course, if it's confidential . . .'

'It's not. It would be, if what happened, hadn't happened

181

– but as it is, it's firmly in the public domain. A lawyer could probably do a better job of explaining, but I don't suppose you're that interested in the clauses and caveats.' He laughed an easy, professional laugh. 'To be honest, I'm surprised we haven't had more enquiries about her over the years. I've been working here since the mid-Seventies. To the best of my knowledge, you're the first writer who's ever rung up to ask about her.'

'Do you have her records there?' I asked.

'We do indeed. I tracked her file down at lunchtime – there's not much in it, but you might find it useful. There's a copy of the adoption form the Fishers had to fill in, a copy of Rebecca's adoption certificate – oh, and a child psychologist's report on Rebecca. It's dated 1964, the year she went into care.' Out of nowhere, I was cotton-mouthed with longing, and it was an effort to concentrate on his next words. 'Looks like quite a lot of documentation's gone AWOL over the years – there's a lot more that should be there, but I suppose there's no use crying over spilt milk. If you like, I could send you copies through the post, or, if you've got a fax machine . . .'

Thank God, we did – the elderly and erratic model Carl had bought years ago, which was now installed in the spare room. I'd never imagined I'd be so grateful for it, that I'd be so hungry for instant information. 'Faxing it should be fine,' I said, and told him the number. 'You've been *fantastically* helpful. Thank you *very* much.'

'Hope it helps with your book,' he said. 'I'll send the pages through now.'

He was as good as his word. When I hurried up to the spare room, a squeaking, whining, grumbling sound told me a fax was coming through. I stood and waited for the pages to emerge – five in total – before taking them over to the desk, lighting a cigarette and starting to read.

Deliberately, I saved the densely typewritten sheet till last, and looked at the forms. The adoption certificate told me Rebecca Fisher had been born Rebecca Jane Sanderson, parents Richard and Marigold Sanderson, deceased. Adoptive parents Rita and Dennis Fisher, date of adoption 18 January 1965. The attached adoption form continued in much the same vein, a three-page list of facts and dates, names and addresses. It had obviously been filled out by one of the Fishers, in small, erratic handwriting that would have been hard to read in the original. As it was, I looked at the poor-quality fax of a poor-quality photocopy, and several words and sentences were indecipherable. Still, the printed questions told me I wasn't missing much. *Name of GP. Name(s) of child(ren) (if any). Criminal convictions (if any. Please give details.)* That box was blank, but clearly announced that this was a form to be completed at the very beginning of the adoption process, something you got sent in response to an initial enquiry. More sophisticated screening procedures would unquestionably kick in later. It maddened me to think of those later, detailed, personal documents lost for ever; to think that, once, they'd been as tangibly real as the papers I had in front of me now.

The Fishers, I thought, had filled this in as soon as they'd seriously considered adopting a child. Something in the idea made me turn back to the front page, check the date of its completion. At first I was convinced that the handwriting and the print quality blurred the numbers, but on closer inspection I saw that there was nothing else they could have been. The document was dated 4 October 1962.

If that's right, I thought, *they waited over two years before actually adopting. Why was that?* I reached for the final page I'd been sent, grinding out my cigarette absent-mindedly, lighting another at once.

PSYCHOLOGIST'S REPORT
Date: 30 April 1964
Name of patient: Rebecca Jane Sanderson
Name of social worker: Bob Mills
Psychologist attending: Edward Leighton

Rebecca shows evidence of deep
psychological disturbance, manifesting
itself most obviously in an unwillingness
to speak, and a complete withdrawal from
emotional contact. Unquestionably, this is
the result of both parents' premature death
in a car accident this January; having
contacted staff at Rebecca's previous
playgroup, I found that her behaviour prior
to this has been 'normal' in every respect.
From extensive liaison with Rebecca's
social worker, I note that she is an only
child, and that her parents, while
exceptionally close, lacked the wider
support network which would have enabled
Rebecca to remain in a familiar environment
following their death (e.g. the home of an
aunt or uncle).

It would be easy to interpret Rebecca's
current withdrawal as an entirely
understandable reaction to the bereavement
process, and to make the assumption that,
given time, her behaviour will normalise.
However, I believe that this would be a
severe and potentially dangerous mistake.
From my observations, there are a number of
factors that imply severe psychological
damage, and that, if left untreated, may
well escalate in later life.

In addition to Rebecca's total lack of

integration with the other children in her care home, she continues to reject the assistance of adult staff, whom she appears to be both afraid of and antagonistic towards. Her rejection, while passive, is nonetheless clearly apparent (e.g. turning her back on care assistants in the home, refusal to eat unless left alone to do so) and implies a suppressed anger that I find profoundly disturbing. While appearing to shun any form of human contact, she has developed a morbid attachment to a stuffed toy, which (I am told) originally came from the home's communal play area. Rebecca entirely refuses to relinquish or even to share this toy, and carries it with her everywhere she goes, insisting on retaining it even during my sessions with her. Tellingly, her only display of violent/actively antisocial behaviour has occurred in an incident relating to this toy, in which (a care assistant informs me) she struck another child who was attempting to take it forcibly from her.

Rebecca also has frequent episodes of bedwetting, but this is relatively normal at her age and, to the best of her social worker's knowledge, could have been going on while her parents were alive.

In summary, I would strongly advise that this child continues to receive regular and comprehensive psychological treatment. It is easy to dismiss the behavioural abnormalities of a recently bereaved five-year-old. However, I believe that Rebecca's problems may result in serious

<u>mental illness</u>, and, as such, must be
treated with the <u>utmost care</u>.

DR EDWARD LEIGHTON 1964

23

When I'd finished the report, I read back through it immediately – bewildered, jarred. While I hadn't consciously been aware of it, I'd assumed from the outset that her adoption had been the result of worried neighbours and social workers intervening – the dark corners of childhood most people only encountered through newspaper articles and NSPCC campaigns, parental violence, neglect, abuse, chaos. It had never occurred to me that she'd been orphaned through a tragic accident, that she'd been happy before that day; a squeal of brakes and crumple of metal marking the brutal transition from family home to care home, from parents to strangers. I imagined the anonymity of the place she'd been sent to with a kind of mental shudder, something in the thought reminding me of . . .

The little room on the third floor of St Edward's hall of residence, Reading. How empty it had looked when I'd first stepped in: whitewashed walls, institutional fittings. The view from the window showing me nothing but other windows across a concrete courtyard, vague shadows hinting at identical rooms beyond them. The drifting, cold horror of standing alone in that place, realising I was five hours' drive away from the only life I'd ever known, that this was home now.

Of course, it wouldn't have been the same for Rebecca when she'd arrived at the care home – I'd been eighteen, she'd been five. I wondered whether the ignorance of childhood would make that feeling of isolation better or worse. On the one hand, you didn't know so much, so you couldn't foresee the horror of it gradually intensifying; on the other, the world looked indescribably huge and alien at that age, and the sudden loss of everything you knew would inspire a bewilderment so intense that most adults couldn't imagine it. A mother's idiosyncratic kindness giving way to the one-size-fits-all care of paid professionals, seeing even that shared out among other children when you were used to being the only one. I could imagine only too well how dark things could take root in that confusion – an obsessive desire for something you could call your own, to belong somewhere, anywhere.

Standing in the spare room, I looked down at the report again, noticing the archaic look of the typescript – a message sent straight from a time when typewriters had been cutting-edge technology, when *electric* typewriters had been the futuristic preserve of the super-rich. I wondered what had happened in the aftermath of its writing, whether further steps *had* been taken to ease out the roots of lifelong trauma. I couldn't see how anyone could ignore a report like this one, with its stark, uncompromising warnings and underlined imperatives. At the same time, though, it was blindingly obvious that Rebecca's psychology *hadn't* been bandaged and fussed over and cured; that it had gone limping out into the world very shortly afterwards, obsessed with concealing the injury rather than healing it.

Perhaps I was reading too much into the report, I told myself. I was doing exactly what I shouldn't do, filling in vast blank spaces with nothing but my own ideas. Still, one fact leapt out quite clearly on its own. Rebecca had been adopted at the age of five, and I was well aware *that* wasn't normal. Babies had always been at a premium with childless couples, older children at the bottom of the heap.

Above the name of the psychologist who'd told me all he possibly could, I saw, with new interest, that of Rebecca's social worker – he'd have all the answers, would know exactly what had happened next.

This time, it was easier to reach the department I wanted – I was relieved not to recognise the female voice that answered. 'Excuse me,' I said, 'I wonder if you can help me. I'm trying to track down a social worker who used to be based in your department. I've got a few questions to ask about a case he was involved in some time ago.'

'Can I ask who's calling?'

'My name's Anna Howell. I'm calling from Reading Borough Council.'

The lie leapt out on its own – incredibly, she seemed happy with it. I could feel her experience filling in spaces with a new multi-agency approach, a partnership initiative she should have heard of, but hadn't. 'We might be able to help. What was the social worker's name?'

'Bob Mills.'

'You mean Robert Mills?'

I spoke cautiously. 'If he was part of your team in the 1960s, then yes.'

'Well, you don't exactly need us to track him down these days. He's Head of Services at the Children's Protection Society.' She laughed. 'Don't you read your CommCare?'

I recognised the title from my Reading Council days; Social Services' answer to the *FT*. Even back then, I'd avoided it whenever possible. 'Not as often as I should, I'm afraid.'

'He got the job in March. I have to warn you, you'll probably have a hard time getting an interview.'

'I can imagine,' I said. 'Thanks anyway. I'll try and reach him there.'

Off the phone, I felt urgency collapse and wither around discouragement. Of all the things Rebecca's old social worker could be doing these days, he had to be the CEO of one of Britain's leading children's charities. The public sector was slightly more democratic than big business, but *only* slightly; in a charity as in an investment bank, top-level managers were protected by an impenetrable brick wall of subordinates, smooth secretarial voices with a distinct undertow of *sod off*. One would say to me, *if you'd like to put your request in writing, Mr Mills will do his best to answer it when he has the time . . .*

I'd try phoning tomorrow, I told myself. I couldn't face that kind of disappointment now, when finding out what had happened felt so important. Maybe, when the psychologist's report had cooled a little in my mind, I'd be able to handle inevitable evasions with the right tone of professionalism.

For now, my day's work was over, and the sunshine past the windows made the room feel oddly divorced from the outside world, heavy with an atmosphere I couldn't put a name to.

'I saw Liz next door earlier on. She's invited us to a bring-and-bake sale on Saturday evening,' I said to Carl that night over dinner. 'I hope you don't mind, but I said we'd go.'

'Some welcome for Petra.' At first he spoke sceptically, then, seeing my guilty expression, laughed. 'I'm only joking, Annie – no problem, that's fine. Anyway, we won't have to stay long, will we?'

'Next to no time – I just said we'd drop by. I don't think it's going to be very exciting. Liz said her friends

Helen and Muriel are going to be there. You haven't met them yet, have you?'

'No. Have I got a treat in store?'

'Well, Muriel seems nice enough. But Helen ... there's something cold about her. I didn't take to her at all, to be honest.' Even now, the thought of her was slightly oppressive – I thought back to our meeting in Wareham Library, her unsettling and perpetual air of silence. Suddenly, I wanted to get the conversation as far away from her as possible, to banish her image from my mind. 'Come to that, I can't really bond with *Liz*,' I went on quickly. 'She's really nice and everything, I know it's great to have such a good neighbour, but I always feel a bit on edge with her, as if I might be doing something wrong. She's such a pillar of the community, like someone from a different species.'

'Give her a chance,' he said reasonably. 'You said you used to feel much the same way about Petra.'

'I *didn't*.' The words came out as a knee-jerk reaction, before a memory returned; three or four years ago in Reading, reminiscing about old times, darker memories of my own slowly drifting into the conversation. 'I suppose I did,' I said unwillingly. 'But that was different. I don't know how, exactly, it just was. There's so much more to Petra than I thought, when we first met. It's not like that with Liz – what you see is what you get. I don't think I'll ever be able to talk to her properly, not about anything that matters.'

'Well, you can never tell. She might have hidden depths of her own when you get to know her better.' He smiled, happy to let the issue go. 'Anyway, it'll be good to see Petra again. Started getting the spare room ready yet?'

'Not yet, we've got ages. I'll sort it out on Friday. It's

never going to look like anything special, but I'll get some flowers and that sort of thing. I don't suppose it really matters, she's only going to be there for one night.'

'It's going to be a pretty short weekend,' he agreed. 'I thought I'd go into Bournemouth when you pick her up on Saturday morning. I need to take the car in for a service anyway, and I know you two will want to catch up in peace for a while.'

I was glad of that – I knew he was thinking in terms of easy gossip and what various people were up to back in Reading, but I had infinitely more important issues to share with her: Mr Wheeler and Socks, things that couldn't possibly be discussed at length while Carl was in the bathroom here or at the bar in a pub. 'Well,' I said flippantly, 'if you insist. Try not to be too long.'

A pause fell as we ate, and I became aware of him looking at me occasionally, almost furtively, split-second-long glances that seemed to check for something hidden. I could see that he didn't really want to speak and that, finally, he had to.

'So, how's the research going? You've been all quiet about it for the past couple of days.'

'There's nothing much to tell,' I said ruefully. 'I'm finding things out. Looking more things up on the internet. I have to admit, it's not quite as exciting as I thought it was going to be, at first.'

My mind reeled before the sheer enormity of the lie, but was instantly soothed by his expression, as if he'd checked back on a fear to make sure it had definitely gone away, and saw quite clearly that it had done. Soon, I thought, he'd be confident enough of its absence to stop checking and, not long after that, my research was bound to come to a natural end.

'Well,' he said, 'I'm glad it's not getting you down too badly. A while back, I was worried you were getting a bit obsessed with it all.'

24

I got the number of the Children's Protection Society headquarters from directory enquiries the following morning. Two rings, and I was through to a main reception desk.

'Excuse me. May I speak to Robert Mills, please?'

'I'll put you through to his office.'

The no-questions-asked tone told me I was about to meet the brick wall. Sure enough, after a minute or so of tinny music, another female voice answered, less friendly, more clipped, ostentatiously busy. 'You're through to Robert Mills' office. How can I help you?'

There was, I realised, nothing for it but honesty. Only the truth could possibly get me through the door here, transferred into the inner sanctum. 'My name's Anna Jeffreys. I'm a writer researching a novel based on the Rebecca Fisher murder case of 1969. I've heard Mr Mills was her social worker at the time she was adopted, and I wondered if he might be able to spare a few minutes to talk to me.'

A pause before she spoke again, her tone slightly dubious. 'If you'd like to hold for a moment.'

Tinkly music again, this time a near-unrecognisable rendition of 'Up Where We Belong'. I was very tempted to just hang up – I didn't have a hope in hell of getting through to the man – but then a new, male voice spoke. 'Robert Mills.'

'Oh, hello,' I said, amazed. 'I wonder if you could help

me. I'm not sure if your secretary told you who I am, but—'

'Don't worry, she did. You've caught me at a good moment, as it happens – I'm free to talk. I must warn you, though, I'm due in a meeting ten minutes from now.'

His voice was quiet, matter-of-fact and rather uninflected, with a slight Northern edge. It was a middle-management public sector voice all the way, making me think of creased Next suits, battered family Volvos, and jugs of bad coffee in boardrooms like staffrooms. I supposed he was the sort of senior manager who prided himself on being approachable. The way he was talking to me now said as much.

For a second or two, I was too surprised to think of a question, then one leapt into my brain on its own. 'How long did you work with Rebecca Fisher?'

'Just under a year. From the time she first got taken into care, up until the time she was adopted. I paid occasional visits to her and her new family, of course, but it was all very much less formal.' His manner was paternal, amiable, rather rambling. 'Thirty years ago – my goodness, that does take me back. I would have been twenty-five years old at the time. It was the first proper case I ever handled.'

'What did you think of her adoptive parents? Rita and Dennis Fisher?'

'They were a very nice couple. It goes without saying that I saw a great deal of them before they adopted Rebecca; I visited them at their home a number of times. They were extremely happy together, very respectable, very settled. Ideal adoptive parents in every way.' I remembered my visit to Teasford, what Melanie had told me about Rita Fisher. 'Also, they were specifically looking to adopt a child of Rebecca's age. That was *very* unusual, and still is today. At the time, Rebecca was five years old, and ninety-nine per cent of people want babies.'

'What made them want an older child?'

'Because they knew that other families wouldn't. They were very kind people – they wanted a child they could make a real difference to. They were on the adoptive parents' register for some time before they found the perfect child for them. They definitely wanted a little girl. The mother was quite adamant about that.'

'Any particular reason?'

'Oh, she simply wanted a daughter. There was nothing *mysterious* about it.'

There was something too-cosy about his voice, somehow false – I had an inexplicable conviction that he was hiding things, and asked something I already knew the answer to, just to see what he'd say. 'Why did Rebecca go into care? What happened to her parents?'

'They both died in a car accident. Rebecca was at her playgroup when it happened. She was their only child – it was extremely sad.'

'How did she react to their bereavement at the time?'

'Oh, as well as could be expected. It's a terrible blow for any child, of course. When she was adopted by the Fishers, that was all sorted out – she was as right as rain, after that.'

'Until she killed Eleanor Corbett.'

I hadn't intended any malice, but the short silence down the line was like a verbal flinch. When he spoke again, there was an almost fearful note that didn't belong in those avuncular tones at all. 'Well, that really couldn't have been foretold, Anna. Who knows *what* started happening in Rebecca's mind?'

'So she had no history of disturbed behaviour before that? She never received any kind of psychiatric treatment between the ages of five and ten?'

'Very briefly. It wasn't considered necessary to continue it after her adoption.'

'It was never advised that she should?'

His voice was sorrowful, soothing. 'Never, I'm afraid.'

If I hadn't known it was a direct lie, I'd never have recognised it as such in a million years – suddenly, his easy manner reminded me of a politician who was far too slick to seem it. I desperately wanted to mention the psychologist's report I'd read, but sheer social embarrassment stopped me.

'Looking back without hindsight, the Fishers were the best adoptive parents she could have gone to,' he went on. 'Eleanor's murder was a terrible tragedy, but it couldn't possibly have been prevented. Nobody could have seen it coming.'

I felt a surge of hatred for his cosy banalities, his papering-over of the truth, and struggled to keep my voice polite and neutral. 'Well, thank you very much for your time, Mr Mills.'

'I hope it'll come in useful for your book,' he said. 'Goodbye, Anna.'

Off the phone, frustration gnawed and raged inside me. Talking to him had told me nothing whatsoever while intensifying my conviction that, somewhere down the line, something had gone very wrong indeed. I pieced together what I knew as hard facts and what I was one hundred per cent convinced of: following Rebecca's bereavement, she'd shown clear signs of disturbance, a psychologist had found them glaringly obvious and his report had been ignored. Whether it had been deliberately overlooked or just lost in a forest of official documents and red tape, I didn't know, and didn't care. What mattered was what had happened next. How the Fishers had reacted to the withdrawn and troubled little girl they'd adopted; whether, in forced initial getting-to-know-you sessions, they'd had any idea what they were about to take on.

They must have done, I told myself – from what I'd read in the psychologist's report, Rebecca's symptoms had been as impossible to ignore as a wooden leg – it wouldn't have taken an expert to notice. At the same time, however, I was ninety per cent convinced that Rita and Dennis Fisher *hadn't*. Robert Mills' description of them was like two hastily sketched stick figures, while Melanie Cook's had been pure Lucien Freud. I couldn't imagine the snobbish, artificial woman Melanie had described knowingly giving house-room to anything damaged, whether the object in question was a vase or a child. And I found it equally difficult to imagine her approaching the adoption process with a philanthropist's selflessness; deliberately selecting the child nobody else wanted, delighted by the chance to *make a difference...*

Questions everywhere I looked, and not an answer in sight. Try as I might, I could think of no further paths into discovery, and was appalled to face a dead end. I found myself hopefully anticipating *A Mind to Murder*, the book I'd bought online which should arrive any day now. Even if it wasn't particularly revealing in its own right, I reassured myself, there was every chance that it would throw up names and places and leads for me to follow. The roadblock ahead of me was essentially temporary. Soon, I'd be able to start again.

On Friday morning I went up to the spare room and set about preparing it for Petra's arrival. The air had a stale, unused smell that I quickly opened the window to get rid of. Even now, in the height of summer, it seemed inexplicably colder than it should have been. With some determination, I struggled to make it look cheerful and welcoming; hoovering, cleaning up hidden corners I'd never touched before, which had grown a thin grey fur of dust since we'd moved in. Making the bed with fresh pastel-coloured linen, I put a bowl of pot-pourri on the bedside table beside a portable radio we didn't use any more, and a copy of *Captain Corelli's Mandolin*. Perhaps there was more of my mother in me than I cared to recognise; it was exactly the way she'd have prepared for a weekend guest herself.

By the time I'd finished, there was a definite improvement in the general look of the place. Only the side of the room by the window looked badly out of place, a sparsely-equipped office in a country bedroom. There was nothing I could do about the computer and printer and fax machine, Petra would just have to live with them; but the bulging folder on the desk's bottom shelf disrupted the look of everything, and demanded to be taken away. I thought about putting it downstairs somewhere, but nowhere seemed quite private enough. While Carl never came in here, there was no drawer in the kitchen or living room he wasn't likely to open, and seeing Rebecca's old school photograph would make him wary all over again. *Where did you get this?* he'd ask doubtfully. *How come you never told me?* And, most damningly of all, *what did you want it for, anyway? I thought you were interested in facts, not her . . .*

While I'd always been vaguely aware of the built-in cupboard on one side of the spare bed, I'd never really noticed it as I did now. Thank God, I thought, there was somewhere safe to put the folder, after all. The door stuck badly, and finally gave with a groaning squeak. I was picking up the folder from the carpet when I put it down again, frowning, reaching in. There was something on the top shelf already.

I saw that it was nothing newsworthy, just a pad of Basildon Bond writing-paper, thick enough to seem virtually unused. I was lifting it out of the cupboard when a neatly folded sheet fell out and see-sawed lazily to the floor. Picking it up and unfolding it, I saw it was the beginning of a letter – a few scrawled lines of wildly erratic handwriting stared up at me. I read through them, cold inside with amazement, and intrigue, and a kind of fear.

4, Ploughman's Lane
Abbots Newton
Dorset DT5 6RJ
27 February 2002

Dear Penny,

   Don't expect you thought I'd write again after what happened, but I thought I'd have to let you know what's going on. Strange things have started happening here, I don't know how else I can say it. Someone's threatening me. I have no idea who they are or what they want from me, but I've been receiving these anonymous letters and today

Nothing more. Just silence, as if I'd heard Rebecca Fisher talking quickly and the sound had abruptly gone dead. I stared at it unblinking for endless minutes, as though looking at an object randomly preserved in time, a fossil, a fragment of pottery unearthed at an archaeological dig. It told me nothing I hadn't known already, but its significance felt overwhelming. To think that it had been here all along, hidden by nothing but an unlocked cupboard door half an inch thick. Studying it more closely, I was struck by the way the words veered off at different angles, and the sheer pressure the black biro had exerted – in places, the paper was almost scratched straight through. And I felt the full weight of her terror and confusion at the moment of writing; the indescribable horror of having an unknown enemy, facing an unknown threat.

Silence had become cathedral-like, multi-layered, as if I could hear a tiny ghost of her voice filtering in on its furthest outskirts. It was then that the phone rang unexpectedly in the main bedroom, a mundane noise from another world, abrupt, insistent, jarring.

I hurried into the bigger, warmer, sunnier room, making an effort to calm down. Sitting on the bed, I lifted the receiver. 'Hello?'

'Hello, is that Anna Jeffreys?'

I didn't recognise the female voice at all, and my thoughts turned suspiciously to telesales, before I realised that she'd used my writing-name. 'It is,' I said, 'can I help you?'

'Well, I'm not sure, really. My name's Lucy Fielder. I got your number from Melanie Cook – she's a neighbour of mine, lives just a few doors down. She told me you were researching the Rebecca Fisher case, and you'd be interested in anything new you could find out about it. I wondered if you'd finished all that now, or if you were still interviewing people.'

The voice was precise, unemotional but pleasant. My imagination showed me another conscientious, middle-aged housewife absolutely in keeping with the estate where she lived. 'Oh, I'm still at the research stage,' I reassured her quickly. 'Anything you could tell me would be very helpful.'

'I'm afraid I won't be any help if you just want to know about Rebecca – I didn't really know her from Adam. But I certainly knew Eleanor Corbett. Would that have any relevance to your book?'

'*Totally*. I'm researching the whole case.' Wonderful as this turn of events felt, I hadn't been prepared for it at all, and struggled to kick-start my thoughts. 'Did you know Eleanor well?'

'Quite well, as it happens. We were in the same class at St Anthony's. After, you know, they found her body, I remember reading about her in the papers, just sad little mentions of how sweet she'd been, how much everyone had liked her. I'd have given a good deal to set the record straight then, and I think a lot of other people felt the same way, but, at the time, it seemed heartless even to think of that. After all, she'd been murdered, and she'd only been nine years old . . . it seemed horrible, wanting to drag out nasty facts about her.'

'What kind of nasty facts?'

'She wasn't anything like the innocent little angel the papers mentioned, I can tell you *that* for sure.' Lucy's voice was matter-of-fact, very slightly awkward. 'In all honesty, I couldn't *stand* the girl.'

I sat up, jolted – while I'd anticipated unearthing fresh truths about Rebecca and her adoptive parents, I'd taken the murdered girl almost entirely at face value.

'We moved to Teasford when I was eight years old,' Lucy went on. 'I joined St Anthony's then, and the teacher put me at the desk next to Eleanor's. None of the other children would have wanted to swap with me, even if the teacher had let them. They all seemed to put up with Eleanor; they were used to her, in the same way you can get used to having asthma or a limp. She'd tag around with them, and none of them ever told her to go away. But she didn't have any actual *friends*, anyone who'd miss her if she wasn't there. Children know about a personality like hers, even if they don't know the right words for it.'

'What sort of personality?' I asked.

'Oh, spiteful, manipulative, devious. You'd normally associate that sort of thing with cleverness, but Eleanor wasn't clever at all – she was like one of those idiot savants, but she didn't have an instinctive feel for maths or art, just petty nastiness. Sitting next to her, you really got to feel that on a day-to-day basis – all sugary-sweet one minute when the teacher was nearby, then hissing at me to let her copy my homework. Then, when I wouldn't, accidently-on-purpose knocking her ink all over my exercise book so it ruined everything, and being so sugary-sweet again when the teacher hurried over to see what had happened. Lots of little things like that, irrelevant in their own right. But they really got to you after a while. It was like having a bad smell next to you all day, and knowing you'd just have to live with it.

'God, she was a loathsome child. I remember her stealing things from my desk and swearing blind she hadn't touched them, even when it was obvious nobody else could have done. Mostly they were just little things like pencils and colouring-crayons, but once she took a brand-new fountain pen I'd got for my birthday – it was quite expensive, and my mother was furious when I told her it had gone missing. Eleanor never had anything like that herself; even compared to most of the children there, her family was penniless. A few of the girls made fun of the Corbetts sometimes, calling them fleabags and things like that. Maybe that was partly why she was so unpleasant. She seemed to resent anyone who had more than her, and that meant practically everyone.

'She wasn't a bully, or even close to one – she was too isolated for that. She was just insidious, vicious. As far as I could tell, she saw the whole world as divided into two groups. There were people she wanted to give the right impression to, when it came to them, she was so sycophantic. And there were people whose opinions didn't matter; she was more than happy to show her true colours

203

with us. As I said, children in her own year could see that quite clearly. It was only older ones and adults who took her at face value – nearly all of them thought she was the sweetest little thing, much as she was described in the papers.'

'I heard she tended to gravitate towards older friends,' I said cautiously. 'Even before Rebecca.'

'You've certainly got the right information there. She had very clear ideas about who she wanted to be friends with, and just bulldozed her way in, offering to do this and that for them till they accepted her. I remember her sucking up to my eldest cousin and her friends – they were two years older, known as the tough girls in their year, although these days, I dare say they'd look less threatening than Just William. She followed them around constantly, till they started thinking of her as a friend.'

Lucy sighed. 'Well, she ended up getting them into no end of trouble. They were in a sweet shop together one weekend, and Eleanor stole all sorts of little things when they weren't looking. The manageress saw her, and was ready to blame them all. But Eleanor said the others had told her to, and she'd been scared not to do what they said. Of course, I wasn't there, but I can imagine her injured-innocent expression perfectly well. If you'd known my cousin and her friends, you'd know what an obvious lie that was – they could be rowdy, but they'd never make a little kid do something like that. Still, everyone believed Eleanor, and they got into far more trouble than they would have done just for stealing sweets. They were furious with her, you can imagine, but there was nothing whatsoever they could do. They'd have been in a hundred times more trouble if they'd tried to get her back for it.'

'I heard about that,' I said. 'From one of Eleanor's sisters. The way she talked about her, Eleanor sounded almost retarded, as if she was hardly able to look after herself.'

'Oh, I saw the way her sisters behaved around her. But in a few highly specialised ways, Eleanor was a lot sharper than any of them. She really encouraged them to think of her that way, always played up to their image of her. It paid off, as far as she was concerned. All the other Corbett girls had to stay at home doing chores on Saturdays, but Eleanor was always free to go out and play – she couldn't possibly be trusted with housework, so someone else would have to do her share for her. I suppose, the way she saw it, the end justified the means. They could patronise her all they liked; she was the one who could go out whenever she wanted.'

I thought back to Agnes Og's living room, suddenly seeing the past she'd described through new eyes; Eleanor deliberately singeing shirts and breaking crockery, smirking inside at the inevitable reactions. 'She sounds so calculating,' I said, 'I'm surprised you say she wasn't clever.'

'She wasn't always as rational as that. A lot of things she did were just pure malice; there was nothing in it for her at all. I remember once, she somehow found out that one of our classmates had a father in prison – of course it had been kept a secret – everyone prized respectability above all else back then, and there was a huge stigma attached to *that*. Anyway, Eleanor spread it all over the school. She seemed to thrive on it. I can still see her, joining in with the catcalls in the playground. That little face. *Delighted*. Like a sweet little girl on Christmas Day.' I could almost feel Lucy's shudder. 'That girl was nothing to Eleanor, nothing at all – she started playing truant soon afterwards, and her mother took her out of school. Eleanor was so disappointed, you could *feel* it. I wouldn't go as far as to say evil, but there was real malice in that child. It was frightening.'

'I'm surprised Rebecca didn't notice that herself,' I said slowly. 'It sounds so obvious.'

'As I said, even slightly older children always seemed to take Eleanor at face value. She just looked so much the part – the cute-little-sister type, tiny, all curls and freckles and gappy teeth. And she certainly pulled out all the stops to get in with Rebecca. She was *Dennis Fisher's* daughter, her mother drove her to school in a *brand-new sports car* – Eleanor sucked up to her like a gold-digger with a rich man. Probably with much the same aims in mind.' Lucy sighed. 'I never really talked to Rebecca, but I always thought she seemed a nice girl – well-behaved, not a bit spoilt as far as I could tell. She was always on her own, whenever I saw her. Until she met Eleanor, anyway. After that, they were together all the time.

'I thought she was making a bad mistake, falling in with that horrible little thing. Ironic, really, that I thought Eleanor was the threat to her. When I heard that Rebecca had killed her, I couldn't believe my ears . . .'

Silence again. I felt shell-shocked. In the space of perhaps twenty minutes, my perceptions of the case had changed out of all recognition; the tragic victim became the villain of the piece, the ostensible villain more enigmatic than ever. 'Eleanor only wanted Rebecca for what she could get out of her,' Lucy went on. 'She just got more than she bargained for, in the end.'

25

When I'd first met Petra on my second day at Reading University, I'd known for a fact that we'd never be any more than casual acquaintances. She was my opposite in every conceivable way, first glimpsed in the centre of a big, noisy group who appeared to have become lifelong friends in less than twenty-four hours. All of them had the same air about them, but she had it more strongly than the others – the unthinking ebullience of well-loved puppies finally let off the leash, the future extending before them in a giddy whirl of Fresher's Balls and Student Union events and coming back at night whenever they liked. A freedom that was wonderful precisely because they were permanently anchored to a secure, unchanging home; there'd always be a heartfelt welcome for them when they went back. They'd never feel, as I did, that they'd finally outgrown their stay in a place where they'd never belonged.

Sitting in the car outside Wareham station and seeing her emerge at last, I remembered that time very clearly. As often before, the circumstances that had led to our friendship struck me as profoundly and almost grotesquely ironic. It had been the very worst of bad times, but had led to something more than positive: the delight of seeing her again for the first time in months, feeling as if we'd met up for a chat only yesterday. Looking round, she spotted me behind the wheel and hurried over, got into the passenger seat.

'Hello, stranger – great to see you again!' She hugged

me impulsively. 'I've really missed you. How have you *been*?'

It was something about me that would never change, my awkwardness with most spontaneous displays of affection – I felt relieved as she sat back. 'Not bad, thanks,' I said. 'How was your journey?'

'A nightmare from start to finish. There weren't any window seats, and I was stuck next to the family from hell. They were still there when I got off, and they'd been screaming at each other all the way from Reading.' Smiling, I started the engine, and we set off. 'It was such a relief to get out,' she went on blithely, 'I thought they were going to start beating each other up any second.'

We talked about this and that and nothing in particular for maybe ten minutes before the picturesque, sunny countryside began to replace dull buildings and residential streets. Out of the corner of my eye, I could see her peering out of the window, entranced.

'God, it's idyllic,' she said, as we turned off the side-road and started up Ploughman's Lane. 'I want to move here myself. It's a whole different *world*, like something out of a Beatrix Potter book.'

'Well, we're almost home now.' We crested the hill and I slowed slightly as we began the descent, feeling more than a little like a tour guide. 'That's us, there on the right.'

'Oh, wow, Anna. It's just beautiful – it's miles bigger than I expected.'

'It's only half ours,' I said hastily, 'it's been knocked into two, but it's still more than big enough. Our next-door neighbour's nice, too. For all the noise she makes, we could be on our own here.' As we drew rapidly closer, I noticed that the powder-blue Fiat wasn't there. 'I'd introduce you now,' I said, 'but it looks like she's at work.

Carl's out, too – he's gone to take his car in for a service, should be back in an hour or so.'

Once inside, Petra wanted to see everything. It felt odd showing her round this place as its chatelaine; the rooms around me felt cooler and stranger than ever, not like *mine* at all. I walked beside her like an estate agent who secretly hated the property, trying to mirror her ecstatic response to various rooms. 'It's gorgeous,' she said, as we went upstairs. 'I'm mad about those oak beams. I'm so *jealous*, I just want to move here – Reading's never going to look the same again.'

'I suppose it is nice.' Suddenly, I found myself unable to feign real enthusiasm, and heard myself speaking frankly. 'I don't know, though . . . it can feel strange, at times. Too quiet. You know.'

'Oh, you're just spoilt. You've got used to it.' We entered the spare room, and she gravitated to the window behind the computer-desk. 'My God, what a view – it looks like there's nobody for miles. No wonder you've started writing in here. Or is the office stuff so Carl can work from home?'

I shook my head. 'My writing-room – well, sort of. I haven't started the actual writing, yet.'

'I've been meaning to ask you all the way here.' Petra flung her overnight bag down on the bed, and the cheerful *home-at-last* gesture made the springs squeak alarmingly. 'How's your new book going? You haven't said a word about it so far.'

'Well . . .' It was an immense relief to hear her bring the subject up herself – as if I'd all but forgotten about it in the joy of reunion, as if it hadn't been itching in the back of my mind throughout our drive from Wareham station. 'To be honest, some strange things have been happening with it. I don't know what you're going to make of them. You'll probably think I'm just being silly.'

'I bet I won't.' She sat down on the bed to another creak of springs, while I took the office chair in front of the computer, swivelling it round to face her. 'Tell me everything – what's been going on?'

'Well ... you know I didn't have any ideas for a new book before we moved here?' She nodded slightly impatiently, obviously keen for the real story to begin. 'It carried on that way for weeks. Then, I found something out from this old lady in the village. You know Rebecca Fisher?'

'Not personally, but I know who she *is*. She killed her best friend in the Sixties, didn't she? Why, what about her?'

'She used to live here,' I said quietly. 'We bought this house from her.'

Petra stared at me for long seconds, round-eyed. 'You're kidding.'

'*Seriously*. We didn't know who she was at the time, of course, but when I talked to some people round here, the whole story came out. Someone had found out she was Rebecca, started sending her death threats. More than that, as well. Apparently, they smashed all her windows while she was at work – and, soon afterwards, they killed her dog.' I took a deep breath. 'That was when she put this house on the market. Obviously, she wanted to get out as quickly as she could – it was why we got the place so cheaply.'

'Every cloud has a silver lining,' Petra said, but the callous flippancy wasn't hers at all; I could see it quite clearly for what it was, a knee-jerk reaction to mask deep shock. 'Jesus, Anna, thanks for giving me nightmares – I'm going to have a really good night's sleep here, after hearing *that*.'

'Sorry, but I haven't told you all of it. Anywhere near all of it.' I'd been alone with my secrets for so long, I had no idea how they'd look to someone else, but, bracing myself for any number of possible reactions, I ploughed on. 'This is going to sound bloody awful, I know, but when I heard that, it gave me the best idea for a new book. Come on, you don't have to look at me like that. I'm still feeling pretty guilty about it myself.'

'I'm not looking at you like anything.' But she had done, for a second, as if I'd just cheerfully announced my membership of the BNP. 'Come on, I'm on tenterhooks here – what's next?'

There was nothing else for it – I told her about my idea, my confrontation with Mr Wheeler, Socks' injury, Socks' death. 'I know how stupid it sounds,' I finished, 'to think he might have something to do with those things. I'm sure he's a perfectly nice man, he just flared up at me because he thought I was being ghoulish, exploitative. It doesn't make sense for me to worry about him – *does* it?'

The silence seemed to go on for ever before Petra spoke at last. 'Well,' she said cautiously, 'I suppose not.'

Looking at her, I experienced a moment of profound unease. I'd been convinced that she'd be reassuringly dismissive of my fears, that she'd even laugh at them, leaving me feeling sheepish and embarrassed and relieved. But her tone and expression betrayed wariness, as if I'd told her I'd found a lump in my breast three weeks ago and it wasn't going away.

'What do you mean, you *suppose* not?' I demanded, forcing myself to laugh. 'He'd have had to be hiding in the woods back there in the dead of night. I heard that noise past midnight, and I found Socks first thing in the morning.

Can you really imagine him on stakeout for hours, lurking behind a tree?'

I'd intended it as a purely rhetorical question, but she didn't seem to take it as one – if anything, her concern intensified. 'I don't know, Anna. He was friends with Rebecca Fisher. If he'd get on with someone like *that*—'

'She was just an ordinary woman when she showed us round here. There wasn't anything frightening about her.' With an inexplicable feeling of urgency, I found myself taking on the role I'd been reserving for Petra: fearless, rational, contemptuous of guessed-at horrors. I'd expected her to give me the reassurance I so desperately needed, and realised I'd have to provide it myself. 'And if you'd seen him for yourself, you'd know that he'd never do any such thing. He's a bloody *vet*, Petra, not a serial killer.'

'I know. Still, it sounds a bit . . .' I could see her biting back words that had haunted my mind for weeks: *odd, disturbing, ominous.* 'What's Carl got to say about it all?'

'He doesn't know. And he's not going to.' Her surprise was palpable, and I hurried on for dear life. 'One thing just led to another – I didn't want to tell him about Mr Wheeler to begin with, and I couldn't go back later and admit that I'd lied. There's no point, anyway. Even if Mr Wheeler *did* do all that, it's over now – he's had his revenge, and that's the end of it. Carl doesn't need to know a thing.'

Thank God, she seemed to understand, and wasn't drawing Carl's instant parallels with that nightmare fresher term; everything in her eyes grudgingly conceded *it makes sense.* 'Well,' she said, 'I suppose it's for the best. But if anything else does happen – not that I think it will – you'll tell him then, won't you?'

'Of course.' The two words came out with a certainty I was far from sure I really felt; I was just relieved to draw a line under this worrying conversation, marking it off clearly as finished business. From outside came the escalating sound of a car engine. 'Speak of the devil,' I said, 'I think that's him now.'

It was. Effusive greetings in the hallway led to coffee in the kitchen, ajar back door leading into dazzling rural summer. If Petra still had misgivings about our recent conversation, she'd tucked them discreetly away out of sight.

'Suppose you've heard what we've got in store this evening?' Carl asked her cheerfully, then, seeing her blank expression, 'You've got a real treat ahead of you. A Women's Institute bake sale in a church hall, no less.'

'We won't have to stay long,' I hurried to assure her. 'The lady next door asked if we'd like to come, and I said we'd put in a showing. You never know, it might even be fun.'

'Stranger things have happened, I suppose,' said Carl dubiously. 'I'm sure I read something about an exploding cow, once . . .' We all laughed. Finishing our coffees, the three of us went for a long, aimless, chatty walk round the village, and talked about Reading, and the handful of people we all knew, and how glad Carl and I were that we'd moved here.

At five to five, Carl pulled up in the little open-air car park on the outskirts of Wareham town centre, and we got out and started walking towards the church hall. The golden sunlight had a slightly faded, sepia edge, and the streets were very quiet. 'That's it, there,' I said to Petra as we approached, 'just past the library, on the left.'

Once there, colourful handwritten signs directed us down a narrow alley that led round the back of the church; propped-open double doors led onto a scene profoundly evocative of childhood, school fêtes and harvest festivals and jumble sales arranged by the PTA. The same air of well-meaning amateurishness hung over everything: the few hastily-set-up stalls, the elderly lady presiding over the side-table laden with tiny beakers of red and white wine. The hall seemed to primarily exist as a Sunday school – pairs of crudely drawn animals had been cut out with some care and mounted on thick card beneath a sign reading *Noah's Ark* in a carefully legible grown-up hand. As a setting, it was slightly but obviously too big for the two dozen or so people in attendance. As far as I could tell, all of them were well over forty and, at first, I couldn't see a single face I knew. Scanning the room, I was relieved to see Liz behind one of the cake stalls, talking with Helen and Muriel. '*There* she is,' I said, then, to Petra, 'That's my next-door neighbour, the one with the brown hair. Let's go over and say hi, shall we?'

Helen and Muriel's presence led to an intricacy of introductions; it seemed everyone was shaking hands and smiling at each other at once. 'I do hope you're enjoying your stay here, Petra,' Muriel said, 'and I must say, it's very nice to meet you, Carl. I'm quite surprised we haven't seen you around sooner.'

'Well, I suppose you're working most of the time,' Liz said to him comfortably. 'I feel I'm meeting you for the first time myself, as it happens. Do help yourself to a slice of cake, won't you? I made it at home this morning, and if I say so myself, it's very nice.'

We all took bits, thanking her. Standing behind the stall, she spoke again to Carl. 'Of course, I've heard a lot about you from Anna – all good, needless to say. We see quite a lot of each other in the daytime – we're always stopping for a nice chat.'

'Shame on you.' Petra's voice was loud, cheerful and

entirely unexpected. I realised she was both talking to me and indirectly addressing our audience. 'Is this when you're supposed to be hard at work on your research? Well, I can't say I blame you – I'd need a few breaks from Rebecca Fisher myself.'

Horror descended, and I felt the slow landslide of confusion beginning around me – Muriel and Liz looked politely puzzled, Helen chillier and more suspicious than ever, Petra obviously wondering what she'd said wrong. Carl knowing, but not really understanding at all. Seconds crawled past without any of them saying a word; all eyes were on me, and I knew I had no option but to confess the truth. 'I'm researching a sort of thriller,' I said quickly, 'based on the Rebecca Fisher case. I got the idea after I moved here – after, you know, I found out about her.'

I couldn't have sounded guiltier if I'd been confessing to the ritual murder of ten small children. Still nobody spoke, and I began to wish the dusty-looking wooden floorboards would creak apart and swallow me whole. From the corner of my eye, I could see Petra's combined uncertainty and guilt, a clear desire to get me off the hot-seat with a swift change of subject.

'Well, it should be great when you've finished,' she said reassuringly, then, turning to Liz, Helen and Muriel, 'she's a brilliant writer. Have you read *A Deeper Darkness* yet? Isn't it fantastic?'

When you're in a hole, stop digging – but Petra had no idea that she was, or rather, that she'd put me in one. For the second time in as many minutes, I knew I'd have to explain. 'I had a novel published last year,' I said lamely. 'It's a sort of thriller, too. I'd have told you about it before, but . . .'

Extraordinarily, Liz rescued me with a cheerful smile, as if she heard similar revelations from her neighbours every day. 'Well, that is good news, dear – well done. I'll look out for a copy when I'm in the library next. What did you say it was called again?'

'*A Deeper Darkness*,' I said. 'I write as Anna Jeffreys. But I don't expect you'll have it in stock – it didn't get an awful lot of distribution, to be honest.'

'That's a shame . . . well, we can always put it on order. And I'm sure it's early days for you yet.' Her voice extended to address all five of us. 'Anyway, do have some more cake, if you want some – there's no need to be shy. It'll only go to waste, otherwise.'

The conversation moved on to other, general things. I felt a mixture of amazement and deep gratitude, realising that Liz had rescued the situation effortlessly. Still, more than once, I noticed Helen looking at me with an unnervingly distant, watchful expression, reminding me how odd it must seem to them that I hadn't said a word about my writing before. I suddenly felt too awkward and self-conscious to take the conversational lead with a faux-casual glance at my watch and a *God, is that the time?*; I hung sheepishly round the edges of chit-chat until, finally, Carl did it for me. 'Sorry to rush off, but we'd really better be going,' he said, with what sounded like genuine regret. 'We're supposed to be going out for dinner this evening. It's been very nice to meet you two – and to meet you properly, Liz. Thanks a lot for the cake.'

'Oh, it's nothing. Have a lovely time, all of you. I'm sure I'll see you soon, Anna, dear.'

Goodbyes all round. As we stepped out into the cooling warmth of evening, Petra drew a theatrical breath. 'My God – I'm so sorry, Anna. I had no idea you hadn't told them any of it.'

'Oh, don't worry. It's not your fault; it was bound to come out sooner or later, anyway.' I spoke with deliberate briskness, trying to convince myself it was the truth. 'I know it was silly of me to hide it – I should have mentioned it when I first met them. It just never seemed to be quite the right time, somehow.'

'You and your writing.' Carl smiled. 'I don't know, Annie – there are probably drug dealers who aren't so secretive about their work.'

I was delighted to see that Liz's apparently unquestioning acceptance of my announcement seemed to have coloured his view of it, as well – before she'd spoken, he'd looked cautious and ill-at-ease, now he seemed to view the evening's events as an amusing irrelevancy. Only I couldn't quite see them in that light, not deep down; part of me still crawled with the embarrassment of half an hour ago, wondered what on earth Liz must really think.

'Well,' I said, rather self-consciously, 'all's well that ends well. Anyway, *shall* we go for dinner somewhere? It's a lovely evening, and there are some good pubs round here.'

We did, driving to one midway between Wareham and home; sat outside in the mosquito-flickering beer garden, where a crowd of cheerful twentysomethings looked like they were on their way to a night's bowling and clubbing in Poole Tower Park. At our rickety wooden table, we talked, ate and drank. Evening came down in rosy gauze layers, wine glasses en route to laughing mouths – a picture of camaraderie so perfect that it could have been a still from a TV ad, frozen above a discreet logo before the real programme began again.

'So what did you make of the locals?' I asked Petra. 'Liz is nice, isn't she?'

'Too sweet for words – wish I had a neighbour like that. Mind you, I could have done without meeting that other one, the Nazi-looking one in the white shirt. My God, talk about a charm bypass.'

I saw Carl nodding humorous agreement beside me and I felt obscurely glad that they shared my reaction to Helen; that it wasn't just me who found her intimidating. 'There was something really creepy about her,' Petra went on cheerfully. 'She hardly said a word. Is she always like that?'

'As far as I can tell. I don't see that much of her, luckily – as little as I can, to be honest.' The waitress arrived with our main course. 'Anyway, let's talk about something nicer,' I said quickly. 'How's work been going lately?'

26

'Good to see her again, wasn't it?'

It was five thirty on Sunday evening, and we'd just dropped Petra off at Wareham station. Pulling out of the little car park, I spoke rather distractedly, even as I twisted round in my seat and waved back at her for one last time. 'Yeah.'

'You don't sound too convinced.' Glancing at me more closely, he saw that preoccupation rather than indifference had created the vague note in my voice. 'What's the matter, Annie?'

'Oh, I just keep thinking about last night – you know, what Petra said about me writing at the Women's Institute thing. I'm not that bothered what Helen or Muriel made of it, but I can't help worrying about Liz.' Even as I spoke, her image came back to me: her unsurprised, cheerful reaction that could only have been a mask for something else. 'We've talked to each other so often, it must seem bizarre that I never told her before. God knows what she must think.'

'Well . . .' He spoke awkwardly and I could see him wanting to deny it, not quite being able to. 'It doesn't matter, you know – it's not as if she's your best friend or anything, there was no reason why you *had* to tell her. It was just a shame it ended up coming out like that, that's all.'

'I'm going to go round and see her when we get home.' I was thinking aloud – the words came out at the same time as I made the decision. 'Try and explain why I didn't tell her before. Just to set the record straight.'

'You don't have to,' he said reassuringly. 'It's really no big deal, Annie.'

'I want to. I won't be able to relax till I've done it. I won't be long, anyway. You'll hardly know I'm gone.'

When we got back, Carl put the TV on and settled down to watch the football highlights while I went round to Liz's back door and knocked rather tentatively. She opened it almost at once. 'Oh, hello, Anna. I wasn't expecting to see you.'

Instinctively, I took a step back. 'Well, I just thought I'd pop round, it's not *important*. If it's a bad time for you right now—'

'It isn't at all, dear. Come on in, I'll put the kettle on.'

I followed her into her impossibly welcoming, nutmeg-smelling kitchen that was cluttered without being untidy in the slightest. Sitting down at the central table, I watched her bustle over to the kettle. 'I suppose your friend's gone home now,' she said. 'It was very nice to meet her yesterday evening – she seems a lovely girl.'

'She is. She said to thank you for asking her along; she really enjoyed meeting you all.' In fact, she hadn't said any such thing, but I told myself that she'd probably meant to. As Liz filled the kettle from the tap, I couldn't help myself speaking slightly more seriously, a new awkwardness entering my tone. 'I suppose I really came to explain about last night,' I said. 'I'm sorry I never told you about my writing before. You must think I'm incredibly secretive.'

'Not at all, dear. Really, it's nothing to feel guilty about.'

Her expression and voice were both matter-of-fact and impeccably diplomatic, but much as I wanted to let the subject go, I wasn't quite able to. 'I know how strange it sounded, coming out like that,' I said. 'Helen was giving me funny looks all evening, after Petra said—'

'Oh, you mustn't worry about Helen, dear. She can be a bit off with people, sometimes – it's only to be expected, really, as I've said before.'

I couldn't help my curiosity from showing on my face; Liz carried on speaking with a kind of cosy, unruffled sympathy. 'She's had a very difficult life, poor Helen. I'm not talking behind her back, you understand, I know she wouldn't mind me telling you. She hasn't lived here as long as you might think, only seven years or so ... before that, she'd spent all her adult life looking after her mother, her father died when she was young and her mother was very ill. No social life to speak of at all, and a rather puritanical upbringing, very religious in an old-fashioned way. Terribly sad, when you think of it. As far as I know, she's never even had a boyfriend – there simply wasn't any time for that sort of thing while her mother was alive.'

It was true, I thought, it *was* a sad story. But her image was still oddly menacing in my mind, and I couldn't banish that feeling no matter how hard I tried. 'She moved here after her mother died,' Liz continued. 'She's very shy, you know. I know she can seem a bit forbidding, but she's just not used to people – she's such a nice lady when you get to know her.'

A slightly awkward pause fell before Liz spoke again, more briskly. 'Anyway, dear, you certainly don't need to worry about last night. I'm sure you had your own reasons for keeping that to yourself.'

'Well, yes, but there's nothing sinister about them.' I was suddenly gripped by an irresistible urge to explain, to make her understand the full story. 'I don't really know why I didn't tell you. I suppose I just didn't want an action

221

replay of the way it was in Reading, before we moved. With everyone who knew I'd written a book. Friends of Carl's. Friends of mine. People I worked with. It was a nightmare.'

Her expression betrayed more concern than curiosity. 'What on earth did they do?'

'Oh, it sounds silly, when I say it. Trivial. But they'd always ask the same questions. How much I'd made from it, for a start – no, *really*, people who'd never have dreamed of asking me that about my job – it was the first thing they ever wanted to know, and they'd never take *not enough* for an answer. They'd just keep on pressing, till I either told them the truth or told them to sod off. And I always told them the truth. And they always looked so disappointed. It was horrible. I always wanted the ground to open up and swallow me.

'But they never let it go, any of them. Every time I saw them, they'd say they'd been looking for my book and couldn't find it anywhere – Carl's own parents said that, and God knows how many other people. They'd reel off this exhaustive list of all the bookshops that didn't have a single copy in stock, and I don't think they knew how much it hurt when they reminded me of that; it meant so much to me, and I had to try and pretend I didn't really care. And then I had to apologise, and explain it didn't have much distribution, it wasn't doing that well – and then they always asked about sales figures—'

I paused for a second, taking a shuddering breath. 'I hate it. I've tried to explain to Carl, but he just doesn't understand – he laughs about me keeping it such a secret, thinks it's something to be proud of. It's like banging my head against a brick wall, trying to make him realise I *would* be proud of it if I was successful, I'd be happy to talk about it till I was blue in the face. But as it is, I just feel like I did when I was a kid, when I used to write then. Like it's something pathetic. Laughable. Something you do to make you feel better about yourself, because nobody wants you around—'

I broke off, amazed and appalled to realise I was on the brink of tears. I hauled myself back as if for dear life, not quite able to meet her eyes. I felt she'd seen me naked. 'Well, that's why I didn't tell you, anyway,' I said, forcing an unconvincing smile. 'I expect you think it's stupid.'

'Not at all, dear. I can understand, only too well.'

My gaze moved back to her slowly, with trepidation – I dreaded a thin veneer of sympathy over dubious incomprehension, but her expression was both frank and kind. '*Really?* Honestly – you're not just saying that?'

'I'm really not just saying that. I've never had a hobby that meant that much to me – you can't really count my gardening, let alone my little part-time job. But if I did, I'm sure I'd feel the same way about it. I'd feel protective about it. I'd want people to understand that it mattered.'

It was extraordinary, dreamlike to find empathy in such an unexpected quarter. At best, I was used to having my secrecy treated as an amusing creative caprice, akin to an actor wearing a lucky pair of socks on first nights. In Liz, I saw understanding without judgement. It amazed me to think I'd taken her at face value for so long, complacent, slightly overbearing, quick to privately disapprove of anything she couldn't see reflected in her own life. There was, I realised, far more to her than I'd suspected – true sensitivity behind the bland, conventional niceness, a slightly guarded but nonetheless genuine warmth.

'I'm really glad you think that,' I said quietly, then, with a determined injection of cheerfulness, 'anyway, I'm hoping it'll be different with my second book. Maybe it'll do better.'

'Oh, *yes*.' She held back for a second, looking simultan-eously curious and embarrassed. 'Tell me to mind my own business if you like, dear. But I can't help wondering – what made you want to write about Rebecca Fisher?'

Normally, I'd have been wary of discussing the subject, too aware of its power to inspire shock and disapproval. Suddenly, however, I felt entirely comfortable describing how it had all started, how I'd read a little more about the case and felt unexpected inspiration take root. How it had quickly begun to interest me for reasons that had little or nothing to do with the book. As I told her about it, I felt we were meeting for the first time, discovering an immediate, unforced rapport.

When I'd finished speaking, she looked thoughtful for a moment. 'It's certainly an interesting story, in a horrible sort of way. I'm surprised you're not more frightened by it. This probably sounds silly, but I still find it quite upsetting to think that woman lived next door. It was the last thing you'd expect to happen in a little place like this. When I first moved here, I'd never have dreamed of such a thing.'

I glanced at her, surprised. Something about her settled cosiness here had made me assume she'd lived here all her life. 'Where did you move from?'

'Oh, the outskirts of Bournemouth – over ten years ago, now. Soon after my husband passed away. The girls had moved out by then, and the house was far too big for me on my own. And even if it hadn't been, it just felt wrong there. I don't quite know how else to describe it.'

'I know what you mean.' I envisioned a many-bed-roomed family home in a leafy suburb, crowded with possessions and achingly empty; its echoes, I thought, must have been similar to those of number four Plough-man's Lane, less sinister, yet infinitely more poignant. 'I'd have moved, as well.'

A grateful glance, acknowledgement that I understood her – then I saw her brushing old sadness away with quick determination, rearranging her familiar smile. 'I took to Abbots Newton at once, anyway. I'd been rather worried that the locals wouldn't welcome a stranger, but they honestly couldn't have been kinder.'

'I've heard they weren't that kind to Rebecca.'

The words jumped out before I'd had a chance to think about them. She didn't try to conceal her own curiosity. 'Whoever told you that?'

It was the first time I'd described my meeting with Mr Wheeler to anyone who knew him. Deliberately, I left nothing out: his fury, his accusations against myself and the village in general, what he'd told me about Rebecca's dog. As I finished speaking, Liz's expression was slightly concerned. 'It doesn't matter,' I continued hurriedly, 'I've managed to track down other people who knew Rebecca – old teachers and schoolfriends and God knows who else – I didn't *need* Mr Wheeler to talk to me. It just shook me up a bit at the time. That's all.'

'I'm not surprised, dear.' She still looked worried, and the pause lasted slightly too long. 'He was *very* good friends with Rebecca,' she said at last, 'so far as I could tell, at least. I saw his car parked outside so often.'

It had the unmistakable edge of a warning, as if she didn't want to sound silly or hysterical, but still wanted her misgivings to come across loud and clear. Looking at her, I felt much as I had done with Petra yesterday morning, in the spare room. Only this was somehow worse. I could imagine Petra's internal casting director putting Vincent Price in the vet's role, but Liz knew him.

Unaware of the cry I'd heard in the night, the day I'd seen him watching the house or my suspicions regarding Socks' death, she'd still found my brief summary of that meeting ominous. The silence had become too heavy, demanding to be broken.

'Do you think he's still in touch with her?' I asked.

'Your guess is as good as mine. Still, I expect so. They seemed very close when she was living here – I'm quite convinced that they knew each other before that.'

I wondered if they could go back *decades*, if he could be as loyal to her as he'd have been to an immediate relative. As furious and vengeful on her behalf. I struggled to submerge the thought.

'Well, I suppose it doesn't matter. I'm certainly not getting in touch with him again – I've got plenty of leads to follow as it is.' I wanted to get this conversation as far away from the sinister ambiguities of Mr Wheeler as possible, to put it back where it belonged, among the spice-racks and cookery-books of a pleasant rural kitchen in summer. 'Anyway, how did your sale go last night, after we left? It was a shame we couldn't stay for longer.'

The change of subject was glaringly obvious, but she didn't acknowledge that by so much as a raised eyebrow – I could see her tacitly understanding my need for normality and reassurance, and blessed her for it. In my mind, we moved another step closer together.

Eventually I caught a glimpse of the clock across the room and did the kind of double-take I'd thought I'd have to feign at the bake sale. 'My God, it's almost seven,' I said. 'I'm really sorry, but I'd better make a move.'

'Don't worry about it. I'm sure I'll see you soon.'

'Well, come round for a cup of tea whenever you like.' Even if I'd wanted to extend that invitation this time yesterday, I wouldn't quite have been able to; suddenly,

226

however, it was simplicity itself. 'I can usually do with a distraction from the research.'

Out of the back door, I walked down her garden path, past the spot where we'd buried Socks. As the sunset came down, the flowerbeds were controlled explosions of colour, as if viewed through a golden-pink filter. Unsettling as I'd found our conversation about Mr Wheeler, I couldn't help feeling startled and happy as I realised how Liz had changed in my mind; she seemed to have crossed some crucial boundary, turning from pleasant acquaintance to genuine friend in the space of an hour and a half. It had, I remembered, been much the same way with Petra, in another time and place completely...

But that didn't matter, not now. I didn't want to think about that time in my life this evening. Quickening my step, I headed back to dinner and Carl as if I could hurry away from terrible memories. That was the worst thing about them, I thought, the way they could jump out of nowhere, the way a tiny part of my mind always had to stand vigilant guard against them.

The following morning, I was stepping into the shower and Carl was getting ready for work when the knock came at the front door. Turning the shower off, I heard him going downstairs and answering it, a brief muffled exchange with a male voice I didn't recognise. Seconds later, the door was closing again, and Carl was calling up the stairs. 'Just the postman, Annie. You've got a parcel. I think it's that book you bought online.'

It was the sort of thing that only ever arrived when you weren't expecting it, and I'd virtually forgotten it existed. I felt ridiculously pleased, as if I'd just received an unexpected present.

'Thanks,' I called back, 'just leave it wherever.'

'Will do – it's on the kitchen table. I'm off, anyway.'

'Have a nice day. See you tonight.'

I heard him leaving, and finished showering as quickly as possible before dressing and rushing downstairs like a small child on Christmas morning. The padded envelope was next to the fruit bowl, *www.truecrimebypost.com* emblazoned in red above our address. As I tore it open, the receipt fluttered onto the table, ignored. I pulled the book out, and studied its cover for long seconds.

A Mind to Murder, I read, *Shocking Stories of Britain's Most Unexpected Killers. By Linda Piercy.* Visually, it could have been designed by an untalented ten-year-old on their class computer – dull red letters on a plain black background, surrounded by a handful of monochrome photographs. Only one leapt out and clamoured for my attention; the posed head-and-shoulders shot, the neat school shirt and tie, the large, pale, expressionless eyes looking directly into the camera. Everything about that cover was as tacky as it was tantalising – it would tell me nothing revelatory in its own right, could all too plausibly infer a great deal.

I made myself a coffee before sitting down, opening the book and lighting a cigarette simultaneously. The sharp, gluey scent of new paper combined with the smell of smoke as I scanned the index for the chapter on Rebecca. Then I flicked rapidly towards the page I wanted, and started reading.

27

From *A Mind to Murder* by Linda Piercy, p. 75.

The ten-year-old girl was crying. Across the living room, the young policeman who'd been sent to question her watched uncomfortably. Constable Brian Willings had known it would be far from easy to break the news that her best friend had been murdered, but at the same time, he had not expected to witness such obvious grief. Especially when he'd glossed over the horrific details with such care, understanding how unsuitable they were for an innocent child's ears.

Nor did his surroundings do anything to put him at ease. Like most of his friends and family in the East Lancashire town of Teasford, Brian was accustomed to small, cramped houses filled with inexpensive furniture, and the luxury of this girl's home made him feel awkward and out of place. Self-consciously, he asked the questions that he needed to, trying his best to speak in a gentle, soothing voice as he enquired whether she'd seen her best friend on the day of her disappearance.

Throughout the questioning, the girl's mother had watched him with coldness and hostility, sitting beside her daughter and carefully monitoring her reactions. As the ten-year-old gave way to a fresh outburst of weeping, the woman rose imperiously to her feet. She was beautiful in an intimidating way: tall, blonde and perfectly dressed. As she addressed Brian furiously, the young policeman couldn't help but remember who he was dealing with.

'She's told you already that she doesn't know anything about it. Why aren't you out catching that poor child's murderer, instead of upsetting my daughter like this? You've taken up more than enough of our time already.'

He tried his best to defend himself, saying feebly that he was only doing his job. But the woman's anger remained implacable, and finally he had no choice but to leave. Driving back to the station, he braced himself to tell his immediate superior what had happened, thinking that Inspector David Howard would order him to go back.

Far from it, however, Howard assured him that he had done the right thing. 'I would have done the same myself, lad. She's only a little girl; she doesn't know anything. And I'm sure you know yourself, there's no sense in getting that family's backs up.'

Brian did know, only too well. Everyone in Teasford was aware of the Fishers. Dennis Fisher owned the town's largest factory, and was reputed to be a millionaire several times over. His wife Rita, who had driven the young policeman out of their home, had been born into huge wealth herself as the only child of a tycoon and his socialite wife. While they had little to do with the town's other residents, their distance from its daily events made them almost legendary figures. Exceptionally close as a couple, the sole tragedy in their lives had been their inability to have children of their own. But when they had decided to adopt, even that problem had been resolved. Angelically beautiful and exceptionally clever, Rebecca had proved to be the daughter of their dreams, and both Rita and Dennis were known to adore the child unconditionally.

'Don't go biting off more than you can chew.' Howard advised the younger man wisely. 'Go and talk to some of the girl's other friends, instead. Surely one of them must have known something.'

Hugh Salter had been a pathologist in the East Lancashire police for almost fifteen years. It was not a job for a squeamish or faint-hearted man, and at the age of forty-one, he thought of himself as virtually inured to horror. He examined the victims of grisly car crashes and industrial accidents on an almost daily basis, and very little still had the power to shock him.

But when nine-year-old Eleanor Corbett's body was discovered in the summer of 1969, even this hardened professional was appalled by what he saw. This had not been a tragic accident, but the brutal murder of a much-loved little girl, a pretty and vivacious child from a large, close-knit local family. Even at a casual glance, the ferocity of the attack left him sickened. Eleanor had been stabbed more than thirty times, the murderer continuing to desecrate her corpse even as it lay lifeless.

'She was only nine, and barely looked seven, if that,' he said later. 'At first, we all assumed that she had been killed by an adult male. I'm not a violent man, but when I saw that poor child's body, I could have torn him limb from limb with my bare hands.'

Of course, Hugh knew the details of where Eleanor

had been found. The derelict house on the outskirts of Teasford, with its long-broken windows, set in overgrown gardens next to a wood. A large group of schoolboys had hung around the abandoned property when it had still had the thrill of novelty, but even they had tired of it long ago. While it still held their interest, however, one of them had captured an exceptionally large spider on the premises, which had since passed into local primary-school legend. Ever since, the house had been known among Teasford's younger children as 'the spider's house'.

It was, Hugh thought, hard to think of any place less inviting to children, particularly little girls. Still there was no doubt that Eleanor had entered it of her own free will, as she'd been seen going in on her own. Furthermore, the room in which she had been stabbed to death held bizarre traces of human habitation. One corner had been crowded with neatly arranged household objects, nearly all of which were damaged in some way. There were cracked pots and plates, and various items of cutlery. Most notably of all, the room had been lined with chipped vases of dead flowers, which seemed to have been arranged with some care.

Unofficially, Hugh was told of the assumption the police were making. They believed that Eleanor had been in the habit of going there with other children, who had brought the various items there as part of some innocent game. Then, on the day of her disappearance, they thought that she had decided to go there on her own, and seeing that she was unaccompanied, a murderous stranger had followed her inside. It didn't quite seem to fit in with their assumptions that there were no traces of sexual assault. But Hugh was well aware that evil was anything but predictable, and while there might be general patterns to the behaviour of child murderers, they would never apply one hundred per cent of the time.

Still, as he began the inevitable examination of Eleanor's body, he was surprised to find other details which challenged his preconceptions. Behind the frenzied attack, there had been far less strength than he'd have expected from a grown man in a murderous rage, and the positioning of Eleanor's injuries indicated that her killer had been smaller in stature than any man Hugh knew. As he worked in the pathology laboratory hours after Eleanor had been found, Hugh felt his certainties of this murder beginning to disappear.

At the same time, the scene of the crime was being meticulously searched by the police. Not just the house itself, but the gardens surrounding it. With sniffer dogs and a crowd of local volunteers, they were combing every inch of the area when the sound of frenzied barking brought two policemen racing over to a patch of bushes by the front doorway. One of the dogs had made a discovery.

The bone-handled carving knife had not been expertly concealed there. The random manner in which it had fallen implied that Eleanor's killer had either tossed it aside casually or in a blind panic. Blood had dried thickly on the blade, and smears ran down the handle itself. Forensic examination revealed that fingerprints had been preserved in that blood, still clearly detectable to the scientists who studied it. The size of those fingerprints told them what Hugh Salter was beginning to realise himself as he examined the dead girl's body.

'At first, I couldn't believe it,' one policeman said later. 'But, when we heard it from forensics and pathology, I knew it had to be true. Eleanor Corbett had been killed by another child.'

Rita and Dennis Fisher did their utmost to protect their adopted daughter, stating defiantly that, on the afternoon of Eleanor's disappearance and death, Rebecca had been in her room the whole time. But their influence only extended so far, even in Teasford. And as details of the case inevitably began to leak out, it was rapidly becoming notorious throughout the country.

The police questioned both parents closely, asking whether they'd seen Rebecca that afternoon with their own eyes. But, while they might do their best to protect the child they'd always longed for, the respectable and law-abiding couple still couldn't bring themselves to tell a direct lie that would pervert the course of justice. Neither of them, they admitted, had seen Rebecca that afternoon at all. Dennis had been at work, Rita shopping for clothes in a nearby city. They had left the ten-year-old in the care of their housekeeper, who had been busy with various chores, and was also unable to verify Rebecca's presence in the house.

The fingerprints on the knife were rapidly identified as Rebecca's. When the police obtained a warrant to search the Fisher home immediately afterwards, the evidence against her became even more overwhelming.

The knife itself was identical to several possessed by Rita Fisher, and had been bought from an exclusive department store as part of a set. Only its white bone handle had become stained, and Rita had thrown it away several months ago for that reason. In the same way, all the odds and ends that had been found in the derelict house could be traced back to the Fishers' own, domestic objects that had been accidentally damaged, and which Rebecca had secretly retrieved from the rubbish before they could be lost for good.

While Rebecca continued to deny any involvement in her best friend's death, she was surprisingly forthcoming on this subject alone. She admitted to taking the broken and chipped crockery and vases, as well as the cutlery which included the knife itself. She and Eleanor, she told the police, had liked to play a game of grown-up housekeeping in the abandoned property, and she had smuggled in these items to make it look more like a home. While she stubbornly refused to admit her guilt, the evidence against her was insurmountable. Rebecca Fisher was taken into police custody three days after Eleanor's body had been found.

It was an extraordinary and unprecedented situation, which the East Lancashire police force had never imagined they'd have to deal with. A ten-year-old child suspected of the most appalling crime there was. As an adult she would have awaited her trial in prison, but as it was, that was clearly out of the question. At the same time, it was equally unthinkable that she should remain in her own home. Finally, the decision was made to keep her in a neighbouring city's police station, which housed a number of individual cells. These small rooms were rarely used, and had been chiefly designed to restrain disorderly drunks overnight.

As news of her arrest became common knowledge throughout the region, details of her whereabouts were fiercely guarded. Public feeling against Rebecca ran dangerously high, and there were fears that a mob could attempt to force entry into the station where she was held. Nonetheless, it was obvious that she posed no immediate physical threat, and in the station itself, security around her was kept to a minimum. The door to her cell was generally left open, and while a female police officer always sat in the corridor leading on from it, this measure was taken more for procedure's sake than for fear Rebecca would attempt to escape.

Most of the time, this responsibility fell to WPC Nicola Harris. At twenty-seven years of age, she was known to be good with children, and her responsible but friendly manner made her an instant favourite with most of them. In the months leading up to Rebecca's trial, she talked to the little girl on a regular basis, and could not help but be surprised at what she discovered.

'Of course, I knew that she'd killed Eleanor Corbett,' she said later, 'but whenever I spoke to her, it was almost impossible to believe it. She was such a quiet, sweet little thing, very well-behaved – I had two nieces of around her age, and both of them were far more trouble than she ever was. She talked about her adoptive parents a great deal, and I got the impression that she loved them very much. As far as I can remember, she never even mentioned that she was adopted, and I never brought the subject up myself. She always referred to them as Mummy and Daddy, and said how much she missed them. It was all she ever talked about at any length, now I come to think of it.'

Forthcoming as Rebecca could be on this subject, however, it was almost impossible to draw her out on any others. Particularly the all-important one of Eleanor Corbett's murder. A police psychologist sent to talk to the little girl was bewildered and frustrated by her complete lack of co-operation. All she would say was that she had had nothing to do with her best friend's death, even when confronted with the overwhelming evidence to the contrary. Following those fruitless sessions, she seemed anxious and disturbed, and WPC Nicola Harris noticed these moods of hers with some concern.

'When Rebecca came back from talking to the psychologist, she was like a different person,' Nicola said. 'Usually she was very self-possessed, but at those times, she seemed distressed and frightened. If I asked her why, she just clammed up completely and swore blind that she was fine. But when I was on duty outside her cell at night, it was obvious that she wasn't. After those interviews with the psychologist, she nearly always wet the bed, and she seemed to have terrible nightmares. The cell door was always left open, and I often heard her talking in her sleep at those times. I can remember her repeating the same things over and over again. 'Don't tell them,' she'd say, 'you mustn't tell them.' When I asked her what she'd meant the following morning, she'd just look terrified and say she didn't know.'

Perhaps it was simply a random collection of words, associated with a nightmare she'd forgotten. Or perhaps, instead, the pressure of her own guilt, as her subconscious mind told her that she could never confess to the evil of her crime.

Even in the weeks leading up to Rebecca's trial, Rita and Dennis Fisher remained fiercely loyal to their adopted daughter, despite the fact that her growing notoriety made the loving couple targets of public hatred themselves. Two nights before the trial began, the fire brigade were called out to Dennis Fisher's factory, where a clumsily-made petrol bomb had been thrown through a window. The fire was put out quickly and the damage was superficial. And as the factory had been deserted at the time, nobody was injured. But there could be no denying the implications of this attack, and it was all too obvious where Teasford's sympathies lay. While Eleanor Corbett's grieving family were treated as tragic figures, the Fishers were vilified as monsters, their financial status only serving to fan the flames of loathing and resentment within the deprived community.

Nor did their initial appearance at Rebecca's trial do anything to increase their popularity. Photographers from every major newspaper in the country surrounded them as they walked up the courtroom steps, not touching or looking at each other, implying new anxiety was taking an immense toll on their previously happy marriage. The impression that Dennis gave was one of unemotional coldness, as he struggled to conceal his true feelings behind a businesslike facade. Rita had constructed her own facade from her finest clothes and jewellery, instantly antagonising people who could not have afforded them in a million years. Perfectly made up and expressionless, she appeared an aloof, snobbish figure, a woman with whom it was impossible to sympathise.

Nonetheless, Rita especially seemed protective of her adoptive daughter as the trial progressed. During recesses, she would appear instantly at the little girl's side, imperiously demanding that the family be left alone with their barrister. It was unsurprising that she should be concerned for Rebecca's wellbeing. Increasingly fidgety and nervous, Rebecca's eyes would dart fearfully round the court while being questioned, and she answered in a monotone so subdued that, several times, the judge had to order her to speak more loudly. While she continued to deny any knowledge of Eleanor's murder, she did so in an increasingly blank and perfunctory way that implied the exact opposite. She seemed to understand that there was no point in lying to the court, while remaining unable to bring herself to confess the truth.

Eleanor Corbett's family were a visible presence throughout the trial. Her widowed mother and older sisters appeared bitter and suspicious, convinced that the Fishers' wealth would enable Rebecca to escape justice. They knew that Rita and Dennis had engaged the best legal representation money could buy and resented it immensely. When the Fishers' barrister suggested that the evidence against Rebecca could have been fabricated, Eleanor's mother Eileen stood up in court and launched into a vicious outburst.

'It was very dramatic,' one court witness remembered later. 'She shouted that it was a joke to suggest any such thing, and she didn't know how he could sleep at night. Then she turned on Rebecca's mother – the judge was banging his gavel furiously the whole time, but I think she was too angry to care. She told Rita Fisher that she was an evil bitch, and so was the little cow she'd adopted – I think they were her exact words. She said something about the Fishers' marriage being a sham, that they couldn't even have children naturally. It could only have lasted three or four seconds, what she said, but it was electrifying. It was only when the judge threatened her with contempt of court that she went quiet and sat back down. I think she'd said all she wanted to by then, anyway.'

Skilled as the Fishers' barrister was, however, the trial's outcome was a foregone conclusion. The jury returned with a unanimous verdict of 'guilty'. Less than ten minutes later, the judge pronounced sentence. Due to the diminished responsibility of Rebecca's age, she was being tried for manslaughter rather than murder, and life imprisonment was out of the question. Instead, she was ordered to be detained indefinitely in a home for young offenders, from which she would be transferred to an adult prison at the age of sixteen.

In the January of 1970, Rebecca Fisher was sent to the Southfield Unit on the outskirts of Birmingham. Only her adoptive father would be alive to visit her there. Devastated by the court's verdict on the child she loved, Rita Fisher had committed suicide two days after the trial ended. Faced with the double loss of his wife and daughter, Dennis Fisher sold his business and started another in a far-distant area, where he could be sure that his neighbours had no personal grievance against him. But while he prospered as he had done in Teasford, he was a deeply unhappy man. The events of 1969 had cast a long shadow, and Eleanor Corbett's was not the only life which had been effectively ended that summer.

Rebecca was finally released in the early 1980s, under a secret and closely guarded new identity. To the public, it remains unknown whether she ever confessed in full to Eleanor's murder, or explained what her true motivation had been on that fateful day. Nonetheless, it was officially decided that the enigmatic ten-year-old killer posed no further threat to the public, and could be freed without fear. Today, Rebecca Fisher could be anywhere.

28

I finished reading the chapter with a deep sense of confusion. Some parts of it neatly dovetailed with what I knew already, while others seemed to directly contradict it. The references to Rebecca's relationship with her adoptive parents particularly frustrated me. I'd longed to discover more about it but, however hard I tried to believe Linda Piercy's account of it, it felt all wrong. Rita and Dennis blinded by parental love, fighting to protect her even when self-preservation must have urged them to distance themselves; Rebecca missing them desperately from her police-station cell, regarding them as she would have done her own mother and father . . .

I wasn't quite sure why it rang so false to me, but it did. Shadowy and blurred as my mental image of the Fishers was, they still looked altogether more complex and three-dimensional than that couple in the book – that cliché of happy-coupledom, perfect in every way. Other elements of the chapter told me quite clearly that Linda Piercy wasn't averse to bending the truth almost double for the sake of a more dramatic story – her physical description of Rita Fisher spoke volumes. I sensed she'd prettified Rita's marriage as she had done Rita herself; I remembered what Melanie had told me back in Teasford, the conversation she'd overheard between her mother and her friend. *They said she'd been the one with the money to start with, and that was the only reason he'd married her*, Melanie had said. *They called him a cold fish . . .*

Suddenly, it seemed that there was too much information in my mind, making it almost impossible to organise. I saw truths and half-truths and outright lies twined round one another like a writhing knot of worms; I couldn't tell where one ended and another began. There was no way of knowing whether Melanie's mother and her friend had been any more honest and reliable than Linda Piercy herself, whether their gossip had been rooted in fact or simply hearsay, guesswork and personal dislike. Somewhere, I thought, there had to be a definitive source of information, objective and unimpeachably *right* as an examiner's answer booklet.

However, I had no idea what that could be. It seemed that my only possible next step lay with the young offender's home the book mentioned, *the Southfield Unit on the outskirts of Birmingham.* There had to be some way I could find out if it still existed, and, if it did, to get in touch with someone who'd known Rebecca there. I put the book down at last, laying it face-up on the table; she watched me from the photograph on the cover, half-smiling as if at my bewilderment.

It was then that the phone started ringing in the living room; recently, the shrill, unmusical noise had started to affect me like Pavlov's bell, and I jumped up from my seat salivating at the prospect of another Lucy Fielder. I hurried towards it through a room whose bareness was beginning to look mundane and unthreatening; clean-cut squares of sunlight fell across the carpet from the windows, and the air was warm and still, scented slightly with air-freshener and pot-pourri. Reaching the telephone table, I lifted the receiver. 'Hello?'

No answer. Just breathing down the line, for maybe four or five seconds – ragged, sexless breathing very close to the receiver, slightly distorted like the sound of the sea in an open shell.

Then, there was nothing but the flat, dead buzz of a severed connection.

Genuine fear could very easily drift out of focus. It was impossible for a threat to stay in the sharply detailed foreground for any length of time when it wasn't growing, or moving, or apparently changing in any way. It was like being alone in a room with a huge, vicious-looking dog fast asleep in one corner. You could only be terrified of its waking up for so long, watching paranoically for the merest hint of movement; after a while, it just became an inert shape on the furthest outskirts of vision, and you'd be able to concentrate on reading or knitting or watching TV as if it wasn't there.

Now terror leapt back into life with heart-stoppingly unexpected speed, a snarl that came out of nowhere. I couldn't take in the enormity of its return all at once. I stood for long seconds, staring at the receiver in my hand – as if I'd never seen one in my life before, and the sight fascinated me – but I wasn't aware of looking at it at all. In my mind, the world held nothing but blank, dull surprise fading too quickly, my heartbeat picking up speed like a train leaving the station and heading out into open countryside. A minute passed in slow motion, beginning with shell-shock, ending with raw terror.

Breaking free of hypnosis with a great effort, I hung up, then lifted the receiver again, dialling 1471 with fingers that felt oddly nerveless. A recorded voice came instantly down the line, cool, sweet, reasonable tones somewhere between a Sixties BBC announcer and a Stepford wife. 'You were called today at 12.07, the caller withheld their number,' I hung up again. While I guessed you could probably withhold your number from 1471 checks as easily as you could go ex-directory, my inability to trace it unnerved me even more – I'd been phoned by someone who knew exactly what they were doing. I had a chilling suspicion that they could see every detail of my life, while I could see nothing at all of theirs.

Walking aimlessly into the kitchen, I sat down and lit a cigarette. I inhaled deeply, the book on the table suddenly forgotten. *It could have been a wrong number*, I tried to tell myself, but the idea looked every bit as genuine as an eight-pound note: wrong numbers didn't stay breathing down the receiver for seconds on end, even the rudest would just hang up when they heard an unfamiliar voice. Someone had called me on purpose, and I found myself wishing I couldn't put a name or face to them. Rebecca might have found it terrifying to have an unknown enemy, but I thought this was somehow worse; having a good idea of *who* and *why*, with every other question left uncompromisingly unanswered.

A picture of Mr Wheeler filled my mind, blocking out everything else. Even if he had wounded and ultimately killed Socks, I'd believed, that had been the end of it. He'd had what he must think of as his justified revenge. With the memory of that ragged breathing echoing in my ears, however, I realised there was no way I could know that – he was a stranger to me, and I had no idea what he thought, how his mind worked. I remembered what Liz had said, that he could have known Rebecca for a long time before she'd arrived here. As I sat and worried, my imagination began sketching out an intricate Gothic labyrinth of possible links between them. They could be long-term best friends as well as lovers, blindly devoted to one another – the bond between then could exist on the level of *Wuthering Heights* or *Othello*, those ancient tales of unrestrained passion that, these days, looked disturbingly close to insanity. If he'd loved Rebecca that much, he could well have decided that *an eye for an eye* wasn't justice enough, that he'd have to go further, do more . . .

I was being melodramatic, I told myself sharply. The parallels with what had happened to Rebecca here were nowhere near that close. Still, the sunshine and peace around me felt unbearable. Going back into the living room, I looked out of the window for Liz's car and saw it wasn't there. The telephone's silence had become appallingly heavy and fragile, dominating the entire house with an unspoken threat; it could be broken at any second. I could lift the receiver and hear that breathing again.

How intimate it had sounded. As if the mouth in question had been a fraction of an inch away from my ear. I should have been able to feel that breath, even to smell it. And at the same time, its source had been entirely invisible, untraceable, in another world.

Inevitably, the rest of that day felt tense and strange; the moment in which I'd answered the phone kept replaying itself in my mind. Several times, I found myself longing to call Petra and tell her what had happened, but I knew perfectly well that I couldn't. She'd be at work and busy, I thought, this new event couldn't possibly be discussed in a five-minute catch-up. And there was something else stopping me from dialling her mobile number – a memory of her concerned voice in the spare room, the day before last.

If anything else does happen – not that I think it will – you'll tell him then, won't you?

Of course, she'd expect me to share this turn of events with Carl as soon as he came home from work, she'd advise and even urge me to; it would seem appallingly unnatural to her that I could even think about hiding it from him. But while I couldn't remember ever wanting to tell him about anything so badly, I simply couldn't. I was beginning to realise that the more tangible the threat became, the more culpable *I* became for not telling him about it sooner; the more I had to fear and longed to share with him, the worse our argument would be if I did.

That night, over dinner, I kept drifting towards the edge of confession, then backing away from it as quickly as I could. I tried my very best to speak and behave as if nothing was wrong, but was painfully aware that I wasn't anywhere near that good an actress. Even I could hear the brittle tension in my voice, could feel preoccupation in every line of my face. Reaching for the glass by my plate, my hand felt clumsy and I knocked it to the floor, where it shattered in a small puddle of white wine. '*Damn*,' I said, rising quickly from my seat.

Carl frowned. 'Annie, are you all right?'

'I'm fine – not cut or anything. I'll just get the dustpan and brush.'

'I don't mean the glass. You've been tense as hell all evening. What's happened?'

Again, the urge to tell him everything. I forced it back down hard, reminding myself how much else I'd have to explain. I bent to get the dustpan and brush from under the sink. 'Nothing,' I said quickly, glad he couldn't see my expression, 'it's nothing.'

'It doesn't look like nothing to me. Come on, Annie, you can tell me, you know. Did something go wrong today, while I was at work?'

I was suddenly reminded of the chapter I'd read that morning – Rebecca's blank, monotonous, increasingly perfunctory replies to the court – and I thought I could understand how she must have felt. Denying everything looked completely unconvincing, and I knew it, but it had become my only option. 'Really, I'm fine,' I said decisively, standing up. 'I just feel a bit on edge today. I'm not sure why.'

He looked at me for several seconds. I could see that he knew perfectly well I was lying, and also that he wasn't going to press the subject any further. 'Well,' he said at last, 'if you say so . . .' And his eyes said, *You're obviously not going to tell me about it tonight, it's your decision. But I know you will, when you're ready . . .*

The rest of the evening was full of a strained pretence at normality, as we tried our best to ignore a tension as unmissable as a tree in the living room; neither of us referred to it again, but the pauses in our conversation were far longer and harder to break than usual. When he'd finished in the bathroom and joined me in bed that night, his hand moved to my breast and he kissed me. At first, I tried to respond as if I meant it, longing for anything that could temporarily distract me. But nothing could – all the time, fear was hanging over me like a lead weight from a too-thin rope. 'I'm sorry,' I said, pulling awkwardly away. 'I'm just not in the mood tonight. I'm sure I'll feel better soon.'

His sigh expressed something far deeper than the frustration of an unsatisfied lover – the bewilderment and worry of having no idea what was wrong. 'I wish you'd tell me,' he said quietly. 'What's the matter, I mean. It's so *obvious*, Annie.'

'There's nothing to tell. It's just a funny mood. *Really.*'

We didn't say anything else, just lay together in silence. He went to sleep shortly afterwards. I didn't. Listening to his gentle snoring beside me, I sensed him lost in some placid dream. His unawareness that there was anything in our surroundings to fear suddenly disturbed me. I kept wondering whether he needed to know, whether I owed him absolute honesty in this matter – whether I could be in personal danger, whether my silence could jeopardise his safety as well.

Part of me longed for the right answers, but at the same time, if I could have consulted some omniscient oracle, I was far from sure that I would have done. I'd be too afraid of what I might hear. I thought of a mournful, blood-houndish face above a buttoned-up white vet's coat, a tone that had changed from affability to fury in the blink of an eye. Much later, as I finally began to doze, my mind showed me a grotesque parody of a sentimental greetings card – with loopy italic lettering, cartoon animal staring perkily out: *someone, somewhere is thinking of you now.*

29

The following morning, I felt appallingly tired. After Carl
had left for work I tried to get some sleep, to top up the
three or four hours' oblivion I'd drifted into at some point
during the small hours. But it proved impossible with the
morning light filtering thinly through the drawn curtains,
and the phone on the dressing-table reminding me all
over again why I hadn't been able to sleep in the first
place. Briefly, I toyed with the idea of taking it off the
hook, but a second's thought told me I couldn't – Carl
might try to call, or Petra, and I'd have no way of
explaining to them why I'd done it. Besides, something
altogether more practical prevented me from disabling the
phone; another acquaintance of Melanie's might try to get
in touch with key information on Rebecca, their impulse
to share it fading minutes after they'd heard the dead tone
and hung up.

Finally acknowledging that sleep wasn't going to come,
I got up lead-limbed, showered and dressed quickly before
going downstairs and making myself a much-needed
coffee. As I sat down at the table, my eye was caught again
by *A Mind to Murder*; still lying next to the fruit bowl.

Odd that it should look so obscurely reassuring, so
divorced from my more immediate, personal concerns.
Everything that scared me most had begun with research
and Rebecca, but, far from my coming to fear them, they
were becoming more important to me than ever; while I
couldn't do anything about the disturbing turn that events
had taken, research was something I could understand,

could control. Picking up the book, I studied the cover again. Rebecca's photograph looked darkly fascinating rather than threatening; no matter how hard I tried, I couldn't associate that enigmatic little girl with a cry in the night, a limp bundle of fur on the garden path, ragged breathing down the telephone's receiver yesterday. I turned to the prospect of discovery like a temporary refuge.

Taking my coffee into the living room, I sat down and reached for the phone. Directory enquiries told me that no such place as the Southfield Unit currently existed on the outskirts of Birmingham; a call to Staffordshire County Council reassured me that it was still in business, under the more user-friendly name of Orchard Lodge. I found the change irresistibly reminiscent of A-level Sociology, evolving attitudes and the rise of political correctness summarised in a few short words; Orchard Lodge sounded so ostentatiously cosy, the Southfield Unit bleak, institutional, archaic.

It took a matter of minutes to track the number down. Once dialled, the ringing tone went on for some time before a man answered. I launched into a lead-in speech that had begun to feel as mechanical and vaguely embarrassing as a cold-calling telesales script. 'So I was just wondering if any of your current staff might have worked there in the early 1970s,' I finished, 'if they'd be able to spare ten minutes or so to talk to me. Of course, I understand that you can't give out addresses or phone numbers but, if you do know of anyone, I'd very much appreciate it if you'd pass my number on to them.'

'Come to think of it—' The sound of the receiver being laid down on a nearby surface, a loud, jarring clunk. The distant sound of him calling. 'Martin?'

There was no switch to tinkly music while my credentials and credibility were discussed – muffled, indecipherable sounds said I was being blocked out by the time-honoured method of a hand over the receiver. It stayed that way for a few minutes, before the man's voice came back on the line. 'I'll put you through to Martin Easton. He might be able to help.'

Another ringing tone began as I was transferred, and I could clearly envision Martin Easton hurrying from a central room into a private office. The number of rings implied some distance to travel.

'Hi,' a new voice said at last. 'Hear you're trying to find out about this place when it was the Southfield Unit. When Rebecca Fisher was here.'

While it wasn't exactly a young voice, it was obscurely redolent of youth – quick and sharp with the placeless patois affected by hard-eyed teenagers, a faint echo of *EastEnders* that you heard just as often in Dorset.

'That's right,' I said. 'To be honest, I wasn't really expecting to get someone who worked there in those days, not straight away. *You* didn't, did you?'

'Well, I was here. But not working. On the other side of the fence, you could say.' His laugh matched his voice, good-humoured but brief, alert. 'I was thirteen when Rebecca turned up – I'd been in a lot of trouble for shoplifting, vandalism, you name it. In case you're wondering, I'm a counsellor here these days. You probably wouldn't think so, but it helps when you've been there yourself. They can see you know what you're talking about.'

'I can imagine.' I paused for a second, not quite sure how to say what I wanted to, then ploughed on and said it anyway. 'You must have seen a lot of changes since it was the Southfield Unit.'

'Christ, yeah. The whole culture's changed. It's a different world, these days.'

'In what way?'

'Oh, just the whole way things get done. These days it's all set procedures, rules and regulations coming down from Home Office level. Every young offenders' home in the country has to do things the same way, pass the same inspections and reviews, that sort of thing. Back in the old days, it was nothing like that.'

His voice was slightly, perhaps unconsciously regretful, and I spoke with some curiosity. 'Why not?'

'It's hard to explain . . . it was more personal, back then. The Head of Unit used to set the tone for the whole place, but now they're just figureheads, pretty much, teach a robot the rules and it could do the job. Back then, though, it was all up to them – how the home was run, what the staff were like, what the kids could and couldn't do during the day. I can guess it created a few little Hitlers, that way of working. But our Head of Unit . . . this probably sounds corny, but he was one in a million.'

My silence clearly demanded clarification and he went on, sounding slightly embarrassed, as if trying to cover over clear traces of decades-old hero-worship. 'Tom Hartley, his name was – *is*, he's still alive today. It says a lot about him that he called himself Tom, rather than Thomas, I mean. He hated the kind of divisions you could get in these places, them-and-us, all that kind of shit – said it just led to distrust and bad feelings, the staff all strutting round like the gods of creation and the kids all acting like prisoners-of-war. Equality was one of his pet words. He didn't just pay lip service to it, either. The staff all ate the same food we did, joined in with all the activities, and he always acted like he was just another one of the staff. We were all in it together, the way he saw it, and we all had to do the best we could.'

'He sounds fantastic.' I spoke cautiously, trying to conceal my own misgivings. 'But didn't any of the kids take advantage of that? In a young offenders' home—'

'Oh, Christ, I must be giving you completely the wrong idea of him. I can just see you thinking he sounds like a pussy, he wouldn't have been able to keep order in a *monastery*.' Martin laughed, a healthy, gutsy laugh that said the idea was ridiculous. 'He was a great guy, but he knew what he was doing, all right. He always believed in looking for the best in us kids, but that didn't mean he couldn't see the worst. There were clear-cut rules, and clear-cut punishments if you broke them . . . no cruelty or abuse, just *rules*. Bullying was just about the worst crime you could commit in there, stealing and lying pretty close to that. He cracked down on them so hard that they hardly ever happened. I don't want to make it sound like Sunnybrook Farm, but I think we were all quite happy there.'

'Was Rebecca quite happy there? As far as you could tell?'

'She seemed it. We were only there together for a year. I turned up the year before they shipped her off to the nick: I was twelve, she must have been about fifteen. Still, it was a small unit, about twenty-five kids, so we all knew each other. And she couldn't help standing out a bit, being the only girl. Not to mention a household name.

'It's weird that that's all changed these days. There's about one girl here for every two boys, I suppose it's a positive step towards equal opps. Back then, I heard they didn't even have a separate shower room for girls before Rebecca turned up; they'd never needed one before. Girls just didn't seem to commit so many crimes. And I'm just talking about the kind of shit most of us were in for, vandalism, persistent shoplifting, that kind of thing. I'm not talking about *murder*.'

'She must have been a bit of an oddity,' I said.

'You're not wrong there. I remember when I saw her for the first time – I was having my first supper in the canteen, and she came in on her own. I just couldn't stop staring. She was so notorious, like Jack the Ripper or something – Christ knows what I'd been expecting, horns, a tail, a triple-six tattoo. But she could have been one of my sisters' friends, from home. She could have been anyone.'

'I suppose you recognised her from that old photo,' I said. 'The one where she's wearing school uniform.'

'I don't know – maybe. I think it was mostly just deduction. I'd heard Rebecca Fisher was the only girl in the place, and she was far too young to be one of the staff. Just call me Sherlock Holmes.' I could sense his grin all the way down the line. 'It wasn't that she'd changed, exactly – when you looked closely you could see it was the same person – but the photograph looked so creepy, and she just didn't. If anything, she looked too prim-and-proper for comfort. Good-looking, very, but not the kind of girl we all wanted to go out with in those days. Like a very pretty Head Girl who'd never dream of *kissing* a boy till she was legally married. I couldn't imagine her wearing lipstick, never mind stabbing a little kid to death.'

'How did the others react to her? The other children in the unit?'

'Well, she was never one hundred per cent part of things – she couldn't be, really, not when she was the only girl. But she got a lot of wary respect, being a *killer*. Some of the kids were scared of that and tried to hide it. A few others were impressed, and tried even harder to hide it –

Tom would have *hated* that, if he'd known. She didn't seem to care much either way. She was quiet, polite, kept herself to herself. Not stand-offish, exactly – if you talked to her she'd talk to you, perfectly friendly in a guarded sort of way – but it was next to impossible to know what she really thought about anything. It felt a bit like having an older sister around the place, in a weird sort of way. We always toned it down in the common room when she came in – the jokes, the language, you know the kind of thing. She seemed the sort of girl who'd hate stuff like that.

'I only saw a different side to her once, come to think of it. I must have been there about two months, at the time. There were five or six of us in the common room, me and Rebecca among them, and we were talking about things we'd done before we'd come here, what our families were like, that sort of thing. One of the kids – he could only have been twelve or so, same as me – started saying about all the foster homes he'd been sent to, how much he'd hated most of them, what a bunch of bastards his old foster parents had been. He was a hard little sod, said it all quite matter-of-factly, but it was pretty sad. Rebecca said something sympathetic, like a social worker might have done, I can't remember what it was exactly. And he said, "Well, you must know what that's like and all. You're adopted yourself, I heard it on the news."

'It was frightening, the way she reacted. She went from calm to furious in about two seconds, flew at him like a wildcat. Scratching, punching. The poor kid didn't know what had hit him, and the rest of us just sat there, gobsmacked. "Don't you dare say that again," she shouted, "you don't know anything about my family, they *are* my family, all that on the news was just *lies*," and she was hitting him all the time and he was coming out of shock, trying to defend himself. Then one of the staff came rushing in to see what was going on and separated them. Took them both off to Tom's office. They both got punished equally, so they couldn't have told the truth about what happened. I suppose the kid was too scared to grass her up, after that, and said they'd just been fighting.'

I remembered something from *A Mind to Murder: she never even mentioned that she was adopted,* I'd read, *she always referred to them as Mummy and Daddy.* 'Did she talk about her family a lot?' I asked.

'As much as she ever talked about anything. She saw a hell of a lot of her father – her *adoptive* father – he seemed to visit whenever he could. I saw him a couple of times. Miserable-looking sod, always looked like a pissed-off wage slave on his way to the nine-to-five grind. It was hard to believe he was as rich as everyone said, he certainly didn't look like a millionaire. But he had money, all right. You only had to see the things he sent Rebecca.'

'She got a lot of presents from him?'

'Christ, yeah – seemed like there was a big parcel for her every week. You had to open your mail in public there, so we all got to see the things he sent her. Funny, they weren't the sort of things I'd have thought she'd like: expensive make-up kits, big bottles of Chanel Number Five, things you'd have expected a vain, tarty sort of girl to ask for. Rebecca wasn't that type at all. She seemed delighted to *get* his presents, but I can't remember her ever *using* them.'

A moment's pause before he spoke again, slightly more briskly. 'That's pretty much all I know about her, anyway. Hope it's been some use.'

'You've been terrifically helpful. Thanks a lot,' I said. Then, unable to stop myself, 'you said Tom was still alive, earlier on. I don't suppose you know how I could get in touch with him?'

'Well, I'm still in touch myself. A lot of the kids kept up with him after they left, and he's been like a dad to some of us. I have to say, though, I'm not sure if he'll want to talk to you about Rebecca. He was seventy-two last birthday, and he's not in the best of health. Still, if you give me your number, I'll pass it on to him . . . can't hurt to ask.'

'That'd be great.' I read our number out, could hear the tiny scratching sounds as he wrote it down. 'Anyway, thanks again. Talking to you has been a real eye-opener.'

'Hope it's helped you. Take it easy.'

He hung up. In my mind's eye, I could clearly see him leaving a small office, hurrying back to a noisy recreation room – a game underway at the pool table, a wall-mounted TV going constantly. I went into the kitchen, lit a cigarette, and lost myself deep in thought.

30

The rest of the morning went by slowly. Bringing down my bulging folder of photocopies and print-outs from the spare room, I sat down at the kitchen table and went through them all; tried to clear my mind, to see the separate pieces as if for the first time. I hoped to discover some crucial unifying factor, some common thread that would tie them all together and show me the real Rebecca. But there was nothing. In fact, the sight of them all spread out in front of me made them more contradictory and bewildering than ever, an impenetrable forest of guess-work, opinions and facts. A corner of the St Anthony's school photograph stared out with a dozen black-and-white faces, behind the psychologist's report on Rebecca Jane Sanderson, and the pad of A4 paper where I'd jotted random thoughts down. In the bright sunlight, the picture was somewhere between collage and still-life; *Confusion*, it might be called in an art gallery, or *Frustration*, or, perhaps, *Obsession*.

At about five to three, I was startled by a knock at the back door. Bundling the various documents unceremoniously back into their folder, I shoved it into a convenient cupboard before answering. I'd known it would be Liz, and it was.

'Hello, Anna,' she said amiably. 'Just thought I'd pop round and see how you were . . . you're not busy, are you?'

'Not at all, come on in!' I was delighted to see her, amazed to think I'd once perceived her as self-righteous or judgemental. 'Want some tea?'

'That'd be lovely. White with two sugars, please.'

I put the kettle on, as comfortable with the short silence as I would have been in Petra's company, or Carl's – when I spoke, it was from simple interest rather than fear of seeming awkward. 'So how's it going? Just got in from work?'

'About half an hour ago. I've had a very nice day so far, actually – I got a letter from my elder daughter this morning.' She smiled. 'That's Katie – I'm sure I've told you about her. She's the teacher in Germany.'

I had an image of what Liz must be like as a mother, never preoccupied, never guilty, always *there* – I felt wistful envy surfacing inside me, ready to reveal itself in a flicker of my eyes, a subtle inflection of my voice. I focused on making the tea, tried to speak with matter-of-fact good humour. 'It must have been good to hear from her,' I said. 'How is she?'

'Oh, very well. She's met a nice new man, apparently, another teacher – I do hope he'll turn out to be the one. I'm probably old-fashioned, but she's leaving it quite late to get married.'

'Does she want to?'

Liz looked thoughtful. 'I'm not really sure. You know how it is, I expect, they don't talk to you quite as much when they're all grown up. Maybe she doesn't, come to think of it. Alice was always the more domestic one . . . of course, she's a mother of three now, over in America. Almost two years old now, her youngest. A little boy called Todd.'

'That's nice,' I said. 'It must have been lovely for you to see him.'

'Oh, I haven't, dear – not in the flesh, at least. Of course, I've got plenty of photos. But I haven't been to visit them in nearly five years . . . it's a shame, I know, but it's so hard to find the time to go abroad.'

I was going to ask why they didn't come to Abbots Newton, but a fugitive look in her eyes forced the words back – of course Liz wasn't *that* busy, she was a part-time librarian rather than a managing director. They simply hadn't invited her.

'They're very good about staying in touch, though, considering,' Liz went on quickly. 'They've both been very good daughters to me.'

Something slightly defensive in her voice told me that her own children might see her as nothing more than a tiresome occasional duty. The silence between us grew gradually awkward. When she spoke again, I could sense her trying her best to sound cheerful. 'What about your family, Anna, dear? Do you stay in close touch with your parents?'

'Not really,' I said quietly. 'We're still *in* touch – we send each other Christmas cards and birthday cards and that sort of thing, but that's about all. I haven't seen any of them for a good six years, come to think of it.'

'Oh, I *am* sorry.' Liz's face was a picture of concern. 'Why ever not?'

'It's pretty complicated.' *Go on*, her expression said, *if you don't mind talking about it*. 'My mother had me when she was very young, a teenager – she wasn't married or anything, and I never knew my real father. She married my stepfather when I was two, and they had three more kids. It was always . . . well, a bit difficult. We all tried to pretend I was as much a part of the family as they were, but we knew perfectly well it wasn't true.'

'Didn't you get along with them?'

'My half-brother and sisters?' She nodded. I took a deep breath, trying to translate incoherent emotion into words.

261

'Oh, we didn't argue, not even as much as most kids do; I got on perfectly well with them, on the surface. But it *was* just the surface. They were all so alike, and I ... I just wasn't. They all had brown hair and blue eyes, like my mother and stepfather did, but it wasn't just looks, it was everything about them. Really confident, but not in an obnoxious way. Just outgoing. *Contented.* They were all very nice; everyone liked them. I liked them myself. I couldn't help it.'

I lit a cigarette, hardly aware that I was doing it. 'It made it worse, in a way, that they *were* so nice. I couldn't really get angry or jealous, just *guilty.* I made everything so complicated at home just by being there. I spent most of the time trying to stay out of the way, really. I think that's how I started writing, looking back. There's not a lot else you can do, when you're up in your bedroom on your own. Maybe that's why I'm a bit funny about it these days. When *you* associate something with something else that much, you can't help thinking other people do, as well. I know how paranoid it sounds, but I always think they're going to know too much about me if I talk about my writing. That bedroom. Not wanting to go downstairs. The whole atmosphere, back then ...'

Taking a drag on my cigarette, I found myself speaking slowly, as if putting it into words for the very first time. 'It would be different, I think, if I was successful – people would be too impressed to think all that; they'd just see a big famous name with books in Smiths. But as it is ... well, I've told you before. It goes too far back. It feels wrong.'

'I can understand that.' Liz's voice was quiet, gentle. 'I honestly can. Does your family know you've had a book published?'

'Oh, yes – it's not as if we're estranged exactly; they

know where I'm living now, that I'm married now, what my husband's called and what he does for a living. But they'll never come here, and they'll probably never meet him. We've never talked about it properly – we never *do* talk about things properly – but we all know it's for the best. We just make things awkward for each other. All they want to know is that I'm all right, that I'm happy. That they don't have to feel guilty about me any more. And vice versa.

'Anyway, they're all fine these days, just like I am. It's not like some tragic separation or anything, it's so much easier this way. I always thought it would be. I remember, after my A levels, I deliberately chose the university that was furthest away from them, out of the ones that offered me a place. I thought things might all be different if I was miles away. I thought I'd be free of all that baggage . . .'

It seemed I'd strayed into deep and treacherous waters while drifting with the current of my thoughts, and I floundered clumsily back in the direction of safety. 'But that's all in the past, now,' I said quickly. 'I don't suppose anything like that happened to *you*, growing up?'

'Well, I'm afraid not, dear – if you can say *afraid*, it sounds awfully ungrateful. No, I had a lovely childhood . . . a perfect childhood, if there ever is such a thing. My parents were very close, and I was their only child. I loved them both dearly; I was devastated when they died.' I caught a sudden glint of tears in her eyes, gone almost as soon as I'd noticed it, and when she spoke again, it was with practical resignation. 'Still, I was well into my thirties then, and I dare say it happens to all of us. It doesn't do to think too much about these things.'

An odd silence began, intensified. I sensed we were both feeling exactly the same way, amazed that an initially straightforward conversation could have taken such an unexpected turn. I'd told her far more about myself than I'd ever anticipated telling her, and seemed to have learned far more about her, too.

'So how's your research going, dear?' she asked at last. 'Come across anything interesting?'

It was ironic, I thought, that Rebecca could be seen as a polite retreat, a diplomatic change of subject. 'Quite a few things, actually,' I said. 'I was working on it earlier, come to think of it, just going over some bits and pieces I've tracked down about the case.'

'What sort of things?'

'Oh, print-outs from the internet, photocopies, God knows what – all kinds of things, really.' I'd got so used to claustrophobic secrecy surrounding my research, it was refreshing to encounter genuine, non-judgemental interest, and I had an irresistible urge to share my private treasure-trove with her. 'I'll show you, if you like.'

'Well, if you don't mind – I'd be fascinated to see them.' Going over to the cupboard, I retrieved the overflowing folder, carried it back to the table. 'My goodness,' she said as I opened it, 'you *have* got a lot.'

'It seems to mount up.' I took out the photograph that protruded a good six inches from the folder's top and bottom, set it down in front of her with a kind of wary, proprietorial pride. 'Rebecca's school photograph in 1969,' I said quietly. 'I got it from her old teacher. It's not the original, I just had it copied.'

Watching Liz's face closely, I saw an echo of my own fascination, the mundane glimpse behind the scenes of horror provoking a deep-rooted chill. It was gone almost at once, and she was interested as she would have been in some TV crime drama. 'All those years ago,' she said. 'It does seem strange, looking at it now. Which one's Rebecca? Do you know?'

'Oh, yes. I'll find her for you.' My finger navigated the maze of faces as Annette Watson's had done in Bournemouth, finding the all-important one almost at once. 'That's her, there. And ... let me see, now ... *there's* Eleanor Corbett. The girl she murdered.'

Liz looked, taking in the sunny smile, the curly hair, the diminutive stature. 'The poor little mite,' she said at last. 'What a terrible thing to happen.'

'It *was* terrible.' But I couldn't quite forget what Lucy Fielder had told me last Friday, the details that changed the picture out of all recognition. 'I don't know, though. I've found a few things out about Eleanor, too ... let's just say, she didn't sound quite as nice as she did in the papers.'

'That does sound mysterious.' Liz smiled; her gaze moved away from the photo, and I could feel her attention going with it. 'I just hope it doesn't start frightening you, finding out about all this ... it's quite a disturbing subject, I'd have thought.'

For a second, I was very close to telling her about my sighting of Mr Wheeler and that silent phone call. But I didn't want to see her vicarious horror; it would terrify me all over again.

The knock at the front door came as a relief as well as a surprise, breaking the mood of imminent confessions. 'Wonder who that is?' I said, then, rising from my seat, 'back in a minute.'

As I walked down the hallway, the frosted-glass panel framed a blurred shape that could have been anyone and, opening the door, I only just managed to stop myself taking a sharp breath. It was Helen. Her smile was perfunctory.

'Hello, Anna. I saw Liz's car parked outside, but she's not answering her doorbell – do you know where she is?'

No matter what Liz had told me about this woman, her glacial inscrutability still unnerved me. It didn't seem at all like shyness, although I knew that shyness could manifest itself in any number of ways. I found it ridiculously difficult to reply confidently, fearlessly. 'She's in the kitchen – come on through. Would you like a cup of tea?'

'No, thank you. I can't stay.'

I hurried back through the hallway, very aware of her silent presence immediately behind me. In these familiar surroundings, she seemed more alien and intimidating than ever. 'Liz,' I called as we approached the kitchen, 'you've got a visitor.'

We came into the room and Liz looked round, smiling. 'Oh, hello, Helen. Were you looking for me next door?'

Helen nodded. 'I was just passing, and thought I'd check if you were coming to the WI meeting tonight. I spoke to Muriel this morning. She can't make it, and . . .'

Her words blurred around me as my attention focused on the table. The contents of my Rebecca Fisher file were still spread out on it, the school photograph staring up at us. Somehow, I didn't want Helen to see it there; it seemed private. 'Well, I'm certainly going,' Liz was saying amiably. 'I'll have to call round on poor Muriel tomorrow morning. I do hope she feels better soon.'

'It's just a summer cold. Nothing to worry about.' With dismay, I saw Helen's gaze moving to the cluttered table. She took a step closer towards it, and looked at the photograph directly. 'That looks very old. Is it yours, Anna?'

I nodded, dreading Liz explaining its history and its significance, but she showed no sign of doing so. Helen's scrutiny left the picture and returned to me. 'How's your book going?'

'Oh, I – I'm still researching it,' I said quickly. 'I've got a lot more to find out before I make a start.'

She nodded, without apparent interest, and I couldn't help but be relieved to see her take a step back towards the door. 'I'll be off, then,' she said. 'See you tonight, Liz.'

Helen seemed perfectly happy to show herself out, but I followed her to the front door all the same. Returning to the kitchen, I reminded myself that I had nothing to fear from *her* direction. And I tried to persuade myself that the phone call itself had been nothing to lose sleep over, either – a dirty old man trawling the directory at random, some kids doing the same thing in the name of primary-school humour. Nothing to do with the random coincidence of Socks' death. Nothing to do with me.

31

Over the next couple of days, more and more of my conscious mind defected to join that pragmatic *nothing-to-worry-about* faction; still, the other side seemed to have all the real power. While the raw terror of Monday night had faded, I was still decidedly edgy in the evenings, and had considerable trouble getting to sleep before the small hours. And the tension got far worse when Carl wasn't there; days when the only car outside was my own, and it was too hot to close the windows, and there was nothing beyond them but miles of deserted summer.

On Friday morning, I was vacuuming the hallway when the phone rang. I turned the Hoover off, and its thin whine died abruptly round the insistent trilling, punctuated by long seconds of silence. It was the most everyday sound imaginable, but had taken on an ominous significance; I stood stock-still and listened to it ring, and it seemed to get a little louder every time it did.

I couldn't just *ignore* it, I told myself sharply – it could be Petra or Carl or anyone. I hurried into the living room, racing to lift the receiver before I could think better of it.

'Hello?'

In the micro-second's pause that followed, I clearly heard an unknown enemy breathing in before breathing out. Then the voice came down the line. 'Hello, is that Miss Anna Jeffreys?'

'Speaking,' I said cautiously.

'Oh, good morning. My name's Tom Hartley. Martin Easton from Orchard Lodge passed on your number to me yesterday, and told me you were researching a book based on Rebecca Fisher. So I thought I'd get in touch. I'm retired now, as Martin probably told you, and I'd be happy to help you with your enquiries.'

The elderly male voice was well-spoken, but not ostentatiously plummy – kindly, level, unemotional. I remembered the first impression I'd got of this man from Martin: a rather naive trendy-vicar type, all hand-knitted jumpers and trusting smiles. I'd known I'd misinterpreted him, but not how badly. He sounded anything but unworldly or impressionable; I could imagine him being nakedly contemptuous of politically-correct bandwagons, of anything at odds with old-fashioned common sense. 'I knew Rebecca fairly well,' he went on. 'I was the manager of the Southfield Unit for all the years she was there, so I dare say that was inevitable. It was very strange, meeting her for the first time. I can still remember that quite clearly.'

The question kept coming back, in various contexts and tones, seeming to echo down the last three weeks of my life: 'What did you think of her?'

'It's difficult to say, exactly.' He hesitated. 'I'd been working with young offenders long enough to know that they weren't *demons* – quite often, they'd simply had a bad beginning in life – so I didn't have the same preconceptions of her as many people might have done. Still, even by the unit's standards, she was a very exceptional case. I couldn't help expecting someone a little more obviously troubled.'

'In what way?'

'Oh, any number of ways. Very withdrawn, or actively hostile, or unusually nervous. But when Rebecca first arrived and one of the counsellors showed her into my office, she seemed remarkably well-balanced for a child of ten, especially one who'd recently been through such a high-profile court case. Very polite, very attentive, very self-possessed. I couldn't help thinking that was a little unnatural in itself; she seemed ten years old going on thirty. You had to keep reminding yourself what she'd done, when you met her . . . it was very easy to forget it completely.

'At the time, I couldn't help suspecting that she was simply a very precocious little actress, keen to make the right first impression. I thought she could well turn out to be the worst kind of troublemaker, the secretive, devious kind. But, as she settled in, I began to realise that I'd been wrong. None of the counsellors could find a bad word to say about her; they talked about her as if she was a little saint rather than a murderess. More than one of them used to say in private, "If only they could all be like Rebecca."'

'How did she get on with the other children there,' I asked, 'when she first arrived?'

'Surprisingly well from the start, as a matter of fact. I must say, we'd all been prepared for some trouble, at least for the first few months – bullying was severely punished in the unit, but when you live in the real world you know you can never stamp it out completely. Rebecca seemed a natural target for that kind of thing, partly because she was the only girl, but mainly because she was the kind of child that she *was*. I believe there's good in most people, if you look deeply enough, but with some of our young offenders, you had to look very deeply indeed. Tough little hooligans, a few of them were, almost uncontrollable before they arrived. And, as I've said, Rebecca could have been a school prefect.

'But she seemed to blend in immediately, in a funny sort of way. Not as if she was trying, either. If she'd tried to take on the more deprived children's mannerisms and street slang, she'd have stuck out like a sore thumb . . . but she didn't do any of that, just kept herself to herself, talked and behaved as she had done to begin with. She found a place for herself in the day-to-day life of the place very quickly. Not part of the general rough-and-tumble – as the only girl, she could never have been *that* even if she'd been as tough as old boots – just accepted as someone who was supposed to be there. Always slightly removed from it all, but very far from a pariah.'

It was odd, I thought, that she seemed to have blended in far better there than she'd done at St Anthony's. In an odd sort of way, I could imagine her status as the unit's sole female and killer making her more confident, legitimising loneliness in her mind. It wasn't personal any more; nobody in her circumstances would have been treated any differently. 'It sounds as if she did pretty well there,' I said.

'She certainly did. In the five years she spent at the unit, I can only remember her getting into trouble once – fighting with one of the boys, apparently, some silly argument in the common room. God alone knows what he must have done to provoke her. She always seemed the most even-tempered of people. In terms of her school lessons, she always did well enough, but nothing out of the ordinary – she was a very old-fashioned sort of girl in that respect, much more interested in Home Economics than any of her other subjects. A proper little housewife in the making. I heard that she kept the tidiest room in the place . . . it was better-decorated than the others, too. Her adoptive father was always sending her little bits and pieces for it when she first arrived, and there was no earthly reason not to let her keep them.'

'I heard he visited her whenever he could,' I said. 'She must have looked forward to him coming.'

A few seconds' dubious silence before he spoke again. 'Well, she certainly seemed to on the surface. She talked about him a great deal, how close they were and how much she missed him. She seemed to have been devoted to her adoptive mother as well; whenever she mentioned her, you could see how upset she was about her death. But I'm not sure she actually enjoyed her father's visits all that much ... I think she preferred the anticipation to the reality of him turning up.'

'What makes you say that?' I asked curiously.

'Seeing them together at visiting times, I suppose. All the visits took place in a specific room with four or five tables, slightly less formal than in a prison, but much the same kind of thing. Sometimes one of the counsellors supervised it, sometimes I did. We didn't interfere, just kept our distance, made sure nothing was being handed over that shouldn't have been.

'I didn't watch Rebecca and her adoptive father, but I couldn't help noticing how different they looked from the groups at the other tables. Most of them sat chatting nineteen-to-the-dozen, as if they couldn't possibly stay long enough, but there was never anything like that at their table; it always looked very uncomfortable. As if they didn't really have much to say to each other, but had to say something for the sake of politeness. You certainly wouldn't have thought you were looking at a father and daughter who loved each other dearly ... if anything, you'd have guessed they were distant relatives. Ones who didn't like each other a great deal, at that.

'She always seemed in rather a strange mood for a few days after he'd been. Slightly more jumpy than usual, unsettled. It was hard to tell, really it was almost impossible to know what she was thinking at any given time. But I got the impression that his visits put her on edge.'

'Did you ever talk to him yourself?' He murmured brief assent. 'What did you make of him?'

'I can't say I took to him. He seemed a very joyless and unemotional sort of man, no sense of humour at all, as far as I could tell. I don't mean that he wasn't some laugh-a-minute joker, although he certainly wasn't – he just didn't seem to have any natural cheerfulness or any real warmth. He was an extremely successful businessman and, when you talked to him, you could tell he was highly intelligent ... but I don't think he took any pleasure in his wealth or brains, either. Not depressive or melancholic, just *blank*, in a way that's hard to define. I couldn't imagine him truly bonding with any child in the world, or vice versa.

'Perhaps that's unfair. He obviously cared about Rebecca very deeply – a lot of *natural* fathers would have distanced themselves from a convicted murderess, and he went out of his way to see her as often as he could. Still, Rebecca always seemed very much more at ease with my own family than she ever did with him.'

I frowned. 'How did she know your family?'

'My job certainly wasn't the kind you could leave at the door when the day ended – my wife and eldest daughter tended to get involved in the unit as well, even though they weren't officially staff members. Occasionally, we'd arrange small group outings for a few of the children, on weekends and bank holidays and the like, quite informal. The outings were something of a reward for good behaviour, although that was never explicit. It was simply a matter of who we could trust to behave themselves.

'After Rebecca had been with us for a few months, it was quite clear that we could trust *her*, and she nearly always came along. Sometimes she'd go on her own with my wife and daughter. My daughter was in her early twenties at the time, and we all felt it would be good for Rebecca to spend more time with women. They'd take her to the cinema, or for lunch in a cafe, or something like that. Of course, they kept a close eye on her, but it was obvious that she wouldn't try to escape. And she certainly didn't pose any danger to the public.

'My wife and daughter liked her very much. It was so easy to forget what she'd done when you got to know her, and they couldn't quite believe she was the same girl they'd read about in the newspapers. She was at the unit far longer than most of the children, so they built up quite a friendship over the years. We had her for dinner in our own home several times, before she moved on to prison at the age of sixteen. Even after that, we stayed in contact. We still send her Christmas cards, letters and family photographs once or twice a year – through a P.O. Box, naturally, her new identity's a secret to everyone, including ourselves. She always writes back. Of course, I can't discuss her letters, but she seems to have built a happy life for herself.'

I remembered the letter I'd found in the spare room's cupboard, and wondered if *Dear Penny* had been this man's wife or daughter. I knew I couldn't possibly ask. Everything about their correspondence screamed *strictly confidential*.

'We all thought that would happen, when she grew up,' he went on. 'There was no question that she'd ever offend again. Well, there was one dissenting voice at the time . . . but the years have proved him wrong, I'm very pleased to say.'

'Who was that?' I asked, startled.

'Oh, some junior psychiatrist from the local authority – Donald Hargreaves, his name was. He came into the unit to talk to her once a month from the day she arrived, and that went up to once a week in the year leading up to her leaving us. There was some debate as to whether she should be sent to the low-security prison I'd recommended, or an altogether more secure one, hence his increased visits.

'Maybe she told him more than she ever told the rest of us – the final decision had nothing to do with me, so I never got to see his findings in any detail. I do know that he was adamant she should go to the highest-security institution possible. His report was overruled by the powers that be, I'm glad to say, so it couldn't have been all that conclusive. Still, misguided or not, he certainly believed in it himself – he actually resigned from the local authority over the issue, I heard shortly afterwards.'

'My God,' I said slowly. 'What did you say his name was?'

'Donald Hargreaves.' I jotted it down quickly on the phone pad. 'Well,' he said pleasantly, 'that's very much where my knowledge of Rebecca ends. It feels rather strange, remembering it all again . . . I hope it's been some help to you in your research.'

'It certainly has,' I said. 'I can't thank you enough for calling – you've cast an awful lot of light on things for me.'

Off the phone, I hurried up to the spare room, sat down at the computer and did a search on Google for Donald Hargreaves, lighting a cigarette absently. Pressing Enter, I waited for a couple of seconds, feeling my heartbeat loud and fast in my ears.

Two results. The first was a listing from the British Medical Council; a name in a long column of names, informing the reader that Donald Hargreaves was a registered psychiatrist. The second was an article on autism, dry as old leaves, from a mental health publication I'd never heard of. A small photograph at the top showed a middle-aged man with shrewd dark eyes and a neatly clipped black beard; a few lines were written beneath it, in italics. *Dr Donald Hargreaves has been a practising psychiatrist for thirty-eight years. He is currently affiliated to the South London and Maudesley Healthcare Trust, where he works as a consultant in the Ashwell Unit.*

I checked the date at the bottom of the article. It had been posted three weeks ago.

32

It was easy to get the number I wanted. After I'd dialled it, a receptionist answered almost instantly. 'Ashwell Unit. How can I help you?'

'May I speak to Dr Donald Hargreaves, please?'

I'd anticipated further questions, but none came – it seemed that public sector psychiatrists were less well-guarded than Heads of Services. A new ringing tone began, continued for some time before a male voice came on the line.

'Don Hargreaves.'

'Oh, hello. I wonder if you might be able to help me. My name's Anna Jeffreys, and . . .'

The familiar speech again. He didn't speak immediately after I'd finished, and embarrassment kept me talking. 'Of course, I understand if that kind of information's confidential. But, if you *were* able to discuss it with me—'

'Don't alarm yourself, Miss Fisher's new identity leaves all that side of things null and void.' Another silence; he seemed entirely comfortable with it. 'I'd be happy to discuss the case with you, as it happens. I could spare roughly an hour, at a prearranged time. When would be a convenient date for you to come to the unit?'

I'd initially anticipated an interview over the phone, was about to say so when something held the words back. Every instinct I had told me this man knew more about Rebecca than the rest of my sources put together and, even at this early stage, I found him difficult to talk to over the phone. A face to face meeting could make all the difference, could unlock some crucial discovery. 'Well,' I said, 'the sooner the better, to be honest. Is there any chance that I could interview you next week?'

Another silence. 'How does next Tuesday sound? Shall we say two o'clock?'

'That sounds fine. Thanks very much,' I said. 'Could I have the address of your unit?'

He read it out, and I wrote it down carefully. 'The nearest tube station's Balham, if you're not driving,' he said. 'I'll look forward to seeing you then.'

The hours passed slowly – I finished off the hoovering with anticipation churning inside me. My mental image of Rebecca had been blurred and shadowy for so long, I'd begun to think it would never alter. But suddenly I felt the picture sharpening, the sheer speed of the change inspiring something close to vertigo. Specific details of the South-field Unit seemed to bring her to life, lending her that crucial third dimension that had previously been so elusive; for the first time, I could see her clearly in the context of different settings. Tense silences over a table in the visiting room, cinema trips with Tom's wife and eldest daughter, that oddly incongruous fight in the unit's common room. Imagining her in those places, I was startled to feel her becoming as real as anyone I'd ever known, as real as she'd been four months ago, when she'd shown us round this house.

I wondered what Donald Hargreaves had known about her, or thought he'd known. Whatever it was, he'd ultimately resigned over it and, from our brief conversa-tion, he hadn't seemed the hysterical over-imaginative type at all. He must, I understood, have seen a completely different side to her, far beyond the girl Martin and Tom had both described – that demurely feminine, politely amenable housewife-in-the-making, fond of home economics and keeping a tidy room. Whatever else he'd seen, it had been disturbing, invisible to the naked eye. Potentially dangerous.

I wondered if she'd told him anything about her relationship with her adoptive parents. As she grew clearer in my mind, that side of her life became more tangled and ambiguous than ever. From Tom's descriptions and Martin's comments, I'd built a vivid picture of Dennis Fisher, but I knew it couldn't even be close to accurate – the man I envisioned would have severed all links with Rebecca the second that the police arrived to arrest her, and scandal threatened. Long before a community turned against him by sheer power of association, before his factory was petrol-bombed by residents hell-bent on a blurred and incoherent revenge. The man I envisioned would have no genuine love for anyone in the world.

Even his wife, Rita. The minor heiress he might and might not have married for her money, whose every possession expressed naked longing for a beauty she'd never had herself. Brittle, snobbish Rita, utterly oblivious to other people's feelings. This was the same woman who'd adopted a five-year-old with utter selflessness, denying herself the beguiling maternal illusion of a brand-new baby. Who'd gone out of her way to give Rebecca the perfect childhood, who'd loved her so much that she'd committed suicide two days after the verdict was announced . . .

It was all wrong, maddeningly wrong. I seemed to be thinking about two completely different couples; it was like trying to solve a jigsaw, not knowing that half the pieces came from another box. Next Tuesday, I told myself, the answers might all come at once. I could see the truth at last, tiny in the distance, moving inexorably closer as I watched.

'I've made us a chicken salad for dinner,' I said to Carl as he came in that night. 'I thought it'd make a nice change.'

'That's great. I've had a nightmare of a day at work. I'll just go and slip into something more comfortable, be down in a minute.'

At the kitchen table, he discussed his colleagues and the events of the day. It all seemed strangely unreal to me, somehow, as if Rebecca and the people surrounding her were draining colour and depth from the present. They leapt out in vivid technicolour, whereas the world he described looked greyish, hazy, dreamlike. 'So Roger was going to complain to the MD,' he was saying, 'but I managed to talk him out of it. It would have been a bad mistake for *him*, more than anything else. That sort of thing never looks good on a store manager's CV.'

'Well ... that's good.' I struggled to conceal my alienation from his story, to maintain a pleasant house-wifely facade. 'I'm sure that was the right thing to do.'

'I hope so. Anyway, it seems to be okay now – when I talked to him this afternoon, he said it had pretty much sorted itself out. From where I stand, it looks like—'

The phone started ringing in the living room, and he broke off. Thinking of Tom Hartley and Lucy Fielder, I willed myself not to move a muscle, not to let my expression change. 'Want to get it?' I asked.

'Sure. Back in a minute.'

Rising from his seat, he walked out. 'Hello?' I heard him saying, then, slightly more irritably, '*Hello?*' Then he was hanging up, came back into the kitchen shrugging. 'Wrong number, apparently. They just put the phone down a second or so after I answered. No bloody manners, whoever it was.'

Foreboding stabbed me hard in the chest – I'd been superstitiously convinced it could never happen in the evenings when he was here, was equally convinced it just had done. If I'd answered, I thought, I'd have heard that ragged breathing for a second time. I became aware he was looking at me strangely.

'What the *hell* is the matter?' he asked abruptly.

I took a mental step back, as if threatened all over again. 'What do you mean?'

'Look, just *stop* it, Annie. You know exactly what I mean.' His voice was full of frustration and concern, reaching boiling point together to create anger. 'You've been a different person for the past week or so, maybe even longer than that. I know you, I'm your husband, I can see when things aren't right. I kept thinking you'd tell me on your own sooner or later, but this is getting beyond a joke – trying to pretend everything's fine, when I can see in your eyes that it isn't at all. Do you honestly think I haven't noticed how you've been acting lately?'

His too-serious expression belonged nowhere but a boss's office – I felt as if I'd been called in for a formal warning on a routine day, and a nightmare out-of-nowhere feeling plummeted my stomach ten floors down. I'd thought I'd been hiding my preoccupation expertly all week.

'It's this research of yours,' he went on forcefully, 'I'm sure of it. Just because you haven't been talking about it recently, it doesn't mean I've forgotten. It seems like it's really getting to you, Annie, it's not doing you any good. I think you should draw a line under it. Forget about it. Start the book with what you've already got, for your own sake.'

The distress in his voice frightened me more than the silent phone calls had done. I remembered his mother's too-solicitous kindness on the rare occasions we'd met, as if I were something that had been broken and mended and still needed to be handled with the utmost care. Fear made me aggressive as if in self-defence; all he knew of that time was what I'd told him, I urged myself, and he had no idea what the reality had been like. 'It's *not* the research,' I said hotly. 'For the last time, I'm *fine*. Why can't you just accept that?'

The flat contradiction effectively stalemated our argument; there was nowhere else it could go without meandering into the endless desert of *are not, am too*. Seeing the knowledge in his eyes, I felt the full weight of his love and helplessness, and forced myself to speak again, more gently. 'I'm just about finished with the research, anyway. There's nothing to worry about, Carl. Honestly.'

The rest of our evening passed in a quiet, resigned atmosphere of mutual denial. Over dinner, it occurred to me that I hadn't told him about my imminent trip to London, my interview with Donald Hargreaves on Tuesday. I certainly couldn't tell him now, when his distrust of anything to do with my research was palpable. I'd leave soon after he'd gone to work, I told myself, and should be home a good hour or so before he returned. Enforced secrecy pressed in around me, tight and hot and claustrophobic. As we sat and watched television, random images from the screen took on the disturbing quality of omens: flickering rain through a car window, a wax-white hand unearthed from black soil, dirty-yellow police tape flapping in a hard wind.

Our smouldering truce with the subject continued all that night and throughout Saturday, while I tried my hardest to *be myself*, the silent phone calls were a constant, niggling distraction at the back of my mind. I wondered if and when a third would come. A growing urge to tell Petra about it began to take hold of me – she knew at least some of the background, would be able to see it in context and advise me accordingly. But there was no privacy to do so on Saturday; I couldn't possibly risk Carl overhearing our conversation, and we were together all the time.

On Sunday afternoon, however, he went out to mow the back garden. I hurried upstairs seconds after the deafening, high-pitched whine began, into our bedroom, towards the phone. While the lawnmower's noise was muted in this room, I could still hear it clearly, would be ready to make a quick plausible excuse and hang up the second it stopped. I pressed out her mobile number quickly, praying she'd be free to talk.

She was. 'Anna, great to hear from you! I just got back from my parents' house. How's it going?'

'Well . . .' My voice tailed off uncertainly. 'I'm a bit worried, to be honest. That's really why I'm calling. You know what we talked about, when you were here – that vet, and Liz's cat dying, and all the rest of it?'

I could sense her sudden alertness all the way down the line. 'What's happened now?' she asked sharply.

From the back garden the lawnmower droned on, insect-like. It hit me that I couldn't possibly tell her about the first phone call, the breathing, the terror. She'd demand to know why I hadn't told her before, and worse, why I hadn't told Carl. 'Last night . . . we got a weird phone call,' I said. 'Carl picked it up. There was just dead silence for a couple of seconds, then someone hung up.'

I fell silent. An expectant pause continued for several seconds. 'And?' she asked at last.

'That's it.' Realising how anticlimactic it sounded, I

found myself faced with an insoluble problem – making her realise its importance, while leaving out any reference to its forerunner. 'Of course, Carl thought it was just a wrong number, but I'm really not sure. He doesn't know about Mr Wheeler and all that; I do. I keep thinking it might have been him, trying to scare me . . .'

Another pause. When she spoke again, I caught a chilling echo of Carl's own voice, a wary note that tried and failed to conceal itself behind pragmatism. 'Anna . . . I don't think you've got anything to worry about there. It probably *was* just a wrong number. Why would Mr Wheeler want to do something like that?'

I felt horribly wrong-footed – she'd been the prophet of doom last Saturday, had suddenly turned into the spokeswoman for hard reason. 'Why would he want to hurt Socks?' I demanded. 'Why would he want to *kill* Socks, come to that? You were perfectly prepared to believe he'd done all that.'

'Oh, I was probably just being stupid. It scared me at the time, but I think just about anything would have done after you told me about Rebecca Fisher. It does pretty weird things to the nerves, thinking a psychopath was in a house before you.' Even in the grip of disbelief, I was about to correct her on the word – Rebecca had been no psychopath, whatever else she was – but then she spoke again, sounding sheepish and slightly guilty. 'If I freaked you out about it, I'm really sorry – you were right, Anna, I was wrong. Like you said, he's a vet, there's no way on earth he'd have done those things.'

It felt like betrayal, as if she'd bailed neatly out of this disturbing situation, leaving me entirely alone in it. 'So don't worry about it,' she went on soothingly. 'Especially not that phone call. Jesus, it was just a wrong number – no need to lose sleep over *that*.'

'I suppose not.' Suddenly, her voice seemed to have come from a very long way away. I spoke to reassure her, as if she was a psychiatrist with the power to classify me sane or otherwise. 'I'm sure you're right, come to think of it – I overreacted badly. I'm feeling quite embarrassed. I'm a bit jumpy about that whole Rebecca Fisher thing, as well ... thinking she used to live here, and everything.'

'I can't blame you for that. Still, it's such a gorgeous house – even if it *was* Rebecca Fisher's, you got a good bargain.' She laughed, and I tried my hardest to join in. 'By the way, how's the research going?'

'Not bad. I'm definitely getting there. Slowly but surely.' The steady background noise of the lawnmower snapped into sudden silence behind me and I spoke quickly. 'Listen, got to run – there's someone at the door. Thanks for calming me down.'

'Any time. You're welcome.'

I hurried downstairs. Through the open back door, I could see Carl lugging the lawnmower back into the shed. The sweet, sleepy smell of fresh-cut grass hung heavily. Watching him from the kitchen, an icy hand gripped my heart. For the first time in almost ten years, I felt alone.

33

In an astonishingly short time, Liz had become very important to me. Perhaps it was partly by default, as the most crucial things in my life couldn't be shared with Carl or Petra. But there was far more to it than that. A new element seemed to have entered our relationship, something vaguely parental that I knew she'd be as embarrassed to acknowledge as I would – indulgent and protective on her side, considerate and slightly deferential on mine. As if each of us was becoming what we knew the other missed most.

Hanging out some clothes to dry on Monday morning, I saw her gardening across the fence. 'Morning, Liz,' I called, 'how's it going?'

'Hello, Anna, dear – another lovely day. I'm not sure all my plants like the heat as much as I do, but I know I shouldn't grumble.' She smiled, setting her watering can down on the grass. 'What are you up to today? More research?'

'Not today. I'm off to London tomorrow, interviewing a psychiatrist who treated Rebecca in the young offenders' home; I've got a feeling he'll have a lot to say.' I suddenly envisioned a casual, chance exchange between Liz and Carl in the front garden. 'I'd really appreciate it if you didn't mention that to Carl. It's a bit complicated, but I haven't told him. He's not that wild about me spending so much time with the research, and I thought it'd be best if he didn't know.'

'Don't worry, I understand perfectly. Not a word.' Her

voice was cheery, creating a wonderful illusion of light-heartedness – secrecy took on the temporary feel of harmless mischief, St Trinian's rather than John le Carré. 'I do hope it all goes well.'

'Thanks,' I said, 'fingers crossed.'

'I'm sure he'll have no end of things to tell you.' She paused for a second, listening out. 'Isn't that your phone?'

'It is – damn. See you later. Do pop round for a coffee this afternoon, if you're free.'

After the dazzling sunlight, the inside of the house took on an odd blueish edge. I hurried towards the phone with far less trepidation than I'd have felt if Liz had been at work. Her presence outside seemed comforting, as if no true threat could co-exist with her watering her plants; lifting the receiver, I felt only a second's fear. 'Hello?'

'Hello, is that Anna Jeffreys?'

An elderly male voice, cracked, quavery, uncertain – a voice I was ninety per cent certain I'd never heard in my life. 'Speaking,' I said, 'can I help you?'

'I thought *I* might be able to help *you*. I heard you were writing a book about Rebecca Fisher, and you were researching it. Is that true?'

Actually, it's just loosely based on her, it's not true crime – I slammed the brakes on that sentence just in time. This man sounded nervous, as though he was talking with a gun to his head; I found it too easy to imagine the abrupt apology, the severed connection. 'It is,' I said. 'Did you know her?'

'Not her. The couple who adopted her ... Rita and Dennis Fisher.' I heard him take a long, shuddering breath. 'I can't give my name, or anything like that. My family mustn't know I've talked to you about this. I've never told them anything about it.'

I felt utterly alert, agonisingly cautious, like a butterfly collector sighting the rarest of rare species on the edge of a leaf, trembling with the threat of imminent flight. The world had contracted to a single necessity: not to startle, to proceed slowly while my instincts screamed at me to rush. 'That's not a problem,' I said quietly, 'anything you tell me is in the strictest confidence. You don't have to worry about that at all.'

A moment's pause, tense as an elastic band stretched almost to breaking-point – I saw the wings stir again, edged closer with my heart in my mouth. 'How did you know the Fishers?' I asked.

'I was their gardener for nearly two years. Before they adopted Rebecca,' he said. 'I left some time before they took her in.'

I still had no idea why he seemed so desperate for secrecy, and struggled to suppress my own curiosity on the subject, hunting for an innocuous, factual question. 'Why did you leave?'

'It's a long story.' A second inhalation; tense, resigned, purposeful, as though he was on the brink of something he dreaded but had to do. 'The *whole* story, really . . . but I suppose I'll have to start at the beginning. I was eighteen when I went for the job. I didn't actually expect to get it. I knew I'd be up against a lot more experienced men, but it didn't stop me. I'd been out of work for a good five months and, well, I was living at home . . . money was tight, and it made things difficult for all of us that I wasn't bringing in a wage of my own. I'd heard that the Fishers paid well, and the job came with accommodation, a little gardener's cottage. Nothing fancy, but I'd just about have killed for it, at the time. Just to get out from under Mum and Dad's feet. You know.'

'I can imagine.' I could, only too well – I'd stopped worrying that he was about to hang up unexpectedly, and the edge of caution had left my voice, unnoticed. 'So your interview went well?'

'It did. It was very strange, as a matter of fact. I'd expected their housekeeper would deal with all that sort of thing, but the first time I went there I didn't even see her. Dennis Fisher showed me in himself. Interviewed me himself, in the living room. The house struck me as odd, too ... at the time, I thought I was just ignorant, that I didn't know what rich people's houses were supposed to look like. But, thinking back, it still looks wrong to me. Big and plain as a box from the outside, no fancy touches at all. Inside, though, it was a different story – frills and flounces everywhere, lacy curtains, everything done in pastel colours. Like it was two different houses, rolled into one.

'The interview took much longer than I'd expected – you'd have thought Mr Fisher was looking for someone to manage his factory, not a gardener. He didn't seem to just be interested in what I could and couldn't do, he was trying to decide what sort of person I was. There was one particular question I remember him asking: "What does confidentiality mean to you?" I haven't got the least idea what I said, I was so nervous. But I suppose it must have been the right answer, looking back.'

'Had you met Dennis Fisher before then?' I asked.

'Oh, no. Everyone knew who the Fishers were, but they weren't prominent in the community at all. Kept themselves to themselves, everyone said. We all guessed they'd mix with wealthy families in other towns; they were really the only one in Teasford. And their house was so remote, nobody saw much of their comings and goings. Of course, the people who worked at Mr Fisher's textiles factory – my mum was one of them – saw him now and then, but he didn't have anything to do with the staff from day to day.

He certainly wasn't the kind of employer who treated his business like a family, for all it was so important to him.'

'So what did you think of him?' I asked curiously. 'When you met him for the first time?'

'I was a bit overawed, like I was with the house. Anything that struck me as odd, I told myself I didn't know any better; it was just what posh businessmen were like. But if he'd just been a workmate of my dad's, I'd have thought he was a cold bit of work. Hardly ever smiled, and even when he did it was like he was making an effort, like he knew he was *supposed* to smile sometimes, to put me at my ease. And he didn't look like I'd expected him to, either. Thin man, he was, forty or so, thick glasses, dark hair. Neatly dressed, but in the same way a town clerk might have been. I'd heard about rich men getting their suits made specially for them, but I couldn't imagine Mr Fisher doing that. I knew next door to nothing about tailoring, and even I could tell his was off-the-rack. He didn't have a big gold watch or gold cufflinks, either, nothing that you'd have expected. He just looked ordinary.'

It was perfectly in keeping with everything I'd heard about Dennis Fisher so far – I felt my mental image of him set and harden like clay.

'Still, I was more than happy to work for him,' the old man went on quietly. 'He seemed as though he'd be a good employer – fair, decent, not the sort of man who'd make ridiculous demands and throw his weight around all the time. When the letter came to tell me I'd got the job, I was over the moon. I think my mum and dad were, as well. We had a bit of a celebration that night, and I moved my things into the gardener's cottage the week after.'

'How did you take to working there?'

'Like a duck to water – at least, I did at first. My duties

were all perfectly straightforward, just keeping the grass short and trimming the bushes back regularly. The gardens had to be kept pin-neat, but were just as plain as the house was from the outside. Not a flower in sight, apart from the daisies and dandelions I had to get rid of. The sort of job you dream of, when it comes with good money and your own cottage. The housekeeper was a nice lady, as well, a widow in her sixties. She had part of the house to herself, but I saw quite a lot of her coming and going – we talked in a friendly sort of way for the first month or so, very much on the surface. About the weather and the area and suchlike, you know the kind of thing. It would all have been as easy as pie. If it hadn't been for Mrs Fisher, anyway.'

'Why?' I asked, startled. 'What did she do?'

'Not very much, to begin with. She called round at the cottage on my second day – I'd say *popped* round, but it was much more formal than that. She was very gracious, in a distant sort of way – a patronising way, I'd say now, looking back. I daresay I'd think it quite offensive today, the way she carried on. She actually said, "This must all be very new to you," meaning the cottage, as though I'd never been anywhere clean and tidy with running water before – like some grand Victorian lady visiting the workhouse. She was dressed like she was off to some big society event, dripping with jewellery at half-eleven in the morning – hair all swept up, made up to the nines.' A brief, reflective silence. 'It's funny that I thought she was so glamorous. If I'd seen her in ordinary clothes down the pub, I'd have thought she looked like the back end of a bus. But I suppose you're impressionable at that age, when you've lived in a shabby little terrace all your life. When she left, I was quite disappointed she'd gone – a real lady, I thought she was.

'Anyway, I didn't think about her much for the next few weeks. I hardly ever saw her coming and going, and didn't have any reason to go into the house. Then, one day, I'd just started trimming back the bushes by the front windows, when I heard voices coming from inside. I couldn't make out what they were saying, but I could tell that they were angry. Furious. One of them was Mrs Fisher's. I couldn't place the second.

'I had no idea what to do – Mr Fisher was at work, and I'd seen the housekeeper leaving for the shops a good hour ago. I didn't want to interfere, far from it, but from what I could hear, things were turning quite nasty in there – anything could be happening, I thought, she might have surprised a burglar or God knows what. Then I heard something breaking, china or something, and I knew I couldn't just pretend I hadn't heard *that*. The voices were coming from a long way inside, towards the back of the house. So I went round to the back door. It was half-open. I let myself in as quietly as I could, and followed the voices from there.

'The living room door was half-open, too. When I reached it, I just stopped dead. There was Mrs Fisher, half-naked – she was just wearing her skirt and stockings, not a stitch else – screaming abuse at a man not far off my own age, who was buttoning up his shirt in one hell of a hurry. I could see an ornamental plate on the floor, smashed to splinters. I guessed she'd thrown it at him and missed. It was then that something else hit me. She was roaring drunk. Her hair was all over the place, and she could hardly stand up.

'"Go on then," she was screaming, "fuck off back to your wife," – excuse my language, but that's word-for-word what she said. The man mumbled something, started moving backwards, towards the door. I ran for it.

They'd never have heard over all the noise she was making. I went straight round to the front and started trimming the bushes like my life depended on it. I don't think I've ever been so shaken in my life – well, not until much later, anyway. And that was thanks to the Fishers, as well. I suppose I'd led a bit of a sheltered life, up to then ... I'd never known ordinary people could carry on like that, never mind rich ones.'

He fell silent. I felt every bit as shocked as he must have done at the time, struggled to find some way of kick-starting his monologue again. 'My God,' I said, 'what did you do?'

'Well, there was nothing much I could do. I certainly wasn't going to tell her what I'd seen, never mind her husband. Something told me I'd be out on my ear if I did any such thing. I just kept it to myself for the next week or so. I'd have liked to tell my mates on my day off, but something just stopped me. Partly, I was afraid it would get back to the Fishers, what I'd said ... there was more to it than that, though. What Mr Fisher had asked me at the interview, about confidentiality – I *did* understand it, perfectly well. Looking back, I'm quite sure that's why he hired me in the first place.

'The next Saturday, though, the housekeeper came round to my cottage for a cup of tea and a chat – how I was taking to the job, that sort of thing – and I knew there'd be nothing indiscreet about confiding in her. She wasn't surprised at all, far from it. "Well, I suppose you had to find out sooner or later," she said, "I've known what she's like for a very long time. And in strictest confidence, so has Mr Fisher. It's a very odd sort of marriage they've got, always has been. A marriage of convenience in every sense of the word; there's no love there at all."

'Her name was Mrs Brown, the housekeeper. She told me she'd worked for Mrs Fisher's family in her younger days, knew just about all there was to know about them. She'd always been a wild one since childhood, Mrs Brown said, only got attention when she misbehaved. Her dad had been a self-made man, rich as Croesus, and he'd married a real society beauty. Rita Fisher was a big disappointment to both of them; they'd wanted a pretty little princess and, as I mentioned before, she wasn't much in the looks department. She was spoilt rotten financially, but her mum and dad hardly even saw her – she was packed off to boarding school the second she was old enough to go. Hated every minute there, Mrs Brown said.

'Well, apparently she started chasing after the boys when she was barely thirteen. Maybe she was just insecure, wanted attention. Still, it led to some trouble, all right. Her parents were more disappointed than ever ... plain as a pikestaff *and* no end of scandal. She got herself expelled from every school they sent her to, it got to the point where her dad had to bribe the headmasters to take her. She started drinking in her teens, as well. Mrs Brown glossed over that a bit ... "Well," she said, "let's just say she was quite unstable." Her father was dead by the time she met Dennis Fisher, but her mother was only too glad to get her married off. Just to make her look respectable. Anyone would have done.'

'Did she talk about Dennis Fisher at all?' I asked. 'Mrs Brown?'

'I asked, but she didn't know so much about him. Local boy, apparently, razor-sharp mind, scholarships all the way to Oxford, then he went to work as an accountant in London. Met Mrs Fisher on one of his rare trips back home. Came from a big mining family, poor as church mice, and he had next to nothing to do with any of them.

Very ambitious lad, by all accounts.' He sighed. 'According to Mrs Brown, he only wanted her for her money. It certainly paid off for him – a year after they were married, he opened his own factory in the area, and it took off like a rocket. But he was still married to her, and there was no getting away from *that*.'

'I'm surprised he didn't divorce her,' I said thoughtfully. 'When he had what he wanted. What was to stop him?'

'Oh, I didn't need to ask *that*, I could see the answer for myself. You wouldn't know it these days, but divorce was quite a scandal back then . . . you didn't need to see much of Mr Fisher to see how he'd have dreaded that. Ferociously respectable man, in his quiet way; the last thing he'd have wanted was the town gossiping. Mind you, he was caught between the devil and the deep blue sea. Staying married to Mrs Fisher was quite a liability in that department. She was discreet enough with her affairs and her drinking, but you could tell he was worried that might change.

'You had to see them together, Mrs Brown said, to understand what a vicious circle they were caught in – he'd sweet-talked her at first with flowers and compliments, but that all changed as soon as she had the ring on her finger. The colder and more disapproving he was, the worse she behaved . . . the worse she behaved, the colder and more disapproving he got. And the longer hours he worked. He was next to never at home, while I worked there. Mrs Brown said that was completely typical. He'd married a business, she told me. His wife was just extra baggage that came with it.'

'It sounds as if she was close to Mrs Fisher,' I said. 'Mrs Brown, I mean. Did she ever talk to her about it all? Try to help?'

'My God, no. If you're thinking of some devoted old

retainer, you're barking up the wrong tree completely. She was a nice woman, Mrs Brown, and the soul of discretion, which was more important to the Fishers than anything else. But she didn't *care* about them any more than my mum cared about Mr Fisher's textiles factory – you did your day's work as well as you could, kept your head down. Feelings didn't come into it. She saved all that sort of thing for her own family. The Fishers were just the people who paid her.'

'It sounds a lonely sort of place,' I said.

'You've got that right. To begin with, I always supposed they'd be off to parties together at the weekends – Mr and Mrs Fisher, I mean – but, after a while, I realised that wasn't the case at all. He spent a good seven days a week at work, and she didn't seem to have a friend in the world – I never once saw a woman coming to call on her, just the occasional boyfriend sneaking in. Whenever she went out, she always came back with armfuls of shopping bags. It seemed to be her only interest in life, buying things on her own . . . apart from the men, of course. And the drinking. From what Mrs Brown told me, she got drunk every day, if she didn't go out. I don't know, maybe she couldn't think of anything else to do.

'I never knew a couple *could* be that lonely – they were as cut off from everything as if they were on a desert island. They didn't even seem to have acquaintances, and as for entertaining, nobody so much as called round for tea. Everyone in Teasford assumed they must have friends outside the area. But I can tell you for a fact that they didn't.

'And they had nothing in common with each other, either. What I said earlier about the house – how it was so different inside and outside – it was their personalities in a nutshell. He'd chosen the place, she'd had a free rein decorating it. Chalk and cheese.' He sighed. 'It's hard to believe people that rich could be so isolated and miserable, but they certainly were. Well, *she* was, at least. He seemed far too preoccupied with his business to feel anything at all. I couldn't help wondering what he did it all for. He must have worked harder and longer than the local miners, and he didn't seem to enjoy anything about it. Not the wealth, or the power, or anything at all. In a funny sort of way, he reminded me of a rat on a treadmill – he knew he had to keep moving, but for the life of him he couldn't have told you why.

'That was how it was working for them, anyway. I did my day's work and went back to my cottage, talked to the housekeeper, saw the Fishers coming and going. Respected their confidence whenever I saw my mates and my family, just said they were a nice couple, decent employers, it was a good job. There wasn't any harm in lying, I thought. It *was* a good job, and I didn't see why I shouldn't go on working there indefinitely – the pay was above average, the cottage was nice, the Fishers were never any trouble. But then ... one day ...'

The steady, effortless flow of his words dried up unexpectedly and I felt him become anxious again, tongue-tied. 'Go on,' I said quietly. 'I'm listening.'

'It's so difficult to talk about. You'll judge me for it, I'm quite sure. You'll think I should have had more courage, done things differently ...' A new and querulous note had entered that elderly voice, at once supplicatory and self-justifying. 'But you see, I didn't know any better, then. I wasn't to know what would happen afterwards ...'

'I won't judge you. Honestly.' My own voice was almost inaudible, as I tried to sound as gentle as I could. 'What happened?'

'It was summertime. I was working in the back garden.

It was very hot, and I'd been working for hours. I suddenly felt quite faint. I needed some water. Cold water.' He spoke as if under hypnosis, simple, declarative sentences like a witness on a stand. 'I went into the house to get some. I thought it was empty. I knew it was Mrs Brown's afternoon off. I couldn't see the driveway from the back garden, so I hadn't seen them both driving back separately. The Fishers. I'd just let myself in and shut the door behind me to stop it creaking in the breeze. Then I heard their voices. From the living room. I can remember it all so clearly. As if it happened yesterday.

'"Why don't you ever listen to a word I say?" she was shouting. "I *would* stop all this, you know I would. If only I had a child of my own to look after. I'd be happy then – you don't understand."

'I could tell she was drunk again, and I wished I hadn't shut that damned door. I could have just crept out again. But if I opened it now, they might hear, and think I'd been eavesdropping. I just stayed where I was, too scared to move, praying I'd have a chance to get out somehow before one of them came in.

'"You know you can't have children of your own," he said. I've told you he was a cold man; his voice was just like ice. "You shouldn't have had some back-street abortion that ruined you for life – what were you at the time, fourteen, fifteen? Christ, you're an embarrassment. I wish I'd never married you."

'"You don't understand me!" she screamed. I could hear something else smashing in there – it's a wonder that couple had any ornaments left. Then she started crying. Loud, noisy drunk's tears. You didn't need to see her husband's face to see how disgusted he was; it was all in his voice when he spoke. "Oh, for God's sake," he said. "You're like a child yourself."

"'I want to adopt,'" she was sobbing. "It would all be different, then. I want a little girl of my own – nobody needs to know she's not ours, nobody in the town. Nobody needs to know I can't have children. A pretty little girl with natural blonde hair like my mother's. I'd give her everything I never had. She wouldn't have to go to boarding school like I did. She'd go to school in the town, and she'd never tell anyone she wasn't ours. I'd be so happy, Dennis, I'd never drink again, I'd never have lovers. I wouldn't need any of that, not if I had a little girl to look after—"

"'A child's not a *doll*, Rita,'" he said. "How are you supposed to know what it's going to look like? People adopt babies, not children."

"'There must be older ones who need adopting. *Must* be.'" She'd stopped crying and sounded hopeful all of a sudden, like she'd just seen it was possible. "We could get in touch with the council on Monday, we could start finding out—"

"'And what about your history? Do you really believe they're going to let *you* adopt?'" He sounded so scornful, not *trying* to hurt her feelings, he just didn't care. "You spent a year in a mental hospital when you were barely seventeen. They look into your background, these people. They'll rule you out immediately. Can't you even understand that much?"

"'They *won't*,'" she said. "Your factory, this house . . . we'd be ideal, Dennis, of *course* they'd let us. They'll never look that far back, not in a million years—"

'I don't know why I moved then. I'd been standing in the same position all the time I'd been listening. Frozen to the spot, you could say. But I *did* move then, very clumsily, and it was a bad mistake – I was standing by the dresser in their kitchen and bumped against it hard, and everything rattled. It seemed like the loudest noise I'd ever heard in my life, and their voices just cut off. "Who's there?" I heard her shouting, and he came hurrying out before I could take two steps towards the door. He just stood and looked at me. I had no idea what to say. And from the living room, Mrs Fisher sounded close to hysterical. "Who is it?" she kept shouting, "Dennis, who's *there*?" I just turned and ran out, in a real blind panic, you can imagine. Went straight back to my little cottage and sat waiting for one or both of them to knock on the door and give me my marching orders.

'The knock came about ten minutes later. I went to get it, not scared any more, just resigned. It was Mr Fisher. He always looked serious, but he looked more serious than ever, on the doorstep. Older too. He asked if he could come in.

'Of course, it wasn't really a question. We sat down together, didn't say anything for a while. "I have no idea what you were doing in the kitchen," he said at last, "whether you were deliberately eavesdropping, or simply found yourself trapped in a difficult situation. In all honesty, it doesn't matter much one way or the other. My wife's insisting that I let you go, and – in the light of the conversation you've just overheard – that's probably best for all concerned. I'm sure you can understand that yourself."

'I just nodded. I was thinking I'd have to move back in with Mum and Dad, wishing I'd managed to save more money while I'd been working there. I was just sitting there staring at the floor when I heard him writing something, and looked up. He'd got a chequebook out, and was filling one in. "I'm well aware that it's no fault of your own," he said. "You can count on us for an excellent reference. And just to show that there are no hard feelings, this is yours as well."

'He handed me the cheque. I almost fainted. He was giving me close to a full year's wages, as casually as he'd have handed over a pound note. "What you tell people is your business, obviously," he said. "But I'd very much appreciate it if you kept certain details to yourself. I can see that you take my meaning."

'I never went back to Mum and Dad's house, anyway. I had enough money to rent a flat in Manchester, and I got another job not a month later – he'd been as good as his word, Mr Fisher, he'd given me a glowing reference. I felt very grateful to him. Plenty of men in his position would have thrown me out on my ear without a second thought, after seeing me in that kitchen, but he'd gone out of his way to help me. So I never breathed a word to anyone about the Fishers, and what I knew about them. It seemed the least I could do in return. For years, I almost forgot they existed – since I'd left Teasford, I'd got married and started a family, and I had no idea what they might be up to.

'Then, one morning in 1969, I picked up the daily paper and read about their adoptive daughter being arrested for murder at the age of ten.'

It was as if he'd been speaking in a trance and was now coming quickly out of it – as he spoke again, the tremble in his voice was both minute and unmissable. 'I didn't sleep properly for weeks. I kept thinking back to what I'd heard that afternoon, what I'd known for years before *that* – they weren't fit to look after a stray cat, never mind a child. But they'd got hold of one, somehow or other. And God alone knows how badly they unbalanced her, between them. I kept remembering the way Mrs Fisher had talked about the daughter she wanted. Like a doll, like a *toy*. And her husband hadn't cared one way or the other.

'I didn't think Rebecca would have been a killer at the age of ten, if she hadn't gone to them. And I'd never said a word to anyone. I'd just let myself be bought off, told myself it didn't matter. It was a little girl's *life* at stake; I could have got in touch with the social services the day I left, could have given them a dozen reasons why the Fishers weren't fit parents—'

I felt the crushing weight of this old man's guilt, something that had been suppressed for decades finally giving way. His voice was cold and taut with self-loathing. 'Of course, I never told my wife and children anything about it – they'd have seen me in a whole different light if they knew. Everyone thought I was such a good man. But when I heard about your research, I knew I'd have to tell someone the full story at last. I've been wanting to phone you for *weeks*, but I just kept losing my bottle. Thinking you'd need me to give my name, that you'd have to let my family know … I don't know *what* I thought, to be honest. I was just afraid.'

'You don't have to worry,' I said quietly. 'And you don't have to blame yourself. You weren't to know what would happen if you kept quiet. Anyone would have done the same thing.'

The voice down the line had become shy, evasive. 'Well, that's as maybe.'

I suddenly realised that I'd heard those words in the same voice before: Melanie's hallway in Teasford, the old man coming into the kitchen beside his son and grand-children. 'Maybe the Catholics have it right, with their confession,' he said. 'I feel better, in an odd sort of way. Now I've told someone.'

34

Pictures becoming clearer in my mind.

A young social worker at the beginning of his career, the first ever case he'd handled on his own. A twenty-five-year-old fellow named Bob Mills, who had no idea that future years would see his ascent to the pinnacle of the public sector, to the more austere and authoritative *Robert*. A sad case to begin your real working life with, if a relatively straightforward one. A withdrawn and unhappy little girl who'd lost both parents some months ago; an angelic-looking child named Rebecca Jane Sanderson, who was currently living in the authority's care, and was urgently in need of adoption.

A psychologist's starkly imperative report landing on his desk at exactly the wrong moment – when he'd heard that a certain couple were interested in giving her a home, a certain couple who'd first got in touch with them almost two years ago. Who'd charmingly, regretfully turned down all previous candidates for adoption: they were slightly too young, too old, too loud, too shy, too aggressive. A very particular couple, but otherwise ideal in every way – devoted to one another, well-known around the area, with enough money to give a child anything and everything they might need in life. You didn't look into their backgrounds too closely, when you were an overworked young man struggling to stay afloat in a sea of red tape and office politics, afraid despite yourself that you were getting out of your depth. You only had to meet the Fishers to know there was nothing wrong with them . . .

The psychologist's report becoming buried in newer, more urgent paperwork as the wheels of adoption started rolling in earnest. The Fishers *adored* Rebecca. She was exactly what they'd been looking for all along. They'd give her a wonderful home. So there was no need to follow up a certain Dr Edward Leighton's suggestions and warnings and fears – if she'd remained in care, of course, there would have been, but as it was, such measures were obviously unnecessary. Her behaviour was bound to normalise, when the procedures had been completed and the forms filled in and the single, pathetic suitcase packed. As Rebecca Fisher, the child would be fine.

Case concluded. Hands washed. On to the next.

Only, of course, it hadn't ended there. Following the events of 1969, things would have been dragged up again, if only behind closed doors – the corners that had been cut, the background checks that had been dispensed with entirely, the report that had been ignored. Perhaps the threat of a scandal, quickly hushed up by the authority *en masse*. And I suddenly knew why I'd been put through to Robert Mills so quickly – Rebecca must haunt his dreams as she did those of Melanie's father-in-law, if for slightly more prosaic reasons. A skeleton in the closet of his glittering career; the bungled first case that had ended in horror.

Off the phone, I moved round the house aimlessly. Revelation had come like a bolt from the blue, leaving me dizzy. The truth about Rita and Dennis Fisher kept approaching me all over again from different angles – sometimes a full-frontal assault, sometimes an ambush from the shadows. And sometimes it crept up soundlessly behind me, tapped me gently on the shoulder: *the whole picture's changed now*, it whispered, *everything's become unrecognisable.* None of my previous ideas remained intact, and some crumbled into dust as others changed without altering at all. It was like looking into a cloudbank and finding faces; they'd been there all along, only now I could see them.

Unstable, lonely, terrifyingly self-obsessed Rita – the last woman in the world who should have been given custody of such a troubled little girl, who'd been drawn to her by everything that existed on the surface and didn't matter. *A pretty little girl with natural blonde hair like my mother's.* Trying to reinvent herself and her own past, seeing Rebecca as a kind of human Prozac. As Dennis must have seen her as a means to an end himself – something to pacify a troublesome and potentially embarrassing wife, to stop her getting drunk, making scenes, taking lovers. He'd given Rita a child as he'd once given a young gardener a full year's wages in one hastily-scrawled cheque. *This should keep you quiet. You've got what you want, now...*

Of course, they must have realised their mistake soon after they'd taken Rebecca in. She wasn't the answer to anything, and never would be. But by then it would have been too late to turn back. A terrible mistake, caused by her instability and his indifference, had become a permanent fixture in their lives. An unwanted child in that lonely house, a child who really shouldn't have been there at all.

It was my own childhood, grotesquely distorted and defaced – my kindly, preoccupied mother and well-meaning stepfather faced that troubled and troubling couple in a mirror, as I faced Rebecca herself. And empathy combined with pity as I looked, simultaneously savage and as helpless as a child. It had been worse for her. It had been so much worse.

I longed to share these new thoughts and feelings with someone, but there was nobody to tell – Liz had left for work, and, when Carl returned, he certainly wouldn't want to hear anything more about my research. I had no idea how I'd manage to avoid the subject that night, but knew that I would. And, as the quiet hours inched past, I struggled to focus my inner turmoil on something concrete. Tomorrow I'd be travelling into London, preparing to talk to a man who'd known Rebecca better than anyone.

The following morning, the alarm tore me from a dark and chaotic tangle of dreams and I was more than relieved to come back to reality.

'Morning, Annie,' Carl was saying beside me, reaching out to silence the insistent, charmless noise. 'Well, better go and have a shower, I suppose.'

Getting out of bed, he drew the curtains en route to the bathroom. I lay still for long seconds, half-remembered images rapidly fading in the sunlight: Rita Fisher drunk and half-naked in a derelict house, Eleanor Corbett smirking and eavesdropping in the Fishers' kitchen. My thoughts turned restlessly in the direction of London, and things I couldn't possibly share with Carl. When he came back in, he seemed to take longer than usual to prepare for work; I watched him dressing from the bed, trying to hide my own tense, apprehensive impatience.

'See you later,' he said at last, kissing me, 'have a nice day.'

I lay and listened to the inevitable succession of small noises: his footsteps on the stairs, the front door creaking open and closing again, a minute or so of silence before the sound of his engine starting outside. As I heard him driving off, I went to the window and looked out. I saw an idyllic pastoral painting with a single animated detail; the black car shrinking in the distance, crawling up the hill, vanishing over the top of it to leave perfect stillness in its wake. The second of its disappearance changed everything in the atmosphere around me – disturbing new freedom crashed down. I was entirely alone in the world, could go anywhere, do anything.

I showered and dressed quickly, and less than half an hour later I was locking up, driving towards Bournemouth station. Parking in the shadows of a nearby multi-storey, I hurried towards the ticket office. I was twenty minutes early for my train, and killed the time in the sad, quiet little station cafe; a coffee, a cigarette, a dizzy realisation that nobody knew where I was.

At last I was stepping onto the teeming platform at London Waterloo, hurrying towards the Underground, checking my watch. I was due at the Ashwell Unit in an hour's time and, half an hour later, I found myself getting off the tube at Balham.

I had to ask directions several times from passers-by before I found the unit. It was an imposing red-brick Victorian building, set well back from a busy road. Apart from the number of cars in the drive, it looked like a private house until I got a little closer and saw the details that made it institutional, saw that the neatness lacked decoration or personality. A small sign directed me to the side of the house, where glass double doors slid open to let me in.

Inside, rows of plastic chairs faced a small reception desk. A mismatched handful of people sat in ones and twos while a middle-aged receptionist tapped at a computer.

'Excuse me,' I said, approaching her, 'my name's Anna Jeffreys. I've got an appointment with Dr Donald Hargreaves at two o'clock.'

She tapped at the computer again, consulted some notes

I couldn't see. 'Take a seat,' she said at last, 'I'll let him know you're here.'

I sat and waited. To my right, an elderly couple exchanged occasional tense asides. 'I'm sure Nick's all right now, dear,' the man said quietly, 'it'll be nice to see him again,' and the woman murmured something I couldn't quite catch. A new man entered the reception area through the double doors that clearly led to the Unit's inner workings. He was dressed for a casual office, but I recognised the neatly clipped black beard from his picture on the internet.

'Anna Jeffreys?'

'That's me.'

I rose to my feet, approached him – a brief handshake, a quick, meaningless smile. 'Don Hargreaves,' he said. 'If you'd like to follow me.'

I didn't know exactly what I'd imagined existing beyond the double doors; sheer ignorance had hinted at a scene straight out of Bedlam, blood-curdling shrieks echoing down corridors, burly nurses racing in their direction like a crack SAS team. The reality both reassured and disappointed; the atmosphere was quiet and pale and sterile, a sense that mental illness was as mundanely regrettable as diabetes. Our footsteps rang out sharp and flat in the silence until we reached a side-door and entered his office.

'I was a very young man when I first met Rebecca,' Donald told me. 'Starting out in my profession, you could say. I'd graduated three years before, and was working for East Lancashire District Council, dealing with young offenders in various settings, the Southfield Unit being only one of those. Before Rebecca arrived there, I'd had very little to do with the place . . . the majority of its inmates posed no danger to themselves or others. Occasionally I'd be called in for sessions with one, but very rarely. Of course, Rebecca was an exceptional case. I came in to talk to her once a month.'

I sat across from him, facing him over a wildly overcrowded desk. His back was to the window, beyond which I saw a tidy but featureless expanse of empty garden, fenced in with tall, rather overgrown hedges. 'How did she behave during your sessions with her?' I asked.

He was easier to talk to in person than over the phone – frank, grave, courteous – but still seemed disconcertingly comfortable with silence. Seconds passed as he looked thoughtfully into the middle distance; I was about to rephrase my question when he spoke at last. 'She was extremely unforthcoming in the beginning. In fact, she couldn't have been a great deal less cooperative. I'd been prepared for that, of course – I'd had full access to her confidential file before meeting her, and they told me she'd behaved in exactly the same way with the police psychiatrists who'd tried to interview her before. But I had no idea quite how odd her behaviour would be when I spoke to her in person.

'There was nothing aggressive about it, nothing so much as impolite. She simply refused to give detailed answers. Even to the perfectly innocuous questions I asked at the beginning of our sessions, just to put her at her ease: how was she taking to life there, for example, was she enjoying the activities on offer? She'd answer in tense monosyllables, sitting bolt upright. At best she'd look wary, at worst quite terrified. I was reminded of the way I behave in the dentist's chair ... it's a lifelong phobia, I turn into a frightened rabbit the second I set foot in the surgery. Something about the whole process petrified her.

'I can't tell you how hard I tried to get to the bottom of

that fear, over the first few months. To begin with, I thought it might well be to do with the setting – our sessions took place in a rather bleak and institutional side-office, and I'd always been aware that it looked unwelcoming. I had a quiet word with the unit's manager about it, and he set the common room aside once a month for our private use. But, even in such a familiar environment, which she associated with camaraderie and relaxation, her manner didn't change at all. It had nothing to do with the *place*, I realised. She was terrified of the sessions themselves.'

'How did she avoid answering your questions?' I asked curiously. 'What exactly did she say?'

'There were no real answers to give – I kept my questions as open-ended as possible, hoping to draw her out in some way. For example, I'd ask her if she missed her old school, expecting the reference to trigger a flood of personal memories and emotions, but far from it, she'd reply as if she'd learned her words by heart. "I miss it sometimes," she'd say, "but I'm happy here as well." And any other line of enquiry would meet exactly the same kind of response. I can't quite describe how appallingly tense she seemed, as if one wrong word could condemn her to death. There seemed to be no way on earth that I could put her at her ease.

'The sessions quickly began to feel like a formality – I was required to come to the unit, she was required to come to me. For those first few months, no progress was made by either one of us. I couldn't understand her in the slightest. While I could imagine her reasons for being less than forthcoming *before* her trial, they simply didn't apply any more; she'd already been sentenced, and had nothing to lose by cooperating with me. In fact, she had everything to gain. By not communicating, she only made herself appear more disturbed. I pointed that out more than once, after realising that nothing else seemed to work. And again, she responded in exactly the same way. "I'm trying my best," she said, "but there's nothing else I can say."'

'It must have been pretty frustrating for you,' I said.

'It certainly was. It's an appalling situation for any psychiatrist to find themselves in, for the most petty and arrogant reasons imaginable – it makes you question your own professional skill when you meet such a brick wall with a patient. But, after a while, personal concern and curiosity began to overcome that. Sometimes, during our sessions, I could tell that she *wanted* to talk very much . . . you may well think that I imagined it, but I can assure you that wasn't the case. You could sense such a *conflict* in that child. Wanting to communicate and confide, but – for some reason I couldn't guess at – simply not being able to. It was painful to watch her at those times. Painful and bewildering.

'I began taking a different approach. She seemed far more comfortable listening than she did talking, so I started to tell her about my own life. I felt that might help to break down her distrust; she'd realise I was nobody to be afraid of, and that, by association, neither were our sessions. For some time, that met with no visible success either. She seemed perfectly relaxed for a change, but she still wasn't giving anything away. Then I mentioned my brother. My parents had adopted him, and I told her so – I recalled that she'd been adopted herself, and thought it might help her relate to me.

'Normally, at those times, she'd be listening as politeness demanded, passingly interested but no more than that. Suddenly, however, she seemed very alert. "Did everyone know?" she asked. "That he was adopted?"

'"Of course," I said. "We certainly didn't make a secret of it."

'She said something very odd, then. "Everyone must have hated him."'

Another long silence. He sat as if meditating, hands steepled together, chin resting on his fingertips. 'She sounded so sad,' he said at last, 'so sympathetic. I suddenly felt I was on the brink of understanding her. "Why do you say that?" I asked. "What makes you think it?"

'And she said, quite matter-of-factly, "People think you're bad, if they know you're adopted. They think your real parents didn't want you, even if they did really, even if they just died. And if they think your real parents didn't want you, they won't want anything to do with you, either. Nobody will, even people who seem nice."

'I just stared at her, stunned. Her whole manner was so earnest, as if she was explaining some complex fact she'd been taught at school. "Rebecca, that isn't true at all," I said. "Who told you that?"

'"It is true," she said defiantly, "My mother told me. She tells me all the time." And I realised she was talking about her adoptive mother, who'd committed suicide over a year ago.

'She just clammed up after that, during that session. She wouldn't say another word on the subject, no matter how hard I tried to draw her out again. But, when it was over, I went back to her file and read about her adoptive parents, made some informal enquiries of my own, wanting to understand what kind of people they'd been.

'The local authority had unearthed quite a few damning facts about *them*, in the aftermath of Rebecca's trial. I'm surprised jobs weren't lost over the matter. They should never have been allowed to adopt in the first place; I could only imagine the corners that had been cut. The woman was diagnosed manic-depressive in her late teens, spent over a year in a mental institution ... she came from a wealthy family, and they must have effectively bribed her way out. She certainly wasn't stable after she was released ... there were rumours of alcoholism, unhealthy promiscuity. From what I gathered, she'd hidden those things very carefully in public; it seems to have been *morbidly* important to her what other people thought. The little people especially, if I can use such a patronising term. It seemed the only way she could feel secure and superior, hiding behind a certain lady-of-the-manor façade with Teasford's poorer residents.

'A lot of this is guesswork and hearsay, obviously, but I'm quite convinced that it's close to the truth. She had a real terror of those ordinary people knowing the less salubrious details of her life – the breakdown, the drinking, the men. Also, the fact that she couldn't have children naturally. She'd become pregnant in her early teens, and there had been complications with the abortion ... afterwards, she was left sterile.'

So much seemed to fall into place as I looked at him: Rebecca's fury with the boy in the common room, her constant references to *Mummy and Daddy*. 'She passed on her own fears to Rebecca, didn't she?'

He didn't answer directly, but went on thoughtfully, looking into the middle distance again. 'It's extraordinary, the damage that adults can do children. Often, they're unaware that they're doing the slightest thing wrong. Rebecca's adoptive mother took on a deeply traumatised and confused little girl, and poisoned her with her own instability. She was terrified that Teasford would discover Rebecca was adopted, seems to have had some bizarre idea that, if *the little people* knew she couldn't have children of her own, they'd immediately know about the abortion and the mental institution and Christ alone knows what else. So she made Rebecca as terrified of discovery as she was. Brainwashed her with the most despicable lies – nobody would ever love her if they knew, she'd be an outcast in the world – simply in the interests of her own paranoia.

'You can imagine the effect that would have on a vulnerable five-year-old orphan. Soon, Rebecca had become more obsessed with concealing her adoption than Mrs Fisher was, and the roots of that obsession went deeper than I can describe. Even at the age of eleven, they couldn't be eased out. I could explain to her as often as I liked that it wasn't true, but at some all-important level, she simply didn't believe me. She wouldn't have believed anyone who'd told her. I'm aware this goes directly against the principles of my profession, where everything in the human mind is supposed to be mendable and treatable and curable . . . but in some cases, the damage has already been done, and is literally irreversible. Looking back and discovering how and why it happened does nothing whatsoever to change that.'

'So she didn't discuss her adoption any further?' I asked.

'Only in the most superficial way. She seemed to trust me a great deal more after that breakthrough session, when she'd finally acknowledged some key element of herself . . . she'd talk quite unselfconsciously about her earliest memories, how she could remember a small terraced house and a nice fair-haired woman tucking her up in bed at night. She never seemed happier than she did at those times, as if she could somehow transport herself back there. Her early childhood appeared to have been idyllic – everything in her file told me the same thing.

'But when she described her life following her adoption, she was like a different person – stilted, tense – and at those times, we both went directly back to square one.

She'd loved her adoptive mother very much, she told me, she'd been heartbroken by her suicide, she was still devoted to her adoptive father. When you'd heard her discussing honest feelings it was very easy to tell when she was lying, and at those times, I'd have been prepared to swear under oath that she was – perhaps to herself as much as to me. I was reminded of the transcripts I'd read of her trial. She'd behaved in exactly the same way on the stand, denying the most overwhelming evidence in a way that wasn't even slightly convincing.'

'Did she ever talk about Eleanor's murder at all?' I asked.

'Not for a very long time. But gradually I began to understand the events that had led to it. As Rebecca came to trust me more, she began to refer to her old primary school in passing, and then to discuss it in some detail. She said that she'd always felt on edge there, that she knew the teachers would expect her to be perfect. "What makes you say that?" I asked. And she said that people always did, that they'd never love you if you got things wrong. Sometimes at home, she said, she wet the bed, and her adoptive mother was furious . . . she told Rebecca that she hated her at those times, that they should never have taken her in the first place. Rebecca described that so matter-of-factly, as though it was a perfectly natural response from a parent. "Grown-ups always do hate you," she said, "if you make mistakes and cause trouble. I knew the teachers at school would be just the same."

'She'd have been twelve at that time – she sounded so much older than she was, and at the same time, so disturbingly young. "That's not true at all," I told her, "children make all kinds of mistakes, and people still love them. What could you ever do at school so terrible it would make your teachers hate you? You were well-behaved, weren't you?"

"'I tried to be,' she said. "But I got upset sometimes. Usually, nobody even knew; I just felt lonely and scared and kept it to myself. I did something terrible at school once, though. I killed our class pet. He was a hamster.'"

I remembered Annette Watson's description of Rebecca crying over Toffee's cage, and listened intently, utterly alert as Donald continued. 'I was very shocked, mainly because I'd never expected her to confess to anything like that with me . . . I tried not to show it, thinking it might drive her straight back into herself. "What happened?" I asked her. "Why would you want to do something like that?"

"'I didn't,' she said, "not at first. I always came in to feed him at lunchtimes and things; I really cared about him. I got to take him home in the summer holidays and treat him like he was my own pet. But then I had to bring him back next term, and everything changed.

"'It was horrible,' she said, "I'd started thinking he was *mine*, and then it was all different . . . I was just one of the girls who put their names down to feed him. I came in to do that one lunchtime, and I thought – it was like he didn't know me, I could have been anyone – I was just so angry all of a sudden, I picked him up, and—"

'It was the first time I'd ever seen her cry. I tried my best to comfort her. "I don't know why I did it," she said. "I just couldn't do anything else. Not then, at the time . . ."

'It was sad. It was also very frightening. You'd be amazed how easy it was to forget she was a murderess, but I suddenly saw that quite clearly. The *red mist* that's become such a cliché . . . that's what she was talking about, in the voice of a sweet, lonely little girl. "Someone else got into trouble for it," she said. "I felt so bad about that. But I couldn't have told them it was me. My mother would have been furious. Might even have sent me back to the children's home; she threatened to do that sometimes . . .

"'I wish I hadn't done it," she said. "I wished that as soon as he was dead. But I couldn't change what I'd done. Not then."

'I remembered reading about Eleanor Corbett, at that moment – how sweet she'd been, and how small for her age – I knew there'd never be a better time to ask. "Was it the same way with Eleanor?" I asked her. "That you felt you weren't as important to her as you wanted to be?"

"'No," she said. "It was nothing like that, nothing at all."

'I believed her at once . . . I'd got to know her by then, as I've said, and it was easy to tell when she was lying if you knew the signs to look out for. Still, she wouldn't yield another inch on the subject during that session. She seemed fearful all over again. Nervous, as though she realised she'd gone too far, and expected to be punished for it at any moment.

'It was *months* before she really came out of her shell again . . . a good three sessions later. I was talking about this and that as I had done in the beginning, trying to put her back at her ease. She spoke up unexpectedly, apropos of nothing. "I had a nightmare last night," she said. "About Eleanor. I often have them, since she died."

'It was so unexpected, it was hard for me to think of anything to say. "Do you miss her?" I asked.

"'I miss the way she was in the beginning," she said. "When we first met. The other girls didn't really talk to me, but she was so friendly straight away – I liked her so much. She was the first real friend I'd ever had. We always went round together. We went to this house nobody lived in any more, and pretended that we lived there ourselves ... sometimes that we were sisters, sometimes that I was her mother. I brought all kinds of things there, from home. When my mother was ... well, angry ... she broke things, and they all went into the dustbin. I took them out when nobody was looking, mended them with glue. And there was cutlery. That wasn't broken, of course, only the handles had got stained. The big knife was part of that; a knife for carving meat. We just put it in the corner with the rest of our things, and didn't think any more about it.

"'We talked, in that house,' she said. "About our families, and that sort of thing. To begin with, I told her what I told everyone at school, nothing more than that. Then ... I started to trust her. I told her I was adopted, and what a secret it was, and why she mustn't tell anyone else.'"

The picture came together for me – Agnes Og, Melanie Cook, Lucy Fielder – leaping out in brutal technicolour. When I spoke, my voice was almost inaudible. 'She blackmailed her,' I said. 'Eleanor Corbett blackmailed her.'

Donald nodded. 'She changed out of all recognition, Rebecca told me. After she knew ... after she had that hold over her. She seems to have been a very spiteful and manipulative child, and disturbingly skilful when it came to concealing that. But she didn't conceal it any more from Rebecca. She had no reason to.

'It began with requests for small things: sweets, hair-ribbons, little toys. Although, from what Rebecca told me, *demands* would have been a better word. Eleanor made it quite clear what would happen if Rebecca refused – she'd broadcast the secret of Rebecca's adoption all over the school. Which was, of course, Rebecca's greatest fear in the world.

'It was immensely distressing even then, Rebecca told

me. Of course, she felt appallingly betrayed; Eleanor was the only person she'd ever trusted in the school. But it didn't seem a tremendous *threat*, at first. Rebecca had plenty of pocket money, and she could afford to buy Eleanor's silence. Unpleasant as it was, it began to feel like a regular duty. Only, as the months passed, that began to change. Eleanor got greedier. She didn't seem to understand that there were some things Rebecca simply *couldn't* give away without her parents noticing – it sounds as if she was a rather stupid child, for all her slyness. She set her heart on a gold bracelet Rebecca wore sometimes – an extremely expensive item, which Rebecca's mother had bought from a well-known jeweller in London. Rebecca gave it to her in a blind panic, knowing only that she had to keep her quiet.

'When its absence was remarked on, Rebecca claimed to have lost it, precipitating an immense argument. Still that quickly blew over and life went back to normal. Unfortunately, shortly afterwards, Eleanor's mother discovered the bracelet under her bed and came to the Fishers' home to return it. Rebecca had no choice but to admit that she'd given it away – she couldn't possibly admit to the blackmail, much less accuse Eleanor of stealing it. After Eleanor and her mother had left, the argument erupted all over again. Rebecca's mother told her she couldn't be trusted with expensive things if she'd just give them to that little ragamuffin . . . all the jewellery in the house was put under lock and key, and Rebecca's pocket money reduced to a pittance. Leaving Rebecca in an appallingly difficult position.

'"I wanted so much to tell my mother," she said to me, "but she'd have been more furious than ever. If she knew I'd told someone that I was adopted, I really don't know what she'd have done . . ."

'By this time, Rebecca had seen the darker side of Eleanor's personality only too clearly – she knew that Eleanor was perfectly capable of blurting the secret out in the playground, for no better reason than that of malice. So she became very possessive of her at school, waiting for her outside classrooms just so she could lead her somewhere private, out of harm's way. After Eleanor's mother had returned the bracelet, Rebecca took her to some quiet corner, and Eleanor demanded that Rebecca steal it back somehow.

'Rebecca said she couldn't, but Eleanor simply didn't believe her. Told her to bring it to the derelict house that Saturday, at half past two. She said she'd be waiting there.

'And that, of course, was how it ended . . .'

He fell quiet and I sat bolt upright in my seat, electrified. 'Did she tell you about that?' I asked. 'What really happened?'

He nodded. 'Rebecca arrived a full hour before Eleanor did. Of course, she hadn't been able to get the bracelet, and she was terrified. She'd found something else, a Wedgwood ornament from the living room, and was praying it would be enough to keep Eleanor quiet. But, when Eleanor finally came in, she just stared at it. Demanded to know what had happened to the bracelet.

'"I told you," Rebecca said, "I couldn't get it . . ." and Eleanor was furious. "I'm going to tell everyone about you being adopted," she said, "just you wait till I get home. I'll tell my family, everyone in Teasford. Your mother's going to kill you."

'I can't fully describe Rebecca's terror. You could see it in her face as she talked about the scene: total recall, blind panic. Everything her adoptive mother had planted in her mind from the age of five was screaming at her inside. And there was more to it than that. Elements of the hamster she'd killed. That sense of betrayal coming back more strongly than ever. I doubt there was any rational thought going on at all, at that moment. Just animal terror, and fury, and *people were going to know who she really was—*

'The knife was close at hand. Eleanor was tiny for her age. Rebecca overpowered her easily. I imagine it was over very quickly.'

'The red mist,' I said tonelessly.

'She couldn't remember anything after picking up the knife – at least, that's what she told me, and I believed her. Just her terror, realising what she'd done when it was over. She ran home as fast as she could, she told me. It was a minor miracle nobody saw her. Her mother and her family's housekeeper were out that afternoon, so she had the house to herself. Up in her bedroom, she noticed that there was blood on her clothes. Not as much as you'd expect, she said, but enough so you could see it.

'"I wanted to burn them," she said, "but I didn't know how." It dawned on me all over again how young she'd been that afternoon, just a *child*. She'd just pushed them down in her laundry basket as far as she could; she literally couldn't think of anything else to do. After that, she told me she had a bath, and waited for the housekeeper to come home.

'The next day . . . my God, she described it so vividly I could have been there. Everyone was talking about Eleanor's disappearance, and Rebecca's father called her down from her room unexpectedly. Both her adoptive parents were sitting in the living room with the house-keeper, she said, in total silence. And her father said that the housekeeper had been doing the washing that morn-ing and come across her clothes. "You seem to have had an accident," he said. "I'm surprised you didn't tell us."

"'It felt so strange," she told me, "so wrong." Then and there, she understood that they all knew what had happened, to a greater or lesser degree – they knew that she'd somehow killed Eleanor Corbett. "I don't think my parents were even wondering why," she said, "just how they could stop a big scandal. The housekeeper was looking at me like I was a monster, but she didn't say anything. I knew they'd given her money. I don't know how much. It must have been a lot, though, to keep her quiet when she looked at me like that."'

I remembered Melanie's father-in-law, the cheque Dennis Fisher had written out for him – that had disturbed me at the time, but this new revelation was a thousand times worse. 'They thought they could buy anything, didn't they?' I said quietly.

'Including justice. But they overestimated their own powers considerably. I imagine they'd hired their house-keeper precisely *because* she'd be bribable in any situation, but they couldn't silence the police or the papers that easily.' He broke off for a second, frowning, remembering. 'Her father said that the clothes weren't fit to be worn again, and had been disposed of. She remembered what he said next word for word, and so do I: "I hope you'll be more careful in the future."

"'It was horrible," she said, "none of us even mentioned what we were talking about, but we all knew. It was always like that, there – we said my mother was *unwell* when we meant she was passed out drunk, that she'd had a *visitor* when we all knew it was a boyfriend. But I never knew it would still be like that, not if they knew I'd actually killed someone—"

'I don't know if she realised how badly she was contradicting herself, at that moment – the happy family home she'd always described to me, how much she loved

322

both her adoptive parents. I'm not sure if she ever knew. But I'm quite convinced the Fishers weren't going out of their way to protect *her*, love and loyalty don't appear to have entered into it. They couldn't simply have let justice take its course, for fear of what Rebecca might say on the stand. Her alcoholism and promiscuity and mental health problems, his absolute indifference to all of them. I can only imagine how badly they both dreaded *those* things emerging.'

'They did in the end,' I said.

'Not to the public. There was a very good reason for that, as well . . . yet another thing I learned in that single session. The most extraordinary conversation I ever had in my professional capacity, or out of it.' His dark eyes were very remote, at once compassionate and judging. 'Soon, she told me, they all knew she'd be arrested . . . when the police found the knife, it was over. It was then that her mother sat down with her, and told her what would happen if she talked to any of the psychiatrists who tried to interview her. "If you tell the truth about yourself and your home life," she said, "they'll have you classified as a lunatic and sent to an asylum. They're cruel to people there, burn your brain out with electric shocks and leave you for days, not even able to feed yourself. And you'll never get out as long as you live, not then." "'I cried," Rebecca said, "and she held me, and said it didn't have to be that way. If I just kept quiet, said I'd been happy before, that I didn't know what had come over me . . .

"'Of course, I didn't talk to them," she said, "I was too scared. But I can trust you. I know that, now. You'd have had me sent to an asylum when I told you about Toffee, if you were like the other ones . . ."'

I understood too much, too suddenly, and looked at

him, appalled. When he spoke again, his voice was oddly gruff, and I thought I saw a subtle glint of tears in his eyes.

'Naturally, I told her over and over again that no psychiatrist in the world would behave like that ... but it was the adoption issue all over again, she simply didn't believe me. Still, I suppose the most important thing was that I'd gained her trust. She never spoke to anyone else about the things that really mattered to her, but after that extraordinary session, she spoke to me at length, in detail and completely without fear.

'I'm quite convinced that I knew her better than anyone else in that unit, children or staff. She was very different from the girl you might imagine and, as the years passed, she didn't change at all. Extremely sweet, in many ways. Self-possessed on the surface, but deeply shy behind that. She'd have any number of acquaintances who'd take to her, but no close friends at all. She was simply too afraid of opening up to people, to strangers. I liked her very much.'

'But ... you overruled the unit manager,' I said, confused. 'You recommended that she should go to the highest-security prison there was, didn't you?'

'I did indeed.'

He'd never appeared more comfortable with silence, and it had never seemed more maddening to me. I found myself forced to put a glaringly obvious question into words. 'Why did you think that, if you were so fond of her?'

'I said I liked her, and I did. But at the same time I was well aware that she was more potentially dangerous than any patient I'd ever treated ... more than thirty years later, I'd say the same.' His expression was inscrutable, meditative. 'To think where they ended up sending her, a virtually open prison with security designed for petty drug dealers and prostitutes – *that's* frightening enough – you're probably aware that I resigned over their decision, and you can be quite sure I didn't do that lightly. But, as for what happened next – releasing her into the world with a whole new identity – I simply can't describe to you what a mistake those people made.'

'But . . . nothing happened after all,' I said. 'If she'd ever killed again, we'd all know. It would have been all over the papers.'

'Nothing's happened *yet*. Rebecca would be forty-three years old today – hardly in her dotage. I still stand by my original judgement. She is, and always will be, a danger to society.'

'*Why?*' I meant to ask, was aghast to find myself demanding, 'What makes you so sure?'

'Because nothing will have changed inside her from all those years ago. In that respect, she's entirely different from the handful of child-murderers I've encountered in my career, and others I've read about; even worldwide there are surprisingly few. Virtually all of those children have a motive in common: absolute ignorance of what death really means. Their victims are strangers or casual acquaintances, they simply wish to know what it feels like to kill. Evil as that motive sounds, it *never* survives into adulthood . . . it's the darkest of childhood fascinations, outgrown as quickly as the lightest.' He paused for a moment, with the same faraway look. 'Rebecca's motives, by contrast, were only too clear. If she found herself in those same circumstances at twenty, or thirty, or forty, *she'd react in exactly the same way*.'

'But – with her secret identity – she'd be too afraid to do anything like that!' I burst out. 'It would be the end of everything for her. She'd know that—'

'Do you believe she was thinking so rationally when she

killed the hamster? Or Eleanor Corbett?' His smile was enigmatic. 'The red mist I referred to earlier had nothing to do with the impetuosity of childhood. She was as guarded at ten years of age as she will be today. In that state, self-preservation simply ceases to exist. The threat of personal revelation. Betrayal by a loved one. Those are her triggers. The hamster released one. Eleanor released both.'

I watched him sit back in his chair, aware of every breath I took. The silence around us grew deafening before he spoke again.

'You're aware of minefields, I imagine, Miss Jeffreys. The mines themselves are extraordinarily easy to produce and distribute – cheap things, scattered as casually as seeds. But there is no high-tech solution for clearing them from the ground once there. A mine can lay dormant for years, decades, longer. Then, when triggered ... I believe the technical term is *fragmentation*.

'I can't think of a better metaphor for that woman's mind. It will never be safe in her lifetime. The mines are still there.'

35

I was almost the only person in my carriage as the train started pulling out of Waterloo station. There was no background noise at all beyond the half-felt, half-heard rhythm of it settling into motion. The time was five to five. As we emerged from the station's shadowy outskirts, into early evening sunlight, I saw grimy house-backs and embankments frenetic with graffiti. I waited to be gradually taken back to Bournemouth and the world I knew.

The stillness around me was absolute, my thoughts in a state of turmoil. For the first time, I understood the darkness within Rebecca; she was more pitiable than I'd ever appreciated and, simultaneously, far more terrifying. Donald Hargreaves' remembered voice drifted in to me, quiet and authoritative, by turns sardonic and deadly serious. Telling me all over again that she was no pathetic victim to cuddle and console in my mind, that the damage that had been inflicted on her made her nothing short of lethal.

Yet I'd never empathised with her more deeply. I saw her life reflecting my own, and the picture was both fragmented and crystal clear; a shattered, age-speckled mirror showed me vivid elements of myself from crazy angles. My terror of revealing my writing, irrationally convinced that a single truth would give strangers a too-intimate knowledge of my life, and my past, and the things I was in most agony to hide from the world. I looked, and saw it become Rebecca's feverish secrecy regarding her adoption; it would instantly mark her out as an outsider, as unwanted. Her terror ran fathoms deeper than mine. I supposed it wasn't surprising. I'd acquired it on my own, while she'd been painstakingly tutored by an expert in the field: Rita Fisher had known the byways of paranoia and concealment as intimately as anyone could know anything. Nobody must ever know about the mental illness, or the drinking, or the marriage that was nothing more than a grotesque sham . . .

I thought of Rebecca's much-trumpeted love of her adoptive parents, her outburst in the Southfield Unit's common room; her passionate insistence that *she* was the Fishers' natural daughter, that the newspapers had lied. I wondered if she'd cling to her secret identity in the same way these days, and imagined that she would. The longing to become what everyone thought she was, what she longed to be in reality – a beloved daughter then, a blameless citizen now – she'd want to believe the illusion so deeply that she actually *would*, forcing her mind into the thought patterns of an envied stranger. She'd never betray her past in a casual remark, any more than she'd betrayed it at St Anthony's – before, of course, she'd made the mistake of confiding in someone else. Vicious, grasping, doomed little Eleanor Corbett . . .

Of course, Eleanor's hadn't been the only death. Rita Fisher had committed suicide two days after the trial had ended. From what I'd learned about her, I was quite convinced that she hadn't been driven to it by love of her adoptive daughter, or even by remorse. I imagined the effect public loathing would have on someone so insecure and unstable, whose only happiness came from the imagined respect and admiration of *the little people* around her. The firebombing of Dennis's factory would have been reflected in a thousand petty local incidents, intensifying as the trial began. I recalled *A Mind to Murder*, Eileen

Corbett's outburst in the courtroom. How Rita must have felt at that moment ... but, even as I understood her terror and humiliation, I found it impossible to sympathise with her in any way that mattered. She'd sacrificed Rebecca on the altar of her own neuroses. Ultimately, she'd created the monsters that would live inside a child till death.

And Dennis himself had colluded with that evil, if passively, giving her permission to adopt and to damage, indifferent to anything but outward respectability and success. I found it impossible to reconcile that knowledge with the other man I'd heard about, that regular visitor to the Southfield Unit who'd sent Rebecca presents every week. Perhaps he'd simply been driven by guilt, a desire to atone ... but I couldn't imagine those emotions existing in that chilly and joyless mind, no matter how hard I tried. It was the only aspect of Rebecca's life that I still didn't understand, and the realisation tormented me with a thousand lingering questions; discovery wasn't over yet, could never be complete till they were answered.

I got off at Bournemouth station, heading for the multistorey – the chilly bleakness inside vanished the second I drove out, and heavy gold warmth replaced it. Checking the dashboard clock, I saw the time was half past six, and was relieved to know I'd be home a good hour before Carl. Disturbing as it had felt at the time, I'd done the right thing in sneaking off to London without letting him know – I wouldn't have sacrificed that day's revelations for anything.

Beyond Wareham's town centre, I turned onto Ploughman's Lane and started up the hill. After the events of that day, the peace was indescribably soothing – grass ruffling in a slight breeze, a bird singing all alone. The serenity turned my restlessness down to a sub-audible murmur, amplifying a sense that Rebecca's darkness was very far away, that Donald Hargreaves had been describing events from another world.

Rosy-blue sky extended ahead as I approached the crest of the hill.

In the split-second that descent began, shock stabbed me in the heart. Two police cars were parked outside the white house in the distance, blue lights dead, surreal and nightmarish in the gentle evening light. *Something's happened to Liz* was my first terrified thought, but as I got closer, I saw she was deep in conversation with a uniformed officer in my open front doorway. Then I saw the jagged viciousness of broken glass round the edges of the ground floor windows, saw the living room curtains flapping out in a sudden breeze.

'My *God*.' Slamming the car door behind me, I raced towards them. 'What's *happened*?'

'Oh, Anna, I'm so terribly sorry.' It was Liz who answered. She was deathly pale, and sympathy and horror combined in her expression. 'When I got home from work about an hour ago, I saw someone had broken into your house – they'd gone, of course, but I called the police straight away. Your front door was wide open.'

My thought processes felt dazed and sluggish as I turned my gaze to the door itself. Its large panel of frosted glass had been shattered, too – the glass around the edges had been removed with a little more care than that at the windows, scraped away so an unknown arm could reach in, unlock. 'Oh, Jesus,' I said. 'I didn't use the mortice lock. When I went out, I just left it on the Yale – I didn't even *think*—'

'I wouldn't upset yourself about it, Mrs Howell.' The policeman must have got my name from Liz; he was

330

youngish, blondish. 'That wouldn't have mattered. A determined enough burglar could have climbed in through one of the windows just as easily. Without a burglar alarm, they'd have had an easy time doing it, especially with your neighbour out all day.'

'We've never even talked about getting a burglar alarm. We never thought ... the area seemed so peaceful.' My voice sounded strange to my own ears, flat and drugged. What should have been my first thought occurred to me out of nowhere, and I spoke more sharply. 'What have they taken?'

'There was no way we could tell, I'm afraid. Not till you came back. We've got two officers dusting for fingerprints at the moment. If you'd like to look around, let me know what's missing ...'

The rest of his sentence faded into the distance behind me as I stepped into the living room. A familiar domestic setting had become a war zone, broken glass glittering in piles and shards and occasional specks that caught the light like diamonds. *This was home only this morning,* I thought, *I'll wake up in bed and it won't have happened at all,* and I realised what a cliché it was to think that, I'd never have let a character of mine think it in a million years. Behind the dead nothing, hysteria rose like bile; I clapped my hand to my mouth as if to suppress vomit rather than giggles, swallowing them, forcing them back down.

'Mrs Howell?' the young policeman said behind me. 'Can you tell me what's been stolen?'

I stood and looked as if I'd never seen this place before and had no idea what should be where. A single glaring absence reminded me abruptly: the empty shelf where the Tiffany lamp had stood. I closed my eyes and saw the room as it had been. 'Our lamp's gone,' I said in a flat, blank voice I'd never heard before. 'My husband bought it. It's not real Tiffany, but it's very nice.'

'I'm sorry about that.' His tone was both dubious and indulgent, deliberately understanding the eccentricities of shock. 'Is there anything else?'

'The DVD player. The stereo.' I saw their absence without surprise. My gaze returned to the shelf like a magnet to true north; I remembered Carl unwrapping something in the kitchen during our first week here, and felt nothing. 'They don't really matter, they're insured. It's just the lamp. My husband bought it from an antiques shop. He thought I'd like it.'

'Surprising the burglars didn't help themselves to the telly while they were here.' His brisk, jovial voice dragged my attention towards the corner, where the huge wide-screen set was apparently undamaged. 'Well, thank the Lord for small mercies. It looks like a good one.'

I barely heard him – as he spoke, I was approaching the kitchen with slow sleepwalker's steps that clearly mirrored my state of mind. The back windows had been smashed as well. Glass crunched under my feet. Through the window frames, past the jagged shards that still clung to their edges, the back garden extended unchanged, serene in the summer evening.

'Your microwave looks like a write-off,' the policeman was saying. 'It might have been accidentally smashed by whatever they used to break the windows. Whatever it was, they took it with them when they left. Of course, there's nothing to rule out deliberate vandalism. From the look of it, their tastes certainly ran that way.'

The words meant nothing to me. Deep inside, I could feel the thick numbing ice of shock beginning to melt around something else – something dark and rotted and terrible trapped inside it, something I didn't want to see.

'Mrs Howell?' the voice asked loudly. 'I asked you if there was anything missing from this room?'

My gaze panned across devastation, elements of familiarity grotesque in this new context; *A Mind To Murder* had gone, I saw. It had been by the fruit bowl when I'd left that morning, had been there for weeks. I found myself staring at the fruit bowl itself, a surreal still-life in a war-torn landscape. Broken glass had fallen across the table. Tiny shards glinted up from the apples and oranges and bananas. *We'll have to throw them out*, I thought randomly, *they'll never be safe to eat now*, and, as I thought it, I felt the shock-ice melt a little more.

'Mrs Howell?'

The voice again, slightly impatient this time. I pulled myself back to reality; everything felt so wrong, as though I'd been dislocated from the world. 'I don't know,' I said, 'I don't think so. It doesn't matter, really.' Realising that he was looking at me oddly, I struggled to think of what he'd expect me to say. 'Have they been upstairs at all? The burglars?'

'Well, your bedroom doesn't appear to have been touched, which I suppose is something to be grateful for. But there's a bit more damage up there, all the same. They seem to have vandalised your husband's computer. Or is it yours?'

I didn't answer – even as he spoke, I was hurrying out of the kitchen and up the stairs as fast as I could, taking two at a time. I squeezed past two uniformed strangers dusting the banisters for prints – white-gloved, patient, pernickety – and had a bizarre momentary image of the gardeners in *Alice in Wonderland* patiently painting the roses. It vanished as abruptly as it had arrived. I was standing in the doorway of the spare room, my sense of unreality fading with terrifying speed.

333

As far as I could remember, the blinds in here had been open when I'd left the house. Now they were three-quarters drawn. Razor-thin slits of light slanted across shadowy greyness the colour of cold ashes. The monitor's screen had been smashed, and the PC itself lay in the centre of the room, a wide crack along its creamy-grey casing, an ominous intricacy of circuits showing through. The fax machine seemed to have been attacked with even greater ferocity; it had been annihilated. And there was something very important missing. Something that had been on the bottom shelf of the desk.

'They've taken my folder,' I said tonelessly.

The policeman had followed me up without me even noticing. 'What folder?'

His tone implied dubious eyebrows being raised at a colleague, but I couldn't have cared less. Slow, swooning horror overcame me; Mr Wheeler's image floated lazily to the surface of my mind, like something pale and drowned and bloated in dark water. *Only when she got home from work*, Maureen Evans had said to me a thousand years ago, *all her windows had been smashed in. She got the police round straight away.* The parallels were too close, I realised. This could be nothing but revenge.

'What folder, Mrs Howell?'

More than anything, I wanted to tell him all about my research and my fears, but knew I couldn't – Carl could be home any minute, and he'd tell Carl. I was almost certain the policeman wouldn't believe me anyway, this cheerful, straightforward young policeman who hadn't expected me to react anywhere near as strongly. From the corner of my eye, I could see him giving me an appraising, sideways glance, a look that clearly read *caution, lunatic at work*.

'I don't know,' I said finally. 'It doesn't matter. Look – I'm sorry – I've got to sit down. I need to sit down.'

Back downstairs, in the shattered kitchen, we dusted down chairs before sitting at the table. Liz was sweeping up the shards around us with swift, practical ease. I thought of the two of us chatting over cups of tea in this very room, and realised I was crying; the policeman sat stiff and awkward as the tears came, but Liz hurried over, laying down her dustpan and brush.

'Come on, now, Anna,' she coaxed, putting an arm round my shoulder. 'Don't cry. It's not the end of the world.'

'We'll do our very best to catch the people responsible, Mrs Howell,' the policeman said. 'I'm sure you know how hard it is to solve this sort of crime, but you can rest assured that we'll try our hardest.'

I broke off crying with a hoarse, unladylike snort, from embarrassment more than anything else. Across the table, the policeman spoke more gently as Liz released my shoulder. 'What time is your husband due back from work?'

'I don't know,' I said, sniffing. 'Any time now.'

'Well, we'd better stay and speak to him as well. We certainly don't mean to intrude, Mrs Howell, but it's obvious you're very shocked.'

I longed to tell him *why*, but knew that anything I said would be anxiously passed on to Carl; I could tell that the policeman envisioned him as a potential oasis of sanity and rationality, as though he was my guardian rather than my husband. Seconds unwound, in which I bludgeoned my mind for the right words. Finally, I found something that wasn't a secret from either Carl or Liz, that still cast new light on events.

'This happened to the woman who lived here before us, you know,' I said to the policeman, making a huge effort to sound as reasonable as I could. '*She* had her windows smashed too, every one.'

I couldn't quite keep the quiver of fear out of my voice and was appalled to see him smiling indulgently. 'Oh, I know what happened. You must think this house is jinxed – but you don't have to worry about that. That incident had nothing to do with burglary. I can't talk about it in detail as I'm sure you understand, but it was very much a personal matter. In your case, we're looking at simple robbery and vandalism. Teenagers, maybe. It certainly looks that way.'

He didn't understand – but there was nothing I could say, no way I could correct him without damning myself. 'To be honest,' he went on, 'a nice house like this in the country, without a burglar alarm that alerts us when it's triggered – you've really been asking for trouble. I'd strongly advise you and your husband to get one fitted.'

Something maddeningly patronising in his voice forced me to speak. 'It's *not* just a burglary,' I burst out, 'I *know* it's not. It's connected to what happened before, to the woman who lived here then—'

Again, he looked cautious, but in completely the wrong way. He wasn't fearing for my safety, I realised, but my sanity. 'You haven't received any threats since you moved in, have you?'

I was very aware of Liz's discreet but constant presence in the room – she didn't know about the phone calls, and God only knew what she'd think if I told this policeman now. *And anything I said would be passed straight on to Carl.* 'No,' I said quietly. 'There's been nothing like that here.'

'Well, Mrs Howell, there were certainly previous threats made last time. Letters, silent phone calls, that sort of thing. The two incidents are completely unrelated – I can give you my word on it.'

I barely took in the last half of his sentence at all – *Rebecca* had received the phone calls, too, only Maureen's son-in-law hadn't known or hadn't told her. For a second, I thought I was about to black out. The parallels weren't just close, they were virtually identical. Mr Wheeler was trying to drive me out, as she'd been driven out herself—

The door leading on to the hallway was open, the front door ajar beyond that. I saw and heard Carl's Audi turning into the drive. Across the table, the policeman spoke with thinly-veiled relief. 'Well, Mrs Howell. Looks like your husband's home.'

'The emergency glaziers shouldn't be too long now,' Carl said, as he laid the cup of tea down by my unmoving hand. 'They'll be here soon, they said.'

It was eight thirty in the evening, and the police had left some time ago. Outside, it was starting to get dark. We were still in the kitchen, where the worst of the damage had been cleared away – he'd swept up most of the glass with Liz's help before she'd gone home, offering to stay, urging us to let her know if we needed anything. He'd thanked her profusely, but I'd been in no state to do or say anything very much; my own words of gratitude had sounded wooden, scripted.

It was amazing how often the same thing could slam into your mind with fresh shock – every few minutes, the enormity of what had happened struck me. How alien everything looked now, felt now. Even now the piles of glass were gone, I still saw tiny glints of it winking up at me from odd places. Or perhaps I imagined them; I couldn't be sure. Carl had rolled the blinds down in front of empty frames, and they rattled intermittently in the breeze – it had been warm two hours ago, was now chilly, insistent.

I picked up the cup of tea with both hands and sipped at it like medicine. 'Thanks,' I said quietly, setting it down again.

'Come on, Annie. It's all right now.' He came over to the table as Liz had done earlier, putting his hands on my shoulders; it should have felt reassuring, but didn't at all. 'It was just a burglary, at the end of the day. It happens to just about everyone sooner or later. *We* got broken into when I was a kid. We were on holiday in Spain at the time, got home to find half our stuff gone.'

If only it *had* just been a burglary, if only it *had* – the words caught in my throat as he spoke again, resigned, good-natured, practical. 'Everything's insured, everything that matters, anyway . . . Christ alone knows what they wanted with some of the stuff they took. That old camera I had in the hallway cabinet, the clock radio in the spare room – we'd have been lucky to get five quid for them at a car boot sale. For *both* of them.' Breaking off for a second, he smiled ruefully. 'Still, it's a bloody nuisance. I could kick myself for not getting a burglar alarm fitted – I didn't even think about it. Don't worry, Annie. I'll find out about getting one first thing tomorrow. This time next week, the place'll be like Fort Knox.'

I found it terrible to watch his misplaced reassurance, knowing he had no idea what there really was to be worried about. Suddenly I longed to tell him the truth, all of it. Even if it made him furiously angry, I thought, it had to be better than *this*; the weight of secret and solitary knowledge had never been heavier. I felt it pressing down on me, and forced myself to speak.

'Carl, I don't think this was just a burglary.'

He looked at me strangely. 'Of course it was,' he said, 'what do you mean?'

'Well . . .'

My voice tailed off before he spoke again. 'Come on, Annie – tell me, for God's sake. What are you talking about?'

The words were angry, but the tone was just concerned, slightly worried, and it seemed to give me the final push I needed. I reached the brink of confession for the hundredth time, but, instead of backing away fearfully as I'd done before, I positioned myself on its furthest edge and jumped into empty air. 'It's because of my research,' I said. 'I'm sure of it.'

Still he watched me, and I couldn't read his expression. I went on, trying to speak slowly, calmly. 'What I've been finding out about Rebecca's life . . . well, a while ago, I went to interview a vet who knew her while she lived here. Mr Wheeler, his name was, apparently they'd been close friends. It was terrible. As soon as I told him I wanted to find out about her, he just launched into this *outburst*, thought I was asking because I was ghoulish, callous, gloating over the details of her being driven out. Remember that collar we found in the cupboard? He said someone had killed her dog to make her leave. Anyway, he was furious. Practically threw me out of his surgery. Didn't even give me the chance to explain that I wasn't like that, he was *wrong*—'

Huge unfairness overcame me, filling my throat with the hot, dry lump of incipient tears – they pricked my eyes, and I blinked them away fiercely. 'I didn't tell you at the time, because . . . well, I didn't think it was all that important, not then. But a couple of weeks later, I was hoovering our room and saw him standing outside. His car was parked by the side of the road, and he was looking at the house. And not long after that, I came down here one morning, and found Socks dead on the garden path—'

I broke off for a second, lighting a cigarette, inhaling deeply. 'It was just like Rebecca's dog, what had happened to it. And Mr Wheeler had been so *close* to her. I thought it might be his idea of revenge. He'd been so furious with me – an eye for an eye, you know – doing to me what someone had done to *her*—'

I'd been addressing most of my words to the table-top, afraid to see the effect they might be having on him, and as I finished speaking, I dragged my gaze back to his face. I'd expected any combination of mounting anger and deep anxiety, but didn't see either – he looked bemused more than anything, forehead corrugated, eyes uncomprehending. 'Is *that* what's been getting to you so badly for the past few weeks?' he asked. 'What you've been so worried about, and wouldn't tell me?'

I nodded, and saw the creases in his forehead deepen; his scrutiny had become troubled and oddly distant, as if he was looking at me through a microscope. 'Annie,' he said carefully, 'I don't know why you let it bother you. It's just a few coincidences – not even *striking* ones, come to think of it. Just . . . things that happened.'

I stared at him, wrong-footed, disbelieving. I could have been talking to the policeman again, hearing him dismiss my fears with patronising gentleness, the way a psychiatric nurse might react to a harmless schizophrenic gibbering about vampires under the bed. 'Look,' he went on. 'That vet got the wrong end of the stick and got angry. He happened to be passing one day, and thought maybe he'd call in on Liz – he saw her car wasn't here and drove off. And then her cat died . . . it was an old cat, you've said as much yourself. There's nothing out of the ordinary in any of it . . . you must be able to see that.'

'For Christ's sake, Carl,' I said urgently, 'look what's happened. What do you make of all *this*?'

I gestured at the blinds that formed a curtain in front of infinite night, as they rattled again in the wind. 'This happened to Rebecca as well, I told you about that months ago. *Her* windows were smashed; *it's exactly the same.* That vet's behind it all, that Mr Wheeler – it's some kind of revenge, I'm quite sure of it—'

His expression was incredulous but also deeply disturbed. He looked like a man confronting something that he'd read about in passing, but had never expected to encounter in the flesh, a man who had no idea what to do in this situation. We both knew it was his turn to speak, but he didn't say anything for endless seconds. It was as if he'd forgotten his lines.

'That's just *ridiculous*,' he said at last. 'Come on, think about it rationally. It was a burglary, and that's the end of it. What's our DVD player and stereo got to do with your bloody research?'

'They took my book. My book on Rebecca Fisher.' He shrugged evasively, and sudden frustration rose inside me, exploding into rage. I gestured towards the fruit bowl, slightly too wildly. 'It was *there* this morning, *right there.* You've seen it there, I know you have – you've seen it there dozens of times—'

'I have, but *so what*? They took all kinds of things, in case you didn't notice. What about the camera and clock radio? They weren't worth anything either. It looks like they helped themselves to whatever caught their eye ... maybe one of them was a true-crime fan, wanted something to read on the drive home.'

His humour was a knee-jerk reaction, no more or less – he showed no sign of smiling, or even wanting to. Still, it seemed to imply a flippant indifference to my fears, and infuriated me. 'They took my folder, as well. I didn't tell you before, but they did. I kept it in the spare room, and it had all my research notes in it. Why would *that* have gone, if it was just a burglary?' I stubbed out my cigarette viciously, lighting another at once. 'Burglars wouldn't even have *noticed* it, they'd have just—'

'This is insane,' he interrupted abruptly. 'Literally *insane* – I mean, Jesus, Annie, it's like something from the *X Files*. Some world conspiracy about your *research*? An evil vet avenging Rebecca Fisher?' His voice was straight from a management meeting, but he looked as stunned as I'd felt coming into the house that evening. 'Maybe the burglars just liked the look of your precious folder. Why would anyone want to steal your *notes*?'

Suddenly, nothing was too damning to keep to myself – I'd have told him any secret in the world, just to make him believe me. 'There's something else,' I said quietly. 'Something I haven't told you. I got a silent phone call here, the week before last. There was just breathing down the line for a few seconds, then someone hung up.'

I paused, trying to gauge the impact my words were having, but he'd become poker-faced, inscrutable. 'Then, a couple of nights later, the same thing happened to you. Only there wasn't any breathing when you answered. They just hung up . . .'

I watched his blank look giving way to something else, like a Polaroid photograph developing itself before my eyes. As the picture grew clearer, I froze up inside. His expression had become more aghast than ever and, instead of horror, his voice was full of incredulity.

'Annie,' he said, 'you're just not making sense. The one I picked up wasn't a *silent call*, it was just a wrong number. And I'm sure the one you picked up was just the same.'

I was starkly reminded of Petra's attitude towards my

fears, over the phone – only I hadn't told her everything, had been convinced that, if desperation ever forced me to, her complacency would instantly snap into vicarious terror. And I had nothing left to tell Carl, I realised. I'd slammed all the cards down at once, confident of an awed gasp that hadn't come. 'It *wasn't* just a wrong number,' I said furiously. 'I could hear someone breathing.'

'Yes, Annie. People do that.'

'Not *that* kind of breathing, not *normal* breathing. It sounded deliberate.' Even to my own ears, I sounded neurotic, hysterical; the world's worst hypochondriac, interpreting banal flu symptoms as the onset of scarlet fever. Only I knew how serious it really was, and pressed on desperately, trying to make him understand. '*Rebecca* got silent calls here herself – the policeman told me earlier. When I got back from London this evening—'

It was as if I'd been running for my life, and had stumbled straight into a man-trap while glancing fearfully over my shoulder – my sentence tripped over itself and went sprawling. Carl's nonspecific concern suddenly sharpened, focused. '*London?*'

I'd have to explain, I knew; the truth had jumped out too obviously to deny, or even to mitigate with a half-lie. 'I went there earlier,' I said unwillingly, 'to interview someone about Rebecca. I'd have told you, but I didn't think it mattered. I was going to—'

'*Look.*' His interruption came unexpectedly, blunt and utterly decisive, as if he'd been grappling with a huge and intricate problem for weeks, and had finally decided on the only possible course of action. 'I want you to stop this research, Annie. I've said it before, but this time, I mean it. You're making yourself ill. You know what I mean. I don't like to *think* that, never mind say it, but it looks like you're sliding back all over again ... what you told me about your fresher term at university ...'

His voice tailed off, suddenly awkward. I stared at him. 'You don't believe me about the threat here, do you? You don't believe me at all.'

He didn't quite look at me. 'I don't think you're *lying*, Annie. I just think you're ... imagining things. We were burgled today. That's all there is to it. Everything's perfectly safe.'

The suffocating terror of not being believed on a crucial issue by someone who knew and loved you better than anyone in the world – it was helplessness and betrayal and utter isolation all at once. I wanted to scream, to rage at him for not understanding, but could only bite down on that impulse as hard as possible; a hysterical outburst would only strengthen his conviction that he was right, I was wrong, my research had begun to unbalance me.

I nodded without speaking or looking at him. Suddenly, I couldn't bear to see him, and didn't trust myself with words. There was a tense silence before the sound of an approaching van cut through it, gradually becoming deafening through the shattered windows as it turned into our driveway.

'Thank God for that,' Carl said, rising from his seat. 'It's the glaziers.'

36

The following morning I opened my eyes to the half-lit familiarity of our bedroom, and felt Carl stirring drowsily beside me as the alarm went. For a fraction of a second, I couldn't understand why I felt so unsettled, then it all came back to me; the emergency glaziers working late into the night, Carl going next door to apologise about the noise shortly after they'd arrived. I remembered hammering and sawing and loud male strangers' voices filling the kitchen and living room, as if a small invading army had been setting up camp on our ground floor.

They'd finally finished, packed up and driven off at around half past midnight. We'd gone to bed immediately after that. We hadn't said another word about the things that really mattered – they had been abandoned on the glaziers' arrival, and felt like something indefinitely postponed.

'Well,' he said, reaching out to switch the alarm off, 'suppose I'd better make a move.'

'You don't have to go into work *today*, do you?'

'It's a Wednesday morning, Annie.' He smiled. 'There's no reason not to – it was a burglary yesterday, not a bereavement.'

I could see him trying his best to pretend last night's conversation had never taken place – or, if it had done, the issues had all been resolved for good. I found myself trying to do the same.

'I'll find out about getting a burglar alarm today,' he said, getting out of bed. 'I'll track down a decent security firm this afternoon. The sooner we get one installed, the better – for our own peace of mind, if nothing else.'

He went into the bathroom, and I heard him showering. Even here, in this bedroom that hadn't been touched at all, everything around me felt terribly wrong; the whole feel of the place had changed, and something new and alien and threatening had crept in to invade it. I realised that I didn't want Carl to go to work at all, that I suddenly feared being left alone here. And at the same time, I knew that I could never say so without feeding his awful suspicions. *It looks like you're sliding back all over again,* he'd said last night, *what you told me about your fresher term at university . . .*

Coming back in, he started getting dressed for work, and talked to me as he did so. 'I'll get in touch with the insurance people, as well – they should pay up for the missing stuff. I'm not too sure what they'll say about your computer. It might be fixable, God knows I'm no IT expert, but it looked pretty much of a write-off to me.'

'Me too,' I said. 'Same as the microwave.'

'Well, like I said last night, it's a bloody nuisance, but we can always replace them. We might as well get the new DVD player and stereo first, though. Why don't we go into Bournemouth on Saturday, pick them up together?'

Everything between us had become deliberately, carefully superficial – we'd glued our normal relationship together like a vase, it could come apart again at any second if we put it straight back to its intended use. Behind the too-fragile surface existed things that couldn't be discussed at all easily. 'That'll be fine,' I said, 'and we can take the computer for a check-up somewhere. PC World should be able to tell us the damage.'

He left for work soon afterwards. As the front door closed behind him, silence exploded throughout the house; I went to the window as I had done yesterday, looked out, watched him drive away. This time, I dreaded seeing the black car vanish over the horizon, and it was gone far too soon. Around me, I felt the world become as alien and sinister as it had seemed when we'd first moved here, but it was worse now, a thousand times worse.

Washing and dressing quickly, I came downstairs as though something was dragging me – I didn't want to see the ground-floor rooms at all, not this morning. In the living room, I forced myself to draw the curtains. Perfect sunlight showed thorough repairs hastily tidied-up after – specks of plaster dust spotted the carpet by the windows, and one of the workmen had left his half-empty coffee cup by the skirting board. There was a faint, unplaceable smell like glue and wood-shavings. Everything around me looked stripped, abandoned, desolate.

I went into the kitchen to wash up the workman's cup, and it was exactly the same in there: the air seemed too still, and noises far louder than they had any right to be. I turned the tap on, and the sound of running water filled my ears. I could feel the tension around me thickening, coalescing to become a presence in its own right, summoning voices, memories, and ghosts of the past.

I couldn't stay here, I realised. The empty rooms terrified me. I had to get out.

Getting my handbag and keys, I went out to the car and started driving into Bournemouth. I had nothing to do there, but it called to me as a temporary place of safety – somewhere that wasn't all that different from Reading, where there'd be people and places to distract me from this new fear. Even Rebecca had diminished in my mind; there was nothing inside me but panic, and an animal impulse to escape.

Once in Bournemouth, the time passed slowly and far

too quickly. I wandered aimlessly round shops I didn't want to buy anything from, and tried to warm myself with strangers' voices. They came from all sides, in the height of summer and the school holidays, families and couples and groups of friends. I seemed to be the only person in the whole city who was there on my own. In the heat and the cheerful crowds, my mind kept returning to the empty house full of silence, the coffee cup where I'd left it by the sink. And I thought about Carl, frowning in an office I'd never seen, remembering the events of last night. Wondering what the hell was happening to me, and whether I was losing my mind . . .

But I wasn't, I told myself urgently, I *wasn't*. I'd call Petra soon, and tell her all about it. I'd do it that weekend, while Carl was gardening. She'd understand when she knew the full story. There was a crucial difference between her and Carl, created by circumstances alone: he hadn't known me during that terrible fresher term, but she had done. She'd be able to see that it wasn't the same at all, that the dangers surrounding me were only too real.

Outside Starbucks, I sat with a paper I couldn't concentrate on, and a coffee I couldn't enjoy, and a huge clock ticking slowly in my head. Each second brought me a little closer to the inevitability of going home. I got another coffee to delay it, and another, smoking too many cigarettes and trying not to think about the time. But the world seemed sadistically determined to remind me – the clear line where the sunlight ended inching across my table, other tables emptying as the last hour or so of shopping beckoned. Finally, I had no option but to check my watch. It was almost half past five in the evening.

I longed to stay here, but knew I couldn't. I'd have to hoover up the plaster-dust round the windows before Carl came home from work, and I'd have to make a start on dinner. I couldn't bear the thought that my having been out all day could confirm his worst suspicions, that they could rapidly set into cast-iron certainty. He'd see my actions today as bizarre and irrational – scared to return to a comfortable home, running away from it like a child playing truant . . .

All the way back to Abbots Newton, I tried my utmost to see the situation through his eyes – there wasn't any danger, we'd just been burgled – but it didn't work at all. I knew he was wrong. The closer Ploughman's Lane got, the colder I felt inside. The inexorable drive up the hill dragged out for minutes.

No police cars, this time. Liz's car wasn't there, either. Just the white house in the distance, empty and waiting. And the things that would greet me inside it: the coffee cup, the plaster dust, the silence.

I'd never known Carl to put anything important off, and getting the burglar alarm fitted was no exception. On Friday afternoon, two men arrived to install it. They accepted occasional cups of tea with thanks and asked about the burglary with exactly the right combination of briskness and sympathy. I found it oddly reassuring to submerge my fears in the normality of the situation – a down-to-earth young wife taking positive measures to prevent a second break-in, untroubled by anything but the loss of an expensive stereo and DVD player.

'Well, it certainly won't happen again now, Mrs Howell,' one of the men said. 'When this alarm's set and triggered, it'll alert the local police straight away. You'd best be careful you don't set it off yourself, by accident – if that happens, you should call the station in Wareham, let them know ASAP before they send a car round. Be a bit embarrassing, I'd imagine.'

'Thanks,' I said, 'I'll remember that.'

It was easy to smile when they were there. But they were gone only too soon. As the front door closed behind them, the burglar alarm didn't reassure me in the slightest, not in any way that mattered. It had been designed as protection against impersonal greed, not hatred, and loyalty, and vengeance.

We *hadn't* just been burgled. I was as sure of that as I'd ever been of anything. If we had, I thought, our TV would have been the first item to go – it had been far and away the most expensive thing in the living room, and hadn't even been touched. While *A Mind to Murder* and my research notes were gone without a trace. I thought a lot about those notes, with a sense of loss almost like bereavement – the school photograph, the faxed-through psychologist's report, the photocopies of old newspaper pages I'd made in the London library – I knew them all virtually off by heart, but that didn't seem to matter. In an odd sort of way, they'd acquired sentimental value; souvenirs of discovery and fascination, tangible mementoes of the real Rebecca.

In the days following the break-in, I mourned them – but, at the same time, Rebecca had faded from the foreground of my concerns. Recent events had swept her away like a wave, and she'd become a tiny speck on the horizon. The tide would bring her back soon, I thought, she wouldn't be left adrift for long. But I simply couldn't focus on her now; whenever I tried, I saw Socks lying dead on the path, heard those seconds of breathing down the phone, recalled Carl's incredulous horror in the kitchen.

I'd been convinced that, in a matter of days, my fear of the house would begin to fade, but, as the week progressed, it showed no sign of doing so. I couldn't think of anything but what had happened here and what might happen next, and claustrophobic foreboding shadowed every second of every hour of every quiet and purposeless day. When Carl had left for work, I went into Bournemouth or Wareham, trying and failing to forget what I was afraid of. And the final stages of the drive back took on the texture of nightmare, repetition only seeming to make it worse; that slow ascent to the top of the hill, dreading the split-second in which the house came into view below.

The evenings, I knew, should have been better – Carl's presence should have provided a temporary respite from anxiety. But now I'd told him everything and hadn't been believed, it only seemed to make things worse. Added to the burden of my fear was the towering necessity of concealing it – I saw everything I did and said reflected in his expression, a moment of wary reassurance, a flicker of fresh concern. He watched me too closely, and tried to pretend he didn't; I struggled to act as normally as I possibly could, and tried to pretend I wasn't doing any such thing.

I raged at myself for feeling that desperate need to reassure him – I was right, he was wrong, I should drag Tuesday night's argument back out kicking and screaming, and refuse to replace it till he understood the danger we faced. But something stopped me, made me conciliate where I should demand. I couldn't bear to hear him voice his fears about me a second time. Everything he'd said before still haunted me; it made me doubt myself, somehow, even as I knew there was no reason to. So I spent my evenings walking on eggshells, as he did, edging uncertainly round a strange, dark place that neither of us fully understood.

On Saturday, we went into Bournemouth together, and I tried to pretend I hadn't been there twice in the past four days. We took the computer into PC World and explained to the assistant what had happened to it. The assistant said he'd look it over, and told us to come back this time next week. In Dixons, we bought the identical twins of our old stereo and DVD player, and carried them back to the car side by side. I was very aware of how passing strangers would see us – a straightforwardly happy couple, intent on enhancing a well-loved home – but any real togetherness between us had been driven into abrupt retreat. Fear could outweigh love very easily, I realised, when it was this raw. On the drive home, we talked like acquaintances beginning to realise they had nothing in common, before lapsing into the kind of silence that acknowledged the fact outright.

When we got back, we set up our new possessions where our old ones had been. My gaze returned to the television, and I couldn't stop myself from speaking. 'It's strange, don't you think? That the burglars didn't take that, too?'

'Maybe they just didn't have room for it in their car, who knows?' There must have been a dubious quality to my silence – as he plugged in the DVD player, he turned, looked at me searchingly. 'Look,' he said quietly, 'there's no mystery to it, Annie. I don't know how I can make you see that. It's *over*, everything's *fine*.'

I'd intended my question to sound artless, casual – a throwaway statement that would spark doubt in his mind. My heart sank as I realised I hadn't succeeded, that my motivation in speaking had been glaringly obvious. 'I never said it *wasn't*,' I said unconvincingly, 'I was just saying, that's all.'

If possible, that brief exchange made the tension between us even deeper – over dinner that evening, his preoccupation was palpable and unspoken, radiating from him in silent waves. So strong, and so appallingly misdirected. And I felt at once culpable and utterly helpless; an unwitting decoy, distracting Carl's gaze while terrible things rustled in the background.

I filled the long pauses with thoughts of Petra. In my mind, she'd begun to feel like a saviour, a lifebelt – someone who'd known me before, who could advise and understand without judging. I'd call her tomorrow, I told myself, when Carl was busy in the garden, and I was alone.

That night, I drank more than usual, knowing it was the only way I'd be able to get to sleep before the small hours: insomnia had begun to plague me, and I turned to the only remedy at hand. When I woke up on Sunday morning, I felt heavy-limbed and headachey. It took me a second to realise I'd been woken by Carl getting out of bed; half-opening my eyes, I saw him moving towards the door slowly and quietly, obviously trying not to disturb me.

I was going to say something sleepy and incoherent, but could think of nothing beyond the blindingly obvious – *Oh, you're awake* – making me seem wakeful and jumpy and everything I didn't want to. Closing my eyes again, I heard him leave the room. I'd been expecting his footsteps to move towards the bathroom, but, instead, they began to negotiate the stairs. There was, I thought, something oddly stealthy about the way he moved, far beyond simple consideration for a sleeping wife. As if it was very important to him that I didn't hear.

The second I thought that, it seemed to infect me, too. I sat up as quietly as I could, trying not to make the mattress creak as I leaned across the bed to check the clock. Eight thirty a.m., I saw – we normally both lay in for at least another hour on Sundays. And all the time, I was tracing those distant footsteps to the bottom of the stairs, through the hallway, into the living room where I lost the trail completely.

A long silence. Then, a handful of muffled words that I couldn't make out at all. He was on the phone, I realised; another pause extended before he started talking again, more volubly. I was sitting bolt upright now. While the exact words he spoke were blurred to incomprehensibility, I could sense a tone running through them like a strong current: unease, enforced secrecy. It somehow chilled me to recognise that. I was reminded too strongly of how I must have sounded last weekend, talking to Petra while he mowed the lawn outside.

My hangover was gone without a trace and I felt exquisitely, appallingly alert. I desperately wanted to know what he was saying, but couldn't possibly go to eavesdrop at the top of the stairs; everything in his tone said that part of him was listening out for the slightest noise. Before I'd come to any conscious decision, I was inching out of bed and across the carpet, reaching the phone on the dressing-table, lifting the receiver with infinite care.

I found it only too easy to imagine him hearing the tiny inevitable *click* down the line, but his voice clearly told me that he hadn't. There was no sudden wariness, just the quiet, watchful worry I'd already heard. I'd picked the extension up mid-word, and listened to him talking with my heart in my mouth.

'—so, obviously, I'm pretty worried. It's been going on for *weeks* now. I thought it'd get better, but since the break-in it's got a million times worse. After she told me all that crazy stuff, that night, it was like she closed herself off from me completely. I couldn't believe what she said, like I told you, it really freaked me out. She can't even see how irrational it is; she's *acting* as if she can, but she's not fooling me at all . . . she's still terrified about all that, and

354

trying to pretend she's not. Pretending she's all right now, and she's forgotten all about it, and it's so bloody obvious that she hasn't . . .'

Dismay crawled over my skin on a thousand tiny legs. I heard him pause for a second to take a breath. Then, a second voice came down the line, freezing me where I stood. It was Petra.

'It was the same when she phoned me last Sunday. She was really scared, I could tell, talking about some threatening phone call. It just sounded like a wrong number to me, and I said so. She said she felt better now she'd talked to me, and she could see I was right – but I could tell she didn't mean that at all, she was just saying it. She honestly thinks that vet's out to get her, told me all about it when I came to visit . . . does that make any kind of sense to you?'

'None at all. That's exactly why I'm worried.'

Another pause – the world seemed to be contracting around me, becoming tighter and hotter and more claustrophobic every second. 'Look, I'm really sorry to bother you, Petra, but I can't imagine her talking to anyone else about this. I'd say you're just about the only person she still trusts. If she gets in touch and tells you anything else, you'll let me know, won't you? Christ, you know I don't want to *spy* on her, but she's just not talking to me, and I don't know *what's* going on in her mind. I don't know what to do for the best, right now.'

'Don't worry. I'll tell you if she says anything to me. Let *me* know, too, if anything else happens. I really hope she's okay, Carl. You don't know what it was like for her, before . . .'

'I can guess. She's told me about it.' In my mind's eye, I could see his pale, set face, the sudden hunted look crossing it as he checked the time. 'Listen, I'm going to have to go. I'm sorry about waking you up. But there wasn't any other time to call without her overhearing—'

'Don't worry. If you'd phoned four *hours* ago, it wouldn't have mattered. I'm worried about her myself, now. Listen, take care, and—'

I realised their conversation would end in a matter of seconds, and he'd be coming straight upstairs. Hanging up as quietly as I could, I returned to the bed as silently as I'd left it. I pressed half my face into the pillow, pulling the duvet up to conceal the other half. And, as I squeezed my eyes shut, I heard his footsteps on the stairs again; my imagination showed me every detail of his entrance, the flicker of reassurance in his eyes as he saw I was still dead to the world. He climbed into bed beside me, and lay down.

He was so close to me, his skin brushed mine. I felt as if we were separated by a mile or more. I could feel no hatred or even antagonism for my husband or best friend, no matter how hard I tried – I knew they both had my very best interests at heart, and knew that I couldn't blame either of them for thinking what they did. It seemed to make it worse that I couldn't muster any anger or bitterness, leaving me with nothing but a turmoil that was mine alone.

And I was alone. Absolutely. I knew for a fact that I couldn't call Petra and tell her what I really felt, not now. My terror would reach her through a half-trained translator – Carl's phone call would colour any natural response she might have, he'd prejudiced her verdict like a careless editorial. Everything I said would come across as the ravings of an unbalanced mind; a stolen folder, a murdered cat, a campaign of terror against me that nobody else could see.

I lay there, and pretended to sleep. Actually trying to

sleep was out of the question. The world was full of Sunday-morning inertia, the cool, shadowy rooms and drawn curtains around and below me waiting for sunlight to snap them into life. But it felt as if the house, too, was only pretending to be asleep; the atmosphere was not that of exhaustion, but of an animal preparing to spring.

37

Since the break-in, I'd started to think it couldn't possibly get any worse when I was alone in the house. On Monday morning, however, it did. The conversation I'd overheard the previous morning came back to haunt me with new clarity after Carl had left for work, and as I prepared to face the day, my sense of claustrophobia was indescribable.

You can't go into Bournemouth again, I urged myself, *it's ridiculous. There's no escape there; you know you'll only have to come back.* But the dissenting inner voice felt like an argument put up for form's sake only, and had no genuine credibility. Deep down, I knew that the car journey and the interminable, aimless hours round the shops were as inevitable as night following day. I didn't just want to get out of the house, I needed to.

I was making myself a cup of tea in the kitchen prior to leaving when the knock came at the back door, taking me by surprise. 'Hello, dear,' Liz said amiably, 'not interrupting anything, am I?'

In the depth of my isolation, I'd virtually forgotten about her, and it came as an extraordinary relief to see her smiling on the doorstep; to realise that I wasn't entirely alone here after all, that I still retained one true ally. 'God, no,' I said, a little too vehemently – then, in a rush, 'come on in. The kettle's on.'

'I just thought I'd pop by and see how you were bearing up,' she said, sitting down. 'I'd have come before – you know how fond I am of you, dear – but I didn't like to intrude. I knew you'd both have so much to do here.'

'Oh, we've sorted everything out, now,' I said, trying my best to smile. 'Everything's pretty much back to normal.'

'It certainly looks that way. Your workmen did a wonderful job with the windows in here – you'd never know they were broken less than a week ago.' The kettle boiled beside me, and I made her tea and brought it over to the table. 'So what exactly did the burglars take?' she asked as I sat down. 'Nothing very important to you, I hope?'

'Not really. Apart from our Tiffany lamp.' An impulse to tell her the whole truth came raging up inside me – I'd barely recognised it before the words were flooding out. 'They took a book I had about Rebecca Fisher, as well, and my folder of notes, the one with the photograph I showed you. I kept it in the spare room, and they just broke in and stole it . . .'

My voice tailed off as I watched her watching me, clearly shocked. It had been the exact reaction I'd longed to get from Carl; faced with its jarring reality, I found myself struggling to dilute it. 'They took other strange things as well,' I said quickly. 'A camera and an old clock radio; neither of them were worth anything either. Still, I don't know . . . it seems *wrong* that they'd take my folder. It seems *bizarre*.'

'I couldn't agree more.' At first, her voice was quiet and awed, then I saw her deliberately trying to pull herself together. When she spoke again, it was with a new and entirely unconvincing briskness. 'I don't mean to worry you, Anna, but taking that folder . . . it doesn't sound quite like a burglary to me, it sounds more personal than that. This is going to sound hysterical, I'm sure – but it sounds like some kind of vendetta against your research.'

I couldn't think of anything to say; it stunned me that she'd drawn exactly the same conclusions as I had, that she saw my fears as perfectly sensible. Because she hadn't known me as long as Carl or Petra, I'd thought, she'd be more apt to doubt me. Suddenly I realised how flawed that logic had been, the direct inversion of reality. She didn't know anything about that fresher term, her mind was entirely unclouded by subconscious prejudice. As the only objective party, she could see the dangers that they couldn't.

'I can't help thinking about that vet, Mr Wheeler,' she went on, 'and what you told me about him, how angry he was when you mentioned Rebecca. You'll probably think I'm being ridiculous, but ... you don't think *he* could have had something to do with it all?'

For the second time in as many minutes, I was dumbstruck – her suspicions vindicated my own, gave them the unmistakable seal of authenticity. When I spoke, my voice was quiet, slightly unsteady. 'That's exactly what I thought ... I just don't know why he'd *do* that. I can just about see why he might want to drive me out of the village, some kind of twisted revenge. But what on earth would he want with my *folder*?'

Liz frowned. 'Maybe he's trying to scare you into giving up your research,' she said at last.

I stared at her blankly, confused. '*Why*?'

'Well ... I don't know. I'm as much in the dark about all this as you are. But from what you told me ... when he said you were being ghoulish and all the rest of it ... I can't imagine he'd take too kindly to the idea of you writing a book about her. I saw how close the two of them were. *I* know you're not exploiting her memory, but *he* might not.'

'I told him I was researching it,' I said slowly. 'But he didn't believe that I *was* – he thought it was just a lie, so I could talk to him about her. He didn't know ...'

Then I realised how easily that could have changed. Muriel and Helen both knew, could only too plausibly have told someone who'd told him. With the best will in the world, Liz could have done so herself. When she spoke again, she put my half-formed thoughts into words. 'It's hard to keep a secret in a sleepy little place like this, dear. Like it or not, word tends to get out.'

'But how could he know I was still researching the book?' My confusion was absolute. 'If he's just trying to stop me, how's he going to know whether he's succeeded?'

'I haven't got the faintest idea, Anna. I only wish I could be more help.' Again, the expression I'd most longed to see scared me badly: genuine concern for my safety, for my future here. 'You must be worried sick ... whatever does Carl make of all this?'

'He doesn't.' I spoke bluntly, and took a deep breath – I couldn't lie to her now, not when she understood so much of the truth. 'He doesn't believe me. He thinks I'm imagining things, that it was just a burglary. He doesn't even think it's important that my folder's gone. It's putting a real strain on things, actually. I can't talk to him about it – he just won't listen. Since last Tuesday, we've been like strangers ...'

Her surprise was obvious. I could see her trying to find a tactful way of asking further, not wanting to trespass on the private intricacies of our relationship. It occurred to me that I'd have reacted in exactly the same way myself. 'That's a shame,' she said cautiously, 'it's not what I'd have expected at all. From the little I've seen of him, he seems such an understanding man – and quite devoted to you.'

'He *is*, he's wonderful. It's not his fault, exactly. It's just ...' Again, there was nowhere to go but straight ahead, and I steeled myself for the ultimate, shameful confession. 'He thinks my research is ... well, unbalancing me. It happened once before, or *something* like it happened. He didn't know me at the time; it was years before we met. When I told him about it, I don't think he really understood. He seemed to see it as something inside me, something that could just flare up again for no reason. But it wasn't like that at all. Everything was different, back then . . .'

I fell silent, and she looked at me. 'It's a long story,' I said awkwardly.

Her face didn't change at all: *Go on,* her eyes said, just like they had when I'd confided in her before, *if you don't mind talking about it.*

'I was eighteen, at the time,' I began quietly. 'In my fresher term. Remember what I told you a while ago, about my family? How much I wanted to get away from all that, how I deliberately chose the university furthest away from them? Well, anyway, that was how it was. I was so happy on the train there, on my own. Scared, but *happy*. It's hard to describe. As if I was on the brink of something wonderful. A whole new life.

'Only – when I got there – everything changed. I thought I'd feel free, far away from it all, but I didn't. I felt scared. Lost. I'd never belonged at home, and I knew that, but knowing it just seemed to make things worse. There wasn't really anywhere to go back to; I was on my own. It's the worst kind of homesickness, that feeling . . . that there isn't *anywhere* you can call your own, that you're just adrift . . .

'Because I didn't seem to belong at university, either. I'd thought there might be other people like me there, but I had nothing in common with any of them. They all reminded me so much of Emily and Louise and Tim, my half-sisters and brother. Happy families, parents who'd wanted them. They didn't know what *outside* meant. We talked at first, and we were friendly, but it felt so strained to me. I couldn't tell them how scared I was, how anonymous the hall of residence felt – they'd never have understood in a million years, they all thought it was great fun. And the more scared I was, the more I moved away from them. And the more I moved away from them, the more scared I became . . .

'I started spending most of my spare time in my room. At first, I hated that room more than anything – it was *anyone's* room: cold, soulless, sterile. But gradually, I still hated it, but I was scared to leave it. I started feeling terrified of people. It's so hard to put into words. To begin with, it was just shyness and feeling out of place. Then . . . it just snowballed. Day by day. Week by week. I didn't want to go out, and then I was afraid to go out, and then just thinking about going out petrified me. And I knew how irrational that was, and that was the worst thing of all. Having a little bit of you looking out, watching your mind slip away . . .'

As I spoke, that terror came back to me, and I felt it all over again. I wasn't conscious of Liz's presence at all, and spoke as if in a trance. 'Three weeks into that term, I only left my room for lectures and seminars. Four weeks in, just seminars. By that time, I wasn't even going for meals. It was a catered hall, and there were meals three times a day in the canteen, but I just couldn't make myself go in there. Once or twice, I remember telling myself I'd *have* to, trying to force myself to come back – *there's nothing to be afraid of,* I'd say to myself, *they're all nice people, what the hell's wrong with you?* And I'd just freeze up inside that horrible room, and listen to all the strangers trooping down the corridor to lunch or dinner, and I'd only dare open the door when the last of the voices had gone. And I'd take a few steps towards the canteen, and I'd just . . .

scuttle back into my room. As if something was chasing me. I can still remember the way my heart felt, at those times. Hammering. Sometimes, I thought it was going to explode.

'There was a snacks machine in the ground-floor lobby – crisps, chocolate, that sort of thing. Pretty soon, it was the only food I got. I can remember how it was, sitting in my room, watching it get dark. It wouldn't be safe for me to go down till the small hours – there'd be people coming in and out of the hall bar till half past twelve or so. And just looking at the clock, watching it inch past seven thirty – and wanting to eat so *badly*, I'd dream of food. And too damned scared to go downstairs and buy it. Even in the small hours, when the whole hall was in bed, it was like stepping into no man's land. And all the time – walking down those stairs on *tiptoe* – part of me knew I was losing my mind—

'I couldn't even go down there, soon. I'd stopped going to my seminars, too. I just stayed in that room. I can't really tell you how I felt then – it was so hard to think straight, I was literally dizzy with hunger all the time. I just knew that I couldn't go out any more, it terrified me even to think about it. There was a little shower-room alcove in my room, and I drank water from the tap. I'd stockpiled a few chocolate bars and bags of crisps, and I tried to ration them as well as I could. It was only a week or so I spent like that, but it seemed far longer – and no time at all. I couldn't really keep track of time, by then. The whole world was just slipping away from me . . .'

I broke off for a second, lit a cigarette before continuing. 'It was Petra who first got worried about me. She'd been one of the girls I hung round with for the first week or so, and she noticed I wasn't around. Everyone else just assumed there must be some normal explanation for it, I suppose – that I'd been called home unexpectedly, or I'd made new friends in another hall, and was spending most of my time round there instead. But Petra wasn't just in the same hall as me, she was on the same course – we were both studying English Lit. I suppose she'd heard that I'd missed a few seminars in a row. She came and knocked on my door a few times, that week. I only knew it was her later. At the time, it could have been anyone. Of course, I couldn't bring myself to answer; the sound of that knocking froze me up inside. I just sat there as quietly as I could, till she guessed I must be out somewhere, and went away.

'Then, after I hadn't been out of my room for six days, I heard voices outside, in the hall. One of them was Petra's, the other sounded like the hall warden. At first, I didn't really take in what they were saying, but, as they got closer and closer to my door, I realised they were talking about me. "I'm getting really worried about her," Petra was saying. "What if something's happened?" And the warden said, "Don't worry, I've got the spare key to her room right here." Then, I heard it turning in the lock.

'I don't think I've ever been so scared in my life, even *now*. This huge, senseless fear, like a panic attack, only a thousand times worse. And I wasn't exactly equipped to cope with that physically . . . I'd had a couple of Kit Kats and bags of Wotsits in the past six days, and I felt so dizzy all the time. When I heard the warden opening my door, I blacked out. Just like that.

'When I woke up, I was in the medical centre just off campus. They had some private rooms in there, and I'd been out like a light for about twelve hours. Petra had stayed with me there practically the whole time, and she was the first thing I saw when I opened my eyes. She asked me what the hell I'd been doing, and I found myself telling her as well as I could. It was funny, really, but that was how we first became real friends. When we'd first met, I hadn't thought we'd ever be at all close . . .

'It changed everything, somehow. Just being able to talk to someone. It turned out I had some kind of minor-league malnutrition, but nothing serious. Petra and the doctor talked me into going for counselling sessions, to sort out the real problems. But I honestly don't think those sessions made any real difference. As soon as I woke up, I knew I was cured, as if I'd been pulled back from the brink just in time. All that terror of people had just snapped off. I'd never had anything like it before, never in my life. And I've never had anything like it since . . .'

I fell quiet; for the first time in long minutes, I became aware that Liz was looking at me. There was no patronising fake-sympathy whatsoever in her expression, just something grave, understanding, sincere.

'It was a nightmare time for me,' I said, 'but it was nothing like this. I was terrified of going out just because it *was* going out. I never thought someone was dreaming up elaborate plots to hurt me, and I never thought of any specific person as the enemy. Carl just didn't understand that at all – he can't see that there's any real difference between that and paranoid conspiracy theories.

'But there's a real threat here, Liz. You can see it, and you don't even know the full story. Soon after I went to see Mr Wheeler, I saw him outside one afternoon. He was just standing there by the road, watching the house. And I got a silent phone call a couple of weeks ago – just breathing down the line for a few seconds, then someone hung up. Carl's convinced it was just a wrong number, but I swear to you it wasn't anything like that . . . remember what the policeman said last Tuesday, about Rebecca getting silent calls here herself?'

'Oh, my God.' Liz stared at me, appalled. 'Why didn't you tell me that before?'

'I don't know,' I said quietly. 'I didn't want to tell anyone – just kept it to myself, and hoped it would all blow over. But then, with the break-in—'

'I agree with your husband,' she interrupted. 'You should stop this research of yours, Anna. *Now*.'

For a second, I just looked at her, caught in the slow dawn of betrayal. Then she spoke again, more gently. 'I believe you, dear, I believe every word you've told me. What happened to you all those years ago could have happened to practically anyone; it's certainly no reflection on your stability these days. But this research of yours sounds far too dangerous to carry on with . . . it's too close for comfort, the links with what happened to Rebecca. If Mr Wheeler's behind it all – and I can't help suspecting that he *is* – he's almost certainly not going to rest until you've given it all up.'

'But there's no way he can know whether I have or not. Like I said before, how could he know what I'm doing with my time?' Across the table, Liz looked worried, and baffled, and older – I watched her shrug helplessly. 'Anyway, I can't give it up. Not now. There's not much more of it left to do, but I still don't know everything I need to. The full picture's out there somewhere. I *have to know what it is*.'

The worry in Liz's eyes was clearer than ever. 'I don't understand, dear. *Why*?'

'I don't know,' I said slowly. 'It just seems like it's the only thing left that still makes sense.'

38

I hadn't allowed myself to remember the details of that fresher term in a very long time. It was as though I'd painstakingly installed a circuit-breaker in my mind when it was over, cutting off any thought as soon as it threatened to spark specific memories. Over the years, they'd all come together and merged into something huge and amorphous, a loathsome, freakish something that scuttled, now and then, through random byways of my subconscious. The second I saw a hint of it in the distance, all I could think about was driving as fast as I could in the opposite direction. I had no desire to look at it more closely; the moment's glimpse told me everything I needed to know.

After Liz had gone home, however, I found myself consciously looking back to it, steeling myself to reach for detailed memories. It felt like being blindfolded and extending cautious fingers into the unknown, encountering something slimy, and gelid, and pulsing. Frozen tableaux returned to me. I remembered creeping down the starkly-lit, institutional back stairs at two a.m. Silence behind the buzzing striplights, black nothing beyond the windows, nothing else moving. Fear stuffing my throat at the thought that something might do. The empty foyer, the big clock ticking out the seconds with flat indifference as I tiptoed towards the snacks machine. I'd try to get enough for the next couple of days, I'd thought. I couldn't bear to do this again tomorrow . . .

I thought about it and was back there – I could feel how

cold the floor was under my bare feet, that towering and undirected fear which found its focus in everything around me. Remembering was as appalling as I'd known it would be, but, at the same time, became staggeringly conclusive evidence in my own defence; even if nobody else could see it, the fact that I could had become all-important. For all my conscious certainty that the threat here was real, a tiny part of me that punched far above its weight had begun to doubt that – had been afraid Carl knew me better than I knew myself, that his concerns might hold some chilly shard of truth.

As I recalled that nightmare time and compared then to now, the more utterly convinced I became. Everything I'd said to Liz had been true. This was no blank terror, but rational fear of a flesh-and-blood enemy, an enemy as real as I was, as the drifts of glass had been in this kitchen last Tuesday, as Socks' corpse had been on the path beyond it.

Suddenly, my longing to desert this house for Bournemouth had vanished without a trace. For the first time in almost a week, I found myself thinking about Rebecca, and her oddly ambiguous relationship with her adoptive father. The prospect of research was a blessed distraction, but seemed far more important than that. If I knew everything there was to know about her life, I thought, I might be able to gain some crucial insight into the situation *here*. I knew I was clutching at straws, but there was nothing more solid to hand. Just a riddle of fear and guesswork and unanswered questions; the exact nature of Rebecca's connection with Mr Wheeler, exactly how far he might be prepared to go.

Liz's warnings hadn't worried me. There was, I knew, no way that the vet could know what I did in this house, who I did and didn't contact. Like me, she'd simply been trying to make sense of the situation, create some neat, reassuring and illusory way out of it all. In the living room, I went over to the telephone and dialled directory enquiries. I asked for the number of Sandwell Prison in the West Midlands, and jotted it down on the phone pad as it was read out to me.

I rang up at once. The initial voice down the line put me straight through to someone else as soon as I'd run through the too-familiar introductory spiel, and I waited a long time for them to answer. When the second voice finally greeted me, they hadn't been told who I was, and I had to reel off the speech again. After some questioning that felt more than a little like cross-examination, my credentials were apparently accepted; I was told to ring back in a few hours' time, and given an extension number to dial.

Time passed very slowly till the clock told me I could return to the phone. The ringing tone ran on endlessly before a woman answered, a woman I hadn't spoken to before. Again, I explained who I was and what I wanted, was about to say that I'd called earlier when she interrupted.

'Oh, yes – Elaine told me about you. She was the lady you spoke to; we work in the same office. She asked me if I'd mind talking to you – I was here when Rebecca Fisher was.' It was a voice made for complaining in, passive-aggression translated into sound – at once martyred and subtly belligerent. 'It's very busy here, you know. I can't just sit around chatting for long.'

'Don't worry,' I said quickly, 'it won't take long. Just a few minutes, that's all.'

'I suppose that should be all right. I only knew her for a few months, mind you – and not at all well, even then. She wasn't any more than a face in the crowd to me, notorious as she was.'

As a witness, she couldn't have sounded a great deal less promising – everything about her tone was harassed, grudging, irritable. It was an effort to keep my discouragement from showing in my voice. 'Were you a prison officer, at the time?'

'That's right. I gave all that up quite a few years ago, moved into the admin office here instead. If anything, it's even more troublesome on this side of things. Thank God I'm coming up for retirement.' The theatrical sigh had an entirely serious undertone of *nobody knows how much I suffer*. 'Before I moved jobs, I worked on Rebecca Fisher's wing for three and a half months. They were short-staffed on it, and I was moved from another one to help out till they could recruit more people of their own. Typical shoddy management; it's a disgrace the way they organise things here.'

I sensed she'd be happy to follow this side-turning off the conversation for upwards of half an hour, and struggled to return it to its intended route. 'Did you ever talk to her?'

'Not that I can recall. I didn't have any patience with my colleagues who went out of their way to be all matey with the prisoners – they were only paying us to guard them, we certainly didn't get any extra for *chatting* with them right, left and centre. Speaking of which, I'm afraid I'll have to get on. Like I said, it's very busy here.'

'Just one more thing. Please. Quickly.' It was the only question that really mattered to me, and I'd been trying to reach it circuitously, now rushed towards it as fast as I could. 'I've heard her adoptive father came to see her regularly. Did you ever notice him at visiting-times? A middle-aged man, dark-haired, wearing glasses.'

'Can't say I did. You really ought to be speaking to her

old personal officer, if you want to know things like that. I certainly wouldn't be able to tell you.'

I sat up. 'Does she still work there?'

'She certainly does. Her name's Patricia Mackenzie, and she's Chief Officer on C Wing now. God only knows how that woman sticks it.' The martyred sigh again. When she carried on speaking, it was either with conscious helpfulness or the desire to pass an irritating distraction over to someone else. 'I'll transfer you to her office, if you like. I have to warn you, she's likely to be very busy herself.'

Once transferred, another phone rang for some time before Patricia Mackenzie answered in person. As predicted, she *was* too busy to talk right now but, when I'd explained who I was and what I wanted, she told me she'd be able to spare ten or fifteen minutes the following morning. We arranged that I'd call back at half-eleven then. Taking down her extension number, I thanked her, and hung up.

Carl got home that night at half past seven, and we had dinner together in the kitchen. I found myself thinking how strange it was that it hadn't quite been a week since the burglary. After our conversation last Tuesday, a distinct atmosphere had characterised these evenings together, the kind that felt painstakingly distilled and double-distilled over a period of months or years; tension like an unwavering electrical hum, a constant presence in the room with us.

'So how was your day, Annie?' he asked.

More than anything, I wanted to tell him about my conversation with Liz that morning – *someone believes me, it's not all in my mind, no matter what you think* – but I knew perfectly well it wouldn't make any difference, he'd still see things in exactly the same light. He'd think that Liz had been humouring me, or that she just hadn't known the full story.

'Oh, not too bad,' I said. 'Liz came round for a coffee earlier, and I did some housework. What about you?'

'Harmless enough. I had to go and check up on the Dorchester store for the first time in a while. It was straight out of *Night of the Living Dead*. I swear to God, we're going to have to do something about that place, and soon – you'd see more life in a morgue.'

It was his old tone of voice, familiar to me as his face and way of sitting – only it *wasn't*, it wasn't at all. He was trying too hard to be himself, and a false edge rang out clearly. I could sense him trying to ignore his deepening misgivings about me the way someone might ignore the early symptoms of some terrible disease, reassuring themselves as much as anyone else, *look, I'm perfectly all right, I can still do everything quite normally*. And I tried to ignore my own knowledge of that, aware that any reference to it would inevitably spiral into a second, fiercer argument; my simmering frustration at his lack of understanding finally bubbling over into fury.

Silence fell again, and we ate. After we'd finished dinner, we sat in the living room together watching TV. We watched it in a way we always did recently, but had never used to – intently, not talking, barely glancing at each other – as if the predictable Monday-night schedule was packed with the most riveting programmes in the history of television. I'd thought all my reserves of fear were fully accounted for elsewhere, but, as I looked at him out of the corner of my eye, I realised I still had some to spare. Our relationship had been entirely healthy when we'd come here, but freak accidents could kill the healthy as easily as the dying; recent events had swerved into its path like an out-of-control juggernaut, and I watched it clinging desperately to life in a hospital bed.

It could still recover, I told myself desperately. All it would take was some kind of conclusion to these terrible events, a rational explanation and proof that I'd been right. But I knew that, if recovery was to take place, it would have to happen soon. In the not-so-distant future, this tension and mistrust would destroy our marriage beyond repair; every day, I could feel us moving a little further apart emotionally, soon we wouldn't be able to hear each other even if we shouted.

I glanced at him when I was sure he wasn't looking, seeing his profile in silhouette. A tense, distracted look hid just below the surface. And, from time to time, as I looked straight ahead, I thought I could feel him glancing at me too; I wondered what he was thinking, and what he imagined he could see in my face.

In bed that night, I lay and listened to him brushing his teeth, then the bathroom light snapped off in the doorway and I saw him coming in, a slightly darker shape against monochrome moonlight. He got into bed. Wordlessly, we moved closer together, a kind of low-level telepathy inspiring mutual knowledge of one another's need; it was desperation rather than desire, a longing to be together again at any level at all. But while it good in its own right, it wasn't enough for either of us – Sellotape instead of surgical thread, a pitifully inadequate gesture in the direction of healing. As we moved together in the darkness, the pleasure was empty, anonymous. We loved each other in the marital bed, and felt like strangers.

39

'I was Rebecca's personal officer for two years, before she was released,' Patricia Mackenzie told me, 'so I suppose you could say I knew her quite well. I was a bit unnerved when I heard I'd been assigned someone so notorious – she was the only murderess in the whole place. I honestly had no idea what I'd be taking on, before I met her.'

From the woman I'd spoken to yesterday, I'd got a decidedly negative impression of Sandwell's officers, but this voice went a long way towards changing that; Patricia Mackenzie sounded pleasant, serious, thoughtful. A conscientious voice. 'I should have known that, if she'd been the monster I'd imagined, they wouldn't have sent her to Sandwell in the first place,' she went on, 'but it still surprised me, how normal she was. I know you can't always judge from appearances, but she seemed as sane and unthreatening as anyone I'd ever met.'

'How old was she when you first saw her?'

'Oh, eighteen, nineteen. It's funny, really. Prisoners in that age group often seem quite vulnerable – impressionable, you know, not much common sense – but she was certainly the exception to the rule there. Very self-possessed, I was struck by that; not in an aloof way, just kept herself to herself. I don't think she had a single close friend in the place, but I'm quite sure she didn't have any enemies.

'She knew how to handle the staff, as well. She wasn't manipulative, at least not maliciously, but it seemed that she'd struck the perfect balance from her first day here.

Very polite and well-behaved, but not so as she'd be seen to suck up by the other inmates. She had a long-term job in the canteen kitchen thanks to good behaviour, quite a responsible job, and from what I saw and heard, she was good at it. A very efficient young woman. I imagine she's made a good life for herself, on the outside.'

I could see only too clearly how the girl I'd read and heard so much about had become that young woman; Eleanor Corbett had taught her a devastating lesson regarding intimacy, and good behaviour had been drilled into her from early childhood. Again, I approached the only question that really mattered to me. 'Did she ever tell you anything about her adoptive father?'

'God, yes. It's funny you should ask me that. It's what I remember best about her, even now. I talked to her in private every week, for half an hour or so. It was all very informal, more a chat than anything else, just so she could let me know if she was having any problems. She never was, so we mostly just talked. I tended to do most of the actual talking . . . she seemed far more comfortable in the listener's role, and I have to say that she made a very good one. But, on the rare occasions that she opened up herself, it was always about her adoptive father. Not that she ever mentioned the adoptive part. *Daddy*, she called him, when she was discussing him with me. Like a child.

'I have to say, I couldn't help but find all that a bit disturbing – there was something almost incestuous about it, she sounded so devoted to him. How wonderful he was, and how much he cared about her, and how much she loved him in return. How she couldn't wait for his next visit, that she literally counted the days between them, and how they were so close that they could talk about anything. It was odd how *different* she seemed at those times – not self-possessed at all, far from it. She seemed desperate to impress me with it all, as if I was supposed to think, *isn't she lucky . . .*

'I tried not to show how odd I thought it was, to react the way she'd want me to . . . it wasn't just politeness; I didn't want to upset her. She was very sweet in her way, even though I found it impossible to really understand anything about her. I told her it was a wonderful thing to have such a good father, a lot of girls would give anything for that. And she'd smile. I never really knew her look *happy*, as she did at those times – not just as if everything was all right, but real joy. It was very strange, when you saw it for yourself.'

'Did you ever see them together at visiting times?'

'I was just coming to that part. As a matter of fact, I did. I was on duty in the visiting room a few months after I'd first met Rebecca. Normally, I wouldn't really have noticed who was there and who wasn't, but when I saw her at one of the tables, I couldn't help but look closer. Especially when I realised that the man across from her could only be her father.

'God only knew what I'd been expecting – from Rebecca's descriptions, I'd imagined a cross between JFK and the Second Coming. In the flesh, he came as a real disappointment, and a real shock. Older than I'd have thought, more like a grandfather than a father, and gaunt, sickly; he looked really ill. And this might sound fanciful, but the whole mood between them was miles away from the impression I'd been given. I'd imagined them acting almost like some of the women did with their boyfriends and husbands, all hugs and chatter and affection, but the two of them couldn't have seemed much more distant from each other. I remember the way Rebecca was sitting, bolt upright, as though she was in a job interview. She seemed a hundred times more relaxed when she was talking to *me*.'

It was everything Tom Hartley had told me about Dennis Fisher's visits to the Southfield Unit. Patricia continued. 'I thought there must be a lot more to their relationship than met the eye – and I was right, I suppose. About a year later, I was called into the governor's office unexpectedly. He told me he'd just received news Rebecca's father had died – the hospital had phoned, he said, and there weren't any other relatives at all. He said it'd be best if I passed the news on to her myself. I was very shocked. I knew she'd be devastated, and I said so. "Well, of course," he said, "but it won't come as a bolt from the blue for her. Apparently he's been dying for years; he was diagnosed with cancer a very long time ago. The doctor told me it was a minor miracle he lasted as long as he did."

'It amazed me, when he said that. All the times Rebecca had talked about her father, and she'd never so much as hinted at it. Still, I dreaded telling her, as much as I would have done if he'd been killed in an accident. I thought maybe she'd kept it to herself because she just hadn't wanted to think about it, that she'd found it too painful to discuss.

'Of course, I had to break the news somehow, and it was every bit as difficult as I'd expected. She didn't collapse in tears, or anything like that. She was silent, shell-shocked, like it hadn't fully sunk in. It looked the worst kind of bereavement to me, the kind you can't even let out with a good cry. The kind that runs far too deep for that.

'She carried on like that for the next few weeks, anyway. She said next to nothing during our talks, and when I saw her round the prison, she looked like a different person. She hadn't often seemed happy before, but she'd always seemed contented – neutral, you know, as though nothing was actually wrong. After her father died, she seemed indifferent, blank ... she was just going through the motions on autopilot. It's hard to describe that change in her, but it was obvious when you saw it for yourself. I was very concerned about her. But I knew she was never at all comfortable discussing her feelings, so I didn't bring the subject up again for some time – when we talked every week, we both pretended nothing was wrong and nothing had changed. It was hard to know what else to do.

'After she'd been that way for a month or so, though, I couldn't just ignore it any more. I asked her if she was coping all right, if she'd like to talk to someone about it. "You must miss him deeply," I said, "I know how close you were." And she just stared at me. Her eyes looked so lost. '"No, you don't," she said. "You think you do, but you don't. We weren't close at all, never were, never would have been."

'I couldn't have been much more shocked, as she carried on talking – it was like listening to another person, one that I'd never met before. Normally she was so quiet and placid and guarded, but she sounded so bitter that day – cynical and frank. As if she couldn't see the point in hiding anything.

'"If he hadn't been dying, I wouldn't have seen him once since the trial," she said. "I never saw him when I was growing up, I didn't mean any more to him than a bit of furniture. At least it wasn't personal; he was the same to everyone. He'd been the same with his own family, cut them right out of his life – I've never once seen any of them. He didn't even have any time for his wife; it was half his fault she was like she was."

'I don't quite know what she meant by that. I suppose it doesn't matter. "He made out that it was so sentimental," she said, "his sudden interest in me. He came to see me at the young offenders' home soon after I got there. We got a private room to talk in and he was almost crying. He'd been for a check-up at the doctor's, and they'd diagnosed the cancer then – it was just a matter of time, could be years, there was no way of knowing. He said it made him realise he should have been a better husband and father and everything else, he didn't know what it had been *for*, all the work and all the rest of it . . . he talked about it like he'd had some kind of religious conversion, but it wasn't anywhere near that noble. It wasn't *atonement*, or anything like that. At the end of the day, he was just scared of dying with nobody in the world who cared about him, even a murderess he'd adopted to keep his wife quiet had to be better than nobody. He'd driven everyone else away, but I'd always be here to talk to him, a captive audience, you might say."

'That's practically word-for-word what she told me. I can remember it all very clearly. "I wanted to believe we were close just as much as he did," she said, "it was what I'd always wanted most, ever since I can remember. But it was never the same as I'd wanted it to be, not when he was actually there. I don't think he really knew me from a hole in the ground, just saw me as someone who loved him. He sent me things all the time, but he might as well have bought them for someone else, some stereotype of a teenage girl he had in his mind: make-up, perfume, skincare things. They were the last presents I'd ever want, I saw too much of that kind of thing with my mother . . . but he just didn't seem to realise that. Or to care.

'"Well," she said, "I suppose it doesn't matter any more. I can't even pretend there's someone out there thinking about me, not now."'

So much clicked into place for me, a thousand tiny

details suddenly coming together and making sense. Behind the shock revelation drifted something else, a diffuse sense of kinship. I thought of myself in that fresher term, losing my last tenuous connection with a place I'd never really belonged in the first place. Rebecca's bereavement had cast her adrift, too.

'It seemed to – to exorcise it all for her,' Patricia went on, 'letting everything out like that. Afterwards, she went back to normal very quickly, at least on the surface. And, not long after that, something else happened. It had been going on for months without any of us knowing a thing about it, lawyers and accountants and God knows who else working it out behind closed doors. The first I heard was when I was called into the governor's office again, out of the blue.

'He told me I'd have to keep quiet about it, and I understood that perfectly well – if anyone had talked, the papers would have been all over the story, back then. Rebecca's father had left a very specific will. He'd named her as his sole beneficiary.'

'*Could* she inherit? A convicted murderess?'

'I must say, that was my first thought. But you must bear in mind, she was an exceptional case. She was well below the legal age of responsibility when she'd killed that girl, and there were God knows how many cracks in the law there. And you can imagine, a rich businessman like her father had the kind of lawyers who could smash them to pieces. I imagine there were quite a few loopholes to be got round; that's probably why we weren't told straight away. But she could inherit in the end, make no mistake about that.

'It was a huge amount of money by most people's standards, well over a million pounds – and that was almost twenty years ago. I can't begin to guess what the equivalent would be today. When Rebecca finally left prison, she was going to leave as a very rich woman.

'It was hard to tell how she took the news. As I said, she was back to her guarded old self again, and I always found it impossible to guess what she was thinking. I don't think she was exactly overjoyed. Money didn't seem to mean a great deal to her. One thing I was quite sure of, she wasn't going to throw it around when she got out. You only had to talk to her to know she'd end up leading a quiet sort of life . . . she wasn't the sort of person who'd want to attract attention to herself, and she was anything but stupid. She knew only too well how the public hated her. If she was recognised out there, it would be *disastrous*. Of course, she'd changed dramatically since that famous photograph of her was taken, but—'

Silence crashed down, and something in the quality of it implied fast-dawning unease, the realisation that she'd let something potentially important slip without thinking. 'Anyway,' she went on quickly, in a determinedly matter-of-fact voice, 'that's really all I can tell you about her. I hope it's been some help.'

We said our goodbyes, and I thanked her profusely before hanging up. Then I went into the kitchen and lit a cigarette, sat taking deep occasional drags like a form of self-hypnosis, barely aware of my surroundings.

It was extraordinary how obscure the picture had been before that phone call, and how well-lit it had become. Too well-lit, in some ways. The essential tragedy of Rebecca's relationship with her adoptive father haunted me as I sat in the dazzling sunlight. Two people frightened and lonely beyond expression, struggling to discover an illusion of happiness, knowing that its reality would always remain out of reach. Two people who shared nothing whatsoever, apart from complete isolation . . .

But there was something else there, too, niggling away in the back of my mind. An unplaceable sense of unease that intensified as the minutes passed; as if I'd forgotten something crucial, and had begun to realise it, and still couldn't quite decide what it might be. Whenever I tried to focus on the absence, it eluded me like the answer to a riddle. In no time at all, it had swelled to fill my mind completely, and establishing the name and nature of my preoccupation had become all-important.

Then it came to me, in a sudden, vivid memory. The faded, middle-aged woman greeting us at the door of this house four months ago, on a windy, grey, dispiriting March afternoon.

'So do you think it's the sort of property you'd be interested in?' she'd asked, and the question had come out with far more than an estate agent's businesslike concern – there'd been thinly-veiled urgency desperation in her voice. 'It's a very nice area—'

The startlingly, almost implausibly reduced price of this house, a deal no young couple could help but jump at. The kind of offer you'd only make if you were desperate to sell as quickly as you possibly could. The kind of offer you'd only make if you needed the money from the sale to move somewhere, anywhere else . . .

But Rebecca Fisher wouldn't have needed the money at once, would have been able to move on anyway, leave the estate agent to sell the empty house at a more leisurely pace, and pass on the proceeds whenever. At the age of twenty-two, Rebecca Fisher had left prison with more than a million pounds in the bank.

Maybe she'd spent it all by then, I told myself uneasily. For all I knew, she could have gone into a buying frenzy as

383

soon as she was out of prison, when she found herself free again for the first time in twelve years. It happened to some Lottery winners, I knew – I'd read about it in the papers now and then, they'd been known to get through equivalent sums in a far shorter time . . .

Only I couldn't see Rebecca doing that in a million years. Practical, efficient, deeply wary Rebecca with her finely honed sense of self-preservation, only too well aware that it would be in her best interests to lead a quiet life. I struggled to imagine her spending thousands in glossy department stores, drawing discreetly curious stares from saleswomen, from other customers. Stares that would inevitably take in her face, attention that would register her age, her Northern accent. *She knew only too well how the public hated her*, Patricia Mackenzie had said. *If she was recognised out there, it would be disastrous . . .*

Confusion pounded in my mind, calling into doubt something I'd taken for granted up until now – that Rebecca Fisher and Geraldine Hughes had been one and the same person. Because Patricia Mackenzie had also said something else. *Of course*, she'd said, *she'd changed dramatically since that famous photograph of her was taken, but*— And then she'd fallen silent as people only did when they realised they'd said too much, and had changed the subject at once.

But Geraldine Hughes *had* looked like that photograph. Not strikingly, not so you'd spot the likeness on your own, but when you knew she was Rebecca, you could trace clear similarities between them. Small, blonde, blue-eyed, delicate-featured. Any real changes could be easily attributed to the passage of time. Who, at forty-three, really looked the same as they'd done at ten?

Of course, she could have changed back after she was released. Maybe she'd gained weight in prison and lost it again when she was free. Maybe she'd dyed her hair in prison and let it grow back. Anything, I told myself, was possible . . .

It made perfect sense. The only problem was, I didn't believe a word. If Rebecca's appearance had changed, she'd want to *keep* it changed. Even if it meant shovelling down platefuls of food she didn't want, to keep the weight on, dying her hair an unflattering colour for the rest of her life. To a notorious figure like Rebecca Fisher, anonymity would always come first. And the threat of recognition would be the worst thing in the world.

Rebecca was a rich woman, and didn't look anything like her picture.

Geraldine had needed money urgently, and did.

Conclusion: they had nothing to do with one another.

But that was ridiculous, impossible. If Geraldine *hadn't* been Rebecca, why in God's name had she been forced out of her home? Why had someone been so determined to get rid of her that they'd smashed her windows, issued terrible threats, killed her dog? I remembered the letter I'd found in the spare room, the fear screaming from every erratically-scrawled line. She'd been frightened for her life here, had felt the danger gathering, week by week . . .

And something else. If Geraldine hadn't been Rebecca, Mr Wheeler wasn't Rebecca's ally, just the friend and lover of a harmless, middle-aged woman, a woman who'd somehow fallen victim to an appalling mistake. Protective of her, certainly, concerned for her, even furious on her behalf; but there was nothing sinister about any of those reactions – Carl or Petra or Liz would have behaved in exactly the same way defending *me*. There was no earthly reason why he'd have gone to such lengths to avenge her, no reason why I should imagine he'd be capable of that. And I remembered the missing book and the missing folder, the things that would have meant nothing to Geraldine's boyfriend at all . . .

Long-held certainties trembled around me, threatened to fall into dust as I watched; I needed answers more than I'd ever needed anything. There was, I realised, only one person who'd be able to give them, a person who had haunted my thoughts for a very long time. To get to the truth, I'd have to confront Mr Wheeler.

40

It was half past six that evening when I turned into the little car park outside the vet's surgery in Wareham. It was at least three-quarters empty, the handful of cars spaced out like the last few chocolates in the box. One of them, I knew, would be Mr Wheeler's. When I'd phoned up earlier under the guise of *a friend*, the receptionist had told me he was in today, and that he'd probably be leaving at about seven o'clock. I'd thanked her and hung up before she could ask further questions of her own, knowing I'd have to arrive considerably earlier than that; the idea of missing him by minutes was appalling.

I parked near the main double doors, turning off the engine. The air was very hot and very still – the sunlight had taken on a rosy edge, and a sense of temporary peace hung far too heavily. A fly alighted on the dashboard. Nothing else moved. Lighting a cigarette, I took a deep drag and saw strings of smoke drift out of the open car window; there was no breeze to disrupt them, and they rose as if in a closed room.

Watching the double doors some twenty feet away from me, I felt almost sick with apprehension. I had no idea how Mr Wheeler would react at the sight of me, whether he'd recognise me at once or not. And I might be wrong, Geraldine might have been Rebecca after all. I might have driven here only to confront an unknowable malevolence – the shadowy, snarling Mr Wheeler who'd dominated a thousand sleepless nights . . .

My fears increased a little more each time the double

doors opened. First a middle-aged woman emerged, then, several minutes later, a younger one. An elderly man shortly after that. Checking the dashboard clock, I saw it was ten to seven. There were only three other cars left here, now. I had a sudden and panicky conviction that the rest of the world was draining away around us; soon, there would only be *one* other car, and I'd know exactly who it belonged to, and I'd wait an eternity for its owner to emerge. And at that precise instant of thought, the doors swung open again, and he was there.

While I hadn't fully realised it up till now, part of me had been hoping against hope that the sight of him would destroy my lingering unease in a second – of *course* he was harmless, of *course* he was normal, I'd been worrying about nothing all along. The opposite was true. As I watched him walking out, I remembered his expression of cold fury more clearly, tiny details of how his face had changed in the surgery. The unpredictability of the immediate future suddenly terrified me.

He had only to turn his head to the right to see me, but he didn't – he headed straight past, towards the battered off-white Ford some thirty metres away. As I watched his retreating back in the rear-view mirror, the impulse to just drive away was almost irresistible. I forced it back as hard as I could, reminding myself that I simply had no choice in the matter. Opening the car door felt like reaching the furthest edge of a high diving board. Getting out felt like jumping off it.

'Mr Wheeler,' I called. 'Wait.'

He stopped, turned. Slamming the car door behind me, I began to walk towards him. The distance between us seemed the length of a football field. I found it impossible to read his expression, and couldn't tell whether he'd recognised me or not. The closer I got, the more convinced

I became that I'd made a terrible mistake in coming here. I wanted my voice to ring out with straightforward, casual confidence, but the slight tremble in it was unmissable and infinitely telling.

'I hope you don't mind me waiting for you like this. I just had to talk to you, and—'

Seeing recognition in his eyes, I fell silent. It seemed that minutes passed before he spoke.

'I know you,' he said quietly. 'You came to see me in May.'

'I wanted to explain at the time – you've got to believe me – I didn't want *gory details* then, and I don't now. But I'm worried for my own safety. I've been getting threats at home, and it sounds like exactly the same thing that happened to Geraldine. I don't know anyone else who can help, who knew her at all well, who knew what happened . . .'

I paused to catch my breath, and still couldn't tell what he was thinking, what he was going to say. A middle-aged woman came out of the double doors, turning and raising her hand to him en route to one of the parked cars. 'Night, Colin,' she called.

'Night, Lucy.' He spoke distractedly, then turned back to me. I watched his face, alert to the tiniest change of expression as the woman started her engine behind us. 'So what do you want me to tell you?' he asked at last. 'What do you want to know?'

Relief hit me like a physical blow. There was no anger in his voice at all, I realised; he sounded like he looked, curious and slightly concerned. 'My husband and I bought Geraldine's house, a few months ago,' I said quietly. 'When we first heard the village gossip about Rebecca Fisher, I thought the whole Fisher case would make a great basis for a novel – I *am* a writer, I wasn't lying to you, I've had one book published. I started researching the case, finding out more. That's why I wanted to talk to you in May.

'Since then, some pretty frightening things have been happening. We've had silent phone calls at home. The house was broken into. All the ground floor windows were smashed. And a cat I was sort of looking after – I found it dead in our garden. To be honest, I really don't understand what's going on. I just keep remembering Geraldine. Everything that happened to *her*.'

His eyes were cautious, kind, slightly guilty. 'I'm sorry,' he said at last. 'I misjudged you. Perhaps I'm a little overprotective about Geraldine, but with the best will in the world, I can't help that. When she was going through that nightmare, I'm quite convinced I was the only friend she had in the area. When I think about how little her neighbours cared . . .'

His voice tailed off, and he shook his head before looking at me with some embarrassment. 'I overreacted badly when you came to see me before. I felt very awkward about it, after you'd gone. I even thought I'd call on you to apologise, but when I finally reached your house, I changed my mind. It dawned on me that you might consider it very odd . . . that you'd probably have forgotten all about our little quarrel, by then.'

So that was what he'd really been thinking when I'd seen him outside. His smile was slightly sheepish before he went on. 'If you're experiencing the same things Geraldine did, I'm very sorry. I can only assume there's some maniac in that village. Geraldine Hughes and Rebecca Fisher have nothing whatsoever to do with each other – I'd be prepared to swear it under oath.'

I spoke quietly. 'That's what I thought.'

'But why did you wait for me?' he asked. 'Why did you

want to talk to *me*? I'm a competent vet, if I say so myself, but I'm no bodyguard. Surely you'd be better off speaking to the police?'

'They don't understand the full story. If it comes to that, nor do I.' I paused for a moment, watching his expression carefully. 'I really want to talk to Geraldine,' I said. 'I think if I heard her side of the story, it might all start to make sense.'

In a split-second, he was defensive again. 'I can't give you her number.'

'I understand that. I wouldn't expect you to,' I said at once. 'I just wondered if you'd give her mine. If you're still in touch with her.'

He nodded. 'I am.'

'Then, next time you speak to her, could you explain the situation? Tell her what I've told you, and ask her to phone me. The number hasn't changed; she'll know it,' I said. 'If she doesn't want to talk to me – well, that's her decision. But I'd be more than grateful if she did.'

'Well,' he said cautiously, 'I can certainly do that. To be on the safe side, though, I'd better take the number again.'

'I'll write it down.' I fished a biro and a crumpled old receipt out of my handbag and scribbled quickly, leaning on my knee, jotting my name down beside the number. 'Thank you,' I said, handing it to him. 'Thank you very much.'

'It's quite all right. Again, I'm sorry I was so short with you before.' He got his wallet out of his pocket, folded the receipt into it. 'I'll pass this on to Geraldine when I speak to her next. That'll almost certainly be over the next few days.'

I murmured thanks again, and this strange little interview was at an end; there was a slightly stilted, embarrassed quality to our goodbyes. I watched him unlock his car and get in, before walking back across the car park towards my own. In the silence, my footsteps sounded hollow and flat before his engine spluttered into life and drowned them out. As he drove past me, he raised a hand in grave, barely smiling farewell. I raised mine back, and stood and watched the car till it had vanished from sight.

I drove home through Wareham's town centre. The time had just passed seven o'clock, and the streets around me were deserted. They'd taken on a mysterious and slightly sinister edge; a frozen tableau of dummies in a dress-shop window, a single crisp packet blowing lazily along the pavement like tumbleweed. Everything I saw found a distant echo in my own mind: emptiness, and wrongness, and an overwhelming sense of ambiguity.

It was bewildering to feel something as familiar as my fear of Mr Wheeler simply disappear. It was like coming home and finding that home had vanished without a trace; standing and staring at the blank patch of land where it had been with an expression of cartoonish bewilderment. I had no doubt that I'd just been told the truth. Everything in the vet's eyes and voice had had the unmistakable ring of honesty but, deep down, part of me couldn't help wishing I could believe in the lies again. Without them, recent events drained of any kind of rhyme or reason, and there was nothing but a jumbled heap of memories thrown haphazardly together, entirely senseless.

Turning onto Ploughman's Lane, I began the slow ascent to the top of the hill. I was too preoccupied to fear reaching it, and the prospect didn't even register. It was only on the way down that I realised it hadn't done. I parked and let myself in with a mind full of unanswered questions, made a start on dinner and thought about everything.

Carl got home about half an hour after I did. If he noticed my palpable preoccupation, he didn't comment on it, and I was far too lost in my own thoughts to analyse the subtle nuances of tone and expression. For once, that night, the too-long silences in front of the television didn't affect me in the slightest, and the tense atmosphere washed off me like water off a stone. More than anything, I wanted to tell him about the events of that day, but knew it was impossible. He wouldn't grasp their *reality*, never mind their importance. I'd only be able to share it all with him when I knew the full story myself. In the shadows of the living room, I found myself praying that Geraldine would call me, and soon.

Over the next couple of days, I couldn't remember ever feeling more restless. Far from travelling into Bournemouth for no reason, I'd become deeply unwilling to leave the house at all. I was terrified that the all-important call would come when I was out, and that Geraldine wouldn't bother to ring back. When I had to go out for groceries or cigarettes, the first thing I did on my return was to check the answering machine, alert for a Northern-accented voice that never came. And, as I focused on the telephone, I was reminded of those silent calls all over again; remembered that Mr Wheeler hadn't made them, that I had no idea who might have been breathing down the line.

On Thursday afternoon, I was making myself lunch in the kitchen when the ringing tone began, almost stopping my heart. *It could be Carl*, I warned myself, but I was well aware that he never phoned at this time of day, and that he was very much a creature of habit. I picked up the receiver with my heart in my mouth. 'Hello?'

'Oh, hello. Can I speak to Anna Jeffreys, please?'

It was the voice I'd been expecting – I'd first heard it over four months ago, and recognised it at once. 'Speaking,' I said, then, knowing the answer perfectly well, 'is that Miss Hughes?'

'It is,' she said. 'But please, call me Geraldine.'

She hadn't extended that invitation in March, I remembered. It seemed to summarise a subtle change in her whole manner – how harassed she'd sounded before, rushing through inessential small-talk like scenery on the way to an urgent appointment. There was none of that, now; her slight Northern accent sounded chatty and conversational, implying all the time in the world to discuss things. 'I gave Colin Wheeler a ring last night,' she said. 'He told me about you.'

'Well, it's good to hear from you,' I said quickly. 'If I can ask, what exactly did he say?'

'Oh, all about you being threatened. That you had your windows broken, your cat killed, silent phone calls. Almost exactly what happened to me there. It came as such a shock, that it was still going on.' A small, nervous, entirely humourless laugh that belonged to her previous demeanour, recalling tiny details of it that I'd thought I'd forgotten. 'I think that house must be jinxed. There's no other explanation for it, that I can see.'

'I don't know. Maybe there is.' I remembered talking to Donald Hargreaves in person, how much I'd learned during that interview that I'd never have stumbled on over the phone. In terms of my own life and my own safety, Geraldine Hughes was an infinitely more important witness. 'Listen,' I said, 'is there any chance we could meet up and discuss this face to face? I can travel, it's no problem.'

'That sounds fine. I'd be only too happy to talk it over

with someone.' She sounded suddenly reflective. 'Colin's a lovely man, but even he must get tired of hearing about it – he'd never say so, but I've gone over it with him dozens of times. And I don't think anyone else would understand unless they'd been there at the time, or had it happen to them. It was so *strange*. I still think about it a lot. Probably too much. It's hard not talking about something when it's on your mind so often.'

'I know what you mean,' I said. 'I know exactly what you mean.'

'I haven't even told my kids the whole story. I didn't want to worry them.' She sighed. 'It's not that I'm not happy where I am now – I really am – but I can't stop remembering how it was there. I didn't just leave, I was *driven out*. It feels like unfinished business, sometimes.'

A moment's silence, heavy with imminent practicalities. 'So,' she said at last, 'when and where shall we meet?'

'The sooner the better, as far as I'm concerned,' I said warily. 'I don't suppose you're free tomorrow, by any chance?'

Her murmur of casual assent startled and delighted me. 'That sounds fine. How about meeting in Bournemouth town centre?' Another pause, this one slightly awkward. 'I'd give you my address, but after what happened . . . well, you know. I can't help being a bit paranoid with my home details.'

'Don't worry. I'm sure I'd feel the same way,' I said. 'If you had nothing to do with Rebecca Fisher—'

'Oh, she wasn't a *stranger* to me, exactly.' Her tone was conversational again, offhand. 'I suppose I had *something* to do with her.'

The words took me completely by surprise. 'What?'

'It doesn't matter. I'll tell you tomorrow.'

'No, really,' I pressed. 'How did you know her?'

'Honestly, it's nothing particularly exciting. All will be revealed.' The last sentence came out in ironic quote marks, then she spoke again more briskly, in her normal voice. 'Do you know Bournemouth at all well?'

I knew I couldn't ask about her link with Rebecca again without actively nagging, persistent as a little kid yanking at her mother's sleeve on the way past a sweet shop. Still, my curiosity was overwhelming. We arranged to meet at two o'clock in a town centre cafe the following day.

Geraldine's words kept coming back to me, like an echo that somehow grew louder rather than fading with repetition: *Oh, she wasn't a stranger to me, exactly. I suppose I had something to do with her.* Becoming more and more ambiguous the more I thought about it. Back in the kitchen, I realised I had no appetite whatsoever for the salad I'd been making myself before the phone rang.

Questions chased their own tails in my mind: what did she mean; what could she mean, what was she going to tell me tomorrow? I went out into the back garden to escape them, hoping that greenery and sunlight might calm me down a little. Liz was there already, doing some gardening by the fence.

'Hello, Anna, dear,' she said as I emerged, 'how are you?'

'Oh, not bad,' I said. 'Thought I'd come out and make the most of the weather.'

'I can't say I blame you. Isn't it lovely?'

A moment's silence fell, oddly foreboding and incongruous with the nature of our exchange, implying things we both knew, that didn't belong in such an idyllic scene. When she spoke again, her voice was superficially matter-of-fact, with an almost apologetic undertow of concern. 'I take it you haven't had any more . . .'

She couldn't quite bring herself to finish the sentence, but in my own mind, I heard the next words only too clearly – *events, happenings, terrors.* 'No,' I said, trying a little too hard to smile. 'Nothing like that.'

'Well, I'm very pleased to hear it, dear. I've been quite worried since you told me . . .' Again, the awkward tailing-off, as I imagined the rest for myself. 'How's your research going, anyway? Have you been doing any more of it today?'

I could tell she was trying to sound politely and passingly interested, but the edge of worry was obvious to me. I had an impulse to tell her all I knew, that my research had nothing to do with events, that Mr Wheeler had been innocent all along. Still, the sheer extent of my own confusion stopped me; I'd be trying to explain a situation I didn't understand anything about myself, and she'd find it every bit as incomprehensible as I did. I'd tell her after I'd talked to Geraldine, I decided, when things were clearer to me. Then I'd explain why I hadn't told her before.

'Not today,' I said, 'I'm not really in the mood, to be honest. I think I'll carry on with it after the weekend. Maybe I'll feel more like getting back to it then.'

'If you say so, dear. I still think you'd be wiser to let it drop, but, if you just can't bring yourself to . . .' She sighed, her expression thoughtful. 'I don't really know why I feel that way. I'm sure you're right about Mr Wheeler – he couldn't possibly know whether you were carrying on with it or not. But, oh, *I* don't know. It's hard to know *what* to think about something like that.'

She didn't know the half of it. My thoughts circled Geraldine's words obsessively and pointlessly, like a starving dog round an unopened can of Pedigree Chum. 'Well,' I said, 'you can never tell. Maybe it'll all start making sense, soon.'

41

Of course, I didn't tell Carl anything about going into Bournemouth. When he'd left for work the following morning, I got up and got ready, then some hours later, I set the burglar alarm and left the house myself. Opening the car door, a sudden impulse made me turn and look back at it; its blinding white façade and surrounding greenery looked indescribably picturesque in the sunlight. The powder-blue Fiat in Liz's driveway made the picture a hundred times more reassuring than it would have been otherwise.

Still, I couldn't help but be reminded of that nightmare Tuesday last week, how I'd felt leaving the house *that* morning. I'd had exactly the same anticipatory, butterfly-ish sensation as I did now, before going into London to meet Donald Hargreaves, and coming home to broken glass and police cars . . .

I wouldn't think about that, I told myself, as I started the engine. I'd simply refuse to. But my awareness of stark parallels between that day and this wasn't quite that easy to banish. Travelling to speak to a virtual stranger, a sense of crucial revelations waiting in the wings. Nobody knowing where I was.

As I parked in the multi-storey in Bournemouth, the similarities became appalling; the dead silence and the deserted look of the place were exactly as they'd been last Tuesday. Even the shadowy hints of other cars around me seemed to be in the same places. But, when I stepped out into brightness and normality, there was nothing in my mind but the prospect of meeting Geraldine.

While it was a good three quarters of an hour before we'd arranged to meet, it seemed that I couldn't reach the appointed meeting-place quickly enough, as though I could hasten her arrival by turning up early myself. When I reached the cafe, it was half past one. All four outside tables were occupied by chattering groups surrounded by shopping bags. Inside the shadows spilled comforting smells of cake and coffee, and it was virtually deserted. I sat down at the only window table, lighting a cigarette. One of the waitresses came over, and I ordered a cappuccino, sitting and smoking and watching the street outside, waiting for Geraldine to be there.

The minutes dragged interminably, and a steady tide of strangers flowed past. I kept thinking I'd seen her in the distance, then realising it wasn't her at all, wasn't anything *like* her. But then . . .

The woman approaching across the road, was fine-boned and middle-aged, with greying fair hair tied indifferently back from her face. She had a big, shiny, cord-handled shopping bag in one hand, the kind that looked effortlessly chic when new and now looked distinctly battered. As she came closer, I raised my hand in greeting and saw her waving back, quickening her step.

My mobile bleeped abruptly from my handbag. Getting it out, I checked the message I'd just received. HAVE U WON A MILLION? TXT BACK NOW 2 FIND OUT!!! I deleted it, then, on second thoughts, turned the phone off – I didn't want anything interrupting our imminent conversation. I was putting it back in my bag when Geraldine came in, smiled across the coffee shop at me and walked over to the table.

*

'I never had the least idea why they targeted me. Or even who they were,' she told me. 'But when I found Maxie dead, I knew they'd stop at nothing to get me out. I came back from the shop one afternoon and there he was, on my back doorstep. He'd been tied up in packing tape. There was a screwdriver through his throat.' She spoke matter-of-factly, but her sudden, convulsive breath implied a deep and lingering grief. 'Whoever it was, he wouldn't have given them any trouble – he was just a little thing, a mongrel, more Jack Russell than anything else. A bit smaller than a Jack Russell, in fact. Tiny.'

An image of Socks rose in my mind. 'You didn't call the police?'

She shook her head. 'There was a letter beside him, weighed down with a stone so it wouldn't blow away. I remember noticing that. I was too scared even to *feel* scared. I opened it straight away. It was all cut out of newspaper letters, stuck on A4 paper. It told me to move out, or I'd be next – and that, if I went to the police, I'd be next anyway.' That deep, shuddering breath again, entirely incongruous with her calm façade. 'I felt like – I don't know *how* I felt. Up till then, I'd thought having my windows broken was the worst that could happen, and you know *that* had happened already. I'd gone to the police then. I'd told them about the anonymous letters and phone calls I'd been getting, too.'

'What did they do?'

'They didn't do a thing. Perhaps I'm being paranoid, but I really don't think I am – I could honestly see them thinking *no smoke without fire* as soon as they read the letters for themselves. And the notes. Someone had tied them round stones with elastic bands, then used the stones to break my windows.' Her face was blank now, utterly bewildered. 'I could see the police thinking it *had* to be true. Why else would anyone go to so much trouble to force me out?'

'I can believe it.' I said. 'What did the letters say?'

'They were insane. Bizarre. I couldn't make any sense of them. GET OUT REBECCA FISHER, that was one of them. WE KNOW WHAT YOU DID, that was another. And the notes tied round the stones all said the same thing: GET OUT NOW. THIS IS YOUR LAST WARNING. They were all cut out of newspaper letters, like the one I found by Maxie. Newspaper letters stuck on that A4 paper.'

'I can imagine how confused you must have been.'

'Oh, I was. But it's hard to explain – part of me was convinced that it was some ridiculous mistake, that it would all blow over.' A long, uncomfortable pause – I saw my own present reflected far too clearly in the recent past she evoked. 'But when Maxie was killed, I knew it wouldn't. I still can't quite forgive myself for not taking the threat as seriously as I should have, at first. I'd had him for eight years. Of course, I didn't call the police *then*. Would you have done?'

I shook my head, and didn't say a word.

'In a horrible way, it's so ironic,' she continued quietly. 'I'd moved to Abbots Newton because it looked so peaceful and neighbourly, so picturesque. I'd just got divorced from my husband, I didn't work and I wanted a new start. There was nothing to keep me in the old place, the kids had all moved away years ago. And the divorce had really isolated me. I got the dog and quite a generous settlement, my ex-husband kept most of our friends . . .'

She fell silent for a few seconds, looking at her folded hands on the table. 'I'd always wanted to live in Dorset, ever since I read some Thomas Hardy at school. And of course, Colin was here. We were together before I got married, and we've stayed close friends ever since. He encouraged me to move, thought a change of scene would do me good. When I first saw Abbots Newton, I just couldn't believe my luck. When I saw that house in Ploughman's Lane. It was like a different world from Teasford.'

I spoke sharply. 'You'd lived in *Teasford*?'

'All my life, born and raised. It was why I wasn't exactly a stranger to Rebecca, as I told you over the phone. I was at primary school with her, a year above her, but I can still remember her clearly. It was a small school.' The big, battered shopping bag I'd noticed earlier was on the floor by her chair and, unexpectedly, she bent towards it. 'I've got a picture from back then. I don't know why, but I thought you might be interested.' Her voice came from below table-level, somewhat indistinct. 'This bag was all I could find to fit it in – it's not exactly a convenient size to cart about on its own.'

She extracted a foot-long black and white photo mounted on age-grimed cardboard; handed it across the table to me. It was identical to Annette Watson's photo, the one I'd had copied. 'It was taken in the summer term,' she said. 'Less than a month before Rebecca killed Eleanor Corbett. Perhaps it's morbid to keep it, but I don't think *anyone* in that photo threw it away. There I am, right there.'

She pointed, and I looked – saw she was recognisably herself, a pretty fine-featured girl of maybe eleven, with long straight fair hair in a high ponytail. One of dozens of anonymous faces I'd never noticed at all before. Background scenery for the main characters to stand out against.

'You did look a bit like Rebecca,' I ventured at last.

403

'Maybe that's what started it all. A case of mistaken identity.'

'Because I'm about the same colouring and height, and come from Teasford?' It was true, I realised; it was a fleeting similarity rather than an uncanny resemblance. With a small, rueful laugh, Geraldine pointed out the real Rebecca, and replaced the photo in her shopping bag. 'I don't know how anyone came to link us together. But they did. I could tell everyone in the village believed it implicitly, that I was her. At first, they couldn't have seemed nicer or friendlier. I didn't have that much to do with any of them, but when I did, they always seemed welcoming. Then suddenly . . . who knows?'

'People changed when it all started?'

'After I started getting those anonymous letters, they changed more than I'd have believed possible. If I'd known they'd react like that, I'd have kept my worries to myself, but it never occurred to me to do that. I honestly didn't think they'd believe it was true. I remember the lady next door, Liz Grey – you must know her now. She was very friendly at first, we got to know each other over a cup of tea when I'd been there a few days. I expected we'd see quite a lot of each other. Then she just . . . cooled. When she found out about the letters. It was like that with everyone in Abbots Newton. However nice they'd seemed at first.'

Silence fell between us, and intensified. Her gaze moved restlessly out of the window, then her sharp indrawn breath made me jump. 'Oh, Christ,' she said, 'speak of the devil. I know that woman – well, I know *of* her.'

Following her gaze, I saw an anonymous crowd for a second or two, then my attention zoomed in on one person. It was Helen. She was walking in our direction. In a handful of seconds, she'd pass us.

'I can't say I miss *her* much,' Geraldine continued. 'I didn't know her at all well, but when all *that* happened, she was more standoffish than anyone else in the village. Even before it started, she seemed like a cold bit of work ... afterwards, she wouldn't even *look* at me. If we saw each other on the street, she'd just walk straight past with her nose in the air, cutting me dead.'

As we spoke, Helen was coming closer and closer. I found myself hoping she wouldn't notice us – it would have been eminently possible for her not to have done. But, as she reached the cafe, she seemed to sense us both looking at her, and turned her head sharply to the right. I saw her seeing us behind the glass. Saw her recognising Geraldine a split-second after she'd recognised me.

Her smile was directed at me alone, the kind of smile that served only to acknowledge recognition. Somehow, she managed to ignore Geraldine pointedly. As she passed by, Geraldine turned back to me with a rueful smile. 'See what I mean? I had to put up with that sort of thing all the time, in Abbots Newton. Oh well, at least it's all over now. I still remember poor little Maxie, but I'll never have to go through *that* again.'

'I'm glad to hear it,' I said, but, as I spoke, my thoughts returned to Helen. I wondered what on earth she'd thought of this meeting, what she must be thinking now. To all intents and purposes, she'd seen me having a coffee with Rebecca Fisher. 'I only hope it ends that well for me.'

It was quarter to three when we said goodbye outside the coffee shop and went our separate ways. Turning, I saw the summer holiday crowd swallow her up and make her part of itself. An ordinary middle-aged housewife and mother, recently divorced as so many people were. As far as I could tell, before she'd arrived in Abbots Newton,

405

only one fact would jump out of her life and make it newsworthy – she'd gone to school with a notorious murderess, had seen Rebecca Fisher when she was just another face in the playground.

Why would anyone target her? I thought, then, hot on the heels of that, *why would anyone target me?*

In the multi-storey car park, the sense of déjà vu I'd felt earlier leapt back out from the shadows. I'd forgotten all about it, and its return chilled me. Again, I was caught in a memory of last Tuesday, returning from London, approaching the car, eerily perfect acoustics amplifying my footsteps in crystal-clear surround-sound. This time, the feeling didn't loosen its grip as I drove out into the sunlight. I wanted to take a different route back to Abbots Newton just to make it go away, but I couldn't. There was only one way to get there. Beyond the windows, the scenery unwound in exactly the same order and at exactly the same speed as it had done then, an undistinguished residential area giving way to Wareham's town centre, the rapid approach of the side-turning onto Ploughman's Lane.

The drive up that hill lasted for ever. I was full of a leaden conviction that when I reached the top, I'd see exactly what I had last week: the two parked police cars outside the house, Liz deep in conversation with a uniformed officer in the open front doorway. The closer I got to the top of the hill, the more certain I became – this didn't feel at all like apprehension, but simple knowledge – and I forced myself to drive a little faster, needing to see for myself.

The second I crested the hill, relief overcame me, closely followed by amazement – I'd been so sure I'd had a real premonition, and it had been nothing but panic and imagination after all. The house was exactly as it had been when I'd left earlier. Driving down towards it, I felt sheepish and embarrassed and delighted. My heart had been pounding like a hell-for-leather drum solo, but as I turned into the driveway, it had almost returned to its normal speed.

I was getting out of the car when Liz's front door opened and she came out; apprehension jumped back up inside me, then retreated slightly. Her expression was concerned rather than appalled, and there was no real urgency in her movements. 'Anna, dear,' she said. 'Carl came back about ten minutes ago; you've just missed him.'

I stared at her, confused. 'What was he doing here? He's supposed to be at work.'

'He got some bad news from home. His father collapsed earlier, and they've taken him to hospital – a heart attack, apparently, there's no telling whether he'll be all right yet. He told me he'd tried to call you, but your mobile was switched off. He said he was going straight to the hospital, and didn't know how long he'd be gone for. He took a little overnight case with him, so he's probably going to be some time.'

'Of course. His parents live a good five hours' drive away – God, how terrible.' Disorientated by bad news that leapt out from the most unexpected direction, I struggled to find the right thing to say. 'Thanks for letting me know.'

'He said he'd give you a ring later tonight, to let you know what was happening. I'm so awfully sorry. I do hope his father's all right.'

'Me, too,' I said. 'Well, I suppose we'll just have to wait and see.'

When I let myself into the house, the door to the kitchen was ajar, and I saw the folded note on the table straight away. Unfolding it, I read a quickly-scrawled summary of what I'd already heard. *Will try to call between 8 and 9*, he'd finished, *Love Cx*. I thought I could still smell a faint hint of his aftershave on the air.

Going upstairs, I saw a jumble of clothes on the bed, telling me he'd packed the few things he'd need in an all-time hurry – tidiness was as inherent to his personality as pragmatism. I hurried over to the phone, pressed out his mobile number and was put straight through to his voicemail service. *Please leave your message after the tone.* 'Carl,' I said, 'it's me. Look, I'm really sorry – I've just heard. Do try and call later, if you can. You know I'm thinking about you.'

I hung up. As I went back downstairs, my concerns were running on two levels at once. On one hand, I was thinking about Carl, how worried he must be as he began the endless drive to the town where he'd grown up; my heart went out to his whole family, from the brother I barely knew to the mother who'd always made me feel awkward. But, beneath that slightly self-conscious sympathy, other things rumbled – and, while I castigated myself for selfishness, the creeping unease that accompanied them couldn't be denied. No matter what happened, Carl wouldn't be back until tomorrow. For the very first time, I'd be spending the night here alone.

The slow descent into evening lasted for an eternity. I sat in the living room and tried to concentrate on a book I hadn't read for some time, longing for the plot to pick me up and pull me out of the present. But I couldn't have been much less distracted by the Yellow Pages. All the time, I was horribly aware of the shadows deepening around me, the spectacular rosy-mauve sunset beginning to tint everything, and threatening imminent darkness. As I stared at the words on the page, Geraldine's voice drifted back to me, as though from a distant room. *I can't quite forgive myself for not taking the threat as seriously as I should have done*, she'd said. *I'd had him for eight years . . .*

Socks lying dead on the garden path. Ragged, sexless breathing down the receiver. Shards of glass glittering up from this very carpet, in this very room . . .

For no reason that I could think of, an image of Helen flashed hard behind my eyes. How she'd looked at me when Petra had blithely announced the secret of my research, in a WI bake sale a thousand years ago. She had, I remembered, seen my school photograph of Rebecca on the kitchen table shortly after that evening, and she'd seen me talking to Geraldine today. I found myself recalling the things that had always disturbed me about her, practically from the first time we'd met. That stillness. That watchfulness. The forcefield of silence that seemed to surround her, that had never looked like shyness to me at all.

I put the book down and turned on the television to banish the silence, then went into the kitchen. I wasn't at all hungry, but made dinner anyway; it was the normal thing to do, and, alone in this odd emptiness, normality became beautiful, longed-for. The deepening sunset flooded the kitchen with light the colour of fire as I sat down and tried my best to eat. Through the half-open door that led into the living room, a studio audience exploded into raucous laughter.

When I'd finished eating and washed up, it was almost too dark to see properly. I put the lights on and drew blinds and curtains, what should have been utterly mundane taking on a new and ominous significance. The night was beginning. I sat back down in front of the television as I'd picked up the book earlier, with every bit as much success. At five to nine, the phone shrilled beside me, almost stopping my heart.

I forced myself to answer it, tense as taut elastic. 'Hello?'

'Annie? It's me.'

I recognised Carl's voice – it sounded distant and blurred, but that didn't matter, it was *his*. 'How *are* you?' I asked at once, then, a split-second later, 'How's your father? What's happened?'

'He's out of danger, thank God. We only heard a few minutes ago ourselves – I called you as soon as I could. We're at the hospital. They're keeping him in for a few days, to be on the safe side.' He exhaled deeply and I felt his exhaustion, and his relief. 'Christ, it's been a nightmare. I wish you were here right now . . . I should have stuck around, waited for you to get home . . .'

'I know you couldn't do that,' I said gently. 'But it doesn't matter now. It's all right now.'

A moment's silence, entirely devoid of the awkwardness that had characterised our recent conversations. His father's heart attack seemed to have driven us closer together, and whether that feeling was temporary or not, it was real. 'How's your mother?' I asked.

'Badly shaken . . . well, you can imagine. Nick and I are staying with her overnight – he's driven down as well. Anyway, I'll be home as soon as I can. I should be back tomorrow evening.'

'See you then,' I said. 'I love you, Carl.'

'I love you too. I'll give you a ring before I leave. Night, Annie. Sweet dreams.'

I hung up with a melting sense of relief, but, as the minutes inched past, anxiety began to creep in again, replacing it little by little. Now Carl's father was definitely out of danger, there was nothing left but my own fear. It whispered insidiously from everything around me: the cheerful and distant voices from the television, the ambiguous silence beyond them. The shelf where the Tiffany lamp had been. And again, I heard Geraldine's voice: *I can't quite forgive myself for not taking the threat as seriously as I should have done . . .*

Checking my watch, I saw the time was only half-nine, and realised it didn't matter. The sooner I went to bed, the sooner the morning would come. Sitting alone down here with nothing but my own thoughts had become appalling. Turning everything off, I double-checked that all the windows were closed and both doors were locked and bolted – more importantly than anything, that the burglar alarm was set. Upstairs, I washed and brushed my teeth ready for bed, slid in between cool, sweet-smelling sheets, squeezing my eyes shut.

For some time I couldn't sleep, and the cry of a bird outside had me sitting up, heart thumping erratically in my chest. Then no further noises came. Maybe an hour passed in which reality and imagination began to blur, but I still felt a long way away from oblivion. *This isn't going to happen*, I thought vaguely, *I'm never going to get any sleep tonight*, then suddenly I was walking through Bournemouth's town centre in dazzling afternoon sunshine. On my right, the cafe was coming closer. The people inside shouldn't see me, I realised, *mustn't* see me, they were dangerous. As I reached it, I noticed that the windows had been smashed, and couldn't stop myself glancing in quickly; the tables and chairs had been stacked neatly in the corners, and a group of uniformed primary schoolchildren stood posing for a photograph. I recognised Geraldine, Melanie Cook, Eleanor and Agnes Corbett. I couldn't see Rebecca at all.

It didn't matter. I was lucky they hadn't seen me. Besides, I was in a hurry, even though I wasn't sure why.

I turned down a side-road, was unsurprised to find myself in verdant semi-rural greenery, approaching a large deserted house with boarded-up windows and a palpable air of desolation. It was a sad but oddly beautiful picture in the sunlight, under the luminous-blue sky. As I approached, a faint smell of decay and wet rot became gradually stronger. The front door looked like it had gone a long time ago, and the light caught odd silvery glints in front of the darkened doorway. It was a web, I realised, spun across it as if to protect whatever lived inside. Its jagged circles closed in around the thick-legged spider at its centre; grotesquely orange and black and bristly, the largest I'd ever seen.

With drugged and enigmatic indifference, I reached out and tore the web apart. Its clammy strands clung to my fingers. The spider fell to the ground and scuttled into the house, where it was immediately lost in the shadows. Around me, the light was heavy and strange and unnatural, as if the sun was shining through yellow glass.

Through the door, I stepped into the hallway. The smell of decay was overpowering here, but still I felt nothing but vague curiosity. In huge rotted holes in the walls, lavish bouquets of wild flowers had been arranged with a florist's meticulous care. I set my foot on the first stair, and prepared to discover the upstairs rooms.

I was woken by the thin scream of the burglar alarm.

I'd heard it before, when the workmen had first fitted it. Then, it had been a few seconds' demonstration only, devoid of real power. Now, however, it hit me like a bucket of freezing water. That soulless inhuman fire-alarm sound, repetitive rhythmic shrieks that seemed to throb throughout the house, far louder than I remembered – deafeningly, unbearably loud. It was impossible to make out any other noises behind it. It blocked out everything. It blocked out thought.

The taste of raw animal terror filled my mouth, bright and metallic. The scream of the alarm sounded like a rusty nail being yanked free of a board. *Eee. Eee. Eee.* The idea of going downstairs was unthinkable, but the idea of staying here was worse – imagining unheard footsteps ascending the stairs, I inched out of bed. The lamp on the bedside table had a heavy ceramic base, and was the only makeshift weapon to hand. Unplugging it, I wound up the flex and held the base out in front of me like a club, began edging out of the room, across the landing. The alarm shrieked on and on. I saw nobody.

I didn't dare switch any lights on for fear that they'd pinpoint my progress downstairs – the house was solely illuminated by a thin wash of moonlight. The door to the living room stood slightly ajar. As I reached the bottom stair, I realised what had triggered the alarm: not an intruder, but a thrown rock. It lay next to the television in a silvery glitter of broken glass. The sound of the alarm had become a dull augur repeatedly digging into my brain. Putting the lamp down on the hallway cabinet, I went to turn it off. It died in one last electronic scream, before giving way to absolute silence.

I walked into the living room as if in a dream. *The police'll be here soon*, I was telling myself. *The alarm should have alerted the station the second it was triggered.* It was then that I noticed the folded square of paper that had been attached to the rock with an elastic band. I was barefoot and approached it gingerly, checking for treacherous glass slivers at every step. I untied the note, and unfolded it with hands that didn't feel like mine at all. A piece of A4 paper stared back at me in the moonlight, pasted letters obviously cut from some newspaper or magazine. The sight froze me up inside.

THIS IS YOUR LAST WARNING
FORGET REBECCA FISHER
TELL THE POLICE AND YOU WILL DIE

That final word. Three mismatched letters. It seemed to pull at me, to suck at me like a whirlpool – I felt my fears swirling together and spiralling down into it. *Socks*, I thought, *Geraldine's dog. This isn't just a threat, they'd do it, they'd kill me.* And then it hit me: if the police weren't already on their way, they'd be getting ready to begin the journey. I wouldn't be able to lie to them in person at all convincingly. They'd see I was terrified and that the window had been smashed, and they'd ask me over and over again what had really happened. I didn't know if I'd be able to keep the truth to myself, not in the face of that relentless, well-meant questioning—

TELL THE POLICE AND YOU WILL DIE, I read again, and the paper fell from my hand unnoticed – I was hurrying to the telephone, desperately hunting through the phone book for the number I wanted. It seemed to take an age to find it. In my mind, I could see the police car travelling gradually closer. At last, I pressed out the number and heard the voice speak in my ear. 'Wareham Police Station. Can I help you?'

Acting had become life and death in its most literal sense. Frantically, I struggled for the right tone, sheepish, a little guilty, and was amazed to hear it emerge just as I'd wanted it to. 'Well, yes. Listen, this is a bit awkward, but I've had a burglar alarm fitted recently, the kind that alerts you as soon as it's triggered. I set it off myself just now by accident; I opened the back door and forgot I'd left it on.

You don't need to send a car round, everything's fine here.'

Clear disapproval came down the line. 'Can I take your address?'

'Number four Ploughman's Lane. Abbots Newton.'

Another pause, this one longer. At any second, I thought, flashing blue lights could interrupt the moonlight, and I'd hear the police car pulling into the driveway outside. When the voice came again, its irritation was bordering on exasperation.

'Two officers *were* on their way. I've just called them back. You know, it's important that you're very careful with that type of system. We have better things to do with our time than go haring off to false alarms right, left and centre.'

'I know. I'm sorry.' I heard my chastened, conciliatory voice as though from someone else. 'I'll be a lot more careful in future.'

'I hope so. Goodbye, madam.'

I hung up. My relief was as nauseating as my earlier fear had been. The note lay on the carpet by the scatter of broken glass, and its mismatched words reminded me I was in more danger than I'd ever imagined. Looking at my watch, I saw that the time was ten to midnight. I couldn't stay in this house, I realised. Not tonight.

42

Liz's doorbell chimes sounded inexpressibly strange at this time and in this situation. As I stood outside her house in the middle of the night wearing slippers and a dressing-gown, their cheery domesticity rang out, surreal and muted behind a frosted glass panel. Hearing them die away in the unrelieved darkness, panic took hold of me; I pressed the doorbell again, harder, held it down till I saw a light go on in the bedroom upstairs.

A window flew open above me. Liz poked her head out. Her hair was scraped back in a bun, her disorientation palpable.

'Anna? My God, what's going on? When I heard your alarm, I called the police, and—'

'Please, Liz, let me in. Something's happened, something awful – someone threw a stone, and—'

The face had gone. Through the frosted glass, I saw the hallway light go on, heard tiny, muffled footsteps hurrying down the stairs. The door creaked open sharply. 'What's *happened*?' Liz demanded, then, at once, 'Come in. Come on in.'

I did, slamming the door behind me as if to shut out a wild animal hot on my heels. The crowded cosiness of the hallway was as bizarre as the door's chimes had been. Harsh centre lights blazed down on ornaments and picture frames, and Liz's terrified eyes. 'Someone threw a stone through my window, just now,' I said. 'Someone's – they've threatened to kill me—'

'*Who* threatened you? What do you mean?' I was about

to reply when she spoke again, and I could see her attempting to rebuild the only world she knew around her; a world of normality, and certainty, and cast-iron safety you breathed in with the air. 'Come on into the kitchen, dear. I'll put the kettle on.'

I followed her in, aware of the bizarre picture I made – I'd thrown crucial belongings into my handbag in the frantic minutes before leaving the house, wore the bag over my towelling dressing-gown, my nightshirt. Sitting down at the table, I opened the bag and fumbled inside it as Liz put the kettle on. 'This was tied to the rock they broke my window with,' I said, extracting the folded A4. 'Read it.'

She took it, unfolded it. I saw horror in her eyes and the set of her mouth, a mirror-image of my own reaction maybe ten minutes ago. 'Oh my God,' she said quietly. 'Oh my God, Anna.'

'*Should* I tell the police?' The sight of her face brought panic crashing back; there was no safe haven here, just a kindly and frightened middle-aged woman I'd grown to like immensely, who I'd been wildly irresponsible to involve in the matter at all. 'Do you think I should let them know about this, or—'

'My God, Anna. Don't even think that. Don't even *think* about it.' Her words came out in a sudden rush – she laid the note down flat on the table, and I saw her hand was shaking. 'You've seen this, you've read this. You mustn't call the police – it would be insane.'

I looked at the note again, the jagged and brutal disharmony of sizes and fonts and upper-and-lower case. In the stark, overhead light, the words became more terrible than ever. It was a huge effort to speak with composure. 'You're right,' I said quietly. 'Of course you're right. But I've got to tell Carl. He needs to know what's happened.'

'Do you know his parents' number?'

'I know his mobile number. I'll try him on that.' Even at such a time, I felt compelled to continue hastily, 'it's all right, I don't need to use your phone. I've got my mobile here.'

I took it out of my handbag as Liz murmured anxious assent and returned to the kettle. I pressed out buttons that seemed far smaller and fiddlier than the ones I was used to. Finding his number was like unlocking a door after eight pints, but at last I managed. I heard the tiny, anonymous ringing tone begin in my ear, urgent entreaties hammering along with my heartbeat. *Please be there, Carl. Please don't have left the mobile downstairs while you sleep in your old bedroom ... please ... please ...*

'Hello?'

His voice was distinctly sleepy, and I could tell I'd just woken him up – still, the relief of hearing him answer left me speechless for a second. '*Hello?*' he said again slightly irritably, then, obviously checking the display on his handset, '*Annie?* Is that you?'

'It's me,' I said. 'Look, Carl – something terrible's happened. I'm round at Liz's right now. I can't stand to be in that house on my own tonight—'

His voice was suddenly alert. 'What is it? What's wrong?'

Out of the corner of my eye, I saw Liz going into the living room, diplomatically leaving us alone to talk. I felt intensely grateful for that; everything about this conversation demanded privacy. 'Someone threw a stone through our living room window about twenty minutes ago,' I said quietly. 'It set off the burglar alarm. There was a note tied round it – I've shown it to Liz. When I'd read it, I rang the police up and told them I'd set the alarm off myself by accident. I didn't have much choice, really. They threatened to kill me if I told the police, and—'

'*Who* threatened to kill you?' Carl demanded, then, 'what did the note say?'

I read it out to him, and as I finished speaking, there was silence. 'Ask Liz, if you don't believe me,' I said furiously. 'Even you can't argue with *this*. That note's as real as I am, it's right here in front of me, in black and white—'

'*Annie.*' His voice was urgent and horrified and soothing all at once. 'Jesus *Christ*, of course I believe you ... I don't know what to say, I feel so *guilty*. All the time, I thought you were imagining it, that it was all in your mind ... my God, I'm sorry. I've been such a moron, it just didn't seem *likely* to me ...'

It was everything I'd wanted to hear from him this week, and last week, and the week before that, but I felt no impulse towards self-righteous *told-you-so*s. His words inspired nothing but melting relief. 'Do you think I did the right thing?' I asked quietly. 'Not telling the police?'

'Of *course*. For Christ's sake, Annie, don't say a word to them. Whoever this maniac is, it sounds like they really mean business ... if only I'd believed you before ...'

He fell silent again. When he spoke it was with a reasonable semblance of his old, straightforward practicality. 'You'll be all right at Liz's, won't you? Overnight?'

'I'll be fine,' I said. 'Really.'

'Well, I'll come home first thing tomorrow. I'll explain it all to Mum. I'll be back before lunchtime, if I leave early.'

A long pause, heavy with things neither of us were in any emotional state to put into words – guilt on his side of the conversation, forgiveness on mine, our shared under-standing of both. A sense of reconciliation. 'I'll see you then,' I said.

'See you soon. Whatever you do, Annie, take care – and don't call the police.'

Liz came back into the kitchen as I was hanging up. 'I'll make us that tea now,' she said, going over to the kettle. 'What did he say, if you don't mind me asking?'

'He's coming home first thing tomorrow. He said just what you did – that I'd be mad to call the police.' I spoke again quickly, with new panic. 'Liz, you don't mind if I sleep in your spare room, do you? I can't stand going back to that house tonight.'

'Well, of *course*, dear. I'm afraid the sheets haven't been aired, but it's clean and ready.' She brought a steaming cup of tea over to me, setting it down on the table. 'Have you locked up next door?' she asked.

'Yes, everything. The living room window's broken quite high up – nobody could get in through that, not unless they smashed the whole thing again.' The idea that my unknown enemy or enemies might still be outside brought a fresh wave of fear. 'I am sorry, Liz, but do you mind if I smoke? My nerves are all over the place.'

'Oh, goodness, feel free. You can use the saucer for an ashtray.' I thanked her, fumbled in my bag for fags and matches, lit up with shaking hands. 'I'm not surprised you're in a bit of a state, dear. What a terrible shock to have.'

I took a long, deep, indescribably grateful drag. The silence lasted some time before she spoke again. 'Promise me you're not going back to that research of yours, Anna. You've seen that letter – it's far too dangerous.'

An icy and appalling helplessness drifted over me and I couldn't stop myself from speaking. 'Look, Liz – I wanted to tell you before, but it was all too confusing. What's been happening – it's *not* Mr Wheeler trying to stop me writing about Rebecca; it's got nothing to do with him. I went to talk to him earlier this week, and that conversation changed everything. He's innocent. And Geraldine, the woman who sold us our house – she wasn't Rebecca. She didn't have anything to *do* with Rebecca, apart from—'

The cigarette in my hand froze en route to my mouth. Liz's voice filtered in to me distantly. 'Anna, are you all right?'

'Helen,' I said quietly.

Liz sat down across the table. I saw her looking at me closely, without really seeing her at all. 'What are you talking about, dear?'

'It all makes sense. Every last bit of it. Christ, I've been so *stupid* – it's been there all along, just staring me in the face.' Knowledge had come pouring in, like an avalanche in my mind, and preconceptions and guesswork crumbled under the only possible truth. 'Geraldine Hughes wasn't driven out because she *was* Rebecca. She was driven out because she *knew* Rebecca – they'd been at primary school together. She'd seen Rebecca in the flesh.'

'I don't understand. Why would that matter to anyone?'

'It would matter to Rebecca. She's got a whole new identity these days, and it's all-important to her that she isn't recognised. Geraldine might not have recognised her, but she might have done, given enough time. Even though Rebecca looks so different these days. *Even though she's calling herself Helen.*'

I saw Liz's absolute amazement. She stared at me, huge-eyed. 'Anna, you can't think—'

'It all makes sense.' The words came out almost fiercely, and I made a conscious effort to calm down. 'Rebecca Fisher built a whole new life for herself as Helen. She's safe here, she's accepted here. Then, out of the blue, Geraldine moved in. Maybe Helen recognised her immediately, maybe they got talking and Geraldine mentioned that she used to live in Teasford – I don't know exactly how it happened. But it did. Suddenly, Helen knew she'd have to get rid of her somehow, before Geraldine recognised her too.

'And she found the best way to do it. Killing two birds with one stone, you could say. If anyone ever linked *her* with Rebecca Fisher, they'd look hysterical, ridiculous, as if they'd heard about Geraldine being driven out, and it had got their imagination working overtime. She'd be safe here for life, when Geraldine had gone . . .

'Only it didn't quite work like that. Because I moved in, and started researching the case. And when she found out what I was doing, she knew she'd have to stop me before I came across something she didn't want me to. Before I could find out what really happened here—'

Across the table, Liz looked ashen, deeply shaken – but, searching her expression for true disbelief, I found none. 'My God, Anna,' she said quietly. 'It makes sense. You're right, it makes *perfect* sense. But *Helen* . . .'

The pause between us deepened to become an abyss, and the buzz of the overhead striplight seemed far louder than it had been up to now. I could see Liz desperately trying to re-establish normality in her own mind, a world in which acquaintances were always safe and friends concealed no dark secrets. 'We should get to bed, dear,' she said at last. 'It's almost one o'clock in the morning.'

Beside the single bed in Liz's spare room, an elderly clock radio blinked digital red numbers that looked much too bright in the dark. 02:45. I'd been glancing at it intermittently in between my restless turning, assuming various positions in the distant hope of getting some sleep tonight – sometimes seeing that a handful of minutes had passed since I'd last looked, sometimes seeing that quarter of an hour or more had gone by. The sheets were chilly and slightly musty, and there was an unplaceably stale, stuffy edge to the air; it was the way my own spare room had smelt before I'd aired it out for Petra's stay. It was less terrifying than my own bedroom would have been tonight, and I knew it. Still, I was completely unable to get to sleep.

I lay and felt my nerves thrumming and jumping inside me, kept thinking I could hear movements outside. Knew that the window faced out onto Liz's back garden, and Socks' makeshift grave, and the woods. *There's nobody there*, I told myself fiercely, *just try and get some rest.* More than anything, I longed for bright lights and companion-ship, but the idea of waking Liz up again was out of the question. She'd seen twelve forty-five as the middle of the night, would see quarter to three as some strange, parallel-universe ghost-hour, alien as outer space.

I couldn't bring myself to lie still for another minute – suddenly, I didn't just want a cigarette and a glass of water, I *needed* them. Remembering I'd left my fags on the kitchen table, I got out of bed as quietly as I could, tiptoed across the landing and down the stairs. The kitchen light-switch illuminated a scene of welcoming domesticity made alien by solitude and silence, and the shelves of spices and cookery books looked odd in the sterile whiteness. I got a glass of water from the tap and gulped at it gratefully before sitting down at the table, reaching for my cigarettes and matches.

The box of matches felt ominously light, and, opening it, I saw I only had two left. The first guttered out in my shaking hand. The second stayed alight just long enough to singe the tip of my cigarette; I sucked frantically, but by no stretch of the imagination could it be considered alight. *Damn, damn, damn.* Liz must have some more, I thought, even non-smokers kept them around. There'd be a big box of Swan Vestas somewhere in a cupboard. I looked in a few, trying to make as little noise as humanly possible, but I couldn't find any. At last, I went to the cupboard below the shelves of cookery books. The door stuck, but gave just enough to reassure me that it wasn't locked. I gave it a hard tug, and it flew open with a noise like a champagne cork popping out. I found myself praying Liz was a heavy sleeper. If she wasn't, it would have woken her up for certain.

I couldn't see exactly what was and what wasn't inside. A folded lace tablecloth was draped over the top of everything, hinting at vague shapes. Taking it out, I stared, puzzled. There was a Tiffany lamp in there. Of course, it wasn't a real one – Liz would never keep a real one hidden like this – but it certainly looked convincing. It was almost identical to the one we'd had stolen.

I knelt, and lifted it out carefully. It *was* identical. The patterns of coloured glass were the same, blood-red and jade-green and midnight-blue, and so was the shape of the shade, the slender wrought-iron stem of the base. I could clearly see it in our living room two weeks ago, on the shelf by the door, by the books.

Rising to my feet and barely aware that I did so, I stared at the lamp in blank confusion. It was then that the voices began to speak in my mind. First a solo, then a duet. Building voice by voice to a deafening chorus, each person saying their separate phrase at once till the distinct words were lost in an overlapping, discordant babble, the volume turning up a little louder as each new participant joined in.

Extremely sweet, in many ways.

A hamster called Toffee.
A proper little housewife in the making.
A cat called Socks.
She seemed far more comfortable in the listener's role. I have to say, she made a very good one—
'Anna, dear? What are you doing?'

The voice came from the open kitchen doorway. I whirled round. Liz was framed in front of the shadowed hallway, wearing a pink dressing-gown with a rabbit on the pocket. I saw her seeing the lamp in my arms.

'It's you,' I said slowly. 'You're her. You're Rebecca.'

43

'Whatever do you mean, dear?'

Under the bleak white light, her reaction was entirely unconvincing – eyes opening a little too wide, subtle elements of fear in the lines of her face – and I could see that part of her knew she was only playing for time. I hadn't spoken with suspicion, but with flat, incontrovertible knowledge; it was like a blinding flashbulb going off behind my eyes. In that single moment of looking at her, everything changed out of all recognition, and old conversations unwound on dizzying fast-forward: her anxiety about my research, how she'd urged me to put an end to it for the sake of my own safety. I set the lamp down on the table, and watched her, and was aware of no emotion at all.

'I was right before,' I said. 'I was right about everything except who you became. You got rid of Geraldine because you thought one day she might suspect—'

'No, – it wasn't like that! I'd never have done it, anything like it, if I hadn't been forced. You have to understand, I didn't have any *choice*.' The words burst out on their own, and I watched her face as she realised what she'd said, that there could be no going back now. 'Anna, she almost knew. Would have known, given more time. When she first moved in and came round for a cup of tea, we were talking and I asked her where she was from. And when she said Teasford, I suddenly realised *I knew her*, I recognised her from primary school. If I could remember her, she must be able to remember *me*. I'd changed to look at, but nobody changes *that* much—'

The sweet, unlined, regular-featured face, the grey-blue eyes, the small hands and delicate wrists – I saw it all as if for the first time. It was only as she finished talking that I noticed her manner had changed in some immense but indefinable way; it was in her whole expression, the set of her face, the way she stood. While an anxious and conscientious echo of the Liz I knew still lingered in her voice, she'd taken off the cosy middle-aged façade as easily and instantly as a hat. So much of it had been created by her choice of words, her use of language, the unthinking banalities of contented middle age.

'I didn't want to kill her dog. I didn't want that at all,' she went on quietly. 'But I had to make her go away. If she'd taken the letter and phone calls and break-in seriously enough ... but she *didn't*, she didn't leave me with any choice. I've built a whole new life for myself here, it's where I belong. It took me so long to find a place I could feel safe in, and I'm a part of things here. I couldn't bear to think that could all change, that I could be driven out myself ... this is home for me, Anna, it's the first real home I've ever had. It's my whole life ...'

She came further into the kitchen and sat down at the table. Everything around me felt somehow staged. As I watched, her gaze strayed to the silver-framed photograph by the fruit bowl and the longing in her eyes was naked, suddenly helpless to conceal itself. Two little brown-haired girls smiled out side by side, dimpled, pink-cheeked, ebullient.

'They're not your daughters, are they?' I said. 'They're not anything to do with you.'

She shook her head without looking at me. Her eyes remained fixed on the picture. 'The manager of my old young offenders' home sent me all the photographs. They're his granddaughters, really. I always wanted a family of my own, but I had far too much to hide. How could I keep it a secret from a husband and children, who I really was? It's the next best thing to that, though. Imagining. I can almost believe they're my own daughters, sometimes. It's almost enough . . .

'Katie and Alice. I chose those names myself; it doesn't matter what they're really called. I felt so contented here, before Geraldine moved in. I really had the life I'd always wanted. I wouldn't have hurt anything or anyone, not then . . .'

It was like a conversation in a dream. An overwhelming sense of sympathy gripped me, but I forced it back as hard as I could. 'What about Socks? You weren't afraid of discovery then, not at all – and you *injured* him, you *killed* him—'

'I didn't mean any of that!' Her voice was suddenly passionate with regret – it seemed to emerge from that blank face by ventriloquism. 'I never wanted to hurt him. If he hadn't gone round to your house, if he hadn't kept going there when I was at home . . . he didn't seem to *want* me any more. He jumped on my bed late one night when I was thinking about that, and I – I just lashed out. I couldn't help myself. And, soon after that, I saw him sitting at his food bowl in the evening. Looking at me. I could have been a stranger who'd just come in to feed him, I could have been *anyone*. I just picked him up, and—'

How well I understood. In my mind, I was back in Annette Watson's flat, listening to her account of Toffee's murder. 'When he was dead, I just – panicked,' she went on haltingly. 'I was terrified you might suspect me, terrified of what I'd done. I don't know *what* I was thinking, to be honest. So I left him on your back path. That way, you'd be the one to find him, you'd come and tell me. I could try and tell myself it was true, that he'd just died of old age, that he'd gone out one night the same as usual, and—'

She broke off for a second, inhaling deeply. I could see the glint of tears in her eyes. 'But I never meant to hurt you, Anna. Never in a million years. When I threw that stone tonight, I could see that the lights were off, I knew you were in bed. All I wanted was to scare you, stop you finding out about me before you found out too much. It was just a matter of time, I knew that. If you carried on with your research, you'd end up putting two and two together, and . . .'

Her gaze moved to the faux-Tiffany lamp on the table. The silence between us stretched out interminably. 'We've talked about so much together,' she said quietly, 'you remind me so much of myself, sometimes. You'll keep my secret, won't you, Anna – we'll still be friends? You're the only person in this village who really understands me. Does finding out who I really am change so much?'

I stood and looked at her, a sense of numbness fading fast. All the horror I should have felt at first came crashing in out of nowhere. The idea that I'd trusted this woman implicitly, almost loved her; it was as though I'd disturbed a stone in a beautiful, familiar garden, discovered pallid, freakish, alien things trundling blindly here and there. A sudden wave of instinctive revulsion came over me as I remembered the morning I'd helped her bury Socks. I couldn't hide that revulsion; I could feel it in every line of my face, hear it in my voice as I spoke.

'It does,' I said quietly. 'It changes everything. I'm sorry. I can't help it.'

Her face was at once expressionless and utterly tragic.

Slowly, she rose from the table and went over to the counter, where she stood with her back to me. I could see her rounded shoulders shaking slightly, understood she was crying without making a sound.

'I'm sorry,' I said again. 'I really am sorry.'

The broad pink-dressing-gowned back betrayed nothing, now. It was then that Donald Hargreaves' voice came back to me, from a quiet and civilised office a thousand miles away. *The threat of personal revelation,* he'd said, *betrayal by a loved one. Those are her triggers.* And it was in that moment of vertiginous knowledge that she turned, and I saw the madness in Rebecca's eyes as she grabbed a six-inch butcher's knife from the wooden block by the spice-racks.

I moved before I'd made any conscious decision to do so – pure survival instinct hotwired my nervous system and I was out of the kitchen, in the hallway, hammering barefoot up the stairs. I could hear her behind me, and my terror made the split-second decision between all the doors on the landing. I darted into the bathroom maybe three feet ahead of her and slammed the door behind me just in time, sliding the bolt to.

The bathroom was in virtually absolute darkness, and the thin moonlight that slanted in through the window showed me nothing but dark, indistinct shapes. I could feel my heartbeat pounding all the way through me; it seemed to be in my mind, my mouth, my ears, even my bloodstream. Behind it, there was nothing but the sound of beating at the door. It wasn't the kind of beating that implied an urgent *let me in.* It was the kind that attempted to force an entrance.

I stood stock-still, feeling exactly what adrenaline hadn't let me feel on the way upstairs – the blank helplessness of something frozen in headlights. The bolt on the door wasn't strong, the small brass type that a housewife with no specific DIY knowledge could easily fit herself; fitted simply so you could call out a sheepish *sorry* when you turned the handle and the door didn't open. A bolt that was about politeness far more than security, that had never been designed to keep out a killer.

The insanity in those eyes – the memory destroyed my caught-in-headlights feeling in a second. Snapping the light on, I looked wildly round the room for anything that could help me. Brass towel rails, clean, fluffy, pastel-coloured towels, wicker laundry basket. Shiny, pale tiles underfoot. Above the gleaming washbasin, the window faced out onto the back garden, but it was far too small for me to climb through, would have been too small for an exceptionally skinny child of ten. Even if I'd been able to, it was a first floor window in the middle of nowhere, with nothing to climb down on the other side. The latticed glass showed me two pictures at once; a sharp image of this tidy, crowded bathroom, and the black misty nothing outside that acted as its screen.

Call for help? There was no point, I realised, there was nobody for miles around. We were on our own here, just as we'd always been. Then, a deafening crash from the door brought two things home to me at once. She was trying to break the door down with something large and heavy. And the door had given slightly. The dainty, discreet little bolt was now bulging inwards, a tiny change in its angles that made all the difference in the world.

That butcher's knife. The eyes and the expression that Eleanor Corbett must have seen in her final moments.

My eyes scanned for something heavy, any makeshift potential weapon. They fixed on the ornate rack that formed a wrought-iron bridge across the bath. It was an unusual and beautiful item, perhaps antique – I prayed that it was, that it wouldn't have the false weight of the bird-baths you could buy from garden shops which looked like stone from a distance but were light enough for a child to lift. I picked it up, bottles of shampoo and bath-foam and deodorant spray scattering in every direction, some smashing open on the underfoot tiles. I'd been right: the rack was as heavy to the hand as to the eye.

I stood pressed up against the wall next to the door. It would give way at any second, I thought, and was right – at last the bolt gave with a groaning pop, unbroken but no longer anchored to the wall. Rebecca came in. I saw she'd been using a side-table from the landing to assist her entrance, and she pushed it to one side in the fraction of a second that her gaze flickered round the room.

She caught a glimpse of me by the wall just in time to lash out as I was raising the wrought-iron rack over my head and preparing to bring it down. The knife in her hand flashed upwards in the light – I screamed, and my free arm went up to block it. The knife slid in above my elbow, slicing up my forearm. In that same instant, I brought the rack down with all the strength I could muster, every element of my mind contracted in self-preservation before I even had time to register that I'd been wounded.

It was a lucky blow. Rebecca collapsed to the ground like a sack filled with something loose, heavy and inanimate. There was a sharp click as her head hit the tiles.

I stood staring down at her limp, unmoving body in horror. And as the seconds passed, I became gradually aware of the blood pumping from my arm, from the cut that was far deeper than I'd thought at first, fat scarlet drops plinking on the tiles an inch from Rebecca's face.

I realised I was crying.

Epilogue

I'm still infinitely confused by my memories of events immediately following Rebecca Fisher's death, as though I'd experienced them while drugged or cataclysmically drunk. Not blurred memories, but huge black areas empty as outer space – the kind of memories you knew would never be recalled by a random mental trigger, the kind that are lost for good as surely as unsaved data on a computer.

But I can recall some things. Images I can see illuminated in separate flashes, so a picture seems to explode into being before vanishing almost instantly; like a flashbulb going off in a dark room, showing you floodlit details for an eye-watering nanosecond. That's how I remember them, anyway. I don't know quite how I saw them at the time.

An image of a telephone on a table, in a bedroom I'd never been into before. On the outskirts of my vision, a half-recognised impression of ornaments and pictures, the dull gleam of a brass bedstead under the centre light; rumpled bedclothes, tangled sheets. My blood-streaked hand lifting the receiver. The pale apricot-coloured towel wrapped round my arm, slowly darkening to red. Wondering whether to call the ambulance or the police first. Deciding on the ambulance.

The flash illuminates a moment of my disjointed, hysterical account spilling out into the receiver, words becoming intricate, difficult, foreign. The patient, dubious voice down the line turning alert at my mention of the word *dead*. The towel round my arm far more red than apricot, now. A dizzy feeling, the world swimming past me, away from me.

The flash illuminates the scene through the open bathroom door as I walk unsteadily past it. Tiles streaked and spotted with my blood, toiletries everywhere. Conflicting smells of spilt shampoo and bubble-bath and conditioner – a provincial chemist-shop smell, grotesquely incongruous with the sight of Liz unmoving on the tiles. A conscious thought caught in the flash with that image, as I look in. *Not Liz. Rebecca. Rebecca.*

Blue flashing lights through the frosted-glass door panel. The urgency of the voices around me as the colours begin to drain out of everything. A paramedic with sandy-blond hair and a dark red birthmark dripping down one cheek. The unearthly dawn of a summer morning as the ambulance arrives at Bournemouth Hospital.

The wound wasn't as serious as it looked, but I still needed ten stitches in my arm. There would always be a scar. I was lucky it was in a place where my clothes would cover it ninety per cent of the time. That was what the nurses told me, when the frenetic *Casualty* busyness was over and the world was quiet again, the nurses who came and went in a misty, dreamlike, seemingly unending gavotte.

I'd been put in a private room. I sensed that was more for the police's convenience than my own. Two of them came to sit by my bed and ask me questions, and I answered with some distant part of my mind still drifting in and out of reality. They were polite, pleasant, concerned; it was a terrible thing that had happened, they hated to ask me questions at this time. But they needed to know . . . I told them the full story, because I wasn't sure what else I could do.

When they'd gone, one of the nurses showed Carl in. He was pale and dishevelled, his eyes appalled – he'd come home to find the police crawling all over Liz's house, and his horror had only intensified when he'd asked them what had happened. *Thank Christ you're all right,* he kept saying, *thank Christ you're alive.* He seemed as dazed as I was, at that moment; his shell-shocked look said he couldn't quite believe the abrupt turn our lives had taken into a strange and violent world. *If anything had happened to you . . .* And then he'd fallen silent, realising, as I did, how easily it could have done.

I'd anticipated a long stay in hospital, but they told me I was free to go home on Monday afternoon, instructed me on how I should care for the wound, gave me the solutions and dressings I'd need for the next couple of weeks. Carl drove me back home. At first, we talked non-stop of what had happened, then our conversation gradually tapered off – there was more talk than silence, and then more silence than talk, and then there was nothing but silence. I drifted into sleep, vaguely aware of my surroundings so that they edged into my dream – honey-coloured houses and dappled ponies grazing in fields, patches of heavy shadow cast by overhanging trees. Sunshine. Emptiness. Peace.

Of course, you'll have read in the papers what happened after that. The way they were legally allowed to release Rebecca Fisher's secret identity, where she'd ended up and who she'd become. She was in the public domain again, inspiring headlines and editorials – some thundering with Old Testament anger, some ostentatiously poignant. Geraldine wasn't mentioned by name. I wasn't so lucky. I was, after all, key to the tale of her unveiling – the innocent writer next door who'd almost fallen victim to her well-concealed madness.

Everyone now knows Rebecca Fisher died at the age of forty-three, in a skirmish with a neighbour she was trying to stab to death. I suppose that's my fault, really. They'd never have known the full story if I hadn't given those interviews to the *Mail* and the *Sun* and the *Express* and the *Mirror*. The *Mail* one was advertised on the front page. I gave them because I wasn't sure that I had any choice, that I *could* decide not to. Even if I had no legal obligation, I couldn't help feeling that I had a moral one; a kind of guilt made me want to explain. *What* had happened was as clear to the papers as it had been to the police, a clear-cut case of self-defence. The knife on those blood-streaked bathroom tiles told its own story, as did the broken bolt and the table Rebecca had used to force entry. But, perhaps unsurprisingly, they cared far more about *how* it had happened, and what had come before, and if I'd ever sensed something strange about her.

I told them the truth, but it was like giving a priceless present that went entirely unappreciated. It took me some time to realise they didn't want the truth, and never would. What they wanted was some crass variation on *A Mind to Murder*; the sweet-faced, middle-aged housewife and librarian, whose reassuring smile concealed *pure evil*. When I look back to those interviews, the sensationalist headlines and the breathless prurience of the copy, I sometimes find myself wishing I could go back in time and reclaim the truth – not hand these indifferent passers-by the details and emotions that meant so much. And I feel an obscure species of guilt, as if I've betrayed Liz's confidence.

I know there was no such person as Liz Grey really, that she'd been a name invented in a prison side-office, a persona that would draw no suspicion in a village far from home. But I can't help feeling she *did* exist, in a way. As a character in a play can exist when some projection of the actor's own personality shines out through the costume and the make-up, creating something so real you can't quite believe it stops existing when the curtain falls.

I felt she'd been a part of Rebecca. The woman Rebecca had always wanted to be.

We'd had a lot in common.

We still live there, Carl and I, in Ploughman's Lane, Abbots Newton. We got some suspicious sideways glances at first, after I came back from hospital. But, as I've said, the story's been all over the papers since then. These days, everyone knows the facts, and the part we played in events, and our innocence.

Anyway, life's moved on in the fifteen months between then and now. A new couple have moved in next door, a couple in their thirties. He's something in television and she's something in PR – they live in London all week and come down at weekends. On the rare occasions they're here, they keep themselves to themselves, and it's easy to feel the house is still standing empty.

Sometimes I see Helen round the village. It's hard to know what to say to each other, on the rare occasions our paths cross. Our only possible topic of conversation revolves around the friend we had in common, and I can tell she's every bit as uncomfortable with the subject as I am. We'll never be at all close, but I can see her as clearly as Rebecca did, now: an awkward, guarded woman, raised to be moral and dutiful and disapproving all at once. There's no real darkness in her after all, and there never was.

Petra comes to visit, from time to time. Everything

between us is just as it used to be in Reading, as everything is between myself and Carl. We're happy together. We've started to talk about beginning a family in the not-too-distant future, and it surprises me to realise I'm as keen on the prospect as he is. There's nothing that has to come before that, not any more. You could say that my priorities have changed a bit.

Carl and I socialise more, as well – I've become friendly with several women I've met at his colleagues' houses, although Jim and Tina still feel like strangers to me. When I'm introduced to someone for the first time, the conversation inevitably moves towards Rebecca, sometimes tactfully, sometimes with blinding insensitivity. Like the newspapers, they don't want to hear the truth. I've come to accept that, and be patient with it, and move on.

I'm still working on the novel. It's going well, and should be finished in a few months' time. I've come to enjoy the time I spend in the writing-room that looks exactly as it did before the break-in – the radio on beside me and Carl at work, window facing out onto uninterrupted woods that never concealed Mr Wheeler after all.

My agent tells me that the lingering aftermath of publicity from my interviews should do this novel's sales a lot of good. I want to be delighted, but can't quite bring myself to feel that way. Bright hope for its success trails a dark and elongated shadow in its wake; it seems wrong somehow, uncomfortably wrong, a kind of grave-robbing.

I've tried to keep the plot as far away from the realities of the case as I possibly can, far further than I'd initially anticipated. When I started writing it, a kind of self-defence mechanism created my central character unbidden, and made sure she was next to nothing like the Rebecca I'd known.

There are some things I don't want to remember, you see. Even now it's all over.

I had the dream for the first time nearly six months ago. Last night, I had it again. I don't know exactly what prompted it. Perhaps the memory just drifted back on its own, the way memories do sometimes.

For no specific reason, I was back at Teasford station. I saw Rebecca standing on the platform further down, a ten-year-old girl in neat school uniform, little gold earrings, an elaborate velvet bow in her long, pale hair. Beside her, silent and blank-faced, stood Eleanor Corbett. They seemed to be the only two people in the world. Around them, the station and the roads and pavements beyond it were entirely deserted. It was a hot summer evening. The sunset was coming down rosily on the horizon.

I hurried towards them, suddenly jolted. My footsteps rang out sharply. 'Where are you going?'

'We have to leave.' Rebecca's face was expressionless, her voice flat and uninflected. 'They know who we are now. It isn't safe.'

I stared, bewildered. 'When are you coming back?'

'We're not coming back.' As she spoke, a train appeared in the distance, approaching impossibly fast. Then it was there at the platform, and I saw that it too was empty. 'We're not ever coming back.'

There seemed nothing else to say. I watched Eleanor board the train with an intense and unplaceable sense of guilt. On an impulse, I spoke as Rebecca stepped up herself, pulling the door to.

'I'm sorry,' I said. 'I didn't mean to drive you away.'

'You didn't.' She spoke leaning out of the open train-

439

door window. 'It's not your fault. We just have to leave now. That's all there is to it.'

The train began to pull out. I waved. She waved back, solemn-faced. Standing in the silence, I watched the train reach the edge of the world, and disappear.

Then I turned, and began the long walk back to Ploughman's Lane.

All Orion/Phoenix titles are available at your local bookshop or from the following address:

Mail Order Department
Littlehampton Book Services
FREEPOST BR535
Worthing, West Sussex, BN13 3BR
telephone 01903 828503, *facsimile* 01903 828802

DATE DUE

MAR 2 7 2006
APR 2 1 2006
MAY 2 0 2006
JUL 2 7 2009
NOV 2 3 2009
DEC 1 0 2009
FEB 1 3 2010
JUN 0 2 2010
JAN 1 9 2011
OCT 0 5 2012

OCT 2 8 2010

Payment...
Access an...
DO NO
order ma...
Please ad...
UK and...
£1.50 for...
maximum...
Overse...
£2.50 for...
for each a...

name...
addre...

GAYLORD   PRINTED IN U.S.A.

prices and availability are subject to change without notice